Seeking Hilary

Louis Berry

Dear Reader,

Your time and heart invested in my stories mean the world to me. I pour my soul into crafting each novel, driven by a relentless work ethic to ensure your enjoyment shines through every page. As a solitary writer, I humbly ask you to share my work with friends who love a good tale. Your recommendation fuels my journey, and I'm endlessly grateful for your support.

With sincerest appreciation,

Louis

Discover other titles as well as upcoming releases from Louis Berry at:
www.louisberryauthor.com

Copyright © 2024 Louis Berry
All Rights Reserved
ISBN: 979-8-9876139-7-9

1

The sound of the canon from Key West's Mallory Square echoed faintly in Adam Phillip's consciousness. He stood at the end of the White Street pier looking across the water and beyond the horizon. Infinite possibilities for life he'd been taught as a child were replaced by the realization his time on earth approached its conclusion.

Murder was the assignment. It was a task that had been completed nearly one hundred times during his career. Victims were never easy targets. Adam dealt with high level political assassinations. Mostly men who were well protected. The occasional female target proved most difficult.

Personal experience echoed memories of a mother who'd instilled life's infinite possibilities. Women captured by evil proved especially difficult for him to perform assigned tasks. No one in his life had been more nurturing than his mother. He found himself existing in a time when only the intensity of a mother's love could overcome forces working against humanity's survival.

Failures haunted the man who sacrificed his life eliminating evil from the planet. World views had been shaped by parents ignorant of widespread malevolence inhabiting the globe. Innocence was exacerbated by the fact he grew up in a small hamlet in the panhandle of Florida. Isolation during youth slowed the awareness of power structures across the globe and how truly interconnected they were.

Every Saturday as a child was spent at the local library. His mother exposed him to every resource that broadened Adam's mind beyond local circumstances. STEM subjects piqued the young man's interests most. That which could be logically proven through mathematics satiated his innate desire for truth. Facts surrounding the environment in which he was raised never jibed with familial assertions of contentment. Relying on the generosity of others and government assistance weakened those around him. His family never experienced financial independence. Being made subservient never set well with Adam. He wanted to be free to move about the world.

Witnessing the dichotomy of blissful ignorance and his family's descent into poverty drove Adam further from family. No one was willing to acknowledge dire circumstances they'd created for themselves. The boy's logical mind separated failures into that which could have been controlled by his parents and those considered environmental.

Saturdays when most kids were happy to sit at story-time in the library, Adam drifted from the group and sought out advanced material. Physics was his preferred subject. His consciousness was thrust to the four corners of the known universe. It was the only manner in which he escaped an environment over which he had no control.

Blame for financial circumstances beyond his father's control was heaped upon out-of-control stagflation of the nineteen seventies. Adam felt the financial strain placed on his family by a phenomenon no one seemed to understand. Inquiries by the child were met with anger. Curiosity drove him beyond his preferred subject, into that of economics. Soaking in the teachings of Milton Friedman brought a keen understanding of how a monetary base untethered and wildly printed destroyed financial circumstances of all except those rare few who controlled the printing. An increasingly complex world purposefully destroyed intergenerational bonds. Adam was left to seek out life's meaning alone.

Keen intellect exhibited during undergraduate and graduate work at USC and UCLA was rewarded with a scholarship to Stanford University to study Physics. Full scholarships were aplenty and afforded the young student the opportunity to leave his economically depressed hometown for the riches of California. His body matured during his time in Palo Alto. He emerged from his time there with a PhD. Youthful strength sought an outlet for deep seated anger disseminated by a father who embraced corporal punishment over intellectual conversations.

On a whim he took a psychological profile offered a select few students. Initially, it was viewed by the graduate as a means of satisfying burgeoning curiosity toward all sciences. What he didn't realize was it had been administered by the Central Intelligence Agency.

Recruitment into the company was viewed by Adam as the perfect situation. Physical strength thirsted for the opportunity to eliminate those he saw as the cause of inequity throughout the world. Seeds of anger planted into the child grew unchecked. The young man lived solely within his ego. Without consideration of a greater self, he was prevented from making compassionate connections with humanity.

Adam glanced at his Rolex Submariner. It was after 9:00 PM. He began his walk toward Truman Annex. It was a night for executing an assignment communicated through back-channels. From the small Island only ninety miles north of Havana, Cuba, Adam launched into Central and South America whenever his job required. Over the prior decade, several jobs were completed in Key West. It was a place that not only attracted unsettled souls in search of nubile flesh, but those in search of world class fishing and water sports. Its proximity to Miami offered an additional lure.

Adam meandered west down White Street. He took on the look of a tourist wearing baggy cargo shorts and a Guy Harvey shirt printed with blue marlins breaching the water's surface.

His home was blocks away on Southard Street. Whenever there was a job to do, he left its comfort behind and disassociated himself from the relief it offered. Adam tapped into his childhood rage whenever he was tasked with killing another human. It was a hue of energy he never wished to infect his home. He'd witnessed the damage thrust upon siblings in a household filled with anger.

Seeking Trinity

His wife, son, and daughter-in-law had been killed in an accident eighteen months earlier. Only he and his adopted granddaughter remained.

Desperate attempts to maintain a connection with Carolyn, his wife, fused passion and logic. After the deaths of his family, Adam's scientific mind reconnected with his conception of God so eloquently proved in his doctoral thesis. It was based in the purity of energy, and he was certain his lifestyle prevented life beyond his earthly manifestation. He was convinced multiple deaths by his hand tainted his spirit. He feared his soul would be pushed beyond the fruitful upon death, like the negative pole of a magnet. Never would he be allowed to exist among the right and just. Like the energy pushed through the dead circuit of an electric iron, he saw his life ending in a heated rage.

Adam turned on South Street toward the east end of Duval. Foot traffic increased the closer he got to the avenue of a thousand abuses. He mingled amongst tourists and locals seeking debauched pleasures. Judgment was absent the man possessing fresh memories of his own descent into alcohol abuse. During their twenty-eight-year marriage, Carolyn taught Adam the concept of eternity. He witnessed her countenance as it aged but found their bond strengthening beyond potential for collapse. Would the universe allow them to be together after his death?

Three years earlier he'd given up alcohol. No longer numb to the world, his attraction to his wife grew more intense. Thoughts of his ultimate demise entered his consciousness daily. He hoped they would be reunited after death but knew only outright repentance would counter evil deeds.

The only person that prevented willful crossover was his granddaughter, Maritza. She was sixteen years old, and there was so much he needed to tell her about the world. He needed to be her most ardent supporter. She would need to be told of the evil that will always inhabit the world, and how he'd succumb to its siren song. Adam knew he couldn't abandon her.

The assassin turned right on Duval Street and began his trek toward the west end of the thoroughfare. Far from the docks where cruise ships brought families to the island were the less family friendly businesses that occupied this end of the street. Bathhouses and drag bars flourished peddling the flesh so many desired. As he approached these establishments he crossed to the opposite side of the street. His actions were not borne of derision. Months earlier there had been a shooting at the Adam and Adam Club. He simply desired a more defensive position if gunfire broke the night air once again.

A small Sig Sauer P365 9mm pistol felt weighty inside his left pocket. Its small profile alerted no one on the street to its presence. Adam tugged lightly on the pocket's rim to experience the substance of the gun. His action offered assurance to its existence.

Hours were spent meandering. Taking on the aimless path of a tourist acted as camouflage. Circumstances were set for him to take custody of the target of his assassination at 3:00 AM. Orders came down that he would be joined by a young associate. It was the first time in over a decade Adam was made to include another intelligence asset during a mission. But why?

The two met earlier in the day at a diner on Roosevelt Boulevard. The young agent was twenty-five years of age and filled with self-importance. His name was a disguise given to him by the agency, Jim Norton.

As Adam recalled their meeting, echoing in his thoughts was the constant tapping on the table of the man's signet ring. The action was incessant, and the older agent felt its repetition was meant to convey a message. What that was, he had yet to ascertain.

Nearing 11:00 PM, Adam passed the Bison and Flute Pub. Erratic roaming dulled awareness of immediate surroundings. The agent was startled when a couple in their late thirties stepped out of the stairwell that led to the rooftop clothing optional bar. A stalemate ensued as they stopped on the sidewalk in front of him.

Quickly he stepped aside and kept moving forward; until he heard his name being called.

"Adam," the young woman called. He didn't turn and kept walking.

Again, she called but louder. "Adam."

He was forced to turn and extinguish the situation that threatened to expose his identity. Standing and smiling at him were Mary Miller and her husband Lester Goldman. Chills ran down the man's spine at the realization of who stood before him. He shook his head and replied, "wrong guy." Without another word, Phillips turned and walked quickly toward Mallory Square.

Fear prevented him from turning to see if the couple was following him. Hopefully, the message had been heeded. He couldn't be bothered.

Time approached midnight and he stood along the railing at Mallory Square. Only then did he take the time to search the faces of the dwindling crowd for Mary and Lester. They were nowhere to be seen.

Mary was a television journalist. A beautiful woman from South Africa who immigrated to the United States after attending college in country. She'd gained a reputation as one who sought truth. It was a sadly unique trait entering the third decade of the twenty-first century. Troubling was the fact she knew exactly who Adam was, and the job he'd performed for three decades. Not even his wife possessed that knowledge.

Two years prior he'd shared information with Mary concerning a global human trafficking ring that'd been operating out of the Ukraine. When her bosses refused to air the story, she took to social media with her findings. Her account was censored, and she lost all credibility within the media community.

Determination by Mary to expose the truth cost her dearly. Acting on orders, a gang of Taliban soldiers in Afghanistan brutally raped her. It was hoped, by those issuing orders, she would succumb to the brutality. Her death would be martyred and exploited by media narratives. She proved too strong. Adam embraced more respect for the woman he was forced to ignore than anyone he'd ever known.

The aging operative felt responsible for what happened to the woman he considered a friend. He loved her without reservation; like a sister. Exacerbating discomfort was the recollection he'd never been able to visit her in the hospital. Had he, it would have alerted his bosses he was the source of information regarding Ukrainian human trafficking.

Lester stood by his wife and nurtured her physical and emotional being back to health. It seemed serendipitous their first trip as a couple led to an encounter with Adam. Familiarities were cast aside by the couple. Mary was astute and realized their friend possessed a higher calling that night.

More time was spent meandering as a tourist, lost and without direction.

Apparent indecision was discarded in favor of the mission's purpose when he made his way down Thomas Street, to the rear entrance of Truman Annex. Punching the code onto the rear iron gate's lock, he released its hold and pushed open the entrance. He walked down Fleming Street and took the first left onto Porter Lane. Continuing until its conclusion in a parking area, he walked to a black Chrysler 300 that had been parked there to accomplish the evening's mission.

Inside the vehicle were black pants and shirt, into which he quickly changed. He looked at his watch once again. It was 1:00 AM. Adam folded his arms across his chest and waited for Norton to join him.

For two hours Adam sat and thought about his past. Repressed experiences were brought into his consciousness to appease an ever-present desire for critical examination. Strength had left his aging body and he focused on the ethereal. Memories occupying points along the timeline of his life were brought together to create a mosaic of the man he'd become. Although cracked and imperfect, he conceived a path toward an eternal existence with the wife he missed dearly. Murders by his hand muddied that vision.

Adam's memories possessed the potential for destruction. He'd never used his knowledge of the universe to advance humanity's understanding of their place within infinite society. The assassin knew there was a way forward for all of humanity to coexist, and flourish eternally. His only failure was that he'd yet to quantify the concept.

Mary once again filled his thoughts. Until the assault she was forced to endure, he innocently thought her cache could bring about meaningful change to humanity. She had the platform upon which to communicate the source of all that was wrong in the world. She was meant to die that day. The same men who ordered her rape, directed Adam to work with an unknown associate. Was it his turn to die?

Adam was allowed to operate as a lone assassin for nearly a decade. Jim Norton had been inserted into his world for one purpose; or so Adam worried. Decades of rotating politicians promising peace, while simultaneously implementing war, tainted the man's view. No matter the party to which one subscribed, the advancement of democracy through violent means continued unabated since the assassination of JFK. Adam's understanding resolved the source of control emanated from a handful of elite families who'd been in control of humanity for a millennium.

The Nazis' desire for a thousand-year Reich and its connection to elite families was easily conceived by the man with knowledge of global political machinery. Force never provided peace. It was a method; a means to an end; and those in control would not relent until their ultimate goal was achieved. What that final objective was, only few elites knew. Adam had been a mere cog in the machinery.

The assassin understood even though an objective may be reached, violence would be the manner in which hegemony over humanity was maintained. There would never be peace for the survivors; those who aligned themselves with the elite. Desire for destruction embraced by evil could never be satiated.

Adam was startled by tapping of Norton's signet ring on the passenger's side window. He pressed the door unlock button and the young agent opened the door and entered the car.

There was something devious emanating from the young man's eyes as he stared at Adam. "You ready to murder a Cuban national?"

Fear of triggering the younger man's presumed second directive, his murder at the hands of an up-and-comer, was blunted when Adam agreed. "Sure."

There was so much more going through his mind. He looked down at Jim's left hand resting on his thigh. The ring he seemed so fond of populated the third finger of that hand. Did that signify devotion to that which it represented? Symbolism meant something to evil, and its design conveyed several malevolent symbols.

"So, what do you think Project Trinity is?" the young agent asked, impetuously.

Something contained in the energy that connected the two on this night spoke to Adam. His partner's inquiry seemed exploratory, less concerned about the man who'd been targeted for assassination. "Maybe we should ask the Cuban, once we take him into custody."

The two sat silent for several minutes.

Jim fractured the stillness once again. "I bet it has something to do with assassinating the president. You know one-third of the balance of power."

"Hmmm. Maybe so."

"Or it could be about the assassination of the third house of Saud?"

Adam looked sternly at his partner. "What would be accomplished by that?"

The young agent shrugged. "Just spit balling."

Seeking Trinity

Wild theories were cast into the conversation to offer a broad array of possibilities. Doing so was meant to elicit from Adam knowledge as to Project Trinity's stated goal. It was a mission known to the younger agent. His soul had been compromised by promises of eternal human existence. Differences between the men were stark. It wasn't as simple as occupying different stages of life. Adam's perspective was universal. What was to be encountered beyond death and how minuscule human lives were on an eternal timeline was the manner in which Adam approached life.

Norton was all about preserving the pleasures of flesh as long as possible. Beset by desire, the young agent believed those who controlled him possessed universal knowledge that could make immortality a reality. It was how they mocked God; feeling as though they controlled the ultimate disposition of souls.

Any extension of life proved temporary. Adam understood. Jim didn't.

The driver checked his watch. It was time. He pressed the ignition button and the car's engine roared to life. He backed out of the space and made his way to Fleming Street. He took a left, advanced a hundred feet and then another left on Emma Street. Stopping at Southard Street before turning left, Adam considered the irony his house was a mere quarter mile away. Thoughts of his granddaughter sleeping soundly offered comfort to a man heading toward destruction.

He maneuvered the car left and continued past the guardhouse. A right on Whitehead Street propelled the car away from their intended destination. As circuitous as his pedestrian path had been, so was that of the two men in the vehicle. Convoluted courses were meant to disguise intent.

The witching hour passed three hours earlier. Simonton Street was deserted. The asphalt glistened from tropical rains all too familiar to Key West. Yellows, reds, and greens flashed on the road's surface with the intermittent changing of traffic lights. Faint sounds of revelers could be heard from Duval Street. He enjoyed the cover of darkness and its solitude. No one wandered more than a block away from the central party hub at that hour. Operations in the dark were the specialty of the federal government and its minions.

Adam drove the four-door black Chrysler 300 speedily down the empty thoroughfare. Tires hissed constantly on the rain-soaked road as Adam made his way toward their destination. Their mission was to disappear a Cuban national caught passing intel on Project Trinity to a CIA informant in Dubai. His crimes had been committed in a far-away land, but he'd been brought to Key West due to its proximity to his homeland. The appearance of his dead body in these waters could be easily explained. The men were fortunate that green traffic signals lit their entire path.

The agents' destination was the federal courthouse. It was one of the grandest structures on the island, a massive two-story edifice clad in limestone mined from a local quarry. It took up half a city block. Its parking lot sat on the other half. Surrounding the lot were iron spikes, seven feet tall and four inches in circumference. The tips were painted gold and meant to dress up an otherwise medieval-looking threat against unlawful intruders.

The tires skidded slightly as Adam turned into the courthouse's drive at a speed slightly beyond safe. He braked hard, bringing the vehicle to a stop in front of the iron-spiked barricade.

His young passenger got out of the car and approached the gate's gold painted lock as he took a key from his right front pocket. He opened the lock, removed the heavy chain, and pulled mightily to slide the heavy gate open.

Adam drove through the gate and pulled into the parking spot around the rear corner of the building nearest a large, windowless steel door.

The young passenger left the gate open and jogged to the back of the building. He rounded the corner, so he'd be hidden from the view of anyone passing on the street. As an added precaution he pulled his Glock 19A from his belt and a silencer from his jacket pocket. He joined the two.

Adam emerged from the car and hurried to the rear door. He pulled a single key from his pants pocket, unlocked the door, and disappeared into the dark courthouse.

Feeling along the rear wall, he found the switch. The long rear corridor filled with light.

At the end of the hall, he found what he was looking for—a holding cell next to the bailiff's entrance to the main courtroom. It was never meant to house anyone overnight, but inside lay a man on a wooden bench. His hands were cuffed behind his back, and a black hood, cinched at the neck, covered his head.

The startled prisoner struggled to sit up as Adam unlocked the door and stepped inside. Moving quickly, he concentrated on the task at hand. He was forced to keep at bay compassionate thoughts possessing the potential to distract him. Adam blocked out philosophical considerations at moments like this. He'd honed the skill over decades of completing horrific jobs on behalf of God and country. His concept of God and the universe changed greatly throughout life. Constantly changing viewpoints possessed the potential to destroy the man.

He grabbed the prisoner's right bicep, yanked him from the cell, and walked him out of the building. Neither said a word.

When the lookout saw the two emerge from the courthouse, he gave one last glance toward the empty street, fell back from his position, and retook his seat on the passenger side of the Chrysler.

Adam shoved the hooded captive into the back seat. Norton turned around and pressed the end of his silencer to the man's forehead—the only statement necessary.

Adam settled into his seat and closed the car door as quietly as he could, not wanting to draw attention to happenings behind the courthouse building.

Questions about the night's mission popped off in his mind like Fourth of July fireworks. As much as he wished to press the accelerator and be done with the task that lay ahead, decades of experience overcame his impulse. Age changed him. No longer did he simply give over his trust to authority. Contemplating his place in the universe brought him to the realization no one was above God. Why should he trust the narrative offered by a flawed human? He himself possessed many failings. Examining every aspect of his time on earth was supposed to bring him satisfaction his was a life well-lived. But as he controlled the circumstances that would lead to the death of another, Adam wondered if he'd ever made a Godly decision.

The trip east on Simonton Street was not nearly as smooth as the trip to the courthouse. Shimmering green asphalt gave way to frustrating, intermittent red as the car seemed to encounter every stop light on the street. Adam just wanted the night to be over.

Finally, the assassin drove sharply left onto Windsor Lane. Although the task of taking another man's life lay ahead, Adam's anxiety dissipated as the conclusion of his mission grew nigh. He'd become numb to the deaths of others. His own imminent demise weighed heavily on him.

The driver turned left onto Passover Lane and drove the short distance to the three-way intersection of Passover, Angela Street, and Carey Lane. He turned into the entrance of the cemetery.

Slowly, the driver steered the car toward the center of the graveyard. He knew its layout well. He took the fifth path to the left and brought the car to a stop in front of a mausoleum with the name "Robert Otto" inscribed on its façade.

The entire trip had been made in silence. Adam knew words could get someone killed, and the fewer spoken, the greater his chance of survival.

The driver quickly emerged from the car and moved toward the great stone edifice. With the tip of his shoe, he tapped out a distinct pattern on a group of stones that lay on the side of the burial house. The rear wall slowly sank into ground revealing an iron staircase that led down through hollowed out limestone, and into complete darkness.

The driver returned to the car, reached into the back seat, grabbed the prisoner by the upper arm, and hauled him out and onto his feet. He nodded for his accomplice to take control of the prisoner. The three men moved quickly around the mausoleum, through the doorway, down into the darkness, and out of sight.

Adam went ahead of the other two. It was completely dark, but he knew the layout of the murder chamber like it was his own living room. When he reached the landing, he flipped a switch, filling the space with an eerie red glow.

He reached out and grabbed the top of the hood and removed it from his prisoner's head. It took only a moment for the Cuban's eyes to adjust to the softer red light.

Two steps down from the platform on which they stood the prisoner saw an iron mechanism that resembled the jaws of a large shark. Fashioned along each mandible were metal, serrated teeth. It was obviously designed to precisely mimic the bite of a Great White. Farther below ran a stream that had been cut from the limestone. Affected by tides, its level rose and fell with the currents and storm surge that regularly influenced the island.

The Cuban put two and two together and envisioned his shark-mangled body washed out to sea and then back onto a Key West beach. He looked to his left, then to his right. Each of his captors held one of his arms. They controlled what little of his life remained. As a Cuban intelligence operative, he knew this day would eventually come.

"Interesting little James Bond contraption you have set up," he said bravely. "You Americans come up with such unique ways to hide your crimes."

The man's bravado caught even Adam, the veteran assassin, off guard.

The Cuban looked at Adam and smirked. "At least I can go to my grave knowing the United States sent their most prolific murderer after me." Neither captor responded. "What's the matter? Neither of you seem to be having any fun. Isn't this why you got into this line of work? So you can murder bad people? Or at least those your government deems bad?"

"You're getting to be a bit too mouthy," the young captor said, before punching him in the face with his free hand.

The man's head snapped back. Upon gathering his composure, he laughed. "Watch the ring, asshole."

"Okay, let's get on with this," Adam said. "Do you have anything else you want to say to God before we kill you?" His words were sincere.

"I have one question of you, and then I will speak to God. If that's okay."

"Go ahead."

"For what crime do I stand judged by your government and by the two of you?"

Adam was confident and matter of fact. "You were caught passing information on Project Trinity. In other words, you've been engaged in an effort to eliminate most of the world's population." The leader had unwittingly acknowledged his understanding of the global elite's directive.

"Wrong. I was passing bogus information meant to flush out the true perpetrators of Project Trinity."

"Oh?" said Adam. "Who's that?"

"They aren't who you think they are. Just like your bosses have never been the originators of your orders. A consortium of intelligence assets from all over the world have been working off the books to prevent programs like Project Trinity from happening."

Adam's epiphany brought forth the realization his work on that night was merely a repetition of lifelong behavior; an action devoid of critical thought. Seeking greater awareness brought him to this point in life. Aging flesh shifted focus to energy contained within his soul. That which propelled him forward had been tainted by societal impediments. He conceived all humans should be afforded the opportunity to freely express their souls. Was the Cuban's energy pure?

Upon meeting Norton earlier that evening at a diner, he examined the man's signet ring to which the Cuban referred. It had the all-seeing eye surrounded by three black onyxes that formed a two-dimensional pyramid. Rays emanated from the larger, top stone, signifying the black sun worshipped by World War II–era Nazis. The dark star symbolized our galaxy's black hole, destroying all matter approaching its event horizon. It was an evil bastardization of the Christian Trinity. A singular inflection point in a man's life could never have been more obvious.

The Cuban saw through the assassin's eyes and into his soul. Adam's hesitance was all too obvious. He continued questioning the man's actions. "What makes your country better than mine? We don't have the prostitution and human-trafficking problem your country has. We don't have the drug problem your country has. Are Cubans that different from Americans? No! You must ask yourself why is that? Is your government complicit? With the NSA recording every single conversation, text, and website traffic, why is it that the people who are causing so much damage to your country have not been arrested? I'll tell you. Your politicians, judges, and corporate executives are profiting from it. We are both in the intelligence game. Do you honestly think Fidel didn't know these things? Of course, he did. He may have overreacted in tightening restrictions in my country, but he succeeded in many ways. Your own John Adams said, 'Our Constitution was made only for a moral and religious people. It is wholly inadequate to the government of any other.' Or did they not teach you that in your school?" He chuckled. "Americans think themselves as intellectuals. Yet whenever anyone possesses a contradictory ideology, your solution is to eliminate them with some crude medieval device hidden inside a limestone cave." He tossed his head toward the jaws of death.

Norton shifted his feet. "All right. Say adios, amigo." All he desired was the orgasmic burst of vitality felt in taking the life of another.

Adam held up a calming hand.

The Cuban viewed his captor's hesitation as an inducement to continue. "We live in a world where we have to compete. There are no easy ways out. There are no shortcuts. Those who promise such are destroying those who follow them. Think about the timeline of your life. American households in the fifties and sixties could exist on one income. Now people must use a credit card to buy groceries. It's all by design." He saw that he was not getting through to Adam. It needed to become personal. "What kind of world do you wish to leave for your Guatemalan born granddaughter? Do you know how lucky she is? Did you know the adoption service your son used was set up to benefit human traffickers and pedophiles? Women having babies for the sole purpose of making money feeds the supply line. Your granddaughter's soul is fortunate to have made its way into your home. Now it's up to you to educate her properly to the evil that exists in the world, and from where it comes."

Adam never considered assets from adversarial agencies would research him. Simultaneously, it scared him while making perfect sense. Another epiphany rang within his being. He'd become so much an arrogantly blunt instrument, he couldn't fathom himself the target of another agency. Was the Cuban trying to send a message? His enemy's words contained urgency. Did the prisoner know Adam was meant to die that night? Did Norton truly have a second directive?

Wisdom comes from age and experience. The Cuban's thoughts paralleled many of Adam's recent judgments. He realized the murder of this man was meant to further the agenda of evil. How much damage would Adam do to humanity by taking from it this man who seemed to care so much? He gambled with his life every time he accepted a mission. The situation in which he found himself mimicked that of a roulette wheel. Should he bet red or black?

He raised his gun and aimed it at the forehead of his captive.

"Wait," the Cuban pleaded. "You promised one last talk with God."

Adam sighed. "Okay." He lowered his gun frustratingly, allowing it to slap against his leg.

Hands still cuffed behind his back, the Cuban dropped to his knees and bowed his head. "Dear God. The souls contained in these three men have been brought together under dubious circumstances. We ask you not judge us for the failings of human flesh but allow us to exist together in harmony for all of eternity." The captive's tone seemed sincere.

Adam furrowed his brow. The man was about to die, yet he prayed for the eternal peace of his executioners. Just when he thought he'd figured out life, someone did something so surprisingly selfless. Childlike innocence had long been suppressed in favor of acute skepticism. Deep within the recesses of his mind Adam recalled saying prayers each night with his mother. Requests for humanity's happiness were pure to the child. The Cuban's prayer sparked his long dormant faith in humanity. Adam grew in the moment. He understood his intended victim possessed not only wisdom and strength, but love for his fellow man; regardless of circumstances. Spiritual awareness was the only path that would propel the man toward a universal existence beyond his earthly vessel. It was that same peace of mind Adam sought.

Shaking his head, he raised the gun toward his captive's face, shifted it upward and fired. The bullet struck Norton between the eyes. The young man's arm went slack, and his gun fell from his hand and clanged onto the metal deck. Then the man himself slumped and fell to the floor.

Adam hurried to the body. He grabbed the gun off the deck and tossed it into the subterranean canal. Then he grabbed the young man under the shoulders and began dragging him down the two steps toward the death mechanism. He paused and looked up at the Cuban. "If I remove your handcuffs, are you gonna help me?"

"What are you going to do with him?" The Cuban asked.

Adam stood the man up and removed his prisoner's restraints. "The same thing I was going to do to you. I'm going to put his head in that contraption, chop it off, and throw his body into the channel for it to be swept into the ocean. He'll wash up on Smather's Beach, same as you would have. Victim of a shark attack."

The Cuban rubbed his wrists and surveyed the situation. "Wouldn't it be easier to take a chunk out of the side? That would look more like a shark attack."

"Agreed. However, I'm sure there's no way you would've allowed us to simply place you in that contraption so we could take a chunk out of your side, so we'd already rejected the most realistic option. Besides, we have to remove the evidence of the bullet wound. Also, this will play better with the media. Can't you just see the headline? WHERE'S THE HEAD?"

The Cuban laughed. "You understand your culture better than I thought."

The prisoner grabbed the dead man's ankles, and he and Adam carefully made their way down the two steps and positioned the man's head inside the iron jaws.

Adam looked at his new partner in crime. "Would you like to do the honors?"

"I don't mind if I do," said the Cuban. As he approached the machinery he seemed at a loss.

"You release the hydraulic pressure with this lever," Adam said, pointing to a long iron bar that wouldn't have been out of place in Frankenstein's lab.

The Cuban grabbed the control and, without hesitation, released the jaws that crashed together.

Inside the chamber, the sound was deafening. The blood splatter was more than Adam anticipated. It sprayed both men's pants below the knees. The head, its oblong shape and uneven weight distribution, rolled crazily at the men's feet like a Mexican jumping bean.

"I'll take care of that," Adam said.

"What do you want from me?" the Cuban asked.

"Nothing, other than to never see you again," Adam replied as he pushed Norton's body into the subterranean canal by rolling it over with his right foot.

The Cuban nodded and turned away. He double-timed it up the stairs, through the door, and into the darkness.

Adam tried to grab the severed head by its short, gelled, spiky hair. He could not get a good grip and dropped the head twice before finally grabbing it by an ear. He placed it in the cloth hood that once covered the Cuban's head and wiped his hand on his slacks.

Quickly, the aged assassin climbed the stairs and exited the mausoleum. His first stop was at the rear of the car where he placed the head in the trunk. Adam moved back to the crypt and secured it by tapping out the pattern on the stones once again.

Only after he'd slid behind the wheel of the car did the gravity of his actions fully soak into his consciousness. He faced the most uncertain future he'd ever known. Conscious anxiety extended to his granddaughter's life as well.

2

Maritza Phillips sat at the desk in her bedroom. Four double French doors that extended from floor to ceiling were open, allowing the cool morning breeze to swirl about her room. Sheer curtains flounced and fluttered as the wind exerted its influence. Just outside was the second-floor balcony that wrapped the entire home. The girl's bedroom was situated at the front of the house and looked down upon Southard Street.

The teenager had grown to accept the late hours her grandfather's schedule dictated. She had no idea where he went on those nights. If he was to be gone for days a captain from the nearby Navy Base would come and stay with her. The man placed in her father's stead seemed less interested in providing guidance for an adolescent who grew more isolated by the day. To her, she seemed nothing more than a passing acquaintance. That was about to change.

Photographs sprinkled about her room displayed countenances unlike her own. Brown skin burst forth in images containing the only family she'd come to know. Isolation began upon examination of all that was physical. Natural assessments were made by a teenager coming to understand her maturing human manifestation. Seclusion was exacerbated by her only parental figure nearing the impending release of his eternal soul back into the universe as hers was maturing into the woman she'd become. Opposing life forces provided no occasion for conversations meant to merge emotional arroyos flowing in different directions.

Seeking Trinity

    The two Phillips were far apart on life's path. Never had a catalyst presented itself to facilitate even the simplest discourse centered on basic human conditions.

    Logic spoke to her circumstances being much better than if she'd remained in Guatemala. Maritza couldn't help wondering if she'd stayed with her birth family whether she'd be surrounded by loving people daily. Her parents openly discussed all they knew of her Central American genealogy. Nothing was ever kept secret. Two large manilla envelopes contained all adoption paperwork, and information about both birth and adoptive families. The young girl had access to the documentation from the age of ten. There was even a grainy passport photo of her birthmother.

    Occasionally, she took the documents and sat on her bed reading every word filled with hope something she'd missed during a prior review would answer remaining questions. As she aged, the teenager occasionally held a mirror to her face and compared it to the passport vision staring back at her. Post pubescent influences brought forth similarities in the two women's DNA. Although she'd never met the birth-mother upon which she gazed, it gave her comfort to embrace a physical being so like herself. It offered a place in the world.

    Late nights were spent by the teenager gaming with all manner of people across the globe. What little structure the old man offered the girl was the command to be in bed at a reasonable hour. Teenage logic was employed to redefine an acceptable bedtime. One such rationalization was the money she earned from competitions, and contributions from the many followers she touched nightly across the globe.

    The same accident that killed her parents had taken the life of her grandmother. Maritza attributed her grandfather's continued absences as him carrying on relationships with women. In reality there had not been a single woman in the man's life since his wife's death.

    Carolyn meant the world to Adam. He maintained their connection by reminiscing daily. He wasn't opposed to relationships, but there hadn't been a woman he met that struck at his soul the way his wife had. It was instantaneous when they first met, and nothing short of that feeling would be pursued twenty-eight years later.

Little time was afforded to allow the relationship between Adam and Maritza to grow organically and flourish. Life lessons weren't instilled. Meaningful conversations were devoid in their relationship. Time spent together focused on self-defense. Adam wouldn't allow his granddaughter's well-being to be left to the mercy of a humanity he'd come to distrust.

Instructions on how to use a firearm and martial arts were given at the nearby Navy Base. The young girl never knew to question how supposed civilians gained access to a secure facility. It was all like day camp to her and had been so with her father as well. Years of training rendered the girl adequately equipped to defend herself until brute force from oversized assailants gained its advantage. For that reason, focus centered on the deft use of firearms.

Her favorite days were when they drove to Miami for urban assault training at an outdoor course near the Everglades. Innocent and violent targets alternately appeared from the shadows and must be dealt with accordingly. Draw, aim, and fire became second nature to Maritza. That which her grandfather took seriously, she conceived as fun and games.

Self-defense skills were developed long before her foray into the global gaming community. Once acuity of keyboard strokes was maximized, she became a sought-after teammate from those with many years of experience. Barbs were callously tossed about from male members of the community, but only until her skills eclipsed theirs. Maritza took delight in telling the men she'd killed on the meta battlefield to, "go make me a sandwich."

Military precision was exercised throughout every household activity. Duty lists were maintained to ensure the home's continued operation. There was never a time when the grandfather let the girl just be a girl. He viewed frivolity as weakness.

It was 4:00 A.M. when she heard her grandfather's car enter the driveway from Southard Street. Sitting in a dimly lit environment, she quickly bid adieu to her friends all over the world.

Darkness cloaked the room with the exception of her dual monitor computer display. She quickly switched off all electronics, tossed her headset onto the desk in front of her, slid out of her chair, and moved toward bed. She scurried, bent over, so her grandfather wouldn't detect movement through her balcony doors at such a late hour.

Laying still, she listened for the front door to open. Instead, she thought she heard the trunk of her grandfather's car pop open.

Curious, she slid out of bed and walked to her open terrace door. Crouching, she peered through the balcony's railing and saw nothing but his car with an open trunk.

Unbeknownst to Maritza, her grandfather had taken Norton's head into the garage. It had become standard operating procedure whenever the cemetery apparatus was employed. He stood at his workbench. Placing the head on its surface, Adam held both hands just above the face until it wobbled to a stop. He bent over and retrieved a small red cooler from the shelf below.

Opening it, he placed the head into the container. Quickly, he walked to the freezer and removed a large bag of ice. He tore a hole into the plastic at the top and spread the ice evenly over the face until it no longer stared up at him. Slamming the lid closed, he picked up a large roll of gray duct tape and proceeded to wrap it around the top and bottom. Once he felt the container secure enough to discourage casually prying eyes, he walked from the garage and placed it in the trunk.

From her bedroom, Maritza watched as her grandfather gently closed the trunk. The man minimized noise to prevent awakening his granddaughter. When she saw him move from the car to the sidewalk, and toward the front door, she scurried back into bed.

3

After assassinations there was never any communication. Not from Adam to his handlers or they to him. No tips about a dead body to the cops. The whole thing was just left to play out as if a random occurrence. Somebody would eventually trip over the body on the beach while on an early morning jog. Cops would get involved; the media would tell the story. It was always the same.

Adam never failed a mission; until that night. He never considered consequences of his work, outside of his own death. He'd always faced that possibility believing its eventuality to be God's will. Zeitgeist within the intelligence community portrayed objectives as a winnable fight between good and evil. What he thought to be righteous was in actuality furtherance of a malevolent force.

Concepts centering on an omniscient being were always believed, but never fully understood. Those who wished to exist eternally possessed the spirit. Adam was certain if humanity connected respective energies in a positive light, an impenetrable shield of contentment would encase earth.

Because he'd never disobeyed an order or failed an objective, there was never any reason to fear his granddaughter was in danger. His wife and son had died nearly two years earlier, and his granddaughter's well-being became paramount. The Cuban's assertion she'd been part of a human trafficking ratline rang in his psyche. He couldn't shake it. Had his son and daughter-in-law repeated poor judgment Adam displayed choosing a career in intelligence? His doctoral thesis had come from a place within him that understood humanity to be temporary, and souls eternal.

Abandoned upon graduation was his conception of the perpetual in favor of immediate gratification. Elimination of those conceived as working contrary to Godliness brought forth carnal elation time and again; mission by mission. As Adam aged he understood how short-lived the vivacity of youthful pursuits. He'd come to understand that societal principals had been inverted. Supposed good deeds throughout the world actually advanced the agenda of evil.

The Key West home on Southard Street was ringed with a white picket fence. Lush tropical landscaping hid most of the façade from those wandering past on the sidewalk. Spanish style architecture gave the home a distinctive look. It was two stories. Glass doors ringed both floors and were occasionally opened to experience cool ocean breezes. Wrought iron poles extended from the ground and provided support for the balcony and roof that were cantilevered from the main structure of the house.

Adam leaned against the iron railing of the second-floor balcony as he sipped his morning coffee. It was late morning. Unusual for him. Given the events of the early hours of the day, he needed to assess his next move. If the Cuban ratted him out, he would have no time. Somehow though, he felt he could trust his adversary. He might have another day to plan. Regardless, Adam knew he had to get out of Key West; where he and his granddaughter were easy targets.

He'd trained for this kind of confrontation. Selfishly, he had not considered the sixteen-year-old girl who lay sleeping in the bedroom on the other side of the full-length glass door behind him.

Successful missions relied on factual intelligence. Lies became apparent, and Adam did not retreat into his fleshly being. He chose to seek that which lay beyond human understanding. Age dictated he look beyond the body that slowly failed him. Viewing earth from a universal perspective, he embraced the notion that all who lived and prospered on the planet were part of the greater good. Each being was a sovereign unto themselves, and he embraced the concept. He teetered between two possible approaches. He could continue deceitful behavior in order not to scare Maritza, or he could be completely honest with her.

It was decided there would be no way for his granddaughter to express her innate value to humanity shrouded in a cloud of lies.

"She mustn't know how grave our existence has become due to my stupid decision," he thought. "No. I've lived lies my entire life. I have to be honest with her. I can be honest with her." He took another sip of coffee. "I just need to introduce our situation slowly."

"Good morning, Papa," called Maritza from behind Adam.

He turned to see his beautiful granddaughter.

Maritza wore flannel pajama bottoms and a Key West High School Conchs T-shirt. Her long black hair was braided to prevent tangles during sleep.

"Hey, sweetie." His gut fluttered nervously. The visage appearing before him acted to exacerbate impugned wisdom of murdering a fellow intelligence asset. He attempted to shake off the nerves with lite-hearted banter. "I see you were up late last night."

"And you didn't get home until four a.m.," she replied, indignantly.

He smiled, hoping her innate Latina fire would bode well for their upcoming adventure. "Listen, we're going to take a little trip up to the panhandle. So, if you can get packed in the next hour that'd be great."

It was Saturday morning, and she considered weekends sacrosanct. "What about school on Monday?"

"I'll take care of that."

"Are we going to the farm in Carrabelle?"

Adam smiled and nodded his head.

"Nice. I like it there."

"Good, because we may be camping there a while." Fun camping thoughts succumbed to the serious nature of their trip. "Oh, and don't bring your cell phone."

"What?" she said, looking at him like he was crazy.

Adam smiled at her playfully. "If I told you our lives depended on you leaving your phone behind, would you do it?"

"Yes," Maritza replied sheepishly. "Okay." She knew her grandfather to be a man few words. If he was asking her to abandon her phone, there was a valid reason.

Adam's smile broadened. "We leave in an hour."

"Okay, Papa."

As Adam packed his necessities, he drew upon his over five decades of life to script the dialogue that would lead Maritza to an understanding of their uncertain future. How could he condense life's experiences into something she'd understand during the course of a one-day drive? Would that be all the time they had left? He'd crossed people who saw murder as the purest form of self-preservation. Memories flickered in his mind—childhood to adult challenges and back to his teen years. In all that, he tried to find a narrative she'd understand. He was surprised to find there didn't seem to be a common thread to tie his experiences with hers.

Times and technology advanced too quickly. Teenage challenges were too dissimilar. All that was familiar centered on simple human expression. It was a strengthened connection between their souls that would bring about survival.

Maritza left the house while Adam was still upstairs in his bedroom. She pulled her wheeled suitcase behind her. It clunked down the steps then clacked along the driveway as she made her way to the rear of the car. She glanced over her shoulder to the balcony of her grandfather's bedroom and the open French doors. "Papa, can you open the trunk?"

From inside the house, and without thinking, Adam fished the key fob out of his pocket. He pressed the release button and satisfactorily heard the trunk pop open.

Thirty-seconds later his granddaughter called up to him again. "Papa, what's in here? Do we need to take it with us?"

Adam stepped out onto the second-floor balcony. Below he saw Maritza holding the small red, duct taped cooler above her head. His heart jumped into his throat, but he forced himself to respond calmly, "Yeah, just shove that into the back of the trunk. I'll take care of it later."

Maritza returned the cooler to the trunk. She moved to the car door, opened it, and sat in the front passenger seat. The teenager watched as her grandfather emerged from the home with a duffle bag in one hand. Tucked under each arm was a rifle and shotgun. He struggled to put down the duffle bag, remove the house key from his pocket, and lock the front door. Then he walked down the steps to the rear of the car. Maritza listened to his footsteps as she stared blankly at the house.

As soon as Adam slid into the driver's seat, Maritza asked, "Why did you bring all of your guns?"

"I thought we'd do a little hunting while we're up there."

"Really? We need *all* the guns. How much hunting are we going to do?"

"I just don't know what mood I'll be in when we get there. Deer? Dove?" He shrugged for effect.

Adam backed the car out of the driveway and headed down the street. He made his way through the one-way streets of Old Town, turned onto US 1, and headed north out of town.

Not a word was spoken as the two drove over the bridge, off the key, and onto Stock Island. Maritza happily fiddled with the car's stereo, searching for music suitable to her young tastes.

Adam grew uneasy, realizing every rotation of the car's tires without conversation was time wasted.

He looked out across the endless blue-green waters to either side of the car. The expanse seemed to fall just short of mocking him. At that moment, he and Maritza were alone in the world; isolated, treading water, and unsure they'd break from its dogma. At some point he'd be made to atone for going against those who ordered assassinations throughout the world every day. He did not despair. For Maritza's sake, he couldn't.

He searched for a way to begin the conversation. "Have you given any thought to what it is you'd like to do to make a living?"

Maritza nodded. "I think I'd like to be an influencer."

Adam wasn't quite sure what that meant, but he tried to be encouraging. "That sounds nice. Like inspiring people to do good things?"

"No, Papa. I want to have a YouTube channel so that I can be famous and not have to work."

Sharper words could not have been spoken. An emotional spike was driven through Adam's heart. He was responsible for her, and became concerned she was veering away from the values he thought he'd been teaching her. Could he make meaningful progress righting her life's path during an eleven-hour drive?

Regardless of what happened when the intelligence apparatus caught up to them, he trusted her soul was eternal and benefitted from their short time together. Adam must know he'd done everything to ensure the health of the life with which he'd been charged.

The grandfather decided to take the highest road possible in response. "That sounds like fun for a teenager, but let me tell you, a lot of things that seem like fun now don't last forever. You should focus on building a skillset that lasts."

"Like what?"

"Well, if I were your father—"

"You are my father. Now."

Adam smiled. This was a relationship he'd hoped for after his son's death. Work always got in the way, and Maritza was left without a father figure several times a year. Sadly, lack of direction was showing in her innocent view of how the world worked. He had to be strong for her. Survive. Those feelings had never been stronger—not even for his own son. "My advice would be to gain a thorough understanding of economics. It's the force used throughout the millennia to enslave people. You'll always have to fight the sort of corruption that exploits innocence. As long as there's life on earth, there will be evil trying to control all living beings. Period. End of story."

"Heavy."

Adam gave her a quick glance. It *was* heavy. He realized he was trying to force an epiphany on his granddaughter that he'd only himself recently become aware. Maybe he needed to take a small step back for a moment. "Okay, how about we let you direct the conversation."

"Deal." Without hesitation she asked, "Do you miss Granny?"

"Every day. There's not a day that goes by that I don't think about the things we did and the things we could be doing together if we'd had the chance to enjoy the final stage of our lives together. She will eternally be a part of my soul."

"That's sweet."

Adam smiled. He embraced an innocent, childlike response. "She had pure energy."

"Energy?"

"Did you know I have my PhD in physics?"

"Yes, Dad told me. He was proud of you."

Adam smiled. "Well, Einstein's theory of relativity states that when you accelerate mass to the speed of light squared, it dissipates into energy. That means the base state of the universe is energy. I believe that holds true for humans. Purely good energy was what made Granny special. The lesson here is to make sure you find a life partner that possesses good energy, or a good soul, if you prefer." He paused. "I fear that your generation focuses too much on the physical."

Maritza contemplated what her grandfather said, attempting to visualize a life partner worthy of commitment. It was a difficult assessment when so many of her friends struggled with finding their own individual way in life.

Coming of age in a human manifestation presented varied challenges. Outward expressions driven by youthful exuberance wrested significance from inner reflections. Could teenagers be expected to seek that which was universal when their flesh tingled with desire constantly? The lesson her grandfather sought to instill in her was the same her parents repeated regularly. She understood good people were few and far between.

When Adam considered the thought of people embracing good energy, he remembered a dream he'd had a week earlier. His instinct was to share it with Maritza, but he hesitated. He feared she wouldn't understand the point of it.

Just as missions had to be based on factual information, his relationship with his granddaughter had to be based on complete honesty, no matter how awkward. He believed honest communication was the foundation of all successful relationships. So, he divulged an inner-most secret.

"I had the oddest dream the other night. Would you like to hear about it?"

"Sure."

"All right, but this is crazy." Adam glanced over at his granddaughter.

She smiled and nodded, eager to hear the story.

"In the dream, I walk into a Bennigan's, and—"

"What's a Bennigan's?"

Adam smiled. "It's where your grandmother and I met. There aren't many of them around anymore. I guess you've never been to one. It's like an Applebee's. I know you've been to an Applebee's."

Maritza still seemed bewildered.

Adam knew the eatery had been a favorite of her father. Maybe he'd never taken her there.

"A chain restaurant."

"Oh. Okay."

"Anyway, I walk in, and the place is crowded. It's standing room only, and I'm wandering through the throng aimlessly. I'm not really looking for a place to sit, and there's no organization to the chaos. No host or hostess. I don't even think there were any servers. Just confusion. Just when the energy of the crowd became unbearable, I see this woman walking across the room toward me. She had an angelic glow that set her apart from the entire room.

Finally, she made her way through the crowd and stood in front of me. That's when I recognized her. She was one of the most important people ever in my life."

"Granny?"

Adam shook his head and smiled. "No. Kathy."

Maritza knew her grandfather was a serious man who didn't smile much. It pleased her to see him express happiness.

"Kathy was an old lover of mine. If it weren't for her, I might not be here today. I may not have met your grandmother, recognized the beauty in her, gotten married, and been so happy for our last twenty-eight years together."

"What was so special about Kathy?"

"In a nutshell, she showed me that a stunningly beautiful woman was capable of possessing a good soul. It was that which she focused on, in herself and in me." He nodded affirmation. "That's the point in my life I began to refocus on my own soul. It's taken me decades to shed the dogmatic expression of my being that had been defined since birth."

"Oh, come on. You're exaggerating."

"No, I'm not. This woman was so beautiful that I often thought she was what Eve must have looked like. A creation from God. What better way to ensure the survival of the species?" Adam smiled, impishly.

"Is that all you took away from the dream?"

"No, hang on." He glanced at his granddaughter. "As my awareness of the situation inside the restaurant grew, I realized every woman I ever had sex with was there. And, by extension, every man that had ever slept with one of the women I'd slept with was there. And let me tell you, there were a lot more men there than women. Some of them my friends."

"Eew."

"Yeah. It happens. The sad realization is that humans are like a colony of rabbits, crawling over one another to have sex." He became distant. "People just can't seem to conceive an existence beyond the physical. You should seek better for yourself."

"Why? You didn't."

"True, yet another aspect of the dream was I saw these women I had sex with, but I couldn't recall any of their names. Sexual…physical encounters were all so insignificant. They obviously meant nothing to me because I could barely remember them. But the one person who gave me continued life and happiness stood out. I'm just saying, you shouldn't have to deal with the bullshit associated with casual relationships."

"But what if I just want to have some fun. Isn't that what you were doing?"

Her question made him consider connections between his upbringing and his view of life. Adam paused to make sure he found the right words. He was afraid he'd confused his granddaughter. "When a child is abused by a parent, by someone that's supposed to love them more than life itself, the effects last decades. I would guess a lot of times the abuser is one who believes they are instilling much needed discipline." He paused in reflection. For a man who embraced stoic strength, confession did not come easily. "It skews that child's view of the world, of God, and can negatively affect all relationships that child will ever have. He'll end up seeking relationships to make up for what he never got from his family, and it's impossible for anyone to fill that void. That's what Kathy, and your granny, gave me—a sense that my own value in the world extended beyond connections defined by DNA. That allowed me to conceive of myself as a universal being, not merely a physical presence that will simply die."

"If you don't want me to have sex with men that I meet and I'm interested in, how I am supposed to find the right man?"

"It's not that I'm telling you not to have sex, what I am saying is that instead of focusing only on the physical attributes of a lover, get to know him as a person. Make sure his energy is good and pure. He'll gain this understanding when he sees himself as an eternal being, not just some dude looking for a good time. Those are the ones less likely to harm you physically or emotionally." He took a deep breath and sighed. "It'll just save you a lot of aggravation. I see that as my job as your parent."

The two sat in silence for several minutes, each contemplating the conversation and digesting exact meanings.

"Papa, I'm not having sex if that's what you're worried about."

"No, Maritza, I don't think you're sexually active. I'm simply trying to correct a pattern in my family so that you won't make the same mistakes we've made for generations. My father never had a conversation with me about how to treat a woman. He never offered the benefit of his life experience in any way. All he instilled in me was avoidance. I avoided confronting reality. And now it's likely to cost us both." He sighed. "Ah, but I digress. As it relates to our conversation, the women of my generation had many sexual partners, it made it more difficult to measure up. No, I'm not saying that my father should have told me the ins and outs of pleasuring a woman during sex, but he could've at least given me a push in the right direction. Hell, buy me a book."

Adam glanced at his granddaughter to see if he could read how she was receiving his message. She seemed contemplative, so he continued. "But I won't lay all blame at his feet. As a young man, I spent a lot of time seeking out the pleasure of women. It was never done spitefully. I was truly looking for Mrs. Right. But the most insignificant quirk would send me on another path, seeking perfection. I guess that's why I liked physics so much. Every relationship between universal elements can be proven mathematically, or it's discarded."

Adam cringed inwardly. He was saying whatever came to mind without thinking. Maybe he was revealing too much about himself. "I guess if you're looking for the elevator pitch, it's this: Make sure you choose a spouse that renders all other potential mates irrelevant. And, if your spouse isn't your best friend, you're doing it wrong."

Speaking about sex to his granddaughter made Adam uncomfortable. Awkward conversations he'd missed having with his father might have sent his life along a more fruitful path. Regret over saying the things he'd said wasn't allowed to stifle conversation, but he decided to bring the topic to a close. "All I'm saying is, don't rush it. Don't be afraid to express your needs to your lover. And if they denigrate you for doing so, that's the clearest sign their souls aren't settled into their eternal existence. They won't be right for you. These people will cause you more pain than their attention is worth. Conceive of love as being eternal, a gift from God. And find someone who feels the same way. Then the two of you will live in harmony for eternity."

The grandfather glanced at his passenger once again. Maritza appeared deep in thought and Adam had no idea what she was thinking. He fell silent too.

Over the next hour Adam considered the tactical defense necessary to ensure survival. As deeply as he concentrated on that, Maritza never left his thoughts. Trying to fill the roles of both parent and General MacArthur proved maddening.

Out of the corner of his eye, he saw his granddaughter continue to fiddle with the stereo, always seeking out her favorite music as they moved from town to town. The soundtrack to her life was always heard emanating from her bedroom. It all seemed to have the same rhythm and was built from computer algorithms. Names of artists weren't recognized by Adam, and he had no desire to learn them.

He wondered whether Maritza had taken their conversation to heart. She didn't need to understand it completely, but Adam hoped it was a conversation she would embrace for the rest of her life. He would never know for sure. Such was the nature of being a parent.

Adam navigated onto US Highway 41, the Tamiami Trail; known colloquially as Alligator Alley. He still had no idea how to save his own life, much less that of his granddaughter. Guilt began to pulse within as regret for killing Norton grew. His actions of the previous night had been impetuous. He'd long questioned the nature of his business and how he'd lived his adult life on the evil end of the universe's energy spectrum. The ultimate demise of the two refugees, whether it occurred within days or in years, would never prevent Adam from trying to be the best possible grandfather to Maritza.

If one were to mark the point at which Adam turned away from evil and embraced a life of decency, that moment could be marked when he met Carolyn. Reflecting on their time together brought a great deal of clarity. Those twenty-eight years were a period of personal growth like Adam never experienced. He understood that, for him to experience a blissful eternity, he would have to embrace the truth, infinite love, and the happiness it brought him in the earthly embodiment of his soul.

It was okay he'd set in motion the events that would end his life. If the company he worked for murdered them both, would Maritza's soul flourish afterward? Would youthful innocence overcome ignorance of God, creating a path for her eternal spirit? He felt he truly knew God, and his energy would remain coalesced and happy at the time of his death. His granddaughter's fate concerned Adam most.

For decades as an assassin, he'd felt as though he were eliminating those who wanted to defeat God. In reality, he'd spent that time doing evil's bidding. He came to understand how adept malevolence was at making falsehoods seem true. It pained him to understand he'd spent his entire career eliminating warriors for God.

Adam turned off of Tamiami Trail and onto a two-rut road, catapulting his thoughts from his past to the task at hand. He drove the car several miles, glancing occasionally at his sleeping granddaughter. It had been dry in Florida for a month, and as Adam sped down the narrow path, the car's tires kicked up a huge plume of dust behind the vehicle. These were not ideal conditions for anyone to perform a clandestine operation. He had no choice.

Adam brought the car to a stop in front of a dilapidated fishing shack.

The trip down the undulating lane jostled Maritza from her deep sleep. As the car settled and gently swayed, she awoke fully. "Where are we?"

"I have to drop off this alligator bait to a friend's shanty," said Adam. He popped the trunk and without hesitation, got out of the car. He walked to the opening and pulled luggage and guns out to expose the small red cooler tucked into the back.

He walked slowly toward the shanty as his mind raced, attempting to solve the problem of a discrete disposal.

Entering the shack, Adam placed the cooler on a small, rickety wooden table just inside the door. He found a gap between the slats of wood that made up the front wall of the place and peered through it to see if his granddaughter's curiosity propelled her from the car and toward the building.

She seemed oblivious to what he was doing; sitting in the car and bobbing her head to the rhythm of the music.

Adam walked to the center of the shack. It was built upon stilts; three feet above the water to account for muted tides and storm surges. On the floor was a trap door he opened exposing the swamp below. He watched as the black water undulated gently. If he simply dropped the head here, he risked the small tide from the nearby estuary not being sufficient to take the orb deeper into the Everglades. Regardless of how he disposed of the head, Adam wanted it to be consumed by one of the many alligators that populated the swamp.

Nearly one hundred yards farther down the dirt road was a small wooden dock that extended into the marshland a mere ten feet. Adam removed a knife from his pocket and cut away the duct tape that secured the cooler. Flicking away two ice cubes that settled in Norton's eye sockets, he exposed a ghostly white and frozen stare. He grabbed the head by both ears and removed it. His former subordinate continued to peer condescendingly at him. He flipped the head over so that its palpable contempt faced away from him.

The grandfather walked out of the shack orienting his back toward the car while holding the head at his stomach. Adam had to leave the cooler in the shack to support his assertion of leaving bait for a friend. If his granddaughter asked, he would say he was simply chumming the waters. He clung to singular threads of truth in developing pretext. As he moved down the dirt road, he consciously shifted his path to keep his body between the head and Maritza's stare.

Adam walked to the end of the dock, looked around the swamp for the familiar ridges of an alligator's back or the telltale black eyes protruding from the water's surface. He knew if he saw one there were at least twenty. The hot Florida sun would rot and bake the head, filling the air with a putrid odor. Attracting more than one alligator to dispose of the evidence seemed crucial. Let them fight over it.

It didn't take long to spot a friendly reptile. The alligator was a mere adolescent. He looked to be about six feet long, which made him about six years old. He'd reached the reproductive age for the species, so Adam deemed the animal adequate to accomplish his goal. Additional comfort was drawn from the fact that where there was a young alligator, there had to be a mother and father nearby.

Overcome with a sense of urgency, Adam repositioned the head in his hands, holding it on either side of its face as one would grasp the face of a toddler. Its skin was cold and clammy. The eyes had begun to dry, shrivel and became cloudy.

As if conducting a funeral, he felt compelled to say a few words. "I can honestly tell you; the next thirty years of your life would not have been very productive in advancing your soul toward a peaceful eternity. You're a reflection of the man I used to be." His soul was callused. It was the closest he came to expressing remorse.

Wishing to not startle the young alligator Adam took aim twenty degrees east of the beast. He plunged his middle and forefinger into the nostrils and pressed his thumb against Norton's forehead. Drawing it back like a bowling ball, he flung it far into the swamp.

At the moment the head splashed into the water the young gator jerked. It took off like a shot, slicing through the water and into the sawgrass. Any questions from his granddaughter would be met with the explanation he found a dead raccoon in the shack. A better lie developed within his conscious mind.

Adam trotted off the dock and back up the dirt path toward the car. He grabbed the luggage off the ground and loaded it into the trunk again. Then he closed it firmly and made his way back into his all-too-familiar position in the driver's seat. Eager to put the episode behind him, Adam threw the car into REVERSE and backed quickly away from the shanty.

"I'm glad you left that stinky cooler in the shack." Maritza said.

Adam slammed on the brakes. "Shit," he muttered under his breath. He brushed aside the curse, shifted the car into DRIVE and pulled up to the dilapidated shack again. He popped the trunk, hurried into the shack, grabbed the cooler, came back out, and tossed it in the trunk.

When he'd retaken his spot behind the wheel, he glanced at Maritza, who was staring at him. "What?"

"Why do you even want to keep that thing?"

"Sentimental reasons." It wasn't a complete lie. The vessel had been used several times to dispose of the heads of victims, He was more concerned about leaving DNA evidence. "And besides, it's not stinky. Why would you say that?"

"Doesn't all bait stink? Isn't that the nature of bait? It's supposed to stink to attract fish…or whatever."

The grandfather shook his head, not answering Maritza's inquiry.

A small sense of relief spread through Adam's soul as he finally maneuvered the car back onto the Tamiami Trail. He'd never been so happy to be on the long stretch of road that splayed endlessly toward the horizon.

No matter how many times he'd driven this route, there always came a time when he wondered, "Is there an end to this thing?"

Slowly his thoughts drifted from the head in the swamp, back to the granddaughter he so gravely endangered. Adam knew every assassination team and their tendencies in situations like this. He looked at his watch and thought, "They must be ransacking my house by now."

How would he protect his granddaughter? Surely, if he offered his life without a fight, they would spare hers, but what then? There was no more family left to take care of Maritza. He was all she had. A mental note was made to provide for her in the event it was only him that met his demise.

When Adam saw the sign for Carnestown on US Route 29, he decided to force an end to the Tamiami Trail. He steered the car north toward Immokalee and chuckled to himself for getting one over on Alligator Alley.

"Papa, what kind of business are you in?" Maritza asked. "I mean what kinds of tasks do you perform daily?"

"I am a global buyer for a telecom company," he said, unconsciously repeating the lie he'd put forth hundreds of times.

"So, you really never felt compelled to do anything with your PhD?"

Adam was impressed that his sixteen-year-old granddaughter thought to ask the question. "Sometimes in life, you get sidetracked, Maritza." He glanced over at her and smiled.

"What was the subject of your dissertation?"

Damn. Another great question. "It explores the theory that energy lies along a spectrum. At one end is pure energy. It's a place where light rules, and there are no impediments to the energy exacting a positive outcome to any stimulus applied to it; a place of creativity and growth. At the opposite end, energy is cluttered with hurdles, barriers. All kinds of obstacles are placed in its way. At that end of the spectrum, nothing positive happens. It's consumed by constant destruction. The two poles struggle mightily for survival, pulling against the other in an effort to wrest complete control."

His words embraced the technical and he knew Maritza deserved a better explanation. "Search on YouTube, the Masaru Emoto Water Experiments. His study encapsulates my theory perfectly. He took droplets of water and said loving and kind things to one set, and mean, hateful things to another set. Each were immediately flash frozen. The visual differences are stark. Those who were spoken to kindly formed the most amazingly beautiful crystals. Those spoken to harshly were ugly and malformed. It really is a truly amazing representation of how beauty is created in the world." Adam thought about all that had gone on in his life from the time he'd completed his PhD until that moment. "At the time I was researching my dissertation, it was all about the mathematics. These many decades later, I believe one hundred percent that God resides on the positive end of that spectrum." Once again, he looked his granddaughter in the eye. "Please. No matter what happens, always embrace positive energy."

"So, the dark end of the spectrum is kind of like the Illuminati mantra, 'Order through Chaos?'"

"Exactly." Adam grinned with satisfaction. He knew his son had done a good job raising his granddaughter, but he also understood his daughter-in-law deserved most of the credit for the quality of the child they raised.

Adam's advice to find a settled soul was borne of the realization his own soul only recently settled into a Godly existence. He'd known several acquaintances during childhood and adolescence who embraced a happy existence, and Adam was never able to understand from where their blissfulness came. It made him happy that he could offer Maritza peaceful guidance while she was still so young. It would benefit her.

The conversation between grandfather and granddaughter continued when Maritza asked a question that bothered her since the death of her father. She brought it into the conversation piggybacking on topics already discussed, as if it had just occurred to her. "Okay, we've talked about sex and math. Let me do some math. You're fifty-five years old. I'm seventeen years old. My father was twenty-five when they adopted me. That means you were thirteen when my father was born."

Adam dismissed the fact he thought his granddaughter was sixteen years old. He smirked and shook his head. "Oh, we can't get anything past you, can we?"

"Nope," said Maritza, her chin raised.

"Your father was orphaned at fifteen. That's when we adopted him." Adam wasn't ready to admit he was the reason his son was orphaned. Feeling responsibility and showing remorse and compassion were red flags to his superiors and changed the trajectory of his career. He was seen as soft. "It's almost as if the universe wanted us together, beyond our inherent physical constraints. You know, as if our souls were linked by prior existences."

Maritza smiled, and the conversation waned.

The joy Adam felt at beating Alligator Alley turned into the realization he and his granddaughter were traveling on just another two-lane stretch of road that seemed like it was squeezed by the swamp surrounding it. He looked at his watch again and grimaced. Most of the day's eleven-hour drive along the length of the state still lay ahead.

As the car approached Immokalee, Maritza decided to see just how far her grandfather would go with his apparent willingness to communicate openly. "Papa, have you ever gotten high?"

Adam glanced sharply at his granddaughter. He lost sight of the road, and the right tires left the pavement. The sound of gravel pinging against the undercarriage snapped him back to reality. He regained control of the car and looked in the rearview mirror. A cloud of dust billowed and hovered over the road behind them.

He considered the teenager's question. He knew this was an opportunity to show the kind of honesty that would help free his soul from his troubled past. "Yes. Once." He was so stunned by the question he forgot his own advice and didn't ask about her experiences with marijuana.

"Well?" Maritza held her palms skyward and opened her eyes widely, waiting to hear the story of an old man getting high.

Adam chuckled at the situation and decided to give her as many details as he could recall. "It was just before I met Kathy. I was with my friend Johnathan David Armstrong." Adam developed the habit of using all three names from reading mountains of dossiers over the course of his career. "This guy was one of the funniest human beings I've ever been around. He had a humorous take on just about everything. Johnnie could have people laughing at a funeral, and not one person would be offended by it."

He took a moment in his own thoughts, drinking in memories. "All I remember was laughter. I couldn't stop laughing. I would look at Johnnie and he would look at me, expressionless, and I just knew something hysterical was about to come out of his mouth. I was laughing in anticipation the entire time I was high. And there was not one thing I remember him saying that night that was remotely funny."

"That. Is. Hilarious."

The two laughed together. Maritza realized she had a little something in common with her grandfather, and Adam appreciated their openness—a sincerity he'd not experienced since Carolyn's death.

"You know, I would've been petrified had your father asked me that question, but with you I'm perfectly comfortable talking about most anything." Adam glanced over and smiled at his granddaughter. "Maybe an old man can learn new tricks."

Time crawled slowly as the car sped along a myriad of never-ending, two-lane roads. The scenery didn't change. There was nothing tangible in the world outside the car that gave any indication they were making progress. Adam could've sworn he was doing nothing but driving on an asphalt treadmill. Florida's length took an emotional toll.

As the two approached Sebring, the first song Adam recognized during their trip began to play on the stereo. Maritza scoffed and reached toward the dial to change the station, seeking something more suitable to her taste.

"No!" Adam shrieked. "Don't change the station."

"Grrr." Maritza responded, jokingly.

Adam paid no attention to Maritza's derision. He just sang along with the lyrics, as best he could remember them.

"What's the name of this song?" Maritza asked.

"Sundown," Adam said. He took a break from his sing-along to explain. "This song reminds me of Kathy, and it's written by one of the greatest songwriters ever—Gordon Lightfoot."

"Why does it remind you of Kathy?"

"She was the desire of every man. She could make faded and torn jeans look as wonderful as any evening gown." Adam embraced the memory of Kathy. All communication channels were open, so he chose to share. "She was walking out of the mall one day. There was a guy sitting in his truck parked next to her car. He asked her to stop and stand still. She did, waiting for him to ask whatever question he had. He said nothing for a long time, and then she realized he was masturbating."

"Eeeeeewwww. Gross."

Adam laughed again. "I would never have done something like that, but she was that stunning."

Maritza nodded. "I guess that explains that." She didn't really understand her grandfather.

He sensed her disapproval. "Forget that. I'm gonna tell you why my music is better than your generation's music. All that crap you listen to are nothing but computerized pulses. Back in my day, to create music you needed a group of men and women to come together with ideas; to work together and create. My music had a soul back then. Your music lacks exactly that."

"My music speaks to my generation, Papa."

He ignored her retort and bathed in the memories stoked by the song. Once it was over, Adam allowed his granddaughter to control the stereo once again.

They continued their journey.

Maritza occasionally remarked about an interesting sight along the way. Adam frequently asked if she needed to stop to go to the bathroom. In most ways, it was a typical road trip. But the pall of that which lay ahead did not escape Adam. Eventually he would have to address it.

There would be no one at the agency willing to help Adam with intel concerning company plans. How long could they wait out a team of assassins camping at the farm? How long could he take Maritza away from a typical teenage life without doing irreparable damage? His psyche became heavier with every rotation of the tires speeding them toward uncertainty.

Avon Park, Frostproof, Lake Wales, Haines City. Points on a map lay ahead of them in a seemingly never-ending string. Adam folded and refolded the paper map his granddaughter retrieved from the glove compartment.

"How many times am I going to have to refold this map?" Adam asked himself.

The length of the state became more perceptible with every fold. He could've hired a plane, like he'd done so many times in the past, but that would have left a trail too easy to follow. Gas and food were paid for with cash. He always carried an emergency bundle of thousands of dollars. It wouldn't last long.

"How did you get so good with a gun?" Maritza asked. "I mean, I bet you could shoot a guy right between the eyes from thirty yards?"

Her question seemed to come out of the blue. "Why do you ask such a question?"

Maritza noticed a corrugated tin building along the side of the road. She fixated on the structure as the car passed swiftly. "We just passed a gun range. It reminded me of all of the times you took me to shoot guns. You're really very good. I was just curious how you got so good?"

He smiled at the fond recollection. "There was a neighbor when I was a boy that used to take me hunting with him. As a matter fact, he took me a lot of places. Gave me a lot of experiences." Adam chuckled. "I guess he also used me as slave labor sometimes. There was a time when he took me for an entire day to build a quarter-mile barbed wire fence along one edge of his property in Carrabelle. And then there was the time he took me to the cattle auction, but we began the day loading cattle onto trailers. I'm quite certain I've never smelled as bad as I did that day." He paused briefly. "Carl Stephens. Good man. Great, positive experiences."

"Did he teach you how to use a handgun too?"

"No. It was rifles and shotguns, but that definitely piqued my interest in guns. I had friends who'd borrow their father's pistols, and we'd go out to the dump and shoot at trash piles. I had a natural ability, so after college I took it up as a hobby."

Adam really did not enjoy lying to his granddaughter. How could he move his life to the positive end of the spectrum if he kept lying? "Carl was a Marine and did three tours of duty in Korea. I was warned by his wife never to ask about his time during the war. It was something he wished to forget. I'm sure he killed many men. I've seen him shoot a rifle. He was an excellent shot." He became pensive. "I've often wondered if he was ever forced into any close-quarter kills?" And then he told another lie to bring the concept of murder into his granddaughter's consciousness. "I know that would affect me greatly too. Can you imagine looking into a man's eyes as his soul leaves his body? I don't know who gets the better end of that bargain—the one who gets to travel to Valhalla or the man who has to live with his actions for the rest of his life?"

He wondered if his experiences with Carl influenced his desire to become an assassin. For the first time he considered the possibility of having soaked into his soul the energy of a man who'd so readily committed murder. Their conversation offered a natural segue into what potentially lay ahead.

The car's engine struggled. The tail end of the Appalachian Mountains extended down through the center of the state into Central Florida. Olympic runners came from all over the world to train on the hills of Clermont. The reason why was made apparent by the car's tachometer revving as it struggled to climb short hills. Relief came only when the car crested the highest point in the state and coasted into shallow valleys. Undulating terrain dissipated into the flat landscape behind them. Higher elevations lay ahead.

"Okay, Papa. We know that Granny and Kathy were positive women in your life. Did you have any difficult relationships?"

Adam took a deep breath. "Yeah. There was one really bad one." He thought a moment, choosing his words carefully. "She was one of my first serious girlfriends. If it'd been just a few years later, we would've seriously considered marriage. Maybe I was too young to recognize the warning signs of a bad relationship, but the emotion was there." He glanced over at his granddaughter. He realized he might never have another chance to discuss such things, so he choked down decorum and proceeded. "And then there was the sex. I only had a few girlfriends at that point in my life. I thought the sex was really great."

"It wasn't?"

Adam shook his head. "No. Sex is spiritual. The connection your grandmother and I had was purely transcendent. It's never better when lovemaking is about a man and a woman becoming one." Once again, he glanced over and gave her a stern look to make his point. "All this crap you see on TV and your phone about sex being purely physical, that there is nothing more satisfying than stimulating your genitalia—that's crap. They say that if an internet platform is free, you're the product. Free porn is meant to shape your mind and make you believe the physical is all there is in life. Sex isn't like what you see in pornography. It's meant to be gentle, soft, and caring."

"I know."

Adam gave her another quick glance. He continued without acknowledging her confession. "Develop a critical mind and ask from where does the money for these websites and their content come, and what is the purpose? The people funding these sites are dumbing down humanity to the point people are roaming around a pasture like cattle, eating, and having sex." He knew the money came from the same intelligence agency for which he'd worked for decades. "Unwanted pregnancies are aborted, and fetal organs are sold for profit. That is their business model. Focus on your energy not your physical desires. Make sure your soul is good and pure of the harm associated with pornographic abuses. Because it's your energy that will last eternally."

Maritza asked, "What made sex with your first girlfriend so bad?"

Adam took a deep breath. Once again, he'd gone off on a tangent. Times of complete honesty was when the façade built upon lies crumbled. He wanted his granddaughter to benefit from his experiences, and there was no way to accomplish that other than utmost candor. "Thirty years later, I see that it wasn't so bad. When you reach my age, you'll appreciate all experiences, since they help shape you into who you become. I'll just let you know what I found out over a decade after that first relationship ended. Given my job, I had access to some sensitive information. It was about a priest, and the children he sexually abused. His dossier caught my eye at first because he officiated at one of the churches in my hometown. I was horrified by one account after another of this priest abusing the young lady I had been so in love with. When all this came to light, the priest swore up and down the relationship was consensual. There's no way a fifteen or sixteen-year-old girl, or boy, can truly understand the gravity of their actions. In retrospect, it explained her casual attitude toward sexual relationships. I'm not sure what that asshole told her during these encounters, but I'm sure it was something to the effect that sex was her only conduit to God, and he the ultimate connection."

He was silent for a moment, and then he expressed his true feelings. "Fucking horseshit! That man damaged that young girl, and several others, period. Just fucking period." Adam glanced and stared into his granddaughter's eyes. He realized he'd confessed to having access to intelligence.

He brushed past the admission and continued. "Remember, sweetie, churches need you a lot more than you need them. Without your acquiescence, they have zero value. Relationships with God are personal, not contingent on the approval of a pedophile."

Maritza felt the anger and hatred emanating from her grandfather. "I'm sorry. I didn't mean to bring up bad memories."

Adam chuckled nervously. "I guess you don't need to ask why we don't go to church." After a moment, he went on. "Do you know what trumps a bad relationship? A stunningly beautiful woman."

"Kathy?"

He nodded. "Do you know what trumps a woman who's stunningly beautiful in the physical sense? A woman who has a beautiful soul."

Maritza smiled. "Granny?"

Adam smiled. "Oh yeah. Be the beautiful woman with a good soul. Happiness comes from within. Seeking it elsewhere is fruitless. Therein lies the key to eternal contentment."

There was a distinct change in landscape as the two moved beyond Central Florida and into the northern section of the state. Sawgrass, swampland, and palmettos gave way to pine trees and cow pastures. This part of the state had been dotted with paper mills in the more industrious age of Adam's childhood. Over the decades politicians had given away competitive advantages to overseas firms. The wealth of small North Florida towns and their respective manufacturing bases had been replaced with the tidal wave of fiat money meant to accomplish nothing more than keeping residents at subsistence levels.

Perry was a town that had been fortunate to keep their mill, and their way of life remained intact. The town was not immune to financial hardships, but most family-owned shops remained open in the downtown area.

Adam chuckled softly as they passed the McDonald's on Highway 98. Childhood trips between Panama City and Gainesville to visit his grandparents flooded his memory. He'd always insist they stop there when he was a kid. The wave of nostalgia almost made him turn into the parking lot, but he shook his head and kept his foot on the gas. There was no way he would allow his granddaughter to eat whatever it was they served.

Nearly a mile later, Highway 98 turned west toward the panhandle. Woods and underbrush were thick in this part of the state. Only well-worn paths gave humans the ability to negotiate their way through the brush.

It was such a wild environment Adam often thought it wouldn't surprise him to see Bigfoot or a Chupacabra emerge from the dense woods, growl mightily, cross the road, and disappear into the woods on the other side. The surrounding natural environment provided a tough backdrop for life, and the residents of the small towns in the area met its terms of survival.

Their trip was well into its tenth hour. It was eight o'clock, and darkness had fallen. Adam knew there was only an hour left. The cumulative effects of the drive from Key West pushed his emotional state from behind and he wanted to make it to the farm as quickly as possible. The pasture represented the only place on earth he felt safe. His foot became heavy on the accelerator.

There were no oncoming headlights and no lights in his rearview mirror. They seemed to be alone on this two-lane highway. His head was heavy, and he forced himself to remain focused.

Briefly he thought of the Dexedrine and Modafinil he'd used as a young operative to stay awake and alert on important missions. Once again, he glanced at his granddaughter, who slept with her head against the window. He felt his age. There was something strong inside that compelled him to be the all-American dad. Maybe because he felt he'd failed his son.

Adam became so determined to get to the farm quickly that he dropped his guard. When he saw a pair of oncoming headlights, he ignored them and kept his foot on the gas. As headlights streaked past the left side of the car, he saw that it was a sheriff's deputy. He watched in the rearview mirror as the headlights swung around, lighting up the woods before centering in his rear-view mirror. Over the next quarter mile, the lights grew larger and brighter. Finally, the cop car's blue lights flashed.

Adam knew the officer was calling in his tag number. He pulled the Chrysler onto the shoulder of the road, shifted into PARK, and rolled down his window. He patiently waited for the officer to appear at his window.

He was startled by the tapping on Maritza's window. Adam pressed the switch to lower the window and watched to make sure his granddaughter's hair didn't get caught between the glass and window frame.

Maritza shifted her weight, lifted her head slightly, and stared at her grandfather through bloodshot eyes. Never achieving full consciousness, she grunted softly and returned her head to its resting position. She was asleep again before the officer spoke.

"Good evening, sir," said the female cop in a thick southern drawl. "Deputy Sally Cole with the Jefferson County Sheriff's Office."

"Good evening," Adam said, feigning inferiority. It was a skill he'd witnessed many of the women in his life execute deftly to avoid being ticketed. It wasn't so much the citation he wished to avoid, as it was a game to be won. He was winless in this aspect of life.

"I clocked you going eighty-seven miles per hour."

"That's probably right," he said. He glanced in his side-view mirror. Headlights approached from behind, and they were closing fast. "I've just been driving since Key West, and I'm eager to get home."

"I'm gonna need to see your license and proof of insurance."

Adam leaned across the passenger's seat and handed her the items she'd requested. He possessed several different IDs, all of which were known by the agency. He offered his real identity as determination grew that his life would embrace truth moving forward.

As he leaned back into his seat, the vehicle in the side-view mirror disappeared from its reflection. He glanced to the left as it passed. It was a blacked-out suburban; out of place in this part of the state. Tallahassee was only forty-five minutes away. The state's capital offered many situations necessitating privacy measures bordering extreme. Self-preservation dictated he treat the unknown as a threat.

His mind flashed forward to the cabin at the farm and how it could be defensively maximized. Gamesmanship dictated Adam consider all possibilities. Maybe it was simply someone who'd had an illegal level of tint placed on their windows? In that case he wondered how fast they were driving and how much of a ticket he'd saved them by occupying Deputy Cole's time.

The deputy finished writing the ticket and handed it to Adam as she gave him a lecture on safety.

Adam drove the car back onto the highway and proceeded toward the farm at a legal speed. Again, his mind drifted to the cabin, and then the property as a whole. Its boundaries were mentally defined as was its topography. Would the only potential threat he'd encountered on the trip be waiting for him and his granddaughter?

Glancing over, he saw Maritza was fast asleep. How could she have gone back to sleep and stayed so through that entire episode? He appreciated the fact there appeared to be zero stress in her life. Adam knew that would change. How soon? He had no idea.

A wave of relief washed over Adam when he saw the bright streetlight standing just before the last bend in the road. It was the figurative signpost marking the end of their drive. Adam pulled off the two-lane asphalt road and onto the two-rut road that led to his property. He stopped at the gate, turned to his granddaughter, and gently shook her awake. "Can you please open the gate?" he asked, a little perturbed he wasn't able to offload worry onto his passenger.

Once the car was through the gate, and Maritza was back inside the car, Adam drove the length of the two-rut road. They passed through a stand of pine trees until the car and its passengers breached the opening in which the cabin was centrally located. To the west there was a burned-out patch of earth; used for decades as a fire pit.

The shelter was wooden and consisted of nothing more than a frame and meticulously placed cedar siding. Insulation from the elements was non-existent. Paradoxically, the roof was brand new and well maintained. For all of Adam's macho concerning his ability to brave the elements, one thing that wouldn't be tolerated was being rained on inside the cabin.

Finally parked in front of a structure at the opposite end of the state from where they began their journey, the two emerged from the car and began unloading the trunk. Adam left the car headlights illuminated until he was able to activate the single light switch inside the cabin.

The only source of light was a bare bulb screwed into a socket shell that hung from an electrical wire fastened along exposed roof trusses.

The cabin consisted of two symmetrical rooms, one used as a kitchen, living area and one a bedroom. The bedroom had a similar lighting configuration. The only structural difference between the two rooms was a fireplace and chimney in the outer room. It was large enough to provide heat for the entire cabin; as well as occasionally used for cooking on days it was too cold to grill outside.

Maritza moved through the outer room into the bedroom and pulled the string that brought forth light.

Once belongings were completely unloaded and they settled inside the cabin, Adam and Maritza began unpacking their luggage.

A chill ran down the grandfather's spine when he saw his granddaughter retrieve her cell phone from inside her suitcase. For all the possible reasons for seeing such a securely constructed vehicle on the road, the one possessing his greatest fear was suddenly and seemingly confirmed. The agency had been able to track them all along.

The only thing he didn't know was how many assassins surrounded the cabin. His dread doubled when he realized all of his weapons were still in the trunk of the car. He'd brought his granddaughter to a place they'd been together many times. Failure echoed in his soul when he realized he'd treated their trip as another family outing. His guard dropped briefly, and death could be the price. He couldn't simply go outside to retrieve his guns without first telling Maritza exactly what was happening. She had to be prepared.

He looked around the cabin for anything he could use as a weapon.

Standing beside the single basin, metal kitchen sink, Adam reached down and retrieved a fillet knife used to skin and disembowel deer. Facing a sniper, he would have no defense. Adam's only hope was to be confronted by an angry group of former coworkers who wanted to look him in the eye and express how disgusted they were with him. Knowing the egos involved, he felt his chances of that were greater than fifty-fifty.

Adam slapped the flat side of the knife blade against his leg repeatedly, punctuating each of his scattered thoughts.

"What's the matter, Papa?"

"We've got issues, sweetie."

Maritza looked nervously at her grandfather as he continually slapped the knife against his leg.

With his left hand he reached across and gently, yet firmly grabbed her shoulder. "There are some very bad people after us, and they're most likely surrounding this cabin."

Neither said a word for several moments as Adam continued to slap the flat knife blade against his leg.

"I guess now's the best time for me to be completely honest with you. I'm not an international buyer for a telecommunications company. I worked as an intelligence asset for the United States government."

Adam was sure this news would freak her out, but instead, Maritza appeared pensive.

Adam knew his granddaughter was smart. He saw the analysis happening through her eyes. He witnessed the events of the prior twelve hours come together like a mosaic and manifested before him in her changing countenance. "This is because of me, isn't it?"

"How do you mean?"

"It's because I have my cell phone. They were able to follow us?"

Adam had never been a protector of people. Shifting sensibilities focused on ensuring Maritza's safety. Decades of experience spoke to the need for a strong will. A defeated mind guaranteed death for them both. "Your cell phone is not the reason they're here. It's all my fault. We're facing inevitable consequences of a decision I made."

Adam's age stared him in the face. He was angry at the sudden awareness. "Sweetie, I'm still living in the last millennium. My partner in Key West had a tiny computer implanted that constantly fed his biometrics to our headquarters. When he died, they knew it immediately." He fumbled for words to enhance his explanation. They became more philosophical in nature. "I've made so many poor decisions throughout my adult life. I was never there for your father, and the day he and your mother brought you home and I held you for the first time, I promised myself I would be one hell of a grandfather compared to the poor father I'd been.

Yet here we are, and exactly the opposite has happened. I've directly endangered your life."

Defiantly, Maritza's retort was filled with innate Latina fire. "You're not the grandfather I've known for the last sixteen years. My grandfather taught me to never give up. My grandfather told me he was certain our souls had known each other for thousands of years. My grandfather told me if you allow your mind to be defeated you may as well give up. I'm telling my grandfather I'm not ready to give up. You taught me to shoot, and I can shoot well. You give me one of your rifles, a pistol, and some ammunition, and I'll do my best to take out as many as I can."

Adam looked directly into Maritza's eyes. "Let's do it, sweetie."

He needed to solve the problem of possessing no weapons. "All of our guns are in the trunk of the car." He paused to give his granddaughter the time to digest his words. "I'm sure they've got the cabin surrounded. There's no way either of us can get out there safely. As much as I hate to say it, we are going to have to stand and fight with whatever we find in this cabin." The man made sure to train his son and granddaughter in the use of tactical weapons, yet his brief lapse in judgment acted to isolated them without necessary tools for survival.

"Isn't that what families are meant to do? Fight to the death for one another?" Skills honed at a firing range where no one shot back convinced the adolescent she possessed greater credentials than the reality of her situation.

Adam held up the blade. It was the only item that possessed lethal energy. "We've only got one knife? I guess we could make do with that."

One manner in which he used the knife to their advantage was to hold it by its blade and swing the wooden handle at the bulb hanging from the ceiling. Thin shards of glass rained down on the floor around the two. The outer room went dark. He repeated the procedure in the bedroom. Downside thoughts brought forth the assessment the squad outside verified targets inside the house knew of their presence.

Adam moved to the window at the front of the cabin and took up a position at its lower edge. Complete darkness was juxtaposed to the yard, lit by a streetlamp mounted on a telephone pole at the edge of the woods. He saw no movement in the clearing in front of the cabin. His gaze shifted to the edge of the woods. Zones of perception adjusted to varying and confusing levels of light across his spectrum of responsibility. He looked into the dark woods, and then deeper, and then deeper, seeking any signs of human activity.

He turned to his granddaughter again. "I can open the trunk remotely from here, but that will alert them I'm coming out. So I'm going to give you the key fob. I want you to take up this position where I am now. Stay below the window frame. Don't let them see you through the window." He pointed toward the back of the cabin. "Behind the refrigerator, there's a two-by-twelve-inch plank that's been broken for years. It's set in place, but it's loose. I can crawl through it, move around the cabin, and make my way to the trunk of the car. When you see me on the ground at the back of the car, pop the trunk, and keep your eyes peeled for any movement. Anything that moves must be accounted for. Maintain a mental image of everything surrounding us. Three-hundred-and-sixty-degree field of vision, Maritza."

The granddaughter nodded at the same time the phone tucked halfway into her back pocket vibrated. She gave her grandfather a puzzled look as she pulled out the phone and looked at the incoming number. "It's a three-oh-five area code. Definitely South Florida, but I don't recognize the number. What should I do?"

Adam took the phone from Maritza's extended hand. He had no recognition of the number either. "Maybe somebody wants to tell you your car's warranty is about to expire." He handed the phone back to her and shook his head. "Answer it. We've got nothing to lose."

"Hello?"

Adam watched as Maritza furrowed her brow. Then she handed him the phone. "It's General Eason asking for you." She shrugged her shoulders.

Neither had heard the man's name before.

Adam put the phone to his ear. "This is Adam Phillips."

The man on the other end of the line spoke commandingly and without fear. "Phillips, this is General John Eason of the United States Army. I'm a special envoy stationed at the Navy base in Key West. We've been monitoring your granddaughter's cell phone since early this afternoon. We heard your plan to take out the assassins and I must say it's an adequate one given the circumstances. However, I think I've got a better one."

Adam listened intently. All he could think was, "thank God for total surveillance of humanity." He had to risk Eason being a white hat employing that which was meant to tag humanity like a herd of cattle. It was his only option.

"Look above your head in the roof trusses. You'll see the two one-by-twelves you'd placed there to use as a shelf. Reach up and you will find two Marlin .30-.30 rifles, and several boxes of cartridges."

To a man confronting a deadly situation, the lever action rifles seemed nothing more than a step above the knife he held in his hand.

"My apologies, but it's the best we could do on such short notice. We have a Comanche stealth helicopter hovering around three thousand feet above you. The crew has marked six heat signatures at various points encircling your cabin. They're all about a hundred yards out from your position. Obviously, we can't take them out without blowing the woods all to hell. This situation is of your making, so you're gonna have to extricate yourself from it. But we'll do what we can to help. So keep this line open."

Adam peered through the window and focused on the tree line, cocked his head to the left, and then right. "Next to impossible shot, general."

"Like I said, you're responsible for the situation. You get yourself out of it." The general continued, "I can offer any visual assistance you need."

"Have you got your AirPods?" he asked his granddaughter.

She grabbed them from her front pocket and handed them to her grandfather.

Adam set the phone on the table and put the listening devices in his ears; they automatically connected to her phone. He stepped to the spot below where the guns had been hidden, reached up and removed them. He tossed one to Maritza, then a box of cartridges.

She caught them like a boss and started loading rounds into the side chamber without hesitation.

"Go to the two windows in the back of the cabin and raise them only high enough to get a clear line of sight to your target. I'll cover the windows in the front of the cabin."

They moved to their respective positions, and Adam asked for an update from the general. "Can you tell from their movements how they plan to attack the cabin?"

"They seem to be waiting for something. Maybe orders from Langley?"

Adam called toward the back bedroom. "Maritza, you keep an eye out for anything that moves."

"Yes, Papa." Her voice quivered, not as confident as before.

That worried Adam. He spoke to the general. "Are you sure you can't blast the shit out of the woods?"

"Sadly, no. There will be too many questions to answer among local and state authorities. We value you. We want you to work with us. But some value is finite. You thought the last thirty years of your life were clandestine? If you survive this, you'll understand what it means to completely disappear."

"Back to your assistance, please. I imagine the targets are equally spread out in a three-hundred-sixty-degree circle. How many degrees west of the chimney is the first target?"

"Seventeen."

Adam called once again to his granddaughter, "Maritza, you know once the first shot is fired all hell will break loose?"

"Yes, Papa."

"Since that's the case, our best approach is to shoot simultaneously and make damn sure we each hit our first target. That will take out a third of their force."

"Uh," said Maritza. "What's the best way for us to do that?"

Adam shook his head. He began speaking rhetorically and to no one in particular. "We have to identify all six targets. They'll be communicating through earpieces, but there's no way for us to tap into their signal. They'll be dressed head-to-toe in black. There will be no way to distinguish them in the darkness."

"There are different shades of black," Maritza called from her spot.

Adam almost smirked. It took a teenage girl to tell him that. "You're right. And if we have different shades moving against one another, we'll see them. They'll look shadowy, or ghostlike."

"Kinda like that movie Predator."

"Exactly. Cloaked, but still visible to a small degree."

Adam scanned the woods. His focus jumped every fifty degrees from the initial target based on Eason's directions. There simply wasn't any movement or any shade of black that stood out.

Suddenly General Eason became a little more animated—maybe even astonished. "Hold on a minute. We now have ten heat signatures." He paused to make a more complete assessment. "We've got two more on each side of the cabin, and they're a good forty yards outside the circumference of the attack team. We'll call them six originals, and now four peripheral."

Adam contemplated the meaning of the additional men. "So," he said. "We've got…what?"

Eason grumbled in frustration. "I can't tell if there are ten bogeys, six bogeys and four friendlies, or four bogeys and six friendlies. But maybe the reason nobody's made a move yet is that they've been waiting for a second team."

Adam called into the back room. "Maritza, remember, they'll be using some form of night vision or infrared. Don't expose your whole head in the window. Just peek with one eye."

"I will, Papa."

"The two on the outer perimeter west of the cabin are fanning out," said Eason. "They seem to have the two in front of them locked in. If they're friendly, the two bogeys in the inner perimeter at the southwest and northeast corners of the cabin are your biggest threat."

"Maritza, do you trust me?"

"Of course I do, Papa."

Adam drew in a deep breath and exhaled. It had come time to force the issue. "Do you see the well pump about twenty yards straight out from your window?"

"Yes."

"I want you to look between that and the picnic table farther left for the bad guy. Don't make any hasty moves and be one hundred percent certain the target you pick out is a bad guy. Can you do that?"

"Yes, but how do I know if it's a good guy or bad?"

"Anybody who approaches aggressively and looks like they want to do you harm...shoot them."

"Got it," she said.

Adam heard her voice quiver. "I need you to be strong for both of us, sweetie." There was no other way to communicate this final directive without placing the burden of their entire operation on his granddaughter's shoulders, but it had to be said. "When you fire, I'm going to fire as quickly as I can afterward. If we can take out the first two, we might have a chance with the other four. Or eight."

As Adam searched for a target among the palmettos that sprang up throughout the woods, Carl Stephens's voice echoed in his mind. "Remember deer are small," his friend told him. "A lot of people make the mistake of looking above the deer. They miss them in the brush."

Adam turned his head toward the back bedroom again. "Remember each time these guys stop and take up a position they're assessing the situation from their vantage-point. They are most likely laying on their bellies. Look and aim low. I love you, Maritza."

For the first time Adam heard fright in his granddaughter's voice as she called from the bedroom. "Papa. I'm not sure I can do this."

"You've got this, Maritza. You're an excellent shot."

"But these targets are armed and will shoot back."

The grandfather thought back to his first kill. What was it that pushed him beyond the threshold between fear and certainty his target should die? Blind trust in the government he worked for consumed mechanical thoughts back then. Still, there was something that convinced him it was okay to kill another human. Abuse suffered during childhood provided the requisite hate to eliminate his first adversary. He knew exactly how to tap into that emotion within his granddaughter but had no desire to damage an otherwise well-adjusted teenager. "Maritza, whenever anyone takes on a new task, or starts a new job, it will always be scary. You're never certain what exactly to expect. I promise you; you have all the skills necessary to do this. Just shut off your mind to all emotion, think logically, and focus intently on your job."

"But you're asking me to kill someone."

It was as though her comment provided the needed permission to justify murder. Adam went somewhere he never anticipated with his granddaughter. "What if I told you the men outside are the same ones that killed your parents…and your grandmother?"

There was a vast pause Adam had no idea how to assess. Was his granddaughter ready for the task at hand?

"Papa, there was a time I resented mom and dad taking me away from my birth mother. It was as if I would never be able to see her; to understand her motivations for putting me up for adoption. They assured me whenever I was ready, they'd take me to Guatemala so that I could meet her." The teenager paused. "I'll never see my parents again. That opportunity has been taken away."

Teenage logic escaped Adam. The grandfather knew she would get to the point of action on her own schedule. He did not wish to press her but needed to be aware of true circumstances. "Are you okay to do this?"

"It's a mindset, Papa. These people are vermin who need to be eradicated."

Adam grew hopeful as time crept on. His granddaughter was taking her role seriously. There was nothing impetuous in her actions. She was a wise girl. He couldn't help but give her more advice as he went through the checklist in his mind. "Remember the checklist I taught you. Hold the bead on the target through the recoil of the rifle. Just before you fire, take a deep breath, hold it, and squeeze the trigger gently."

Movement near the edge of the woods became apparent.

"Got it, Papa." This time she gave him instruction. "I see my target. I'm going to give you a countdown."

"I got one too, so I'm ready when you are, sweetie."

Mere seconds later, the young girl's voice spoke firmly and confidently. "Three. Two. One."

Two gunshots rang out milliseconds apart and echoed through the woods.

"My screen has come alive with activity. You've got four advancing on your position now, Phillips. Cock that lever action antique and fire at will. The two you shot at are still in place. I can't tell if you've hit them or if they've hunkered down."

Adam and Maritza each chambered another round. Adam called out to his granddaughter, "Start looking toward your right, sweetie. They should be coming out of the woods soon."

Adam moved his gaze to the right as well, searching for the first to emerge from the edge of the woods. He knew his car parked outside would provide perfect cover for the advancing enemy. His greatest chance for success would be to focus on the assassin who emerged nearest the vehicle before he could take cover.

Another shot rang out from the bedroom. "I got one," yelled Maritza. "I nailed that motherfucker!"

"Good job, sweetie."

Confirmation came from General Eason. "I think your granddaughter has downed two. Neither are moving on my screen. The second advancing assassin has stopped just outside the tree line."

"Can you give me a landmark where the third assassin is so I can tell her where to aim?"

"Two trees to the right, there appears to be a five-gallon bucket at the base of that tree."

"Maritza, can you see a five-gallon bucket at the base of a tree outside?"

"Yes."

"Behind the tree that is two trees left of the bucket is where the assassin is hiding," said Adam. "Be patient. Don't shoot until he exposes himself."

Just as he finished speaking, Adam saw an assassin running from the tree line toward his car. Calmly he drew a bead onto the torso of the man and fired. He couldn't tell if the man had been hit or had simply dived behind the car, but the attacker was on the ground.

"Sweetie, I know we feel like we've hit some of these guys, but please don't lose focus. Please don't let your guard down."

"I won't, Papa."

Suddenly four gunshots rang out. Both Adam and Maritza ducked for safety beneath their windows, shielded by the wall of the cabin.

Something didn't seem right to Adam. He couldn't figure it out. He distinctly heard four gunshots in quick succession. If the assassins had automatic rifles, they would've peppered the walls of the cabin without hesitation. The gunshots came from four different directions. Four distinct shots.

"Good news or bad, I don't know," said Eason. "But the four peripheral heat images are now closing in."

"Shit," Adam muttered. He was losing track of all of the players on his mental chess board. He began to doubt his ability to save his granddaughter.

Quiet. Quiet. It was too damned quiet for too damned long.

"Stay down for now, Maritza. I need time to think."

Calmly he took a fresh cartridge from the box that lay on the floor next to him and loaded it into the breach of the gun. He wanted to ensure his gun possessed its maximum load.

The most they'd hit was three. Adam couldn't count the one behind the car as dead.

There was an eerie calm outside, given there were potentially three assassins still alive. Or was it seven? It struck him odd the assassins' guns had fallen silent.

Once again Carl's voice echoed in his mind. "Mama used to give us four twenty-two cartridges," he'd once said. "And she expected us to bring back four squirrels." These assassins were trained, almost brainwashed, to hold fire unless certain of a kill. Otherwise, evidence of their presence and location would ring out in the night.

Adam heard someone call from outside. The voice seemed familiar, but he figured all that was recognizable was its burdensome southern accent. The kind of drawl he'd grown up listening to and speaking. It was the same accent he'd worked hard to eliminate and that grated on his nerves like fingernails on a chalkboard.

"Hello in there," called the man. "We don't mean you no harm."

General Eason's voice rang in his ears. "All four are standing at the edge of the clearing holding their rifles well above their heads."

"My name is Tommy Owens," said the man. "Me and my grandkids seen these people attacking you, and we took 'em out for you."

"Tommy Owens?" Adam yelled still crouched beneath the window.

"Yep."

"What's your sister's name?"

"Carol."

"Did you graduate Central High School in Panama City?"

"Yep. Are you Adam Phillips?"

Adam didn't answer immediately. He sat up and peered through the window. All he saw was a countenance he didn't recognize. And then he chuckled at the realization a high school friend would have changed over a thirty-seven year period, just like him. "Tommy, can you do me a favor? Have your grandkids come around where you are and lay all your weapons on the ground?"

"Sure thing, Adam."

He watched as the oldest child of fifteen came into his line of sight and took a position next to his grandfather. The boy was thin yet muscular and resembled the figure Adam remembered Tommy possessing in his youth. Slowly, two more came around from the east side of the cabin and joined the other two. They appeared to be a year or two younger than the eldest.

"I'm coming outside," yelled Adam. "I'm gonna have my gun in my hand, but I won't raise it up unless I'm threatened."

"I understand," said Tommy in his slow, baritone, southern drawl.

Adam turned toward the back bedroom and spoke only loudly enough for his granddaughter to hear. "Maritza, you stay in here and shoot anything that looks threatening."

"For sure, Papa."

Adam stood, making sure not to expose himself in the window. Slowly, he opened the door and took a tentative step outside.

Growing up in the South in the latter half of the twentieth century, a man knew to approach every situation with extreme caution. In the South, men had been known to murder friends over the pettiest of disagreements—even those decades old. But Tommy Owens possessed answers to at least some of the questions racing through Adam's mind.

With every step, Adam searched his mind for conflicts he may have had with Tommy. Were there any women in which they had a common interest? There were never any school fights, or heated exchanges on their high school football team. Adam quickly came to the realization if he had to choose one of his friends from school to help him out in a situation like this, it would be Tommy.

Tommy stepped over his gun and began walking toward Adam. As the two men drew closer together, each extended a hand to the other in friendship.

"I can honestly say, Tommy, that I have never been happier to see you."

Tommy chuckled. Even his laugh was burdened by a southern drawl. "Yeah, we were passing by on the highway out there and saw these fellas pulling into your property. So, we decided to take a little look-see. I wanted to see what these fellas was up to. They certainly didn't look like they belonged around here." The friend paused. "Then we saw them unloading all of their weaponry and knew they was up to no good. The grans held back, and I was able to get close enough to the cabin to see you and your little lady get out of the car."

"She's my granddaughter," Adam felt compelled to say. "I will be forever indebted to you and your grandchildren."

"Well, I'm just happy to help."

The tension dissipated as the two men stood talking as if they had come together after a long day of hunting to compare notes. Tommy introduced his grandsons. Handshakes were exchanged. For the briefest moment, it began to feel like home again.

And then the pleasantness was shattered.

"Papa!"

Adam turned to see Maritza standing in the doorway of the cabin. Behind her stood an assassin, bleeding from his left side.

His blood-soaked left hand held a nine-millimeter pistol to her temple. He'd wrapped the girl's long black ponytail around his right hand and was pulling up on it, lifting her onto her tiptoes.

Adam felt a kind of rage beyond anything he'd experienced before. For the briefest of moments, and with the help of an old friend, he'd felt as though he could give his granddaughter a future. That was in jeopardy. Three decades of training took over. He set aside emotion and began to consider scenarios for getting Maritza out of this situation alive.

"Why don't you just let the girl go?" Adam said. "You're in an unwinnable situation."

Adam held his gun at his side in order not to appear threatening. He saw Tommy and his grandchildren in his periphery as they slowly stepped back.

"What do you want with a Mexican girl anyway?" asked the assailant.

Adam knew the man was trying to goad him into making a move that would give him an excuse to shoot Maritza. It was a move only a blunt instrument employed by a government could conceive as a successful play.

Adam shook his head. "She was born in Guatemala, and she's my granddaughter."

Against every bit of situational training Adam had gone through, he slowly raised his rifle and drew a bead on the man's forehead. It was the single action that could cause the death of his granddaughter. He simply couldn't help himself.

The man pulled back the hammer of his gun with his thumb.

Maritza screamed a bloodcurdling scream that pierced every cell in Adam's body. He'd known parents to have a sense of empathy for their children that compelled them to experience every pain felt by offspring. He'd never experienced it fully until that moment. It occurred to him Maritza's death would take away his reason to live. Tears welled up in his eyes as he realized he may have just caused her demise. He was incapable of focusing on his target.

A shot rang out. But it wasn't from Adam's or the assassin's gun.

The grandfather dropped to a defensive posture on his right knee. He tried to sort through the million thoughts racing through his mind. Slowly he realized what happened.

His granddaughter ran toward him and fell into his arms. As he embraced Maritza, Adam looked past her. The feet and legs of the assassin protruded from the doorway. Blood soaked the door frame and the floor around him.

"Mister, are you okay?" said what sounded like a child from behind him.

He turned to look.

A girl, no more than twelve, was holding a .270-caliber scoped rifle. Smoke drifted from the end of its barrel. This was not one of Tommy's grandchildren he'd met. She must have stayed back, hiding in the woods. He wondered if that had been part of Tommy's strategy or just a move to keep her safe.

The little girl shot the would-be assassin between his eyes. Adam had never been so happy to see a twelve-year-old so completely competent with a firearm.

"Dammit, Darla," bellowed Tommy. "Didn't I tell you to wait in the truck?"

"But they needed my help, Grandaddy. You always say to help your neighbors in a time of need."

Adam continued to hold Maritza tightly. He had no interest in ever letting go. It was a forever together for which he wished.

Finally, they broke their embrace.

Tommy let them have their moment, but there were issues to address. He moved slowly to his old friend and placed a hand on his shoulder. "Have you got a minute?"

The two men walked away from the group that gathered around Maritza and Darla. They stopped just short of the woods.

"So, rumor over the last thirty years is that you got yourself involved with some intelligence operation," Said Tommy.

Adam simply smiled.

Tommy nodded. "Okay, I'm sure you can't talk about that, but let's discuss how this affects me. Now these boys laying dead around here appear to be part of assassination team, if I'm not mistaken. So they don't have any family waiting for them at home, or at the very least, they won't be missed by anybody. Now, since four of the six boys are dead at the hands of me and my family, I'd appreciate being able to keep this whole situation out of the court system."

"I can understand your position," said Adam. "But we have professional cleaning crews for just such occasions." It was an excuse based on distrust. No longer did he have access to an apparatus that erased all evidence of his existence. He'd planned on borrowing a backhoe from a neighbor to dig a hole adequate to conceal all bodies eternally.

"I can appreciate that, and I'm hoping you can do an old friend a favor, because it would give me a little peace of mind." Tommy gestured at the dead bodies scattered around. "What your team sees as paperwork and the cleanup, I see has pork chops, bacon, and pork bellies." He smiled. "Let me take them to the hog farm."

"Tommy, if I didn't know any better, I'd say you've done this before."

The man flashed an impish grin. "Naw. I just watch a lot of television," he said, deflecting ideas concerning current and prior guilt.

"But look at it from my perspective. I have to trust that the job is done correctly as well."

Tommy smiled and nodded. "You see, the difference between you and me is that you're asking me to trust some nameless, faceless government bureaucrats to have my well-being at heart. I'm asking you to look into my eyes and trust an old friend. The world would be a much better place if business were transacted like this again, don't you think?"

Tommy's wisdom was undeniable. All he needed to do was convince Eason. Shit! He'd forgotten about the general. The Air Pods lost the connection to the phone still inside the cabin. Eason was unable to eavesdrop on their conversation outside. "I've got to go, Tommy."

As Adam approached the cabin only sparks of conversation came through on the AirPods still secured in his ear. "Phillips...there?"

Nonchalantly stepping over the dead body in the doorway, Adam moved into the cabin.

"Phillips, are you there?"

"I'm glad to say we're all here and alive," replied Adam.

"I don't have a janitorial service to send to the cabin. We're operating on a bare bones budget."

"That's okay. I can get it taken care of."

"Do you have your encrypted phone with you?"

"Yes."

"Let's move our conversation there. I'll call in five minutes. I gotta pee."

Adam went to the front door again. He grabbed the dead assassin by his shoulders, dragged his feet along the ground, and tossed him into the center of the yard. "Maritza, come inside. You have to pack." He went to his car and opened the driver's door.

"Where are we going?"

"I don't know, yet. We'll know in five minutes."

Dutifully, Tommy and his grandchildren dragged the bodies of the other dead assassins into the center of the yard and piled them on top of one another. A call had been made to his wife who was in route with the flatbed trailer and a tarp. He'd meet her at the gate to the property and exchange vehicles. Tommy's desire was to keep her innocent of the affair. Promises were made to never again feed human flesh to their hogs. The woman couldn't stomach the thought of someone being a part of their Christmas ham.

Adam opened the trunk of the car and removed a satellite computer and phone. Each possessed state of the art encryption technology to prevent anyone listening or reading correspondence.

He took them into the cabin and set them on the small wooden kitchen table. He opened the laptop and logged in. He opened the map application on his computer. The cabin was a hot zone. Instructions from Eason would come, and he'd have to follow them, post haste. The map showed the cabin as their current location. He zoomed out to get a good look at nearby roads, searching for the quickest way out of the area.

Adam looked across the room at his granddaughter. "Are you not packed yet?"

"Papa, it takes time."

"Time is a commodity we don't have. Have you not learned from the past half hour what we're up against?"

Without a word, Maritza continued to pack.

Adam retrieved his duffle bag from the floor in front of the sink. Exactly five minutes after he hung up with Eason, the satellite phone rang.

Adam hurried to the kitchen table and picked it up. "Yes sir."

Without any greeting, Eason began offering instructions. "There's an international airport located west of Gainesville."

Adam moved southeast on the map until Gainesville was in the center.

"It's northeast of Newberry on County Road 235," said Eason.

"Geez! There are several international airports west of Gainesville."

"That's because there's a lot of drugs flown into and out of that area. As a matter of fact, I'm gonna be sending you a CIA plane that was used for just that purpose. The hope is you'll go unnoticed, given the history of that plane using the Newberry airport. Look for a Gulfstream G650. Be there in an hour."

Adam was used to changed plans and hurried exits, but with his granddaughter tagging along, there was an added sense of urgency. In addition, there was an overzealous officer Sally Cole he must avoid in Jefferson County. "Can I ask where we are going?"

"Cuba," replied Eason.

Cuba was one country in which he'd never operated. He had no contacts there. He was blind to everything about his immediate future. He hated not being in control. He knew Eason's final directive was as good as goodbye. He hung up the phone without another word.

Adam drove the car as quickly as he could down the myriad of two-lane highways without risking being stopped again for speeding. Conventional wisdom of teenagers learning their limits spoke to the fact Highway Patrol wouldn't stop anyone unless they were doing more than ten miles per hour over the limit. Adam's speed teetered above and below that inflection point in an effort to close the distance between them and the remote airport. Nothing could delay their timeline. From here on out, movements would be executed with military precision, or lives could be lost. How does one instill a sense of urgency into a teenager?

Retracing lonely, two-lane, north Florida roads didn't appeal to Adam, and he could tell Maritza wasn't thrilled either. As long as they were alive, forward movement was a good thing. Adam thought how lucky he was to have escaped this part of the state as a young man.

For the second time in his life, he considered himself fortunate. He'd never been able to shake the nostalgia he felt for these small communities and the people who inhabited them. They'd always be a part of his soul. If he hadn't the experience of life in the panhandle, he wouldn't understand how basic human existence could be. For most of his adolescence, he knew there was something more to experience. His reality was based in human conditions controlled by others.

As death became a daily consideration, he worried that only when his soul was released from its earthly confines could he once gain regain influence over his existence. The concept of eternity was the only notion that brought peace of mind.

Adam no longer had the physical strength to affect change among adversaries. Situations involving hand-to-hand combat would prove fruitless against younger, more virile opponents. Why had he never been given a desk job? Many of his peers were in DC working for one of the seventeen intelligence agencies, gathering, processing, and reporting on global happenings. Why did the federal government need seventeen agencies? Why not two—one international and one domestic? It was obvious to the critical thinker such a vast spy network was meant for only one thing, and that was complete control of the global population. The question remained. From what level did control emanate?

The drive offered time to continue reflecting on his professional life. Maybe that was why Adam had never been promoted? Awareness of reasons the home office kept him in a field role into his fifties brought clarity. It was hoped the weaker, senior agent would meet his demise during an operation. Adam's epiphany drove him to act rashly and murder his counterpart in Key West.

The frustration of realizing the nature of corruption in the world was only eclipsed by the knowledge he'd beaten them at their own game. He remained one step ahead of his adversaries. He'd played the role of pawn for thirty years. Joy was tempered by the realization with every passing day, he existed in a world controlled by elites. Centralized control brought humanity closer to the fulfillment of Project Trinity. Had the Cuban been given the same objective from his country's intelligence apparatus? Regardless of the circumstances of others, he hardened his determination to take out the true dictatorial class. If he only had an elite team with whom to partner.

Maritza stared at the McDonald's on Highway 98 in Perry. She realized this was the second time in the last three hours she'd passed the same store. Gaming trained her mind to accept only movement into successive levels as progress. Frustration burst forth at the recognition of stagnation. "Kids were never meant to travel in cars for more than ten minutes," she barked, illogically.

On the way to the smallest international airport in existence, they passed through a number of small, quaint communities. Towns like Mayo, Branford, and High Springs. Adam had driven through this area many times over the decades. It was four in the morning and traffic signals ceased to change from green to yellow to red. They simply blinked cautiously yellow until morning traffic affected sensors that regulated flow.

He remembered the times he'd driven through these towns to see his grandparents in Gainesville—past small houses with swing sets and bicycles in front yards. He wondered if parents who occupied these homes were challenging their kids to think critically about all that surrounded them. He felt it imperative kids think not only of their immediate circumstances but of the lives of those throughout the world. Innate compassion dictated empathy first for everyone he encountered. Affinity for the human race pulsed ethereally and Adam envisioned everyone's connection as being bound by an indestructible fabric. His generation lost the ability to think critically. They'd lost vital human connections; trading them for electronic pulses displaying software driven games and 24-7 sports programming.

He felt his face flush with anger as he thought of the many times he'd questioned his mother concerning global events. She never had any answers. "I just don't know about that," she'd say, comfortable in her ignorance.

Five decades later that tragic viewpoint continued to affect him negatively. Was it the worst form of child abuse to teach your children to aspire to nothing more than being a petty functionary? As an assassin he'd mindlessly embraced taking orders and executing tasks. Outside of Carolyn and his family, there'd never been any growth toward becoming a universal being.

Something compelled him to search for answers his parents couldn't provide. He learned to push beyond circumstances relatives simply accepted. Their biggest failure was to view their child as a mere carbon copy of themselves; not allowing Adam to grow in his own right. In the latter part of his life, Adam conceived how he'd fulfilled that predetermined destiny over which he had no control.

Looking toward a future whereby all humans controlled personal providences, that part of God that pulsed within everyone, provided his only salvation. It was that accomplishment toward which he dedicated his remaining time.

The young girl that sat next to him bobbing her head to the rhythm of the music on the stereo represented his last opportunity to build the foundation of a successful family; one that would prosper for generations.

Adam turned off of County Road 235 and onto a two-rut driveway that ended at a closed iron gate. He looked at his watch. It was 4:35 a.m. There was a man holding an AR-15 standing at the gate, waiting to let them inside. Adam knew this show of force was standard operating procedure.

Maritza sat up straight and peered through the windshield. She exclaimed disgustedly, "this is nothing more than a cow pasture."

Her grandfather remained silent and maneuvered the car uphill. Once they reached a natural peak, a long, flat runway came into view. At the near end sat a plane awaiting their arrival. The familiar sound of jet engines idling brought comfort to Adam. They were close to escaping their brief ordeal.

"Ooh! A private jet," Maritza remarked gleefully. "I feel like Ariana Grande."

"Well, I'm glad something has gone right for you today," her grandfather replied, rolling his eyes.

Maritza's cavalier attitude gave Adam pause. In the last three hours she'd learned her grandfather was a career assassin, murdered two people, and he'd placed his life in danger to ensure her safety; yet someone called Ariana Grande held more sway with his teenage granddaughter. He laughed as he recalled ignoring his father in the same manner when he was a teenager. Being a parent was a thankless job.

5

Adam and Maritza bolted from the car, grabbed their bags from the trunk, and jogged to the plane. The young girl struggled up the stairs carrying a suitcase that added half her weight to the challenge of ascent. Her grandfather steadied her with a hand on the middle of her back. She faltered a bit at the top step, and he gave her a little push. Once the teenager breeched the opening, Adam entered behind her.

The plane was equipped with a single tan leather seat on each side of the aisle near the cockpit. Behind them, a luxurious sofa was positioned parallel to the port fuselage. Across from it was a credenza styled entertainment center complete with forty-inch flat screen television. Aft was a configuration of six chairs. Three by three facing each other; two on the starboard side and four on the port.

Maritza placed her bag on the floor behind the right front seat and sat down.

Adam shoved his duffle bag into the luggage closet at the back of the plane. He walked forward and took the seat to the left of his granddaughter. Being close to the pilot offered a modicum of peace that calmed their tumultuous psyches. Each clung to the realization they'd need help from others for mere survival.

Adam looked forward and witnessed the captain pushing open the cockpit door. The man was strapped into his seat and twisted himself to face his passengers. "Is everybody secure back there?" he asked.

Adam checked to see that Maritza was strapped in. "Yes," he replied as he buckled his own seatbelt.

"All right," said the pilot as he latched the door into the open position. "Here we go."

Almost immediately, everyone on board felt the power of jet engines revving. The plane accelerated quickly. Force pinned Adam and Maritza to the backs of their seats.

Maritza traveled internationally with her parents many times, but this takeoff felt different. This wasn't a jumbo jet lumbering down the runway, almost begging to pick up enough speed to become airborne. The Gulfstream shot down the runway for what seemed a matter of seconds before the plane tilted as it climbed into the air. It quickly leveled off. She heard the hum of the wheels retracting and then a thunk as landing gear doors closed.

Adam looked through his window. Even in the dark, he could see they were skimming treetops. He smirked, knowing the pilot was flexing his skills. Evasive maneuvers didn't seem necessary given the plane's history in the area.

Adam looked across the aisle and through Maritza's window—toward the east. The sky on that side of the plane was a shade lighter as the sun affected the new day's horizon. He knew they'd be in Cuba in time for breakfast.

He called up to the pilot. "Where are we going, anyway?"

Only the profile of the man's face was exposed as he turned to answer. "Mariel," he remarked before facing forward again.

Adam knew that, at this extremely low altitude, the pilot had to maintain a direct visual of the terrain.

The rest of the captain's reply was broken into choppy, verbal lobs he tossed over his shoulder a couple of seconds at a time. "There are abandoned airports," he said. "All over Cuba. Like at Mariel. That will get us. Close to Havana. Then you can skirt. Around the city. To the safe house."

Adam knew Mariel. The boat-lift that brought a 125,000 Cuban refugees to the shores of south Florida occurred when he was a young and impressionable teenager. It became one of the reasons he chose to join the agency. Once in the service, he researched the clandestine operation through old, classified reports.

A senior field agent, Rafael Ferguson, told him he possessed evidence the CIA was involved in the coastal incursion. His report included the history of the CIA and the Nazi influence that was brought from Germany to combat the bogeyman the United States feared most; Russia. The report detailed the creation of the CIA in 1947 and how most Central and South American countries were prosperous at that time. Country by country the CIA funded revolutions, influenced elections, and organized coups. Force, coercion, and murder were only a few of the tools they used to achieve their objective. According to the agent, this was a CIA led operation meant to destabilize the United States. 2024 offered a perfect perception of the long-term project to destabilize the country he'd risked his life to protect.

Adam considered the irony of flying to Cuba in a luxurious private jet owned by the CIA. It made him antsy. The plane had been bought and paid for with money from an illicit drug trade that destroyed the lives of millions of US citizens. It was how the agency made money to fund black operations. Dirty money wasn't part of any official budget. There was no congressional oversight of its spending. In addition, it made those in control extraordinarily wealthy. Once again, age offered hindsight to juxtapose an idealistic youth with the jaded cynic he'd become.

He thought about Rafael. It made him sad. The fate of a man working for God and country appeared expendable at the direction of those in charge. He was killed on his very next mission. His death had been a lucky break for those in charge. In Adam's mind, it was too fortunate to be coincidental.

Adam looked across the aisle at his granddaughter. MP3 player in her hands, wired earbuds in her ears, she was immersed in unrealistic dreams embracing the superficial life of a pop star. Adam retrieved the MP3 player from deep within his glove compartment. Her phone had to be left at the cabin. She had no idea what his life was about, what this plane represented, or what life in Cuba may hold for them both.

Adam reached across the aisle and tapped his granddaughter's arm. She pulled herself back into the present from some far away place in her imagination. This was how she'd always appeared to her grandfather—oblivious to what others around her were doing; seemingly without a care in the world.

Being on a plane triggered Maritza's thoughts of all the countries she'd been with her mother and father. She looked at Adam. "I've never been to Cuba."

"Well, that would be because it's illegal for US citizens to travel to Cuba." He had so much to teach this young lady. Time was the unknown variable. She appeared strong, but he would not shirk his responsibility to her.

The nature of Adam's business meant he had to lie as standard practice. When he was younger, he could manage his feelings concerning those lies. He could either prove himself better than the lie, or its impact on him dissipated over time. That was no longer the case. The frequency of energy resonating within his soul would affect its well-being after death; or so he believed. His scientific mind rationalized associations with like-minded spirits operating at the same level of understanding is what brought humans together. Whether alliances coalesced for good or evil, it was common energy that bound participants together. So many lies he'd put forth emanated negative energy. He needed to cleanse himself of those dregs, and soon.

Maritza's resilience puzzled Adam. She'd been a part of their family since she was five months old. Nothing about the environment in which she grew up prepared her for such a nasty existence. The home in which she lived was purposefully safe. Her shell hardened after the death of her mother and father. Awareness of the inequality of human existence had been thrust upon the teenager.

Adam considered her soul. He knew her energy had been around since the beginning of the universe. How long had it been coalesced into the consciousness he'd grown to love? What were her experiences throughout time that allowed her to kill people deemed a threat? There was strength in her eternal being. How else could she have experienced the last four hours, and then gone about her teenage life as if nothing happened?

He thought about his doctoral dissertation. Was his granddaughter a unique human being who could slide down to the evil end of the energy spectrum, complete her business, and then slide right back to the Godly with little or no effort? It was a skill he believed he needed to perfect for mere survival. Adam grew to understand his granddaughter's strength was enduring.

His scientific mind craved clarity. He needed logic. He was open to being taught by whomever embraced truth. He glanced over at Maritza again. She still appeared oblivious to outside influences. Her soul was awash in music blasting through ear buds.

Adam reached over and tapped her arm again.

Maritza removed her left ear bud and looked at him with raised eyebrows.

"I just want to make sure you're okay with everything that went on this morning?"

Ambivalently she shrugged her shoulders. "Yeah. Sure." Uncharacteristic of a teenager, she continued examining the question. "I'd always considered the possibility my parents, and granny were killed purposefully. Using a phrase you used earlier, I feel like my soul was unsettled having been ripped from Guatemala. I grew to love my parents, and to understand their motivation for doing so." She paused, not wanting to admit to homicidal thoughts. "When you told me the men coming after us were the ones who killed my mother and father," she shook her head, "Let's just say it scares me to have that kind of anger and hatred toward another human."

"You know you were forced to kill those men. It was either them or you."

"Actually, I only wounded the second one. Darla got credit for the kill."

Then it dawned on Adam. She was equating her experience to a video game.

"Is that it?" she dismissed him with the brashness of a CEO with more pressing issues to deal with than the prattle of an underling.

Adam nodded, looked forward, and lay his head back against the headrest. He closed his eyes and visualized what life in Cuba would be like. Exhaustion consumed him and he fell asleep.

6

Adam was jostled awake by gentle rocking as the plane touched down on the runway. He became momentarily disoriented.

Once he'd gathered his wits, he looked over at his granddaughter. She was asleep, and in the most uncomfortable position imaginable. Her chin rested flat against her chest. Her head hung so low it was as if her neck had been severed and only hung by the slightest sliver of skin. He reached over and gently stroked her arm. Fear gripped his awareness if she jerked awake, she might hurt herself.

As Maritza transitioned into consciousness, Adam peered through his window at the runway. Grass and weeds grew between slabs of concrete that made up the tarmac. In the distance were several hangers constructed of rusted, corrugated tin. Sheets were missing in places, exposing the skeletons of the structures. To Adam, it appeared as if the buildings had been abandoned for decades.

The plane turned off the runway and onto the taxiway. It bounced as it rolled over each strip of grass in the gaps between concrete slabs. The changing angle of the plane gave Adam an unobstructed view of a four-door 1950s-era car that awaited them. It spoke to the minimalist environment in which Cubans were forced to exist under Castro's dogmatic regime. He made it out to be a Plymouth but had no idea the model. Its exterior was covered in rust. Adam suspected the engine would purr like the proverbial kitten. Vehicles were meticulously maintained due to scarcity. Outward appearances spoke to the fact there was no escape from elements exerting influence for decades.

When the plane came to a stop and the sounds of the engines cascaded into silence, the couple's driver approached. The man twisted the door's handle and pulled down, exposing the stairs fashioned into the inner curve of the fuselage. Maritza grabbed her bag from the floor and moved to the doorway in front of her grandfather's seat.

Adam made his way to the rear of the plane and grabbed his duffle bag from the locker. Joining his granddaughter quickly at the front of the plane, he followed her down the steps.

The driver was a handsome young Cuban who offered Maritza an especially friendly smile as she descended the stairs.

An uncomfortable pall washed over the girl's psyche. She'd yet to understand how attractive men found her.

After Adam joined the two, without a word the driver led them to the car and loaded their bags into the trunk. Adam took the front passenger seat.

Maritza chose to sit directly behind the driver and pinned herself against the door; hiding from potential glances in the rear-view mirror.

The young driver engaged the ignition and drove toward the airport's exit that appeared to be nothing more than a mere gap in a rusted chain-link fence.

Adam nodded his approval of man and machine who both appeared worthy of alliance. The car may have looked like a hunk of junk, but it ran like a dream.

"Papa," Maritza said. "Can we stay for a few days wherever it is we're going?"

He smiled. "I think so." Adam turned to the driver, who still hadn't said a word. "Can you tell us where we're going?"

"Finca Vigia," he offered with a proud smile. As if a docent for the museum, he continued. "It was the home of your American writer, Ernest Hemingway, from 1939 to 1960."

"Nice," Adam replied. "But I thought no one was allowed there?"

"We have special permission."

"Duharte-Ranero?" Adam asked, referring to the country's current president.

The driver gave Adam a stern look. "No," he said. "He is on his way out."

Adam knew there was a lot more to the story, and that he would be both briefed and debriefed whenever they got to Finca Vigia. It worried the operative there may be a coup in the making. The Cuban people had been actively protesting convictions, so it may be nothing to concern Adam. In political situations, lines are blurred, and no one ever truly knew allies from adversaries.

He turned and peered into the back seat. "Maritza, do you know what Finca Vigia means in English?"

"No."

"You have to learn Spanish. I told you. I even bought you Rosetta Stone ten years ago." He waited briefly for some teen-angst-driven response, but there was none. "It means 'Lookout Farm.' Quite apropos, don't you think?"

"Sure." It'd been nearly sixteen hours since she was able to be stimulated by her cell phone. No matter how her grandfather attempted to inspire conversation it'd been a constant companion upon which she relied for global interactions with people she'd befriended via the internet. Maritza was lost without it.

"You know, you're always staring at a screen driven by some program. You need to understand the people who are programing that software are also programming your brain."

When there was no response, it became obvious his granddaughter was exhausted and not interested in chatting.

The trip around Havana's city center took them through rain forests and past grand plantations. Although the road appeared to be in good repair Adam noticed they passed more bicyclists and pedestrians than motorists. The fact was the average Cuban couldn't afford a car. Mounted to each bike were oversized baskets, and most were also equipped with saddlebags. These bicycles were less about recreation and more for utility.

Adam was struck by the lush green landscape. Tropical rains kept plants well nourished. They passed through a few small towns. One indistinguishable from another; except for names posted on signs at city limits. Brightly painted buildings dotted the towns. Adam found it curious colors chosen weren't pastels. Instead, dark blues, oranges, and greens dominated façades. Harsh colors confronted his senses. Adam laughed, realizing he shouldn't expect townspeople to employ professional designers. Colors were hideous and obviously made from the cheapest paints available. What else should one expect from a communist country that stifled innovation and creativity?

Mountains jutted up through the lush forest and were just as green as the rest of the landscape. Underlying surfaces were hidden beneath the vegetation. Tobacco plants seemed to thrive in the red soil that resembled Georgia clay.

The driver maneuvered onto the National Highway of Cuba. It was a well-maintained three lane highway. Few automobiles were encountered during their drive. The ones Adam saw were late model Mercedes and BMWs. It appeared a great deal of the country's resources had been diverted to this road for elites to use, easily moving between huge tracts of land. He witnessed not only the past but one possible neo-feudal future. Steely determination welled within the man's soul. The desire to stop Project Trinity before its execution guaranteed such a miserable existence for humanity flooded back into his consciousness.

Along the route they encountered a few billboards featuring Castro, clad in his drab-green revolutionary uniform. The signs proclaimed him *Comandante en Jeffe*—Commander in Chief, many years after his death.

Adam questioned how much history had been kept out of schoolbooks in order to obscure the US government's involvement in Cuba. It was sickening to a man who'd been complicit in perpetuating lies during his career. Thoughts naturally progressed to consideration of his soul—that which would live on after his death. He was less concerned with how his deeds would negatively affect his afterlife. It was his belief every human's energy was connected to the universe. Succumbing to the effect of lies dragged souls away from that which was Godly.

Part of that connection was the link to absolute truth, which Adam believed could not be hidden at the universal level. He wondered if the catalyst for unsettled souls were caused by an inner conflict between human energy and lies put forth as reality. For anyone who sought facts, lies became painfully obvious. It was clear to Adam that Castro had been funded and protected by the same forces that controlled US politicians for decades. How else could they have flown a CIA plane into Mariel unmolested?

The results were dire for the average Cuban. As with most of humanity, they only wished to lead productive lives and be a part of beautiful, successful families. How could the US have allowed this poverty to go on for so long? The Monroe Doctrine was not adhered to, because the US was the shadow colonial power when it came to Cuba.

Adam recalled learning the differences between capitalism versus socialism versus communism in school as an adolescent. It never made sense a country's people would choose anything other than complete freedom. Continued inquiries offered his first epiphany as to how the hidden hand of the elite stoked a population's inability to conceive personal success. Cards were stacked against those unwilling to force change. Watching others succeed exacerbated frustration. Increasing societal despair drove misery, and it loved equally miserable company. Populations allowed themselves to be consumed by hardship and wished the same for everyone around them. Sinking emotional states dragged communities away from God and toward that which can only be tactilely satiated. Only those providing physical sustenance, politicians and other false idols, were revered. The cabal counted on people's unwillingness to place their bodies in harm's way for humanity's eternal preservation. Martin Luther King said, "when you lose your fear of death, they can no longer control you." It was the Godly to which humanity must return. Communism's foundation was built on base-level human existence, and changing that mindset would be paramount in creating a free and fulfilled populace. Its desperation was easily witnessed on the faces of citizens of an otherwise beautiful country.

It had become obvious the degree to which any society in history was enslaved depended on its citizens' willingness to fight for freedom. His understanding offered the perfect example as to why humanity must battle tyranny. Saturated negative energy soaked into the souls of entire populations and dragged down entire societies. Humanity needed a new enlightenment. Very few controlled most of the planet's resources. The United States was the last bastion of freedom on the planet, and Cuba provided the launching pad for importing equally distributed despair to the proletariat.

Adam shook away his reverie as the car turned off the road and onto the bumpy driveway of Finca Vigia. It was a grand home, and Adam was overcome by its stately appearance. Its construction was nineteenth century but conveyed strength; that which was built to last. A pergola encompassed the majority of the front patio. Red, flowering bougainvillea flourished and draped over the sides of the structure. Beauty was protected by limbs adorned with vicious thorns. The uninitiated risked extreme pain blindly reaching for that which was perceptually attainable. This was a home worthy of a man of Hemingway's stature. No wonder he loved it so. Concrete steps guarded the right half of the home and wrapped around its side. The third step offered a wider landing as did the sixth.

"I'll bring your things inside," the driver said, as all three emerged from the car.

Without acknowledging him, Adam climbed the steps, overwhelmed by the home's resplendent nature. Its exterior was the soft pastel yellow Adam thought should have covered the buildings in the towns they'd passed through. The entry was guarded by two stately columns. Another five steps between the pillars serviced the front door exclusively.

As they approached, the door opened, seemingly on its own. Into the breach stepped a black man standing six foot four and dressed in Loudmouth golf slacks and a white golf shirt emblazoned with Tiger Woods' logo.

"Welcome." The man's voice was deep and strong. There was something familiar about it. Adam knew this voice, but before he had the chance to put a name to it, the man introduced himself, and extended his hand, "I'm General Eason."

A wave of relief washed over Adam that was expressed through humor. "Did your wife dress you that way?"

Eason chuckled. "You'd be surprised how many tourists dress this way. Besides, we're too far out in the country for anyone to notice." He stepped aside to allow the two to enter.

The inside of the home was just as intimidating. Its walls were white, and the ceiling was the same yellow as the exterior. Tiles on the floor were twelve-inch terra cotta squares. Its appearance was clean and earthy. And then there was the ghost of Hemingway.

Adam looked at his granddaughter. She appeared in awe as well.

General Eason led them to a back room. Dark brown bookshelves lined the rear wall beneath a bank of windows that encompassed the length of the wall.

Sunlight lit the interior. Trophy heads of several species of animal were mounted along the walls at various spots.

Maritza shuddered. "Papa, those heads on the wall freak me out."

Adam nodded. "Yeah, I've never been much for trophy hunting. Hunting for basic subsistence is a human right."

General Eason listened but did not offer comment. He strolled over to one of the two large armchairs upholstered in a floral print and sat down. Adam chose a cane chair across the coffee table from his new boss.

Eason smiled. "These chairs were made from Cuban Mahogany trees felled in the area."

"Nice. This kind of workmanship lasts forever," Adam replied as he patted the wooden arms of his chair.

Eason glanced at Maritza and then Adam. The young girl stood at the back of the room, gazing through one of the many windows.

Adam acknowledged the man's cue. His chair creaked as he turned toward the girl. "Maritza, why don't you go find your room and put your things away."

The teenager drew in both lips and bit them closed to prevent verbalized disdain. There was a great deal of strength in her glance as she looked between both men. "Sure." Her response was tinged in sarcasm with a hint of skepticism.

The men watched her leave. "That's one strong young lady you have there," General Eason said.

"Yeah. I've always known she was strong willed, but I never truly understood how strong her soul was until she was forced to display it."

Eason leaned forward and sat on the edge of his chair. He glanced through the doorway, reassuring himself they were alone. "You've obviously come to the conclusion that your career has been spent advancing the agenda of an unelected body across the globe."

Adam nodded.

"There's a faction of the military that has come to the same conclusion, and we've put together a select group to combat it. We're building communication channels and a report sharing apparatus, but most importantly, we've secured all nuclear weapons from being launched without our authorization."

"Do you think this will come to a nuclear exchange?"

"No. But we must make sure we prevent the cabal from destroying the earth."

"I'm not sure it's that easy."

Eason stroked his chin with his left hand. "What if I told you the elite unit we have in the United States military is connected to the same types of units in Russia, China, Japan, Australia, New Zealand…and Cuba?"

Adam heard the front door of the house open and then close. He assumed it to be their driver bringing luggage inside. He sat back in his chair and mentally digested what he'd just heard. Noticeably absent from the general's list were key allies. He still had no idea who he could trust, and who he shouldn't.

When a third figure appeared in his periphery, Adam glanced toward the entry across the room. It was the Cuban he was meant to assassinate in Key West. He knew his name from the dossier he'd read before almost assassinating the man who stood across the room from him—Reinier Fernandez. Information contained in that file spoke to the meaning of the man's name, "wise army." It was of German origin.

When the Cuban saw the recognition on Adam's face, he smiled, moved across the room, and took a seat in the second floral-printed armchair next to Eason.

The seating arrangement imparted a me-versus-them feeling in Adam's psyche. That night in Key West replayed in his mind. "I guess I was right in letting you live?"

Fernandez smiled and gave a little nod. "Si, and I thank you for your gift of life. I got sloppy while visiting a friend in Miami. Too many cervesas. His house was bugged, and they captured me the night before I was to fly back to Cuba. Stupid of me." He made a sweeping gesture toward Adam. "Never underestimate the grace of God. He brought me to you."

Adam looked at Eason, and then Reinier. "Maybe the three of us were brought together for a reason."

"Okay gentlemen," General Eason barked. "Enough of old-home week. We need to get down to business. We're getting a lot of chatter on encrypted channels about Project Trinity. We need to know exactly what Trinity is and how they intend to deploy it."

Adam thought aloud. "I know from my research people who practice satanism love the number three. Could it be a three-pronged attack on humanity? Jim Norton had a three-pointed pyramid, and the black sun on his signet ring."

"The number three appears all throughout the world. Many religions embrace its concept," Reinier offered.

Adam nodded. "Agreed, but I feel like evil uses it and displays it mockingly. It's as if they want the world to know they control all trinities."

He glanced at the other two men as all three sat in silence. They needed more intelligence to act, but where should they start?

"Wait a minute," Adam looked at the Cuban. "The reason for the wet work against you was that you passed information about Project Trinity."

The Cuban nodded. He opened his mouth but hesitated.

Skepticism forced Adam into the belief he was trying to concoct a story.

"The information I passed was meant to draw out those who directed Project Trinity. Cuban intelligence thought we are onto something. We traced the movement of three elite couriers into Dubai. Suffice it to say, we rolled the dice and I lost. The only thing we accomplished was that I exposed myself as an intelligence asset." He looked stoically at Adam. "And you were the one who drew the assassination card."

"Is there anything else to go on?" Adam asked.

"Let's go into the dining room," Eason said, standing and leading the way.

The two agents followed dutifully.

The men moved into a large rectangular room containing little furniture. A wooden dining table was surrounded by three chairs. There was room for at least six diners at the table. Three additional chairs were drawn away and placed against the wall. Adam knew the room hosted the likes of Ingrid Bergman and Gary Cooper. A buffet stood against one wall. Above that hung a favorite painting of Hemingway's. It was La Ferme by Joan Miro and had recently been repatriated from the National Gallery in DC.

Eason snatched up a remote control from the table. He pointed it at the painting and pressed a button. There was a faint hum as the painting slid down, exposing a screen. General Eason moved around the dining table and took a seat at its head.

Adam and Reinier sat in the two chairs next to Eason on opposite sides and shifted them so each man could see the screen.

The screen showed a map of the world. There was a red dot on London, one on Berlin, and another on Buenos Aires. "This is all the intelligence we've gathered so far that can be attached to Trinity." Eason's deep voice echoed in the empty room. He lowered the volume attempting to soften the echo. He wished to prevent Maritza from overhearing their conversation. "We deciphered phone calls from these three locations mentioning Trinity. All three calls mentioned a depopulation event. Their goal for a successful operation is a 'hoped for' death count of between five and seven billion people."

"Oh my God," Adam said.

Reinier followed with, "Dios, mio."

Adam pointed to the map. "Were these calls made between these cities, or were other cities involved?"

"That's what is so disturbing," Eason said. He pointed the remote at the screen again. Three more dots appeared, this time in blue, on the cities of Washington, DC, Beijing, and London. The last was right next to the original red dot.

The two operatives sat silently staring at the map, contemplating the implications of what they'd been told.

"But you mentioned China as being a part of our coalition?" said Adam.

"The Premier is. However, there's a great cabal that remains. President Vasily rid Russia of most of the cabal members he identified. He's still working on it, but the remaining moles have buried themselves so far underground they won't have access to anything lethal." Eason looked from Fernandez to Phillips. "But that doesn't mean we don't need to stay vigilant."

Maritza called out from an adjacent room. "It could be a marker of some sort, or an Easter egg. Or it could be the three wise men?"

Adam leaned forward to try to see her through the doorway, but he couldn't quite spot her.

She continued from the other room. "Maybe it's their way of eliminating Christ from the equation? The human manifestation of God. Christ is the earthly example of how to live a Godly life." She paused. "I streamed the movie Elmer Gantry a few months ago. The very last lines in the film equate the belief in God as childlike behavior. Mocking of faith in movies has gone on for decades."

Adam looked at General Eason and shrugged.

Eason nodded his approval.

"Come on in, sweetie," Adam called.

Maritza strolled into the dining room. She spent most of her life staring at screens, examining messages constructed by billions of pixels. Solving this puzzle might be a task for which she was better suited than those seated at the table.

The teenager came around to the far side of the table and stood next to the general, as if she belonged in such a high-level meeting. She pointed to the pin placed at Germany's capital, and then the one in South America. "Berlin was the center of Nazi power, and Buenos Aires was where they took Hitler to safety after the war."

The men looked at each other.

Reinier shrugged. "Maybe she's on to something?"

Adam gave his granddaughter a skeptical look.

"What?" she asked. "It's based on the video game, *The Final Solution.*"

General Eason closed his eyes and let out a sigh. "A video game? We can't base our mission on a video game, young lady."

"I don't know, General," she said. "But the facts you just stated were all played out several times in this game. I watched it all unfold before my eyes."

"You saw seven billion people murdered on earth every time this game was played?"

"No, of course not."

"Thank you," the general said, smugly.

"It would vary between four and seven billion. Seven billion occurred very infrequently, and that seemed to upset the overlords." She laughed. "Oh boy, I remember playing one day and the death count didn't even reach a billion. The overlords were angry. Cussing like sailors on that day."

Reinier asked, "So you were just allowed to play with these —overlords—as you call of them?"

"No, that's what they called themselves. And we had to hack in to play. They thought we were an elite group of players, and part of their intelligence apparatus." She nodded satisfactorily. "We were that good."

Eason sat forward at the realization. "I read some intel a few years ago that world leaders, corporate heads, and politicians play encrypted video games so they could communicate offline. Maybe they did play out different scenarios in order to perfect a plan?"

"Holy shit," Adam exclaimed. "Maritza, in what ways did they kill seven billion people?"

"Ways? It was mainly through the health care system, but it centered on weakening immune systems. Of course, the fast-food industry helped to a great extent. The only thing that saved anyone is that digital soldiers educated people of the true intent of the Nazi health care system developed during the Holocaust. How effectively the white hats' message was delivered, and what percentage of the population was open to it, determined how many people were saved. But," she said, and then she gazed across the room, seemingly lost in thought. "Of course, there was a time, before I began playing, when the elite placed nano-bots in gel-caps of popular over-the-counter medications. These bots were activated by satellites and killed people that way, but I was told the technology just hadn't advanced quickly enough. Maybe they've finally perfected mass genocide. Lord knows they've spent billions researching better ways to kill humans with bombs, guns, and even sonic weapons. It isn't such a stretch of the imagination to believe they've secretly accomplished that which will be used for such a heinous purpose."

The three men again looked at one other.

Adam broke the stalemate. "We still don't know what Trinity is. Or how they intend to deploy it?"

Maritza meekly raised her hand, as if she were in a classroom.

Adam nodded toward her and she let her hand fall to the table. "If you can believe what internet sleuths are saying, Trinity consists of any vaccine; flu, Covid, any manner in which they can place their technology inside your body is utilized. DNA services that everyone voluntarily submitted saliva samples with promises of finding one's heritage, or relatives across the globe you didn't realize you had. This maps out individual DNA with common characteristics. Their profiles are used against them. Speculation is that the elites can isolate huge swaths of the global population based on this information. From space. Mass global genocide."

Reinier looked from Adam to Eason, "Do we have nano computers that can be injected and complete these types of tasks?"

Eason nodded at the pieces of a mystery coming together. "And I can guarantee you there is that kind of evil on this planet. There are people who would formulate that plan and work their entire lives to make it happen."

"Truly evil," Adam offered rhetorically, and speaking as if only he could hear his words.

A long silence descended on the group.

Maritza broke it. "General Eason, what is the Wi-Fi password?"

He held up his index finger. "Martha Gelhorn, no spaces, but give me your old phone." He stood and went to the buffet against the wall. He opened the top left drawer and took out an Apple iPhone box. "I have one here that's exactly like your phone

—an exact clone with all of the same apps and games. It even has your game progress to date. The only difference is this one is fully encrypted and can't be traced." He walked over and handed her the phone. "I'll need your old one," he said, looking her in the eyes as he held out his hand.

"And my complete playlist?" she said, head cocked arrogantly and ignoring the general's demand for her old device.

"And your complete playlist."

Adam chimed in. "We left the old one at the cabin to prevent being tracked again."

"Excellent," Eason said. "You're actually going to like this one because it operates faster than your old phone. Without all of the spyware, why wouldn't it?"

"Cool." She took the new phone, and without a word exited the room.

General Eason again took his seat at the table. The three sat in silence, trying to determine the veracity of the statements of a sixteen-year-old. If there was any credibility to what Maritza said, how would they prove it?

"Can we get vaccines from all manufacturers to test them?" Adam asked rhetorically and continued speaking to no one in particular. "Can we download programming from global satellites to examine it?"

Eason sighed. "We might have to steal samples of every vaccine known to man. We do have scientists that can examine it."

"Talk about a needle in a haystack," Adam said. "Maybe there's a stockpile in a warehouse somewhere. We just have to find out where? But what do we do with it once we have it in hand?"

Eason stood. "Come with me, gentlemen." He led the others out of the house and onto the asphalt driveway.

The men followed the driveway's downward slope around the side of the house. At the bottom of the hill stood a large outbuilding. It was two stories at one end. Windows ran the length of the building. In the bottom half of a single middle window was an air conditioning unit. Its weight was supported by two steel posts angled from the appliance's outer corners and toward the foundation.

"I know it appears dilapidated. But it's quite useful. Its appearance is meant to satisfy the casual observer that nothing of value is contained within its walls."

The men stepped off of the asphalt driveway and onto a concrete path that led to a door at the end of the building. Inside were two long rows of computer stations with a long aisle down the center of the room. At each computer, an operator tapped away upon keyboards. Computer cables were bound by zip ties and strapped to load bearing poles. They were strung up to the roof's exposed rafters. From there they ran back toward a small server room encased in glass.

Adam beheld the modern room. The temperature was kept at sixty-five degrees, monitored by a digital display all could observe for the benefit of continued operations.

Eason led his visitors to the opposite end of the room where stairs led to the second floor. At the top of the stairs, Eason unlocked a door and ushered his guests inside.

Adam soaked in every detail as he'd been trained when entering new environments. The room was an office with a single desk at one end and a conference table at the other. Stacks of manilla folders containing varying amounts of paper were scattered on every flat surface in the room.

Eason chuckled. "I really should make the transition to the digital age." He waved his hands over the mess. "All of this represents intelligence that those folks downstairs have gathered. Are you men ready to dig in and see what we can find?"

"What are we looking for?" Reinier asked, bordering sarcasm. "Evidence to prove some internet conspiracy theory?"

Eason hated to admit internet hackers seemingly had been successful where their intelligence failed. "I've seen some of the evidence Maritza is referring to, elites using gaming platforms as communication backchannels. There have been a lot of conspiracy theories that have been proven factual. For all the evil in the world, ninety-nine percent of the population hopes for the best for all humans, and some use their skills to protect their fellow man. I think it's worth looking into. Yes."

The men sat dutifully around the table for hours, searching through reports and laying them aside. Sometimes pages were marked with Post-it notes, referring any reader to something contained in another document that might be linked. Time passed but focus never wavered. They knew what kind of evil lurked in the world, and the potential for destruction of innocent lives was greater than it had ever been. Subconsciously, they knew they were placed on earth by God at this moment in time when their souls could do the most for humanity's survival. Faith dictated they move toward a purpose that was right and just.

Reinier sat back and jabbed at the paper in front of him with his index finger. "I'm looking at these calls between London and Buenos Aires."

"What have you found?" Eason asked.

"They always occur on the third Wednesday of the month at fifteen hundred hours."

"Three-three-three," Adam said. "Definitely symbolic of something, but what?"

"Only if the satanists believe Monday is the first day of the week," Reinier quipped.

The general looked at the paper calendar that hung on the wall next to his desk. "The third Wednesday is three days away," Eason said. He stood, went to the door and jerked it open. "Kennedy, get up here," he yelled down to someone on the floor of the computer room.

Adam heard quick footsteps up the stairs, and a young man breezed into the room. He looked like a field agent, fit and strong. He could definitely take care of himself in a fight. He held a laptop at his side like a book. "Yes sir?" he responded, standing in the doorway.

Eason settled into his chair and gestured toward an empty one. "Come on over here and sit down." He glanced at Adam and

Reinier. "This is Kennedy. He's the best hacker working on our side." He looked at the young man who entered the room and smiled. "Maybe the best in the world, huh Kennedy."

Kennedy ignored the accolades, moved quickly to the table, and took his seat.

"Bring up the calls into Buenos Aires." Eason barked.

Kennedy opened his laptop and tapped on the keyboard. "Got 'em."

"Can you confirm what we're seeing on these reports, that all calls involving Buenos Aires were incoming calls? None outgoing?"

Kennedy spent ten or fifteen seconds scrolling through data. "Yes, sir. You're right. Never any outgoing calls on these encrypted channels."

"What is the location of the receiving phone when these calls are placed?"

An indiscernible cluster of pins were clumped together on the computer tech's laptop screen displaying a map of Argentina. Individual markers grew into several distinct locations all over the city once Kennedy honed its focus on Buenos Aires. He shook his head, unable to offer a single solution. "They're all over, sir."

"Any commonalities you can see?"

Kennedy tapped at his keyboard some more. "It appears all the locations are cafés."

"Great," said Adam. "There have to be ten thousand cafés in Buenos Aires."

"I've got an algorithm I can run to look for narrower commonalities. The program draws upon all information on the internet about each location," Kennedy remarked as he tapped his keyboard.

After several minutes of silence, the hacker offered his assessment. "Hmmm. That's odd. All these cafés do have something in common."

"Spit it out," barked Eason.

"They all have liver dumplings on their menus."

"Liver dumplings?" asked Reinier.

Eason's face soured. "I've never had a taste for liver."

"How long is the average call?" Adam asked.

"Average?" He banged on his keyboard. "Three and a half minutes."

Adam nodded toward the laptop. "Can that program tell you whether the phone is on so we can trace its signal? Have we recorded these calls?"

"First question, no. The user always powers down the phone when not in use. Second question, we do have recordings but haven't broken the encryption," Kennedy said. "Once we identify the protocol used—MTProto, Viber, Wickr, or an internally developed one—we can apply our algorithms to break the audio."

Adam turned to the general. "You don't have access to a quantum computer?"

"That's easier said than done," Eason replied sarcastically. "You can't just order one from Amazon."

Nobody laughed. The Trinity problem garnered all of their attention. Adam considered every option. In his decades of experience, he'd seen many examples of horrific human behavior. Politicians were the polite face of it all, but there was an invisible hand at work.

The mere fact that a gaming company would name one of their products *The Final Solution* spoke volumes. Was it that of a global elite? His life equated to nothing more than that of a knight on a chess board. He'd only recently come to understand both sides were controlled by the same families. It was a friendly encounter for elites who instructed knights to take out pawns on a whim. They controlled the game of life as quietly as they could so as to not awaken Godly opponents.

Adam had assessed his true purpose for decades. Mostly, he'd kept his thoughts to himself. He felt it was time to speak up. "Maybe Maritza's onto something. Maybe Project Trinity was a continuation of Hitler's final solution? We can't think of history in the small, chewable bites it's been fed to us in school. We can't be horrified about the Holocaust. We can't be shocked at the atomic bombs dropped on Hiroshima and Nagasaki, which happened to be the Japanese cities with the largest concentration of Christians. We can't talk about how many Christians were put to death in ancient Rome without also acknowledging that twenty-seven million Russians were murdered by Hitler's troops in World War II. Even if we don't subscribe to any religion, we must understand that religions are made up of people who love God, and their fellow humans. And now the destruction of humanity is a fucking video game. Whatever it is we're fighting has been working for centuries to destroy all that is good in humanity."

Eason leaned back in his chair and interlaced his fingers behind his balding head. "Pretty bleak assessment, Phillips. But I can't say I disagree." He glanced back and forth between the men. "This is why we chose this line of work." He leaned forward and picked up the next report in his stack. "Let's keep working until we find something we can sink our teeth into." He turned to the computer expert. "Kennedy, have you heard anything about world leaders playing video games?"

"Video games? Really?" The man chuckled, but then he saw that the general was completely serious. He cleared his throat. "Oh. No, not really. But they could have a private group and communicate privately. Hell, with the encryption they have access to, it might be the most secure method to communicate. And strategize." Realization of another pathway to gather intelligence grew in the hacker's mind.

Eason leaned forward again. "Put your best hacker on it, Kennedy. If that group is out there, I want it hacked, and I want to know exactly what they're saying."

Compelled by both the general's orders and the gravity in his voice, Kennedy shot out of his chair and moved quickly back down the stairs.

Adam turned back to the stacks of paper in front of him. He riffled through the pages in one stack and sighed. He knew the answer was there, but his mind just couldn't make any connections.

"Money!" Adam shouted. "We're looking in the wrong place. We need to be following the money."

"How?" said Eason.

"We know the Mastermach family owns every central bank across the globe." Adam channeled his inner Milton Friedman and continued. "And with money that can be printed in any currency and whatever denomination they wish, they control all world markets. If we can find the accounts that funnel toward Buenos Aires, we might have our man. Figuratively speaking, of course."

Eason leaned to the side to yell past Adam. "Kennedy, get back up here."

After a moment, they heard Kennedy scampering up the stairs again.

Eason barked instructions before the young man had even cleared the doorway. "I want you to see if you can find large sums of money wired into Buenos Aires and see if you can tie it in any way, even if it's paper thin, to our Trinity caller. Make sense?"

"Yes, sir, but please define large."

"Ten million or more."

Kennedy nodded and nervously contemplated his instructions. "Yes. That's…Okay, ten." He shot out of the room and again hurried down the stairs.

"This is probably a good time for us to stop and have lunch," Eason said.

All three stood and made their way out of the command center.

7

Breaking for a lunch that consisted of a tropical fruit salad and grilled snapper offered a brief respite, but the men couldn't ignore constantly echoing thoughts. Time was spent on the patio staring across green fields and into the mountains and forest that surrounded the estate. They gazed into the lush jungle as if the answer to their problem would present itself from the trees. The ice in their lemonade melted quickly, resulting in a two-tiered concoction—murky yellow at the bottom and clear on top. All three were mired in the sediment and pulp of petabytes of information, hoping to latch onto that one fleshy tidbit from which the key to stopping Trinity would burst forth. Too much work. Too great the consequences.

Eason smiled. He was confident the two men at the table would fight to their dying breaths for all that was right in the world.

Adam heard movement and turned. Kennedy walked briskly around the back of the house and ascended the steps to the elevated patio; waving a stack of papers as he came. "General Eason."

The general cleared a landing zone on the table, and Kennedy dropped the pile of research in front of him.

"Yeah," said Kennedy, a bit out of breath.

"Yeah, what?" asked Eason.

"Money. There's a lot of money being moved into Argentina. And when I isolated the Bitcoin transactions—"

"Ah, Bitcoin," Eason interrupted. "The currency of choice for drug dealers, human traffickers, and money launderers."

Kennedy shook his head. "That's fucking bullshit."

General Eason slowly lifted his head to look at the analyst.

"I'm sorry, sir. What I mean is that drug traffickers, human traffickers, and money launderers don't use cryptocurrency to hide their ill-gotten gains. The nature of the blockchain is such that anyone can trace every transaction, every coin from its genesis block. If a bad guy did that, when he finally turned it into fiat currency, all authorities would have to do is be waiting at the bank, so to speak."

"All right, hot shot," said Eason. "So tell me why the Bitcoin transactions are important." He gestured toward an empty chair at the table.

Kennedy sat down and leaned forward. "These people are the elite. They aren't worried about the authorities. They're worried about the masses waking up. If they were to wire a half a billion dollars, that would have to go through several steps and intermediaries along the SWIFT system. Many people would have to authorize that single transaction. Suspicious Activity Reports would be filed. If they do it that way, they run the risk of just one human realizing what's going on. It would be like a spark to kindling. They can't afford that kind of wildfire awakening. To send a half a billion dollars in Bitcoin, all you need is two crooks—one to send. One to receive."

"Color me intrigued," said Eason. "But so?"

"So," Kennedy said, bouncing in his chair and grinning from ear to ear. "I've traced almost ten billion dollars of Bitcoin transactions to a phone that was pinging off the same cell towers as all of our intercepted calls, at the same time."

Eason, Reinier, and Adam all smiled along with Kennedy.

"Ding, ding, ding," said Eason. "We have a winner. Kennedy, have you ever been to Buenos Aires?"

"No, sir."

"Well, you're going now. All three of you are."

8

    Maritza sat at the edge of her bed. Her room was the most understated in the home; one assigned to a teenager existing amongst high-level bureaucrats. Lack of modern décor was a phenomenon she was accustomed. Her grandfather's home on Southard contained the same energy. It spoke to a simpler time. All that secured her from surrounding elements, natural and man-made, were of quality construction.

    An eight by four-foot closet was positioned into the southeast corner of the room. It was built into the structure but appeared as an afterthought; placed in the corner like so much dirty laundry. Maritza stared at the boxy cabinet and imagined if it'd been removed and replaced with a classic armoire. "That would look much better," she thought.

    The same terracotta tile found throughout the house covered the floors. A large throw rug covered the room's rectangular configuration, except for twelve inches along each wall. The carpet's appearance added to the angular, uninspired feel of the room.

    Walls were painted turquoise and ringed at the ceiling by white crown molding. The east wall opened to the world outside with three large double-hung windows. Twelve panes adorned both upper and lower half. One window along the southern and two along the western walls assured sunlight throughout the day. The frames and muntins were painted stark white. The contrast of colors was two-dimensional and did nothing to stimulate the teenager's creativity. There were no window coverings to block out sunlight. The room was naturally lit and ill-afforded anyone the opportunity of sleeping the day away.

Seeking Trinity

A small two-shelf bookshelf sat adjacent to the closet and underneath the window along the south wall. Next to it, in the southwest corner, was a curio shelf painted white. A small brown wooden desk was situated in the center of the western wall. On the space above the desk hung the head of a gemsbok. Its long straight horns extended up-and-back to a point nearly touching the crown molding.

Maritza stared at the animal. Neither appeared especially comfortable in their environment. She looked to her right, through the open bedroom door. Another bookshelf was positioned between it and the edge of the bed. Books. Damn books. There was even a completely filled bookshelf next to the toilet in the bathroom.

The new cell phone was shoved into her back pocket on which she sat. Gravity of circumstances took control of her psyche. The stark change in her environment took her from the comfort she'd known her entire life. Longing for her cozy bedroom on Southard Street, and even the farm she'd gone to camp dozens of times welled within her soul. It was all she'd known during her time with her grandfather. Excitement waned and she took stock of the alternative path her life had taken.

Maritza removed the phone from her pocket, stared briefly at it, and tossed it onto the bed next to her. Interest was focused on the new environment she found herself in and how it affected her immediate future.

She'd watched through her window as her grandfather, Eason, and Reinier walked from the house to the outbuilding. Curiosity drove her mad considering the possibilities of that which was contained within its four walls. If they wanted her to accompany them, they'd have taken her.

Trance-like, Maritza stared into the gap just outside her bedroom door until the stillness ahead was broken by Kennedy's presence.

The young analyst walked toward her room, smiling. In his arms he carried a computer central processing unit. As he breached the doorway, he introduced himself. "My name's Kennedy."

"Maritza."

He nodded. "Yes. Your grandfather is so very proud of you."

Kennedy walked to the small desk and placed the CPU on the floor beside it. "We have to leave pretty quickly, but I wanted to bring you a computer to help with your homework while you're away."

"Thank you," replied Maritza.

The young agent stood before her and offered his hand in friendship.

Maritza looked up at him from her seated position and smiled.

The two shook hands.

Kennedy leaned in toward the young girl. "Don't tell Eason, because the whole house hasn't been wired, but this room has state of the art fiber-optic internet. You can do anything on this computer in an instant. It's like having the library at Alexandria available with a mouse click."

"Why this room, and not the rest of the house?"

Kennedy smiled. Evidence she possessed a keen intellect appeared to him first-hand. "It's mostly about not having the time to get the house wired. However, I did do this room first because it is where my buddies stay when they visit."

The two acknowledged their secret with a shared smile.

Kennedy bounced his head gently as he looked around the room. He pointed to the desk. "Rafael will bring up a monitor and optical mouse. Make sure to ask him if there is anything else you need."

"I will."

Kennedy extended his hand one last time. "I really have to go. It was nice meeting you."

"It was nice meeting you too."

She watched as the young agent disappeared around the corner outside her bedroom door.

Moments afterward, Rafael appeared laden with monitor and mouse. Without a word he moved to the desk and began working on assembling components.

"No hay otro lugar para configurar la computadora que este escritorio."

Sheepishly, Maritza spoke to the man's back as he continued to work. "I don't speak Spanish. I mean, no habla Español."

Her admission brought an abrupt turn. Rafael looked directly at Maritza and furrowed his brow. "Lo siento…I'm sorry. You just epitomize the beautiful Spanish girl to me." He turned and began to work again. "I said there really isn't another place to put this computer than on this desk. It was built to pen letters and read books, not hold a large flat panel monitor. But I can assure you it's the best available tech we have."

"I appreciate you doing this for me. I'm sure it will alleviate many hours of boredom."

"I would invite you to the data center, but we have to have permissions especial."

Maritza nodded her understanding. "That large building at the foot of the hill is a data center?"

Rafael nodded. "Si."

Maritza's mind began to fathom possibilities of the work conducted in that outbuilding. Boredom was pushed aside by an increasing heart rate. "Do you mind if I download software onto this computer?"

"Download away, young lady. We have developed an in-house spy-bot second to none in the world. It can actually reprogram software. If you're downloading something and it detects malicious code, it will remove it and actually enhance the programing. It's no longer a simple yes or no when encountering viruses while downloading. Alternative Intelligence is a wonderful thing."

"Whoa." The possibilities conceived within her teenage mind became endless.

Rafael finished setting up the computer, stood and offered a half-hearted salute to Maritza. "Don't hesitate to let me know if you need anything."

"Do I come down to the data center if I need something?" Maritza searched for any excuse to get into that building and satisfy her curiosity.

Rafael straightened his back. "No. You'd better go through General Eason."

The teenager nodded her head. She sat meekly until Rafael disappeared around the corner outside her room. Once gone she stood and shot across the floor to the desk. She quickly sat and turned on both CPU and monitor. As the machines warmed up and went through startup commands, she picked up the mouse and switched it on. The red optical laser on its bottom glowed and she flipped it over and placed it back on the desk. The conception of what she wished to accomplish grew in her consciousness.

Several programs were downloaded. It took hours to set up her new computer to accomplish her goals. Nowhere in her consciousness was the cell phone that had been her constant companion. Although it was an exact replica of her own, she'd tossed it carelessly onto the bed and chose to focus on the strange environment in which she found herself.

Not until she was ready to launch her personal mission to save humanity, did she acknowledge the phone's existence. Dread overtook her when she realized this was the phone Eason had given her. He said it was an exact replica. Usernames and passwords for individuals she'd hacked were contained in the notepad function on her phone.

Hurriedly and nervously, she leaned back in her chair and reached toward the bed. She retrieved the phone and began tapping the screen to bring it to life and enter her PIN. She swiped the tip of her index finger across the screen until the home screen containing her notepad stared up at her.

Hesitantly, she tapped the icon. Maritza needed to know if the information was there. She was unsure if her years of work had gone for naught. When the application came to life in front of her, she saw a comprehensive list of all entries made into the program. It was a single entry she scrolled to find. She was awash in relief as she spied its title—GAME FREAKS.

Experiences of the prior few days opened her eyes to the kind of evil populating the planet. When she played with elite gamers in their Final Solution fantasy, she only conceived them as being freaks.

Hours upon hours were spent in front of the screen. Meals were skipped. Occasionally, Eason breached her doorway asking if there was anything she needed. The man looked upon her as his own daughter. A charge of which he not only welcomed but for which he longed.

A modern headset was requested and delivered. Maritza sat at the desk like a pilot, winding her way through the meta environment created for the benefit of evil. To her advantage there were far fewer players to contend with than a normal gaming environment.

11:00 PM. Eason breeched her doorway once again carrying a tray of food. "You missed dinner."

Maritza nodded short, sharp, and quick strokes of her head acknowledging she hadn't eaten.

"Can't you stop long enough to eat?"

She shook her head.

"Okay. Well, I'm going to leave this food on your bed. Please take time to eat."

As she moved through the game, seeking out information, she saw an icon appear in the upper right-hand corner of her screen. It read—POST GENOCIDE POWER STRUCTURE. Curiosity took control. She slid her pointer to the hyperlink and clicked it. Exploding onto her screen was a map of the globe. Color coded, it showed the division of the world's continents into six regions. Each was labeled. North America and the Arctic Circle contained the name of ROCKLAND. South America contained BRAUN. Europe contained WALSINGHAM. Asia contained

LING. Africa contained MBEPO. Curiously, the Antarctic was separately coded but contained no name, just a series of hieroglyphic characters indiscernible to the youth.

2:00 AM brought forth uneasiness as Maritza found her meta-avatar venturing beneath the earth in Patagonia. She was tired and unsure she could continue much longer. Curiosity pushed her forward. She descended an elevator, down a long corridor, and into a conference room. Seated at the table were five avatars. Each represented by an animal head atop a human body. All animals were fierce and imposing creatures.

"Those must be the false idols Papa told me about," she thought to herself.

Conversation echoed in her headset constantly. The experienced gamer thought it odd there seemed to be no competition between the five players. Instead of taking pleasure in capturing one another, royalty appeared to collude with each other in the destruction of their own armies.

Maritza felt camouflaged by taking a position as an American general. It was the only way to mask the fact she only spoke English.

Hours staring at the screen allowed her to understand the flow of conversation. It was rhythmic and moved up through the ranks to the five self-appointed sovereigns. Assessments were made, and consensuses reached. Orders flowed back down through the ranks. A ticker on her screen's header counted population figures in real time. Only when drops of one hundred million were estimated were offers of congratulations given.

As communication worked its way up to those considering themselves demigods did English become prevalent. Those at the top of the genocidal pyramid cautioned generals to not be hasty in their execution of the plan. It was estimated they could plausibly murder a half a billion through nuclear world war. It was mentioned that had been their mistake when destroying Mars in one felled swoop. Such a mistake must be avoided at all costs. The purest souls were released into the universe on that day and found their way to earth. Innate in these sentient beings was a healthy skepticism of unnatural death.

Maritza drifted in and out of awareness of the myriad of conversations, until a voice rang loudly in her ear. It was as though the person speaking had the ability to communicate directly to her. The teenager was no longer veiled by stillness.

A female voice rang loudly, laden by a heavy German accent. "Who are you? You are new to the game."

Nervously, and without discernment, Maritza blurted into her microphone, "I'm Trinity."

A brief silence was broken by the voice. It became angered. "*I* am Trinity, and you are not to speak that word outside this simulation."

"Yes, ma'am."

"Who is your superior? Who let you into this meta-genocide?"

Maritza's heart raced. She had no idea how to answer. Certainly, she was safe at Finca Vigia. She was surrounded by intelligence assets. Did these elites possess the ability of moving beyond the meta environment and into her reality? She wondered if she'd ever be able to go outside her home again.

A Russian male voice broke into the conversation. "She is with the Eurasian delegation, Trinity."

"But she speaks English?"

"Yes, we have assets across the globe. Her expertise is in simulation programming. This is her first time as an observer."

Silence denoted contradiction, until it was verbalized. "But her avatar has been active for eighteen months?"

"Yes. We reuse them as people…die suddenly."

"Very good."

Maritza wasn't sure Trinity's approval was of recycling identities, or whether she was happy people were dying suddenly.

Prolonged silence spoke to the teenager's assumption Trinity left their chat. Slowly her heart rate returned to normal.

Once she was able to think critically, she wondered who the Russian was that came to her rescue.

It didn't take long for the man to introduce himself. "My name is Vladimir Tupolev."

Maritza's heart rate spiked once again. She had no desire to remain a player in the metaverse. "Thank you," was all she could muster before removing her headset and tossing it onto the desk. Quickly, she switched off the monitor and then the CPU. She paused briefly and then unplugged the machine and ethernet cable.

The teenager took a deep breath as she stood. Peering through the eastern windows she saw the sun exerting its influence on the morning sky.

She took two steps to the edge of her bed and stood staring at her cold dinner. It had dried and become all too unbecoming; appearing more like that projected forth during reverse peristalsis. "Yuck."

Maritza leaned over and picked up the tray off her bed, turned, and slid it onto the desktop, pushing the headset and keyboard away with the platter's edge. She walked to the head of the bed and jerked the comforter away. The young girl crawled into bed, laying between the sheets. She pulled the top cover over her head to block out oncoming sunlight. For three days lack of sleep was a trend brought on by the acts of her grandfather. Maritza could only hoist blame upon herself. She had thrust herself onto the playing field of a game she was ill-prepared to play.

Eason sat alone at Hemingway's dining table. Occasionally, he glanced at the sideboard against the wall. Centered on top was a silver platter. Several bottles of the finest liquor available anywhere in the world adorned its surface. Young Eason never touched a drop of alcohol. He'd witnessed what it did to his father and how it affected his parents' marriage.

Thirty-nine analysts populated the property with him. They lived in temporary trailers scattered about. No one ever came to the house unless the visit was predicated by urgent business. The outbuilding buzzed with activity twenty-four-seven. Three shifts rotated through and intelligence gathering never ceased. Neither did the emotional weight that burdened the man's large frame throughout his career. Advances in career were supposed to make things better for his family. To the contrary, it wasn't financial freedom provided by promotions that increased stress. It was access to information contrary to the reason he joined the military out of college.

Eason shifted his gaze through the dining room doorway, across the living room, until it rested on the green hills seen from the rear wall of windows. He tried to ignore imagined and phantom bitterness of alcohol on his tongue and the numbness it offered.

For the briefest moment being in the house alone with Maritza acted to quell exacerbated loneliness. The general had a daughter her age he hadn't seen in over a decade. Days filled with work offered balance provided by the role of father figure to a teenager. Breaks in the day were filled with fantasies of conversations with Maritza he'd missed having with his own daughter.

Anger burgeoned within the man when Kennedy requested the young girl be flown to Buenos Aires to aid in intelligence gathering. Word arrived upon Kennedy's landing in Buenos Aires, the young girl successfully hacked the elite's Final Solution video game. The man whose career advanced due to his ability to motivate and advance stated objectives, never felt more inadequate.

As Eason's career progressed, idealism gave way to alcoholism. The younger man viewed his life as valuable and was certain by its end he would be able to point to accomplishments with pride. He realized evil humans were like weeds. Seemingly appearing from nowhere, they consistently destroyed all that was beautiful. Higher ranks did nothing more than expose the man to ever-increasing awareness of the destruction humans thrust upon one another. Conviction of due process shifted to quick and decisive elimination.

As he aged, tolerance gave way to a psyche embracing mass execution to rid the planet of that deemed unworthy of human existence. His only saving grace was the realization he'd allowed himself to embrace the same tactics of those he wished to eliminate. Sobering logic prevented decisive action.

Solitude granted clarity of thought. Hours spent alone in the dining room offered the chance to recall the career he enjoyed and the family he destroyed. Measuring its timeline via hindsight offered the ability to witness inflection points. Focus had been global. Strategic moves were devised to manipulate, corner, and eliminate those who perpetrated crimes against humanity. Destructive energy permeated the man's soul and was carried home nightly. Splintering rebellious factions of evil fragmented the relationships with his wife and three children.

Two sons were in their twenties, and his daughter was sixteen. He had no contact with any of them. Child support deducted from his paycheck provided the only reference to the little girl he was thrilled to hold at birth.

No matter the post at which Eason found himself stationed, commiserating over drinks after work with other officers isolated father from family. Major catalysts for his destructive behavior moved from the clandestine to mainstream. Innocently viewing a news program with his wife, Eason witnessed a presidential cabinet member declare the death of five hundred thousand children worth the cost of the Middle Eastern incursion of which he'd been an integral part. Never had he witnessed such a vile and evil declaration that went unchallenged by the journalist. Self-criticism echoed in his mind. He should have known at the time when the American flag was sewn on soldier's uniforms backwards, intent was not what it seemed. That which was touted as signifying troops constantly moving forward, was nothing more than the elite's contradiction of the American ideal; the concept of power emanating from the people.

The country John Eason grew up in was considered the beacon of freedom for the world. Its decline was facilitated by the apathy of its citizenry. Long term considerations had been tossed aside in favor of immediate gratification. Critical thought gave way to listening idly as overlords implanted their narrative that it was humanity destroying the planet. Messages delivered 24/7 seemed innocuous but were more destructive than the collective megatonnage of the bombs dropped in all US conflicts. He witnessed friends and family who once embraced discourse, bristle and argue at anything deemed contrary to officialdom. Exchange of ideas had been lost to personal dogma. "Pride goeth before a fall," Eason thought to himself.

As a seasoned officer Eason possessed an understanding of historical military campaigns and their significance to humanity. It was easy for him to see how the beacon of freedom had been turned using vast military power. The Military Industrial Complex, as Dwight Eisenhower warned, took resources from every area of society and turned its might outward. In the name of nation-building, campaigns were waged to gain control. An unwitting participant, the man understood the country he loved had become the greatest impediment to global prosperity.

Eason glanced at the liquor bottles standing steadfastly beside him. Maybe a taste would settle his soul?

His sons went away to college and never bothered to contact their father. All he had to do was pay for it. Upon graduation they began their lives. Eason had no idea if they were dating, engaged, or married. He didn't even know if he'd been made a grandfather. The general could utter a command and divisions of men would mobilize. Yet he couldn't make a call and gain an audience with estranged family members.

Exacerbating frustration was the secrecy with which his job must be conducted. His wife and three kids had no conception of the forces that fueled alcoholic genes passed down through generations. Just as his parents never instilled coping mechanisms, he'd lost all opportunity to educate his children of the silent demons lurking within their flawed flesh. It was important they do not allow innate malevolence to wrest control of their futures. There was no way to communicate; to be their father.

Not until the man defeated his demons, did he see the world more clearly. A decade of sobriety coupled with increasing global responsibilities offered Eason the opportunity to speak with men and women of equal authority and conviction. Aiding his recovery was the understanding he was not alone. Military forces across the globe began to see themselves as the puppets the elite manipulated for centuries. Narrative and emotion were stoked to create fires of conflict. A stressed population was a compliant one. Leaders of armies knew it their duty to preserve their way of life for each country's citizens.

Military leaders from different backgrounds redirected the conversation from differences to similarities. Eason was a part of that group. A collective consciousness developed between them. Reductive analysis brought forth the realization differences were only slight. Humans don't possess an innate desire to control one another or force beliefs onto infidels. It was the narrative put forth by the few to control the many. The internet connected the youth of the world. Old men and women in positions like Eason were quickly becoming extinct. They would not go down without a fight for relevance.

Of the population of military commanders who were hip to the global chess match, few could be trusted. Constant encroachment on unconquered territories offered the sadistic an orgasmic-like sense of accomplishment. It was those generals leaders like Eason knew to avoid when building the coalition.

Eason examined his life's path; that which brought him to a place where he found himself alone in a man's home he'd never met. The thirty-nine analysts who occupied the outbuilding daily were the best in the world. An arsenal of military equipment had been secured and stationed across the globe. Logistic skills were beyond reproach. Needed armament and supplies could be delivered to any destination within hours. Sympathetic bankers hid needed finances. Shields to the identity of those possessing funds were sophisticated and would make the most seasoned Swiss financier sit up and take note.

Echoing in Eason's consciousness was the realization for all he'd accomplished with his band of rebels, the global elite had a several decades head start. Hindsight offered the mosaic of control they'd successfully employed to encroach into every aspect of human life.

The dollar's spread as the world's reserve currency was touted as bringing stability. Conversely, its intent was to become the biggest rug-pull in history. When deemed optimal, its valued would be crashed, erasing trillions of dollars of wealth accumulated by families across those same decades. Desperation among the masses ceded control to those who craved its destructive tendencies.

Internet kill switches, manufactured electromagnetic pulses, and power blackouts had all been planned to prevent civilizations from connecting. Communication among those embracing love for fellow humans could not be allowed.

Most sinister was the takeover of healthcare systems across the globe. Centralized control over medical schools rewarded soon-to-be physicians whose only lofty skillset was the ability to memorize mountains of data and regurgitate it. Those were the ones easiest to control. Prescriptions, procedures, and inoculations were prescribed, not by doctors, but by billionaires who feigned benevolence in their actions. If it furthered the coming genocide, it was codified and distributed. Doctors prescribed that which they were told and were paid stipends for their trouble.

If the rebel's intelligence was factual, billions of people had nano computers coursing through their veins. Signals sent from off-earth satellites could murder instantly, metastasize several types of cancer, or heart disease. It was reasoned the global elite wanted to rid the earth of nearly seven billion people. Doing so slowly was the preferred method. It offered plausible deniability. If their plan became known to the remaining half billion slave race, there would be no way to control them. It was deemed judicious by the elite to set the wheels in motion in one felled swoop. A single signal that affected billions had been developed and programmed over decades. Just as Robert Oppenheimer deemed the first test of the atomic bomb, Project Trinity, so had the elite. Destruction was seen as creation by those embracing evil.

General Eason stood, walked over to the sideboard, and retrieved the bottle of Jewel of Russia Ultra Black Label Vodka. "I could have one drink and still be able to function tomorrow," he said aloud to no one.

10

Adam didn't appreciate the notion of flying on yet another private jet purchased with drug money. Expediency was the objective for this mission.

Viewing the city as he had several times during his career, Adam thought of Paris. The cities' architectures were quite similar.

The taxi pulled up to the Argentinian estate; the safe house where they would stay. It sat on a corner and took up half a city block. Iron fencing ringed the entire property, supported every twenty feet by concrete columns. Atop the pillars were globe lights. Inside the base of each lamp were hidden cameras that increased security.

The entrance was equally grand. It looked more like a church than a residence. Three archways made of limestone blocks gave way to an equally impressive fourth which framed the oversized entry. Keystones marked the center of each overhead curve. Filling the doorway were two massive wooden doors. Intricate leaded glass pieces were set in the top-center of each.

Adam's soul became more disquieted when they entered the home. The place could easily be hyperbolically mistaken for the Palace at Versailles. Expensive tapestries hung along the walls. No matter what room he walked into, he found all manner of fine art. The opulence on display was like a dagger twisting in his soul. He thought about his age and wondered if there was time for redemption.

An independent documentary team consisting of military intelligence sought to find definitive evidence Hitler had in fact survived the war and made his way to this part of the world. High ranking Nazis who were supposedly killed were found living in comfort by Simon Wiesenthal, and a group of dedicated Nazi hunters. It seemed implausible their Führer would be left to die, and fueled speculation. The contemporary team came very close to discovering the safehouse, and it lay abandoned for fear of exposure.

Adam knew moving closer to danger necessitated leaving Maritza in Havana. It was felt she would be safer there. The Trinity Project's intent and the evil that controlled such forces on earth caused the grandfather to wonder whether Maritza would have the opportunity to live a happy and productive life. It would be difficult to create a world where a good number of people wouldn't be lured into a life of crime motivated by the benefits of ill-gotten gains. The luxury of the home was intoxicating. Contradictions abounded witnessing the comfort of riches paid for by destroying humanity. Untraceable stores of value were available to those involved. Could their small band of warriors really make a difference?

Conversely, young Kennedy was like a kid in a candy store. He walked from room-to-room, eyes wide-open and mouth agape. Every so often, he'd mutter something under his breath like. "This is way cool." Or, "Unreal." Or, "You gotta be freakin' kidding me."

All three men eventually wandered together into the living room. Kennedy practically ran to the Steinway baby grand piano, lifted its cover, and began to play.

"I'm not sure we have time for that," Adam barked.

"Agreed. But watch this."

Kennedy played a light, airy, happy tune. At that moment Adam recognized it as "Camelot." A computer program recognized it too. A wall behind the piano slid open, exposing a cavernous room.

"The CIA set up this code, poking fun at the fact they'd murdered JFK and gotten away with it."

"How do you know this?" Adam asked, skeptically.

Kennedy smiled, and responded boastfully, "I'm the best hacker on the planet. Haven't you figured that out yet?"

Reinier looked at Adam. "This whole house is spooky. I sensed it when we walked in the door, and now we have secret rooms. I feel like I'm in a Vincent Price movie."

Adam smiled, shook his head, and walked toward the ever-growing opening in the wall and peered inside. It was a communication and computer center equipped with the latest technology. This room was the only thing in the house that gave any indication this house was a center of operations for a corrupted CIA. Until that moment the only suggestion concerning the home's sordid past was the dark energy that soaked the men's souls. It took on mass as well.

Still embracing childlike energy, Kennedy hurried into the computer lab and began turning on as many machines as possible. Screens lit up, and various beeps and clicks signaled the equipment coming to life. These would be the machines needed to track and identify Trinity.

"I guess we're at your mercy, Kennedy," said Reinier. "Let us know what we can do to help you."

Kennedy nodded and smiled. "You guys chill for a few hours. It's gonna take me a while to set all this up, but once I do, we'll definitely start working."

Reinier and Adam retrieved their luggage from the grand foyer. Each man moved through the home silently, searching for a bedroom in which to place their luggage.

After he'd unpacked his toiletries, Adam wandered aimlessly through the house. The sun had set for the day. Windows appeared as dark paintings whose only relief was provided by various lights outside along the avenue.

As he strolled, he found himself humming the song "Camelot." For the hardened man who'd shown little, if any, sentiment over the past thirty years, he was surprised to find himself brushing away tears. It was as though there was a beast inside him trying to escape.

As had been the case throughout his adult life, he used logic to maintain control and force down whatever emotions he felt. To do that, he needed to understand from where emotions emanated.

He remembered his mother pulling him away from his schoolbooks one night so they could share Sir Richard Burton's rendition of "Camelot." The actor performed on one of the many variety shows prevalent in the 1970s. Adam envisioned the red curtain and the wide-open stage that Burton filled and commanded. Adam was all ears as he listened to the story of a place where happiness reigned supreme and where that which was contrary to contentment had been outlawed.

Parental faults were considered when attempting to understand the man he'd become. Disadvantages had been placed upon Adam's youthful incarnation. Yet there had been a sensibility instilled at a young age that had a profoundly positive effect on Adam. Contained in Burton's countenance, and the words he sang, the youth understood all of humanity sought personal Camelots. It was that which led him to use his physical skills when choosing to forgo a career in science. Ignorant of the global power structure, he wanted to be the catalyst for making the world a better place. It was the importance of human expression. All humans must be given the opportunity use all available mediums to create that which their souls envisioned. If Adam could guarantee that existence for humanity, he would gladly sacrifice himself upon whatever cross the cabal desired.

After his self-guided tour of the house, Adam settled into a big chair in the living room in front of a large floor-to-ceiling window. The view was of Villanueva Street. It was a road that existed since the city's inception. Centuries old large homes lined one side of the street; cafés and shops the other.

Trance-like, he watched as everyday Argentinians walked past. He wondered about individual circumstances. People he didn't know meant something to him—always had. He was jostled back to reality when Reinier walked up behind him. He felt the man's presence and slowly turned to look up at him.

Reinier was the first to speak. "Looking for Trinity?"

Adam laughed softly, brushing aside the query. "Why did you get into the intelligence game?"

"Truthfully?"

Adam nodded.

Reinier scratched his eyebrow while formulating his next sentence. "I was young and idealistic. I bought into the propaganda that there was this giant beast ninety miles north of our shores that desired to consume our country and all its resources. It made sense to me we had to operate our country on bare minimums and that Cuban citizens must sacrifice their freedom in order to channel resources to fight the beast."

Reinier moved to the adjacent chair, sat down, and shifted his gaze through the same window. "From a historical perspective, Ernest Hemingway piqued my interest. He was a man's man, an American man. He loved Cuba. That didn't make sense to me. The more I researched the more I understood that Hemingway backed Castro because he thought Castro was truly going to rid the country of its mafia-related corruption. He was double-crossed by Fidel. The Cuban people's suffering began, and he felt a responsibility for that. Ten years ago, I became less of a blunt-instrument and more of a Cuban historian. Physical abilities began to fail me. Access to classified documents was not a problem for me. I saw bank transfers from New York financiers' banks into Castro's coffers."

"Revolutions are expensive," remarked Adam as he continued to stare through the window.

"I guess my superiors felt the revolution was so long ago the information I had access to was useless. I saw correspondence between CIA officers detailing how they orchestrated the Bay of Pigs fiasco to embarrass your president and bolster Castro's popularity among Cubans. All to keep them in servitude." He turned to face his newfound compatriot. "It was then I realized Castro's purpose was that of a clown for US Communists. They needed communism close, and to be viewed as successful for decades. They needed to be able to point and say, 'See. It works.'

All of these decades later, there are documentaries about how successful the Cuban Revolution has been. How Cuba has the greatest healthcare in the world." Reinier shook his head. "I can tell you the Cuban people continue to suffer. It's up to guys like us to stop it."

Adam gazed through the window. A man over a decade younger from another country had come to the same realization about the subjugation of his country's citizens. Common occurrences were not coincidental to Adam. More evidence presented itself that power structures existed at least one level above sovereign nations. He feared they went higher than that.

"The defining moment for me was when I found documents concerning bastard children of many dictators like Fidel, being groomed and placed in leadership roles in several countries around the world," said Reinier. "Then I understood the elite's plan was truly global." He smiled. "But you see the Cuban people now taking to the streets in protest. If you believe in the universe's energy, maybe we are entering the age of Aquarius?" He shrugged.

Adam nodded. "According to science, it takes as much energy to dismantle an apparatus as was required to build it. These cockroaches are all over the world and have been doing this for decades. They've successfully recruited new members promising riches beyond their dreams to oppress the global population. The only way we can ever hope to win this war is for the citizens of the world to wake up and understand what's been going on. That volume of united energy would be unstoppable." He pointed at the people on the street in front of the house. "How many of those people do you think are aware of the true power structure of the world?"

Reinier smiled. "The advantage we have is that this is Argentina. This is where they brought Hitler and Eichmann after World War II. I believe the everyday Argentinian knows this and has a better grasp on reality than we do in Cuba or America."

"I can only hope you're right. Right for their sakes but, more importantly, for Maritza's sake and the sake of all young people who just needed a chance to live their lives." Adam paused. "How many kids do you have?"

"You know that's classified," Reinier joked, but was still unwilling to say.

Adam nodded. "Well, I don't have any. My wife, son, and daughter-in-law were killed in an accident. You met my granddaughter. She's all I have left. Being in this situation has given me a lot of time to think about what I've contributed to the world. My career has been a farce, and now I realize that I don't have much to offer in order to sustain humanity."

"But you have a beautiful, intelligent granddaughter."

He slapped his thigh. "I thank God for her every day. But my scientific mind has joined with that of God, and it's made me realize that one of our greatest responsibilities is to create happy families so humanity can survive and thrive."

Adam stared past the people on the streets and into the Buenos Aires night. Sparse lighting from the columns that ringed the lawn reflected a growing understanding emanating from the darkness. "My greatest regret is that I didn't have more children. I haven't done my part to ensure our civilization's survival. When I was younger, I brushed aside any sense of failure by bullshitting myself that no one should bring kids into such a horrible world. That plays right into the globalist's hands. We must make the world better, Reinier."

The Cuban nodded. "Five. I have five kids."

Adam smiled. "Thank God for men like you. Maybe one day I can be their American uncle?"

"You already are, my friend."

Kennedy bounced into the room motivated by youth and enthusiasm and did not wait to be recognized to speak. "Okay. I've got all the algorithms set up and running. They'll gather data all night, and we can begin analyzing it in the morning."

Adam continued to stare into the night. "Thank you for all of your hard work."

Attempting to lighten the mood, Kennedy said, "How about we go get some dinner? Maybe some sangria?"

Reinier stood, walked to his new friend, patted him on the shoulder and gave Kennedy a big smile. "Yeah. Let's go."

Adam wasn't so enthusiastic, but he knew it would be good to get out.

As the three men exited the grand home, Adam picked up his wallet and keys from a table by the front door. It was a life-long habit; an unconscious act. He wondered why the minute he walked into this strange house he felt at home enough to fall into that particular practice. Questions remained regarding the frequency of his personal energy and how he'd allowed it to deteriorate throughout his life.

It was a cool night. Adam could have used a jacket. He noted that none of the men wore one. Instead, they hurried down the sidewalk with their hands shoved deeply into their pants pockets.

The city bustled with pedestrians. In some places, the people were so thick that Adam and his friends had to walk single file, weaving their way through the crowd.

When they reached the corner of Avenida 9 de Julio and Avenida Corrientes, the three looked into the middle of the intersection and stared. They were looking at an obelisk that was an exact copy of the Washington Monument. It was lit in light purple. Cars and pedestrians hurried along like a swarm of ants avoiding the massive impediment in the middle of the intersection.

"I had no idea they had a replica of the Washington Monument here." Adam said.

"Actually, it commemorates Argentina's quadricentennial in 1933," Reinier said. "It was built by a German company. Can't recall their name."

"Yeah, 1933," Adam pondered. "Ironically, the same year Hitler came to power."

Kennedy nodded, admiring the knowledge of the other men.

Adam took in the obvious Egyptian influences of the piece. He imagined all the points around the globe where structures like this had been constructed. During his travels he'd seen similar designs in London, Paris, Istanbul, and the ancient city of Rome. Were they meant to harvest energy from the environment or project it from inside the earth? Physics taught him to formulate a million questions but there was never enough information to answer any of them.

Purposefully lost was the history of such structures and their reason for existence. He did know energy was the base state of the universe and that if a man like Nikola Tesla could have harnessed it, the human race would have thrived. The genius' life's goal had been to provide free energy to humanity. Access to energy would propel humanity forward without constraints. Individuals would be free to express themselves in a manner unique to distinct souls. Without that liberty, humans were forced to exist in a construct not of their making. The destruction of Wardenclyffe Tower by Tesla's banker provided another bit of anecdotal evidence of profuse global corruption.

The three continued aimlessly, passing the opera house built in 1936. Centuries-old buildings lined the streets, interrupted here and there by a ground-level Starbucks and McDonald's. Early evening rain caused the street to shine, reflecting a rainbow of lights from buildings and traffic signals.

The men finally settled on a café that offered outdoor seating. The tables were made to look like picnic tables, but were constructed of aluminum. Six could comfortably occupy one table and the three assembled and spread out. Adam sat on one side, and Reinier and Kennedy took up opposite ends of the other.

A waiter hurried from the café to deliver menus and asked about their needs. Reinier spoke on everyone's behalf since he and the server shared a common language. After the waiter disappeared into the café, he turned and looked at the other two. "Why do neither of you speak Spanish?"

Adam and Kennedy glanced at each other, sharing the uneasiness based in each man's lack of a worldly focus.

"You're right," Adam replied. "I wish I'd learned to speak many languages. I even bought my granddaughter Rosetta Stone, but apparently her life has been overtaken by the American exceptionalism propaganda, and she has no desire to embrace other cultures...even one she was born into."

An hour was spent making small talk while they picked at their food. Hollow were the words spoken. Adam knew they were all preoccupied by the mission to identify Trinity.

What kind of information would they get from the algorithms? What were their expectations? Would any prior research be supported by these new reports? If so, what pieces of intel possessed newborn foal legs; only requiring the support of additional data? Would that data be present in tomorrow's reports? Two things they didn't have were time and resources. That worried the older American.

Breaking the monotony of singular thoughts, Adam spotted a woman walking down the street and lost all work-related focus. The greater the intensity of a woman's beauty, the farther away one can be and still appreciate it. The distance between Adam and the woman was a hundred yards. His view of her was intermittently obscured by other pedestrians. As she sliced her way through the crowd, nothing hindered Adam's ethereal enjoyment of her. Extraordinary female beauty warmed Adam's psyche.

Her dress was black and tight against her body. Hurricane force winds wouldn't cause a ripple in the fabric. The dress' hemline didn't reach mid-thigh. She strutted down the sidewalk. Her legs moved scissor-like. The bending of knees became lost in the length of her legs.

Adam's gaze didn't waver as he examined her gate and everything about her. The closer she moved to the men the more obvious it became she was no Argentine. Adam surmised she was at least six feet two inches in heels. Her body was ultra-slender and carried not an ounce of fat. Her face was round and full and beautiful; and her hair light blonde. Her countenance spoke to Adam of Siberia.

The woman moved toward the men. Adam dropped his gaze to the table. He felt embarrassment warm his face. He was too busy faking ambivalence as he ate Choripan and drank from the beer mug in front of him to notice the young lady moved behind him and turned to face the table.

She sat side-saddle on the bench Adam occupied and settled in front of him. "Hello boys," she said, startling Adam. "Are you gentlemen drinking away your sorrows tonight? You all look as though you have a lot on your minds." Her English was perfect and unbroken.

Maybe he was wrong about her nationality.

Out of the corner of his eye, Adam saw that Kennedy was getting fidgety.

"Well, hello," the younger man said, attempting to project a suave persona.

The woman gave him a disinterested nod and turned back to Adam.

Reinier gave a half-hearted wave.

Adam replayed the sentences she spoke in his mind. Her accent appeared American, but he couldn't figure from which region of the country she hailed.

The woman smiled and shook her head. "My, my. I can tell that Trinity has all of you bamboozled."

Adam sat up straight. "What do you know about Trinity?"

"I know everything I'm allowed to know. Just as you know no more than what Eason allows." A beautiful disarming smile grew on her visage. "Make no mistake, superiors are there to control the dissemination of information. That is all."

Adam glanced at Reinier. The man gave him a sheepish look, as if he'd been caught in a lie. "You knew she was working with us?" He shook his head. "I feel like it's halftime of a football game, and I've been forced to purchase a program to find out who the players are."

The Cuban's lack of response acted as confirmation.

Adam glared at Kennedy. "Why does everyone know everything before I do?"

The young man shrugged his shoulders and pursed his lips. "I didn't know there were more people working with us."

Adam sighed. "So where do we go from here?"

The beautiful blonde seemed unphased. "I'll start by introducing myself. I'm Sofia."

"I'm sure you already know our names," Adam said, shaking his head slowly.

"I know you two," she said, pointing to the field agents. "But I don't know him." She nodded in the direction of Kennedy.

Adam actually saw the kid attempting to emanate an air of sophistication.

"I'm Kennedy."

"Of course, you are." Sofia turned to Adam. "I read your doctoral thesis on the plane from Moscow. Interesting proposition."

Adam nodded.

She continued. "It's best to understand how the mind of the man you work with conceives the world around him."

Kennedy cleared his throat and shifted in his seat. "My dissertation was on the ability of encryption and the blockchain to eliminate the need for centralized control by all institutions."

Adam waited for his young colleague to close the sale. Or try to close it. Or do *something*. When he realized that wasn't going to happen, he went back to business. "You seem well briefed, Sofia. Tell us where should we focus our efforts?"

"If you're looking for the quickest solution, the populace needs to wake up to the kind of evil that controls every aspect of their lives, but that's not so simple. One of the worst creatures on this planet is a sycophantic male who worships others and produces nothing himself. Alpha males will ask tough questions and expect honest answers. If people would think critically while examining the decades of their experiences, they would see how their lives have deteriorated. That would be a good first step. Yet, it's up to small groups of people like us to exterminate the bad guys." Sofia displayed a fervor for humanity. It was a trait seemingly innate in all of them.

Adam thought if she hadn't been an intelligence asset her passion for the elimination of evil could be mistaken for emotion.

"Americans think they saw evil in Hitler," continued Sofia. "They lost a little less than half a million men in that war. Hitler and his Nazis murdered twenty-seven million Russian men, women, and children. You can see where his malevolent energy was focused."

"Why do you think that was?" Asked Kennedy.

"Because Russians believe strongly in God."

"Why did Hitler not bomb the shit out of the royal palaces in each country he fought?" said Sofia. "He chose to terrorize everyday citizens instead. You need to understand who is truly pulling the strings and who are the puppets."

Adam nodded in agreement, but he was skeptical. Sofia's monologue proved one of two things. Either she held many of the same beliefs as Adam, or he'd been the subject of Russian surveillance. He could never fully trust her, but her passion was comforting. She seemed to possess a conception of humanity he could work with.

"Where do we go from here, Sofia?" Reinier asked.

She smiled. "We have a saying in Russia. 'Don't go to someone else's monastery with your own rulebook.'"

"Rulebook?" asked Kennedy.

Sofia rolled her eyes and smirked.

She was about to explain when Adam stepped in. "Sofia means that it will be left to our own psyches. We have to get into the mode of thinking like they do. We have to understand what it takes for someone to desire to murder everyone on the planet because…just because."

Sofia nodded and sat forward. She jabbed her index finger into Adam's chest. "Dr. Phillips, we need to know what it's like to exist at the destructive end of the energy spectrum, as you call it in your dissertation. The place where everything is consumed by fire. But we must never lose sight of the light, love, and happiness that exists at the other extreme." She gave him a few extra jabs for emphasis. "Only that will save humanity. Otherwise, we risk everything and everyone."

Regardless of her apparent zeal, Adam was dubious. His skepticism came from professional training, but was tinged with decades of hateful anti-Russia propaganda. His entire career had been performed in secrecy. No outsider had ever been allowed inside, not even his wife.

Eason was the only visible leadership presence he'd experienced since his handler was killed in the Pentagon on September 11. It was an inflection point that rendered Adam rudderless. It was that moment he felt a sea change in the intelligence apparatus for which he worked.

Formal lines of communication had been replaced by tables at sidewalk cafés. Trust in historical allies was gone. Cuba and Russia had seats at the table. Adam was experiencing a paradigm shift like never before, but he realized it was that kind of tectonic transformation needed to make the world a better place.

After dinner glasses of fernet gave way to pitchers of sangria as the four talked into the late hours. Conversations became more personal. Each participant wished to know with whom they dealt. One's fate would be placed in the hands of the others. Inebriation exacerbated Adam's suspicion that death never appeared more imminent to everyone there. Uncertainty among the newly formed team regarding the level of each member's convictions compounded collective insecurity.

11

There were only a few hours until daylight by the time the three men made their way back to the house on Villareal. Adam rationalized the night's frivolity, exacerbated by alcohol, by telling himself there would be no work to complete until Kennedy finished his data farming operation. That would take hours. The young analyst was better able to operate effectively when no one else was around to distract him.

Adam shook his head as he witnessed the young agent sit down at the piano and tickle the ivory combination that exposed the data center. There were times in his youth he could have worked continually for days. Those instances were fueled by company issued drugs. He wondered what long-term damage they'd done to him and had no desire to push himself to that extent. No longer could his flesh withstand such trauma.

As Reinier walked up and stopped next to him, both men watched Kennedy disappear inside the computer room, and then as the wall closed behind the young agent.

Both men made their way silently past the secret room and beyond the grand piano.

Adam stopped and looked back at the seams of the wall, ceiling, and floor. No light escaped from behind the wall. He marveled at the workmanship and pride of those who constructed the secure vault. He'd once embraced a similar devotion for his job.

Adam glanced at the doorway that led to a vestibule from which individual suites were accessed. Reinier disappeared beyond the frame and leftward toward his room. Adam moved toward his bedroom down the hallway to the right.

Inside his suite, he picked up his suitcase and placed it on a chair in the corner of the room. He flipped it open and began feeling his way through neatly folded clothes to retrieve pajama bottoms. He undressed and kicked that day's clothes under the chair.

He smiled as he moved toward bed, anticipating the comfort it offered. When he tugged at the edge of the sheet and comforter, they barely moved. He wondered what kind of military plebe made the bed. The sheets were tucked so tightly Adam had to slide inside them as if he were inserting a piece of paper into an envelope.

He slipped his arms under the covers and by his side. He chuckled, imagining he appeared as a middle-aged babe in swaddling clothes with only his head exposed. He felt trapped yet comforted.

Adam wondered how Maritza was doing in Cuba. He wasn't concerned about her missing school. Knowledge came from experience, and she'd been involved in life well beyond her peers. It gave him peace-of-mind to know she was safe with Eason and the other analysts and agents at Finca Vigia.

Streetlights outside his window flickered as branches swayed in the breeze. He watched for a moment. Finally, he closed his eyes, blocked out all distractions, and began to drift off to sleep.

In the stillness and quiet, he heard something from another part of the house. Some kind of music. And then he snickered. Kennedy was playing Camelot on the piano.

Exhaustion quickly pushed Adam into a deep sleep.

A few hours later, just before sunrise, Adam drifted from REM sleep into the delusional. Someone was sitting on top of him. The tightness of the sheets and the burden of his visitor made it impossible for him to roll away from his predicament.

He opened his eyes and was bewildered by what he saw. It was a man dressed in a Soviet-Army-issue uniform. The weight of the dark overcoat seemed to pull his shoulders down. The adversary's Siberhat was emblazoned with a red star surrounded by a gold wreath of oak leaves. Within the star sat a hammer and sickle. And the assailant's face? The man's glower created a mask of hatred.

As Adam pondered the nature of the visit, the man punched him in the face. Once, then twice, then three times. A trinity of abuse.

He had no defense, much less a chance of mounting an offense. The man's hatred struck him as odd. Wasn't the Russian team on our side? His subconscious mind blended realities. The timeline of his life collapsed into that moment.

"Why is a man who is supposed to love me beating me without provocation? I'm only a child in swaddling clothes. How can someone with such an advantage in size viscously beat a helpless child?" questioned the man existing in a delusional state hovering between reality and fantasy.

"Goddammit, Dad. Stop!" Adam awoke fully from the nightmarish experience. He took a moment to right himself in the awakened world. "Man, that's fucked up."

Effects of the abuse he suffered as a child remained fresh decades later. Inability to trust a father colored his perception of apparent allies who'd once been enemies. Such a specific fantasy caused Adam to question whether his father began corporal abuse at a time when he was helplessly confined to a bassinet. Was it possible for repressed memories to include that of an infant?

The first of the morning sun's rays drifted into the room. He wriggled violently to remove himself from the sheets that held him in physical and emotional check.

Finally, he stood next to the bed, ripped the sheets off, and threw them to the floor. No longer would they control him.

Adam wondered about the meaning of the dream while he showered in his ensuite bathroom. He then turned his attention to that which required action. As much as he wanted to trust Sofia, something about her gave him cause for doubt. His entire life taught him the only person he could truly trust was himself. That lesson had served him well, but he knew there was more to life. In order to make a difference in the world, he would have to put his faith in others, and that did not sit well with Adam.

He made his way to the living room and saw the hidden door to the data center was open and activity bustled inside. Adam saw the tops of a few heads above computer monitors situated throughout the room. Several analysts had been flown overnight from Finca Vigia.

One head, with long, straight, black hair looked eerily familiar.

"Maritza?" He called out.

The girl popped up from behind her monitor with a grin on her face. "Hey, Papa."

She was wearing a T-shirt he'd bought for her on one of their many trips to the gun range. It read STAY CALM AND SHOOT LIKE A GIRL.

"What are you doing here?"

"I can answer that," said Kennedy as he breezed into the room.

Adam turned to the analyst and raised his eyebrows.

"You see, Maritza spent a lot of time at Finca in Cuba working with our analysts. She has quite the aptitude for the work." The young analyst didn't have the courage to admit Adam's granddaughter successfully hacked the elite's gaming platform.

"But you're placing my granddaughter in harm's way. If Argentina is ground zero for Trinity, she would be much safer in Cuba."

"Actually, this is one of the more secure locations in all of Argentina. Short of a nuclear blast, we're all very safe in this reinforced bunker," Kennedy rationalized, but wasn't sure Adam approved of his rhetoric.

Adam smiled sarcastically. "Yes, but she would be even safer if she wasn't in Argentina, at the center of the storm." Decades of missions dictated he move toward danger. He'd sensed the onset of trouble and didn't want his granddaughter anywhere near it.

Kennedy held up an index finger and shook it, as if he were about to disagree. Then the gravity of the situation seemed to dawn on him. "Point taken. However, what your granddaughter brings to the table is her youth, and that's an asset. She's grown up communicating with kids from all over the world and has ground level contacts anywhere we might wish to go. And she has a deep knowledge of the dark web. This is all second nature to her."

Adam glared at Maritza. "Drugs?"

The girl sat down and sunk into her chair.

"Drugs are only a part of the dark web," said Kennedy. "We all know governments are heavily involved in trafficking drugs and humans for their own benefit. Your granddaughter is a benefit to this team."

"But she's only sixteen years old."

"More like seventeen," she said.

"No, less like seventeen than sixteen. You don't round up from sixteen and a half, Maritza."

She stood again and looked her grandfather in the eye. "No. The day we eliminated bad guys in Carrabelle was my birthday, and I'm seventeen. And in case you hadn't noticed how mature I am, I didn't ask you to buy me anything." The ever-present yet small vein of immaturity showed itself briefly.

Adam was embarrassed he didn't know his own granddaughter's birthday. The grandfather dropped his head and shook it. "I'm sorry I missed your birthday, Maritza. When we get back home, I'll do something special for you." He turned to Kennedy. "If anything happens to her, I will torture you in ways only I know how."

"Yes, sir."

12

Dining room chairs had been pulled away from the table to make it more accessible to those adding to the growing stacks of reports and dossiers placed upon its surface. Adam and Reinier sat at opposite ends, meticulously reading page after page. Each man took notes on a legal pad. Silence was only disturbed by the turning of pages or scribbling of notes.

Noise radiated from the data center adjacent to the dining room. Printers hummed and analysts tapped keyboards. Shared ideas were voiced by the young staff without regard for those tasked with concentrating on details.

Sporadically, analysts flitted into the dining room carrying the freshest intelligence bound in manilla folders by thick rubber bands. Each new report was alternatively placed on the unread pile next to each agent. An efficient balance of work was desired and based solely on volume. Occasionally, new material contained information deemed important enough to bring directly to an agent's attention.

Adam concentrated deeply on his work, but he noticed among analysts who continually breezed in and out was Maritza. Pride for the contribution she made and the truth she learned pulsed in his soul. Regardless, he couldn't shake his sense of fear for placing her in harm's way.

Adam finally rationalized having Maritza in the war zone was the best way to protect her. Together was the only way he could hover over her like the papa bear he wished to be.

Throughout his career, Adam understood trust couldn't be offered beyond his own ability to carry out a job. His granddaughter displayed deft skills at the cabin in Carrabelle. Her maturity offered an additional source of comfort. Adam knew he would protect her until his dying breath, but feared life without him posed challenges she was ill-equipped to manage. It wasn't until his fifty-fifth year that he completely understood power dynamics of the world and the universe in which they lived.

Adam shook away concerns and refocused on the mountain of reports that lay in front of him.

Hours of the same repetitive work drained him. Trouble remaining centered on task created an inefficient imbalance. When he found he could no longer focus on reports containing the most heinous of human activity, he threw down his pen and rubbed his eyes.

Adam brought forth, from the recesses of his memory, those many years spent as an assassin. He analyzed the elimination of high-level individuals in hindsight. Details of orders were traced within his consciousness, from their genesis, through the chain of command, to their culmination. Decades long understanding of the world's power structure had been shattered. He had been the tip of that spear, aimed and launched according to the whims of unelected elites. He felt empathy for fellow workers situated along that information chain, the shaft of the spear.

His feelings drained him of even more energy. He sorted through the same questions he'd asked himself many times before. Did everyone involved in missions carried out during his career know their true purpose? Had he been unwittingly thrust into darkness? Facts and circumstances surrounding one job triggered thoughts of another, and then another, until it became overwhelming.

He came to the same resolution he always had. Elites arrogantly controlled a population that outnumbered them one hundred million to one. That level of hubris could only be borne of the possession of the same brand of wonder-weapon sought by Hitler. For the first time he feared those controlling the planet had extra-terrestrial help. The physicist knew the universe was infinite, and that there was obviously intelligent life throughout. It wasn't until that moment he conceived the same evil populating earth was pervasive on a universal level.

Politicians had come and gone over the 30 years of Adam's career. There were however those who remained in office nearly his entire lifetime. It was those politicians who shaped public narratives. Government control of every aspect of one's life would purportedly lead to a serene existence. From the other side of their mouth hatred was heaped upon those who spoke of individual freedoms. Us versus them proved effective in Nazi Germany. The rhetoric was the same but the population was divided further. Subsections of society busily squabbled with one another as power became highly concentrated. Laws and resolutions to address issues were nothing more than cheese in a mouse trap. No matter the myriad of cultural types across the globe, all became dependent upon central authority.

Raising his consciousness to a universal level offered the perspective of humans being nothing more than ants in a jar. Different shades and types living together harmoniously until the jar was shaken. Violent attacks upon one another continued as those peering down from above the fray took sadistic pleasure in the destruction they caused.

Adam considered the military men and women who served with the same passion he held for spreading democracy across the globe. Incursions seemed to be nothing more than power grabs. Evident was the fact whenever new democracy was established, the US Constitution was never replicated. At no time was a new contract implemented between government and its citizens stating power rested with the people. Never were individual rights recognized as given by God. Continued attacks on such a constitution was easily ascertained in hindsight. The US was the only country with such a contract. Its society was the target of the elite's most intense divide-and-conquer strategy.

The history of global chess pieces being moved and manipulated spoke to a relative handful of hidden hands manipulating society. Leaders of multiple nations spoke in unity about the need for a great reset of humanity. The time of switching from benevolent rulers to feudal lords had almost been reached. Adam's mathematical mind easily postulated, that when properly motivated, humanity's Godly energy could easily win out over the evil that controlled the world. Discomfort felt by the elite being so vulnerable to an uprising supplied the motivation for mass genocide.

Medieval alliances among those who prospered from destruction reached a crossroads. Returns diminished when resources must be shared with eight billion others. Threat of a mass awakening would render their media-driven narrative machine inert. Guillotines and gallows held the fate of an outnumbered elite who viewed humans as no more valuable than cattle; inventory to be written off.

The timeline of history echoed in Adam's psyche. Consistency of the path away from the enlightenment of the Renaissance offered proof society's slow descent was managed by families exerting control for centuries. Nazi passion for the thousand-year Reich made sense. Build the human population for a millennium. Profit from their labor. Eliminate them when numbers become uncontrollable. The pall that soaked his soul became unbearable.

Adam stood and made his way to the back of the house, and into an exterior outbuilding. The sounds of activity in the data center faded and were replaced by the sounds of the city. Cars passed on rain-soaked side streets. Voices of passing pedestrians carrying on conversations brought him slowly back to the realization there was a world filled with people who were unaware of the potential danger faced by humanity.

Thoughts of his career faded as he examined the layout of the porch at the rear of the house. At one end was an iron framed dining table with a glass top. It was surrounded by matching chairs; each with a cushion in its seat. At the other end was a daybed covered by a comforter printed with large yellow hibiscuses.

Adam descended the two steps from the house to the porch. To his right was a bamboo sofa with cushions that matched the daybed. He sat on the middle cushion and then slid the coffee table away so he could stretch his legs.

Leaning back, he crossed his right ankle over his left. Adam sighed away all the thoughts that were stressing his psyche. His surroundings reminded him of his youth. This screened porch was similar to one at his childhood home. As he peered into the backyard, he noticed its shape narrowed at the rear property line. A gardening shed with an adjacent iron gate encompassed the entire rear lot boundary. A two-lane road extended behind the homes on the street. It was all too similar, and eerily so.

An hour passed as Adam stared without focus on the physical world that surrounded him. Occasionally, a pedestrian passed by the gate and garnered his attention. He felt tremendous anger at the fact his adult life had been a lie, but childhood memories and recollections of friends helped push away annoyance.

As if washed away by a tide, pleasant, youthful memories gave way to those of the jaded old man convincing himself it served no purpose to teach a child the world was a kind place. Adam knew it never would be. Malevolent energy would always consume those who wished to destroy all that was beautiful for the thrill of watching it burn.

Suddenly, in his periphery Adam noticed movement to his left. Maritza occupied the doorway holding a photograph in her left hand.

When the two made eye contact they exchanged muted smiles. Each was heavy with dogmatic visions of what life had become.

Adam saw doubt reflected in her countenance.

Maritza descended the two steps to the porch and sat to the left of her grandfather. She pulled the bamboo and glass coffee table toward them, showing complete disregard for his outstretched legs. She nonchalantly placed the photograph on the table.

Adam drew in his legs but didn't bother sitting up.

"How's it going for you in there?" he asked.

"Not too bad. However, I don't think they're going to let a seventeen-year-old have access to any really sensitive information. They pretty much just have me running queries. I never get to see the data that comes from my work."

"What's with the picture?"

She picked up the photograph and, without looking, handed it to her grandfather.

"Recognize it?" she asked.

He took it and found himself gazing into his own eyes. Adam did not respond.

"That photograph was taken at three a.m. in front of the US Embassy in London on the night a high-level diplomat disappeared. He was last seen entering the embassy earlier that evening."

Adam shook his head. "They should have never given you access to classified information. Remind me to scold Kennedy." When his granddaughter did not respond he continued. "And?"

"And were you involved in that man's death?"

Adam's first instinct was to lie as he had done throughout his career. Self-preservation wasn't a consideration. Evil was the author of all lies. He realized this might be his final opportunity to set their relationship on a fruitful path. Lies could derail that course. "Yes."

"You know they found him dismembered, right?" When her grandfather didn't respond, she became more direct. "Did you do that to him?"

"Not on that one." He wanted to clarify, but even as he spoke, he knew he was saying too much. "I was more like a technical advisor."

"That was only a couple of years ago. I was fifteen." For the first time in a week, the fundamental innocence of her youth shined through.

Adam hardened his posture. "What did you expect after Carrabelle?"

"In Carrabelle we were defending ourselves. Your job is to murder people, or at least make sure the job gets done. There's a huge difference. It's going to take me a long time to come to terms with that sort of callousness from you."

"I can't argue with you there." He gave up trying to explain himself.

Maritza looked her grandfather directly in his eyes while waiting for an additional explanation.

Adam realized she wasn't going to accept silence. He chose to start from the beginning. "When I was a kid in Panama City, we had a porch, not unlike this one. My grandfather added it to the house several years after he and my grandmother built the home. I don't know what it was about that porch, but to the ten-year-old me, it was a refuge. I could go out there and be almost a world away from the dogma that permeated the energy in my home." He looked at his granddaughter. "You've never been to Panama City, have you?"

She shook her head. "Mom and Dad never took me, and neither did you and Granny."

"I'll take you there one day. It's such a dichotomy, but it reflects the greater world we're forced to operate in."

Maritza furrowed her brow. "How so?"

"Very few people control the vast majority of resources. The citizens who struggle to make ends meet bullshit themselves into thinking they live in paradise because of the beautiful beaches. It's all propaganda broadcast over the television stations in town." Adam shook his head. "I can see now how people can fall prey to a comfortable narrative."

"Which narrative?" Maritza inquired.

"That of trusting people that have no business being trusted. That of giving away personal value to those who use it for nefarious purposes."

Maritza softened. "You have every opportunity to right those wrongs."

Adam sighed. He hoped she was right. Bringing the conversation back to its original context, he continued. "I would sleep on that porch to avoid the random and angry rants of my father. In the summer, it was hot, and I would sweat and stick to the sheets." He chuckled at the memory. "I could hear the flapping of cockroaches' wings as they flew across the room."

"Oh my God. Are you serious?"

Adam nodded and smiled. "You have to understand. I was basically living outside. I could easily escape by pulling the comforter over my head to hide from those beasts. Then there were the winter nights in our north Florida town. They got very cold, and my mother would put four or five blankets on the bed to keep me warm. I liked those nights best. There was a great deal of tranquility on a cold, crisp night. I can remember my mother always supported me in trying to distance myself from the anger and hatred inside the home. I haven't really thought about that time in my life until recently. I think she was taking responsibility for bringing me into an untenable situation."

Minutes passed without a word spoken. Adam needed time to express himself. He needed to think and articulate concepts using his own words. It would come, and his message to her would be the purest, unadulterated advice he could offer.

"Those were the days I began to identify more with my mother than I did my father. She was the one who offered advice and instilled pearls of wisdom. She told me to follow my bliss, but never took the time to define it. Looking back, I can see my passion is for all of humanity and how our souls are connected within the context of the greater universe. When I graduated with my PhD in Physics, I was young, virile, and obsessed with the physical, and that's how I got to where I am today. I aggressively stamped out those I viewed as the cockroaches of society. The naïveté she instilled in me caused me to think I could have the same open and honest relationship with every human I encountered. My father was so absent in my life. I never conceived of him as a representation of how humanity destroys its youth, mainly by not instilling strength in children. Evil saw that trait in me and exploited it."

Maritza shook her head. "I don't understand what you mean by that."

Her grandfather glanced into the back yard and thought before looking at her once again. "It goes back to my energy frequency. It was not pure; therefore, I was attracted to that lifestyle. Evil attracts those of like mind."

His granddaughter nodded her understanding.

Adam glanced away, gathered his thoughts, then continued. "I guess what I'm trying to tell you is, that the world is a façade. Every human tries to paint an image of themselves in the best possible light. If I were giving you advice on how to live your best life, it would be to understand your own energy and the energy of those around you. Also, if you associate with negative energy people, their energy *will* soak into your soul."

Adam stroked his chin with his thumb and forefinger. He dropped his gaze to the floor at his feet. The green indoor-outdoor carpet was worn and reflected a decades old fashion. "Anytime I tried to express my individuality as a kid my father would beat me with his belt. Looking back, I see he felt he had no control over his own life. It made him angry. It made him a hateful person. I believe every lash of that belt opened a wound in my soul. Those emotional lacerations exposed me to a greater degree of influence by those who hate and wish to destroy the world. Energy is like water; it flows freely to the point of least resistance. My damaged flesh was like a sponge that accepted that ethereal concept of the lesser man my father defined for me. I became their minion." Adam glanced at Maritza. "I'll have to take you to my hometown one day and show you the misery that surrounded me as a kid." He chuckled away the pain. "Some people I grew up with thought that was the greatest place on earth, but to me it's the universe's anus."

"You don't mean that, Papa."

"Of course not. I'm just frustrated. No one there ever stood up against the local elite hegemony. It wouldn't surprise me to find out they've been trafficking humans through the port for decades." He paused. "I'll take you there one day. It's definitely a unique spot on the globe." There was so much more he had to say, but he knew when to stop complaining. "Have you ever felt like you didn't belong?"

Maritza's brown adopted face stared back incredulously at her grandfather.

"Hmm. I guess you have." He reached over and stroked her cheek. "As a physicist I understand that energy can't be destroyed and that all of our souls will live on forever. But that makes me wonder if our souls get to choose which family they're born into. Actually, there was one man I've truly identified with in my life. That's my maternal grandfather. My closeness to him and the man he was makes me wonder if my soul was a part of his ancestry. Was I his father, or uncle? It's easy to imagine my consciousness floating in the universe and being presented the opportunity for a human existence with the daughter of someone I may have known personally as my own son or nephew. Man, I certainly didn't get what I bargained for."

"Do you really believe that?"

"I have to, Maritza. If that weren't the case, life would effectively be over at conception. Human existence would be about nothing more than birth, growing, decaying, and then death. That's simply not possible if you understand the laws of physics. Our bodies die, but it's our energy that lives eternally. The question is, does our consciousness remain coalesced at death? I believe it does, and if we lead a rogue life, after we die our energy will drift toward other outcasts. If we ensure our energy frequency is pure and good, we will attract others who are of like mind…or consciousness, if you will." He paused. "I do believe it's never too late to change that frequency for the better." He smiled and brought his thought process to conclusion. "God presents us challenges in life in order to strengthen our souls for our next adventure."

Saying this, he recalled his most heinous act. Adam continued to embrace honesty, no matter how brutal. "There was a girl I knew in high school that got pregnant. She withdrew from school, went away, and had the baby so it could be put up for adoption. When my turn came to be in that situation, I took the easy way out. My father dealt with his anger over uncontrollable situations by beating us. It was a release. It was quick. And it was dirty. But all of his pain was transferred to us, and he walked away feeling like a man. That abortion had the same effect on me. Of all the horrible acts I've committed in my life, that was the absolute worst." He became pensive. "The question remains, was it universally unforgivable?"

Adam fought back tears. "If you're ever searching for a strong woman as a role model, my high school friend is the perfect example. She owned up to her mistake, had a healthy child that a family could love and give a future to, and then she came back to school and continued to strengthen herself. She faced a lot of derision from a bunch of young shits like me, but she didn't buckle under the pressure. That's true strength."

In Maritza's mind, life became less about having a physical presence to love, but a connection of energies; of universal consciousnesses. "I think I understand how humans who aren't related can live together as a family." Questions of varying countenances disappeared. "Papa, do you think our souls have been connected before?"

He nodded. "Most definitely. I believe in Einstein's theory of quantum entanglement. It not only applies to particles, or material, but also to our souls. When you came into our family at five months old, I definitely felt that connection. I believe wholeheartedly we've been together in the past and will be for all eternity. That's why we have to do the best we can to strengthen our family members. I believe that strength will carry over in the energy that is our soul and will fortify ensuing realities. We will be together forever and will be stronger for what we've overcome in this life."

They both fell silent. Adam's childhood issues caused him to drift away from the church. Unfortunate circumstances? Maybe. It was those experiences that pushed him toward the sciences, toward that which could be proven. The irony was his life was nearing its conclusion, and he'd come full circle. Adam embraced God and the eternal life and happiness offered by its positive energy, and believed whole-heartedly that wholesome energy permeated the universe. There was only one change for which he wished—to know the child he'd murdered.

"Papa, if everyone's consciousness exists for eternity and can connect with others, why do we need physical manifestations of our souls?"

Adam smiled. "That's an excellent question." He shifted his position on the sofa so that he faced his granddaughter. Confrontation over a photograph had blossomed into a healthy conversation. "I've told you before the universe is in perfect balance. As part of that balance there must be matter in order to establish equilibrium. When matter and energy are in perfect balance on a universal scale, it brings serenity. There may be pockets of volatility, but the overall universe will continue to grow and expand in a stable manner."

Maritza nodded. "I think I get it. Energy is like water, affected by tidal dynamics. It's pushed where forces take it."

"Yes. You get it." Pride filled his psyche. Adam felt compelled to expand further. "As part of my growth and movement toward a Godly existence, I've given up a lot of vices because I didn't feel they fit into who I was trying to be for the purpose of achieving eternal happiness. However, one thing I haven't been able to give up is AC/DC. I really enjoy their music, but there's no doubt lyrics and even the music contains negative frequency energy. I'll reminisce about my younger days and watch videos on YouTube. There are stadiums filled with concert goers who are all jumping to the rhythm of the music, and I think to myself that is a God given talent to inspire so many people. But then I think about the content of their lyrics. It perplexed me and I was unable to reconcile how I could be so devoted to God and at the same time enjoy this music. I've thought about this a lot, and one day it came to me. AC/DC, in their music and lyrics, are expressing their concept of the human experience, however flawed it may be." Adam paused and tried to express his thoughts more succinctly. "The evil that controls the earth creates the negative energy in which we all are forced to live. It affects all of us. Artists who reflect that in their work are simply trying to understand why. They speak to challenges all humans face."

For the first time he witnessed his granddaughter blush. "You really wouldn't like the music I listen to."

He nodded and smirked. "Yeah, I've been meaning to talk to you about all the negative energy in the sounds I hear emanating from your bedroom." He paused. "I'll speak to what I know. In the song 'Hells Bells,' they say, 'Satan's calling to you.' Well of course he is. Every single day. Their music has been a part of my life since high school, and I can remember friends of mine calling me the devil because I listened to that music. I've been judged by pretty much every human being I've ever come into contact with, so I try to not judge others. Those are my circumstances, but to be a good human you must make an effort to understand others and their struggles."

Maritza's grandfather had always been a stoic and unemotional person. She never knew what thoughts were being processed behind his expressionless and hardened face. He'd always intimidated her so much she felt he didn't care for his own granddaughter. There were times she even allowed herself to believe he didn't like her because she was Guatemalan. After her parents were killed, she feared having to live with a man she'd come to know as one of the most caring individuals on earth. She mistook his strength for a dogmatic expression of hate. It all made sense to her. Her grandfather was a man who loved humanity so much he sacrificed his life to a career that betrayed him.

"Papa, what advice would you give me as to how to approach my life?"

"Maritza, you can't go through life regretting every decision you've ever made. If I could go back and change any decisions I've made, I might not have you, and you're the most important person in my life." He thought more about the advice he'd give her. "The only thing I wish is that I had more children."

"Because Dad is dead now?"

"No. Life isn't a hedge against tragedy. It's more about realizing that I have not done my part in helping the human race flourish. Your grandmother and I didn't have any children of our own. That's a net negative. That's a decreasing population." He paused. "There's no professional contribution you could make to society that would come close to the value of children, grandchildren, and so on."

Adam looked around at the patio that reminded him of a childhood from which he'd worked hard to distance himself. "I'm glad you and I can have frank discussions about life. I never could've had a meaningful discussion with anybody at seventeen years old. Uncomfortable conversations and the ability to have them has to be the most difficult, yet important life-skill. When things go unsaid between two humans, it takes away the honesty from a relationship. If you don't have a completely honest relationship, especially with your spouse, you're inviting other issues to arise and possibly destroy what you've worked hard to build."

Maritza sensed there was something deeper to his words, something concerning her grandfather she wouldn't understand unless asked. "You seem to be referring to something specific? What is it?"

Adam didn't hesitate. "After your grandmother was killed, I was cleaning out some of her things. I came across an old paper calendar. There was only one thing written on each monthly page. No birthdays. No Anniversaries. Just a reference to her menstrual cycle. Fourteen days after every entry was a reference to ovulation. A line was drawn four days back, and four days forward. Above that notation was written, NO SEX. For the first time in our relationship I knew she didn't want to have children. As much death and destruction as I've caused in my life, it pained me to realize she'd unilaterally decided we wouldn't bring any souls into the world. Was that the karma I cast into the universe? As a man seeking out a purpose for my life, I constantly come back to the realization I haven't contributed anything to the growth of the human race." He paused. "I had all the information I needed to understand this as a young person but chose to ignore it." He paused before becoming melancholy. "Your grandmother was a beautiful woman, but she never embraced the ethereal. Because of this, I believe she was unable to conceive of how much I truly loved her."

"Why, Papa?"

"When I was bringing together all the information for my dissertation, my whole world was on campus. God is not welcome at universities. I felt as though my committee would fail me for not being able to prove God's existence; a presence relying solely on faith. It was totally misplaced anxiety. It was me who was searching for God. They didn't care about that. All they wanted was mathematical proofs of the flow of energy, and those particles that affected its transmission negatively." He paused. "I simply could not defend it." He laughed. "The irony is that I was so determined not to make the same mistakes my father did, and damned if I didn't do exactly that, and on a much grander scale."

"How could you have done that?"

Adam looked into his granddaughter's eyes. "I caused so much death and destruction when I was certain it was the right thing to do. I always felt the violence my father exacted upon his family was due to the fact he had no control over his life. I made sure I placed myself in a position where I had total control over not only my actions, but the lives of others." His stare returned to the yard. "Only when I viewed my life from a Godly perspective did it come into focus that I'd become exactly what my father was, on steroids. People controlled me like a puppet, and the destruction I caused to families throughout the world made my childhood home seem like Christmas every day."

When Maritza didn't respond, Adam sat back against the sofa and looked around the room. Its similarity to his childhood home's porch was striking. It aroused disturbing memories. There was even a single bed placed against the far wall, just like the one he slept on as a child. Repressed memories burst forth into his consciousness. These were thoughts he'd suppressed long ago in order to make way for a successful life. To the outside world, his friends at school, he spoke of the fun of camping out on his back porch every night. Representing facts as something other than the avoidance of abuse doled out by a father he'd long stopped considering extended the man's influence into Adam's young adult life.

As a kid, he'd believed corporal punishment was justified in order to provide him with structure and discipline. The energy of hatred and anger permeated all who occupied the house, and the patio was his only means of escape. He'd chosen to travel across country for college as an additional means of escape. There were many schools in the southeast with excellent physics programs. Nobel Prize winning physicist Paul Duroc taught at Florida State University; less than one hundred miles from his home.

Adam's malaise was broken when Sofia appeared in the doorway, breaking the light streaming from inside the house.

Automatic was the greeting he was about to thrust upon the unknown visitor who joined them on the patio. He lifted his eyes to face the person standing behind his granddaughter—a tall, thin, beautiful woman. "My God," he said. "They'll let anyone in here. Is this house not supposed to be safe from people like you?"

Sofia looked at him and smiled. Affecting a thick Russian accent she said, "I am here to take you to SVR Headquarters."

"What's with the accent?"

She dropped the accent and responded. "I thought that would stoke your hatred of all things Russian. You seem to wallow in the anger."

"I don't hate you." Adam shook his head defiantly. "I'm done with that emotion."

"Seriously though, we…the Russians…have found Trinity's safe house and are holding her there."

"Her?"

She nodded her head. "You'll never guess who she is. As a matter of fact, I'll give you three guesses and the first two don't count."

Adam laughed as he stood and walked toward the doorway. "My mother used to say that."

As Sofia disappeared into the house, she said, "Call your mother, and let's go."

Maritza looked at Adam. Her responsibilities to the team burst forth as she admitted, "I've got to get back to work."

The two moved back inside.

Satisfaction welled within Adam's soul at what he considered to be the completion of one of the most difficult tasks of his life. The conversation had been uncomfortable and disjointed, but for twenty minutes, he'd been the kind of mentor that strengthens youth.

13

A cold June wind blew rain against their faces as Adam and Sofia walked away from the CIA safehouse and through the streets of Buenos Aires. Both wore hooded windbreakers to shield them from the weather.

"Do you have a car nearby?" Adam asked.

Sofia turned to face Adam. "No, the house is just around the corner."

"What?" Adam replied incredulously. "Are you serious?"

"It's just a coincidence, I'm sure."

The couple rounded the corner and walked to the end of that block. At the far intersection stood a large estate home, not unlike the one they'd just left.

A six-foot iron gate surrounded the property. Atop each fencepost was a cast iron bear. Each animal struck a different pose. Some were up on hind legs; others lunged forward; still others swiped the air with oversized paws, claws exposed. He counted at least twenty such figures before they turned up the walkway and moved toward the front door.

Two large brick pedestals stood six feet high and bracketed the concrete steps that led up to the house. On each stood the bronze statue of a bear on its hind legs, front paws outstretched in an aggressive manner. Mouths were agape and displayed lethal fangs. "Geez, Sofia. You guys should just go ahead and hang the Russian flag above the doorway."

She laughed as she opened the door and breezed into the foyer. Without breaking stride, Sofia approached two massive wooden pocket doors. The blonde beauty turned and smiled at Adam. Then, holding his gaze, she slid the doors apart.

Adam leaned past her to absorb the grandeur of the chamber he identified as the study.

Ornate chandeliers and wall sconces commanded the attention of those entering for the first time. Persian rugs adorned the floors. Bronze statuettes of fierce predatory animals along with busts of Lenin and Stalin stood on many of the smaller tables throughout the room. Adam laughed at the number of bear sculptures. "These people," he thought.

A small coal fire burned in the fireplace. Occasionally a flame burst forth to lick at the oxygen required for its meager existence. In front of the fire stood a large, ornately carved coffee table. A broad and bulky leather sofa was positioned parallel to the table and hearth. Matching club chairs faced each other from the ends of the table. Four balding and older men occupied all seating. Each held a cigar and a snifter of brandy.

The two subordinate field agents shared a glance as they moved into the room. The connection between them carried with it a mutual thought process. Before them sat the political class. Those who'd never dirtied their hands with the blood of humans but moved pawns and knights to accomplish dirty work. It was men like these who pushed the world toward the brink of disaster. Adam and Sofia witnessed personal satisfaction of those who never entered the playing field but possessed the power and resources to destroy the world. These people viewed themselves as chess masters, though their fingerprints never appeared on any pieces on the board. Dubious energy permeated the souls of the two who'd been tasked with actually saving humanity.

They continued toward the men, each moved around opposite ends of the sofa. Adam looked at the faces of the men. Each displayed Cheshire-cat-like grins. Three of the four he knew only from dossiers he'd studied at various times during his career. The fourth was his current boss, General John Eason, who appeared to fit in quite nicely with a group of men the mainstream media portrayed as his country's most egregious enemy.

Eason raised his glass to Adam. "There he is," he said in a smug, condescending tone. "Aren't you going to thank our Russian counterparts for finding Trinity?" None of the politicos knew Maritza found Trinity's location, days earlier.

Trying to gain some sort of credibility among the elite in the room, Adam smiled as he looked at each Russian and addressed them. "Ambassador Chemyenko, General Ivanov, and Secretary Orlav, thank you for including us in the capture of the genocidal maniac known as Trinity."

All three nodded and silently raised their glasses.

"We'll be joined soon by an analyst who will brief the room," offered Eason.

"Isn't she here?" asked Adam. "Can't we just go interview her?"

Eason shook his head. "No. We decided to keep her at her family estate. It's isolated and built eight floors beneath the surface. Doing so will keep the citizens of Buenos Aires safe. Her bosses wouldn't think twice about murdering thousands to prevent us from obtaining their secrets."

Adam straightened his back, stood tall and commented sarcastically, "Nice."

"Face it, Phillips," said Eason. "They're within days of executing their planned genocide. What difference would a mass murder make now?"

"Because it isn't a part of their plan," Sofia interjected. "For all of their faults, these people do operate by a code. They feel as though covert warnings, no matter how vague or fictionally delivered, allow permission to do as they please to the useless eaters on the planet. We don't have intelligence that speaks to such a warning. I just don't see them endangering humans without offering potential victims the opportunity to object."

General Ivanov looked at Sofia. His uniform was olive in color and adorned with copious medals and ribbons. "So you feel certain these people have scruples?"

"Yes, sir. For decades, all of our intelligence has matched operations with arrogantly published information foreshadowing these events. It's always disguised and coded. It's never meant to elicit a response. We have no such warning for Buenos Aires."

Secretary Orlav sat forward. "So what do you feel will be done to free Trinity?"

Sofia pursed her lips and shook her head. "Nothing. She is as good as dead to them. Their plan will continue. Some subordinate will step into the void and make sure it's executed."

Adam bristled. "Executed. Not a good word."

Without acknowledging Adam, she continued. "The good news is she knows this, so there is no reason for her to not disclose every detail of the plan. She will be boastful in her disdain for humanity."

Suddenly, the doors to the study opened, and a young man stepped inside. He wore a Russian flag lapel pin and carried a laptop at his side. Behind him a member of the housekeeping staff carried two folding chairs, which she set up behind the sofa.

Adam and Sofia knew the chairs were meant for them and moved quickly around and behind the sofa and then sat dutifully. The young agent was to give a presentation while standing throughout.

Ambassador Chemyenko stood and walked to the fireplace. He flipped a switch on the mantel. A panel above the fireplace, moved up, revealing a screen.

The newcomer sat at a desk and opened his laptop. It took him a minute to get his PowerPoint slides up on the screen above the fireplace. Then he stood and walked to the screen. He began to brief the room on the SVR's knowledge of Trinity. The agency researched her for years. Not until Maritza found her inside the meta bunker did the Russians know her location. That fact would be withheld.

The young agent spoke with a thick accent, but his English grammar was without flaw. He was tall, and strong of stature. An intelligence asset that appeared as capable of defending himself as he was comfortable giving a presentation. "To understand where we are today, we must begin during World War II. There are five families who claim to be of ancient bloodlines, a lineage seeded by alien progenitors. They feel as though the earth rightfully belongs to them. These are the same families that backed Hitler and Mussolini." He allowed himself an off-script comment with a hint of anger. "These families funded Hitler's war machine and the Nazis that murdered twenty-seven million Russians during the war."

The junior agent glanced at the faces in the room. They all knew the history. His job was to illustrate what the SVR learned since World War II. "We've been monitoring communications with Trinity for nearly a decade. Her history in Argentina has been documented thoroughly. Her role was cast as an adolescent when she showed proficiency concerning the mindset to execute the longer-term plan of the elites. She was informed by her parents the defeat of Nazism was planned from the beginning. The purpose of Hitler's downfall was twofold. To convince humanity evil had been extinguished on the planet. And, to test their newly created propaganda apparatus on German citizens to see how they reacted to various messages." He editorialized once more. "It worked. These same families are the ones who murdered Richard III at the Battle of Bosworth Field in 1485, just to illustrate how long this struggle has been going on."

"For what purpose was that?" Eason inquired.

"By all historical accounts King Richard was a leader of the people. He knew a coalesced citizenry would be difficult to defeat. The global elite, as we are aware, bank on humanity being fractured and arguing amongst ourselves."

Attempting to impress his counterpart, Adam leaned toward Sofia and whispered, "I'm related to Richard III."

She looked at him skeptically and affected a Russian accent. "I don't believe you. Prove it to me."

He retrieved the phone from his pocket, pulled up his 23andMe account, and pointed to text that read, "You and Richard III are descended from the same European woman that lived thirty-thousand years ago."

Sofia raised her eyebrows and nodded her appreciation she was in the company of royalty.

The young Agent Tupolev glanced around the room and looked for puzzled faces. When he saw none, he continued. "The infiltration of the United States started with Operation Paperclip. The exact number is unclear, but approximately sixteen hundred Nazi scientists were brought over to assimilate into society, but also to begin phase two of the Nazi plan. The approval came from President Truman in the form of what they called a temporary military custody. It's been far from temporary. These men were supposed to be monitored twenty-four seven and then sent home once their jobs were fulfilled. They all stayed and developed a culture that lives on today. These scientists were just as culpable of war crimes as the patsies who were tried at Nuremberg, and they lived out their days freely in the United States. Each possessed a special skill necessary to implement a portion of the plan, which called for every facet of society to be controlled."

Eason glanced at Adam. Both men lived long enough to witness the degradation of American society. Technological advances never solved human issues. They only acted to create a greater web of control over those deemed livestock. Trillions had been spent during their careers developing more efficient means of murdering innocent people. Yet there still was no cure for cancer. Patchworks fashioned from lifetimes of experience created the reality that taxes were spent on that which would profit the wealthiest, most secretive families. Taxpayers paid for the elite to gain greater control. More and more diseases had been identified, for which big pharma offered a monthly pill to counteract symptoms. Americans paid the heftiest price for drugs offered by companies owned by the elite. It appeared to both men the time of value extraction had come to an end in favor of an extinction event that would leave the most beautiful planet in the universe under the control of a few. An inflection point driven by technological advancements allowed for the possibility of mass genocide.

Tupolev paused to digress. "We must remember that during this time, the only method of global communication that wasn't subject to wiretap was via the daily paper. A signal had to be sent to those stationed around the world that control had been achieved. That message came in the form of the Black Dahlia. Elizabeth Short was murdered and surgically bisected on January 15, 1947. How very Nazi to use one's skills to employ precision in murdering that young girl. It almost appeared boastful, arrogant. No one has ever been prosecuted for that crime. The signal meant not only had Hollywood and the Los Angeles Police been captured and controlled, but so had all segments of society necessary to move forward with their plan. Indeed, 1947 appears to be the year in which global cells were activated. The International Monetary Fund began its operations. Israel became a reality. The CIA replaced the OSS. The genesis of the apartheid regime." Agent Tupolev stopped himself. There were several more items to list, but he'd made his point.

He flashed the remote toward his laptop across the room and the next slide appeared on the screen. It was a map of Central and South America. Arrows pointed to various capitals. Callout bubbles hung near each. "All of these capital cities governed prosperous nations before World War II. Once the CIA was created, with the help of Nazis from Operation Paperclip, campaigns of destabilization of the western hemisphere began. The CIA acted surreptitiously to engage in soft coups, and then the IMF would come forth like a white knight and loan the country tens of millions of dollars. At that point the country was conquered. The IMF, controlled by the aforementioned five families, now had control of the continent. The countries were trapped. They could never repay the debt because the elite's apparatus and foot-soldiers also destroyed each nation's ability to export national products under the guise of global warming, or some invented ecological disaster. They delivered Nazi propaganda via a media captured during paperclip."

Adam spoke up. "You've referred to these five families a couple times. Who are they?"

Tupolev smiled. "That's just it. They've so well concealed themselves we cannot say for sure."

The American asked the obvious. "Okay, so how can you tell it's five families?"

The young Russian nodded his head, conceding doubt. "There are endpoints to all communications we receive. The same message is broadcast to five distinct locations and utilizing the same frequency. From those same locations orders are communicated and we've been able to follow them through to execution. We've identified channels in an out of the five, along with communication amongst the five." Vladimir again failed to give Maritza credit. "We hacked their Final Solution game. In it was a post genocide map. Earth was divided into five separate regions…and the Antarctic."

Adam looked around the room, waiting for someone else to ask the obvious. When they didn't, he inquired. "If we know the locations of the five, why not take them out?"

Tupolev looked at General Ivanov. "I'm sorry. It is where my English fails me. The locations are in cyberspace. They could be broadcast from Mars for all we know."

Adam shook his head. "I find it difficult to believe we haven't identified these people."

The young Russian smiled and nodded. "Have you seen your American film Eyes Wide Shut?"

"Yes."

"The elites, when they were having their orgies and sacrifices always wear masks to conceal their identity." Tupolev paused. "The veils are always visages of predators…humans being the prey. It's a simple representation, but I also find it odd Stanley

Kubrick died not long after that film was made. Maybe he was onto something he felt safe to release in a fictional format? The same manner in which the elite offer humanity clues to their planned operations. I think there is more to that film." The young agent digressed. "I'd love to see the director's cut."

Tupolev paused again for questions. When there were none, he continued. "Once the global elite controlled Central and South America, they moved their pieces on the chessboard ninety miles south of Florida. The CIA funded and armed Castro to move communism next door to the United States." He turned to Adam. "And, by the way, Hemingway did not commit suicide. He was murdered because he knew Castro was a CIA asset. If he'd spoken up about that, the citizens of the world would have believed him. He possessed that level of legitimacy."

"How can you be so sure?" Adam blurted out.

"If you don't believe our intelligence, at least entertain a thought experiment. Think of the timeline of events. In the summer of 1960 Hemingway presented Fidel Castro a trophy for winning a fishing contest named for the writer. The men were friends. He supported Castro because the revolution was meant to clear the corruption from the Cuban government. Not long after that, Castro confided in Hemingway that he was a CIA stooge. Hemingway fled in late 1960, or early 1961. The Bay of Pigs happened on April 17, 1961, an operation by the CIA meant to embarrass your President Kennedy. Hemingway knew this and had to be silenced by the CIA. A mere seventy-six days later, on July 2, 1961, the writer was conveniently dead. Silenced forever."

The young man stopped and took a large sip of water from a glass that sat on the coffee table. "If you recall, recently the US media was awash with stories about the wonderful Cuban health care system. According to these stories, it was the leading health care system in the world. The selling of communism to Americans entered its final phase."

He advanced to the next slide, a four-paneled image. In the upper left was a photo of a group of hippies in the 1960s carrying signs that read, MAKE LOVE, NOT WAR. The pane below that showed a picture of the Supreme Court with the caption ROE V. WADE. In the upper right-hand corner was the photo of a less than attractive woman wearing a simple white t-shirt that read, I'VE HAD 21 ABORTIONS. In the lower right was a simple message that almost fifty percent of marriages end in divorce.

"Hindsight makes it easy for us to visualize the destruction of the family. Individuals across the world have gone from feeling humans are eternal beings to feeling like they're animals seeking the next physical pleasure. God owns eternity, and the evil elites the physical; that which can only grow and die. All the control they've seized from humans is tweaked by pandemics, false flag shootings, and in-fighting among various groups of Americans. All areas have been controlled, academia, the media, the judiciary, the health care system, professional sports, the Vatican and other religious institutions. All areas of society."

Eason stood and swirled the brandy in its snifter. It was a drink only he knew shouldn't be consumed. Unchecked secrets possessed the energy of destruction. In deference to his hosts, he declared, "I know that Phillips and I can attest to the degradation of society during our lifetimes. When you collapse those events spread over decades Agent Tupolev spoke of, it creates a pretty clear picture of the evil we face."

Eason walked to the window and stared across Villareal Street.

No one else felt compelled to offer personal assessments.

Wrapping his presentation, Tupolev summarized. "These families are the ones who've enslaved humanity throughout history. They were the robber barons in the US, who wanted all of the New World for themselves. They've denigrated God and called his followers laughable idiots who place their faith in a mythical character like the Easter Bunny. They've marginalized natural remedies in favor of pharmaceuticals that were born of the petroleum industry. They've successfully caricatured people who embrace natural medicine; making them look like kooks."

He stopped suddenly. "I forgot to mention another 1947 incident. The Roswell crash, which gave them the plethora of technology used today to control the masses. So much so, it's the basis of the overarching metaverse that so many companies are developing. I'm not sure how all the individual spaces will interact, or if they'll eventually become one. Once again, that's where the money is being spent. This will be virtual reality that eliminates the need for a flesh and blood body to house our souls. It's where the elites want to trap our souls and control them. They know very well there is a God and eternity. It is somewhat like the mathematical proof of contradiction. They embrace their evil god, so the universe's balance brings forth our God of love, light, and truth. They don't want us to know God and live beyond this human life—outside of their control."

Everything the young Russian presented fit into Adam's belief that since the base state of the universe is energy that was how souls perpetuated eternally. But there were still questions. Appearing like a first grader, he raised his hand.

Tupolev pointed to him.

"Where does Trinity come in?"

The young agent shook his head. "That is simply a nickname that refers to the Third Reich—a continuation of the thousand-year Reich. It was her duty to make sure it flourished and advanced. She did an admirable job, if you're a Nazi. Interestingly, Trinity was also the code name of the first atomic bomb test in New Mexico. It seems to be a term bastardized for any purpose deemed relevant. That's where the six-six-six metaphor comes from. It's their way of absurdly saying Moloch is six times the force of each member of our trinity?"

He looked around the room. "Anything else?"

There were no other questions, so he nodded toward Sofia and Adam. "There's a car waiting out front to take you to the airport to meet Trinity."

Without a word, the two field agents stood and followed the agent out of the house; eager to meet a woman capable of conceiving and rationalizing the murder of seven billion people.

14

Another car. Another plane. It was a life to which Adam had grown accustomed. Prior missions had been about nothing more than eliminating targets of assassination. It was a laser-like focus he'd honed over decades. Now there was a Russian counterpart, and a granddaughter who constantly filled his awareness.

What would Trinity divulge concerning plans of the global elite? Could there really be that level of evil on earth? Most importantly, how would it affect his granddaughter's future? Would she have one? He'd spent his life and career in service of those who felt it time to cull the majority of humanity for the sole purpose of not sharing the planet and its resources. Adam could handle the fact he'd done this to himself, but if Maritza got hurt through his actions, he didn't know if he'd be able to continue in a life damaged by his own ignorance.

Everything he'd learned in the briefing at the Russian Embassy was difficult to fathom. He'd taken each fact presented with a healthy dose of skepticism.

Adam and Sofia were on their way to meet Angela Braun, the sixty-seven-year-old daughter of Adolf Hitler and Eva Braun. Tupolev only identified her as Trinity. Dossiers that Adam and Sofia read on the trip contained shocking confirmation Hitler had indeed escaped to Argentina after World War II.

Trinity had one sister, three children, four nieces and nephews, eleven grandchildren, and nine great nieces and nephews. Sofia warned Adam many Russians in positions of power would champion the need to eliminate the entire bloodline, Romanov style. Hitler had murdered twenty-seven million

Russians. It was a point Tupolev emphasized. Having been judged himself by the actions of others, Adam knew it possible any human was capable of redemption. Any one of Hitler's lineage should be given the opportunity to provide value to humanity.

The Jorge Newberry airport was situated along the coast and offered the speediest exit for the team to make their destination of Bariloche in a timely manner. It was an airport Adam seemed to have entered and exited once a decade. Whenever Argentina went through a hyperinflation of their currency, wet work needed to be performed to cover the tracks of bankers. Crises created opportunities. Those privy to the machinations of markets, or who understood the game played by the elite, purchased land for pennies on the dollar after economic collapses. Unwittingly, Adam acted to destabilize countries and cover the tracks of malevolent men.

Bariloche was a sleepy resort community situated in the foothills of the Andes Mountains. Nothing about its outward appearance spoke to high-ranking military officials occasionally invading the town to discuss furtherance of a global agenda. It was a place where the ultra-rich gathered, and those who endeavored to possess earth were the richest of all.

After World War II, several high-ranking Nazis escaped to Argentina and built families and businesses throughout the Patagonian region. Adam again considered the work Simon Wiesenthal accomplished before his death. Another piece of his personal mosaic came into view when he realized Nazi hunting basically disappeared after Mr. Wiesenthal's death. Had the Nuremberg Trials been a complete sham? Some good came from them, but those executed were nothing more than sacrificial lambs; men who were not a part of the long-range plans of the global elite. The thousand-year Reich was meant to benefit only the elite, and as far as Adam ascertained, it hadn't ceased. Only foot soldiers had been made to pay with their lives. Progression toward global dominance continued throughout the twentieth, and into the twenty-first century. Was the Holocaust a mere trial run to test the effects of propaganda on the German population? Regardless of the Russian briefing, all questions remained valid.

The philosophy Adam expressed in his doctoral dissertation had been intellectually shelved in favor of a lucrative, yet suspect career. It was more obvious than ever his conclusions were correct—that those who exist on the Godly end of the spectrum are motivated to create and share with humanity, and those who exist among evil thrive on destruction and witnessing extreme pain.

Yet another flight carried Adam to a strange airport. There were few airports Adam hadn't flown into during his career. Elites hid where he was not, and his epiphany grew more valid with every new experience.

A driver escorted them to a car, and soon they were entering a ski resort nestled in the foothills of the Andes mountains. As the car moved up the long drive to the resort's porte-cochere, Adam beheld the grand façade. Obviously fashioned after those in the Bavarian Alps. The lodge could have been planted in the middle of Bayern and no one would have thought it out of place.

SVR agents waited by the entrance to escort Adam and Sofia into the building. They all projected the requisite Russian scowl. Adam glanced at all faces, hoping to spot an American. What at first was compelled by the desire for comfort, quickly switched to relief as he recalled the murder of Jim Norton. Understanding grew that national allegiances weren't always without questionable motives. Sometimes the lines delineating teams became blurred.

The couple were led through the resort's industrial kitchen at the rear of the building and to a waiting elevator. Adam noticed the buttons in the elevator went from G downward. Each successive number had a minus sign the left, -1, -2, -3....

The SVR agent accompanying the couple witnessed Adam's puzzlement and explained. "The Germans are masters at building Deep Underground Military Bases."

"Is this where all of the global operations were coordinated?" Sofia asked in English so as to not alienate her companion.

"In the beginning, yes. After the crash in Roswell, and the reverse engineering of alien communication systems, the cabal built these bases all over the globe. They communicated via video long before that technology was released to the world's population."

Adam looked at Sofia. He knew she was thinking the same thing he was. What other technology was being kept from the world and applied as leverage against humanity? Cures for diseases? Water desalination? The free energy Tesla sought? He knew that which would relieve stress from the population would remain hidden.

The elevator continued to the lowest floor it serviced, -8. The doors opened onto a long, well-lit corridor. The three started down the hall.

"Is Trinity the only prisoner here?" Adam asked.

"Yes. All of the others have been moved to various black sites, even some to your Guantanamo Bay." He paused. "What you must understand is these people are merely mid-level managers. The ultimate control structure extends far beyond their authority."

Adam enjoyed the lack of oversight inherent in a career as a lone wolf assassin, but he'd never felt so alone; so exposed. It seemed everyone around him had access to more information than did he. His only resolution was to continue moving forward, embracing the notion of self-preservation.

As the three reached the end of the long corridor, Adam examined the two large double doors that consumed the far wall. He glanced at Sofia, and she at him.

The Russian agent moved quickly ahead of the two and opened the left door.

Adam followed Sofia into the room.

Inside was a long conference table with six plush, leather high-back chairs on each side and one at the far end. Occupying the lone seat at the head of the table was the sixty-seven-year-old Angela Braun. Her shoulder-length, curly brown hair was parted down the middle and hung to her shoulders. It suggested fashion of a bygone era.

She turned her head and watched Adam and Sofia approach. Her curls bounced on her shoulders. The tightly coiled mane exhibited a vibrance that made her appear younger than the lines on her face and the fatigue in her eyes suggested. Angela's lower eyelids sagged away from the eyes they were meant to protect.

Adam walked behind her and around to the far side of the table and sat down.

Sofia sat in the nearest chair adjacent the old woman.

On the table in front of her sat an electronic control panel. Adam examined it intently and looked around the room for the devices it was meant to control.

As he moved his gaze around the room, he wondered how many of the world's leaders had occupied chairs in this conference room. How many Deep Staters had been there strategizing the demise of the world's "useless eaters" via Project Trinity? Irony reared forth in his consciousness as he recalled reading Henry Kissinger's The Final Days. He wrote, 'the elderly are useless eaters.' How could a man so old be so obtuse to the beauty inherent in all human life? It was the wisdom of older humans that would be lost, and one such purpose of targeted genocide. Young people without a connection to history are easier to control.

"All of them," the old woman said, seemingly reading his mind. Her accent was harshly German; bitter in its bridge between humans with opposing viewpoints. Fanatical parents never allowed her to speak a language other than the mother-tongue until their deaths in the early 1970s.

Adam looked into her milky eyes. "All of whom?"

"World leaders. You were wondering if any had attended meetings in this room. The answer is all of them from 1958 until now."

Adam nodded. "I guess we spoiled your party?"

Adam and Sofia watched as this petite, harmless old woman transformed. Her face hardened as she looked into the eyes of each of her captors. "You have spoiled nothing. As a matter of fact, you're late. Very late. Our plan has been in action since 1958, and no one can stop it."

If the old woman was trying to intimidate them, she'd failed. But to Adam, her bitterness offered a glimpse into the malevolence with which they dealt. Any questions of how something as evil as the holocaust could have happened vanished with her display. Channeled through her visage was evidence of the unending supply of earthly hatred.

Softening a little, the old woman continued. "So, you want to debrief me. It will do you no good, because the world's end will begin on June twenty-fourth, no matter what you do."

Adam looked at the date on his Rolex Submariner. That was three days away.

"Why?" Sofia asked.

Angela whipped her head around to face the female agent. "Why? Why not?" She smiled. "Because earthly gods have decided it's time to cleanse their garden of weeds that have taken over."

"Why don't you tell us how we got to the point of murdering seven billion people on earth," demanded Sofia.

Adam nodded. "We have all the time in the world."

The old woman smiled again. "Only until June twenty-fourth. But I can paint quite the picture for you in a couple of hours." She raised her chin pompously like a chess grandmaster who'd just declared checkmate. She folded her arms across her chest and looked down upon the two field agents from just above her lower eyelid and smiled.

Adam and Sofia had been trained to never stop working for their cause and were happy to embrace death for what they felt was right. Objectives shifted from securing the planet for the benefit of the elite they worked for, to ensuring humanity's continued growth.

The provenance of their newfound purpose sat arrogantly in front of them.

Sofia lost patience. "Well, since you have all the answers there really is no purpose to me asking questions. Tell us how you did it."

The old woman's glance shifted between the two. "First, let me show you something." She leaned forward in her chair and began tapping on the electronic panel in front of her. A pane on the wall at the far end of the room slid upward, into the ceiling, revealing a large screen. Adam and Sofia were somewhat astonished to see the logo of the Fourth Reich grow in resolution as the screen warmed up. The 1930s styled eagle had been replaced by one that resembled the emblem of the United States. In its beak was the familiar ribbon, but the phrase "E Plurubus Unum" had been replaced by *Ordo ab Chao*— "Order out of Chaos."

She smiled gleefully at Adam. "Who would like to go first?"

Adam knew she had access to dossiers on them both, possessing information better left in the darkness in which they'd operated. He gestured to Sofia. "Ladies first."

"Ah, chivalry isn't dead." The old woman grinned impishly as she banged feverishly on the keyboard in front of her.

Adam and Sofia stared at the screen on the wall. And then it came into view—the dossier the cabal maintained on Sofia. She glanced at Adam, seeming a bit uncomfortable about that which might be revealed. The screen displayed her name, city of birth, branch of military and rank, and unique SVR identifier. The information was repeated in German, English, Russian, and Spanish.

"Inside this dossier are the details of every assignment you've ever been on," said the woman. "The people you have murdered, or I guess assassinated is a better word when it's ordered by your superiors. Relationships with men, and women. We have it all." She stared at Sofia. "Would you like to delve into this?"

"No!" The revelation of her work history confirmed she'd been working for the same overlords as the old woman. Sofia felt a pain in her gut. Mere minion status deflated what she'd embraced as a purposeful career. She'd been a minor pawn in a global chess match played by people she'd never met.

"I can even show you videos of all of your encounters. It's been a most successful means of blackmail." The old woman grinned impishly. "You are more beautiful when nude. That can't be said of most women." Angela turned to Adam. "Would you like a turn?"

Adam shook his head. "I'm well aware of the crimes I've committed and for whom." His curiosity overtook him and caused him to break Sofia's pledge of no questions. "Where did this plan originate?"

"The gods of the universe. They have seeded several manifestations of humanity throughout history. Tweaking DNA along the way. Now it's time to scrap it and start over. There will only be enough humans remaining to act as donors."

"How is that possible?" Sofia asked.

The old woman continued. "The key to controlling humanity is to control energy and the currency used to sustain life."

Adam looked at Angela. "Let's get to the bittersweet symphony."

The old woman removed her hands from the keyboard and sat back in her chair. She steepled her fingertips and tapped them repeatedly. "There are so many moving pieces in our arrangement, but I'm sure I can present it to you in a manner that you'll be able to understand."

"We're both very intelligent," Adam boasted.

Angela hastily continued. "Oh yes, I've been meaning to tell you, I read your dissertation. I'm impressed. You have a keen grasp on the universe and the energy it contains." She smiled, glancing at them both, briefly offering the opportunity for Adam to accept her kudos.

Seeking Trinity

When there was no response, she nodded. "I guess I'll start now. What you must understand is that World War II went exactly as the global elite desired. It caused a lot of stress for my parents, but it was a testbed for the newly developed theory of mass formation psychosis. You see, the elite have think-tanks whose sole purpose is to develop psychology and technology to control the minds of the masses for profit, and finally for the global genocide that will occur on June twenty-fourth."

She glanced between the two. "Haven't you ever wondered how the German citizens fell into line with murdering six million Jews? It was easy. We gave them someone to blame for their inadequacies. They could have easily defeated my father and the German Army. They far outnumbered us. But as the useless eaters they are, they took the easy path of hatred and cast aside pride for the human race. You see, my father's mission was to be the fall guy. His purpose was to deflect from the grander plan. He and his army could never have conquered the world. That eventuality needed to be subversive in order to work." She looked directly at Adam. "If I'm not mistaken, your dissertation addressed the ease with which one can exist at the evil end of the energy spectrum. It is much more difficult to live a Godly existence." She smiled. "Your words."

Adam nodded. "Because evil wants us all to focus on the pleasures of the flesh. It's a very short-term perspective; living only in the moment. Embracing a concept of eternity and a place with God requires we exist on an eternal horizon. That requires discipline. Human energy cannot truly bind to another if there are other energies distracting them. At least, that's my belief."

The woman gestured to their surroundings. "Although this building was not finished until 1958, its design was finished in 1943. That's when we knew we'd settled on two goals. The first was killing as many Jews as possible, if not all of them. The second was to kill as many Russians as possible." She looked at Sofia. "Do you know why?"

"Because Jews and Russians are the most devout concerning their relationship with God and are least corruptible."

"Another gold star," boasted the woman.

The remark reminded Adam of the gold stars given to Jews in Germany during World War II. Was Angela's assertion coincidental or the purposeful branding of another human target?

Angela continued. "In the interim, we simply watched how the United States handled its victory in World War II. At the close of the war, many veterans who came back from the war bought Harley-Davidsons and spent their remaining days riding all over the country. That opened our eyes. We learned that Americans are inherently selfish. These men had no family and produced nothing of value. The destruction of the manufacturing base along with the family was the easiest path, and after that, Americans' relationship with God would be cast aside."

Adam interjected. "Why try so hard to destroy God? You have the technology to destroy humanity. Why not just use it?"

"When one does not hold God within their soul, it destroys their belief individuals have value. Once our paperclip scientists infiltrated politics, law enforcement, universities, media, and the pharmaceutical companies, we began to broadcast the message the collective was more valuable than the individual. Humans started valuing their favorite sports star more than themselves."

"It still doesn't make sense to me. Why not just kill everyone?"

The old woman smiled. "That can easily be explained by your thesis. If we successfully shift the energy frequency where humanity resides, it will spread to the wider universe when these people die. Instead of a happy and growing environment, these newly released souls will create a dark place. A cosmos that will soon wither and die." She paused. "Soon in a cosmic sense."

"And then what? Your souls will perish too."

The old woman shook her head. "No. There are alternate universes. We can continue destroying all that is meant to grow for all of eternity."

"If this is an eternal circumstance, it doesn't make sense to murder humanity."

"It will take billions of years to move into the next universe. In the meantime, we may as well enjoy a planet that hasn't been overrun by human livestock."

Adam wasn't sure he believed what Angela said. The problem was she believed it, and so did a lot of very powerful people. "Let's get back to the nuts and bolts of Project Trinity. I've had enough of your warped philosophy."

Angela chuckled satisfactorily. "As technology advanced, the figures being projected onto living room walls became more lifelike, and the extraction of value easier. With individual value gone, humans naturally turned to groups to fill the void. It became important which neighborhood you lived in, which company you worked for, and even your preferred method of stimulating your genitalia. Even the most personal act of human expression yielded to groupthink." The old woman smiled. "Of course, that last one was helped along by childhood vaccines that destroyed testosterone in boys and estrogen in girls."

Adam spoke rhetorically. "All to prevent humans from procreating…and thriving."

The glint of evil they'd witnessed earlier sparked in Angela's eyes. "This planet is rightfully ours! So, then we attacked both fronts. Sex, drugs, and rock and roll gave the youth, with their nubile flesh and wanton desires, the catalyst for sliding toward personal destruction. Simultaneously, we attacked their parent's God as some anthropomorphized being; condescendingly watching from every corner of the universe. Once we did that, humans viewed themselves as nothing more than flesh and blood. No longer could they conceive a higher level of consciousness. So many now view their existence as finite, and by doing so their lives end at death. A sort of divine, self-fulfilling prophecy."

"You're absolutely mad…evil incarnate," shrieked Sofia.

"Evil has its place in the universe too. We're simply fighting for our right to thrive." She focused on Adam. "This is where your genius shines. You saw through that charade with your definition of the energy spectrum." Angela regained focus. "And after a couple of decades, the family in America had been destroyed." She laughed. "Personally, I think the single most ingenious part of our plan was appealing to the most intellectual, strong, and beautiful women in the US to pursue a career instead of a family. We rendered childless millions of women who might otherwise have given birth to tens of millions of strong humans. Warriors. It was easier than we thought. You see, we all have that hatred and anger within us; that frequency as you so eloquently put it. All we had to do was stoke it into a burning ember, and we dialed humanity like a radio to the far end of the spectrum."

Sofia sat silently shaking her head. Understanding of how the cabal's plan personally affected her grew. "As soon as we stop Trinity, I'm going back to Moscow and get pregnant." Her words were juvenile but meant to lash out at a woman bent on destruction.

"I told you earlier, you won't be able to stop it. The plan has been ordained." She glanced at Adam and Sofia for any queries before bringing her explanation back on track. "The rock and roll part of the plan came out of Tavernier Grange, just outside of London, and it worked to perfection. In case you haven't figured it out, there are a lot more than four fabulous participants. Also, the hordes of screaming girls at airports were all contrived." As if to inflict harm on fans of the group she barked, "the Beatles were nothing without our machinery pushing them into the global consciousness. Just like today's artists, athletes, and musicians. Giving the world false idols on earth shifted their consciousness away from the eternal."

Adam shook his head in disbelief. It all became overwhelming. "Let's go back to your religion, or whatever it is you call your belief system?"

Angela smiled. "After World War I, there was a great deal of desperation in Germany, which became the genesis of the Nazi party. There was a literal underground society, the Vril Society, that came into prominence with the Nazis and organized them with a singular spiritual focus. The Vrils are the basis of our religion. We are female led, with a high priestess, and our beliefs are based in sex; straight sex, homosexual sex, pedophilia. There really are no constraints on what we deem appropriate. If it stimulates your genitalia, go for it. It's all about extracting energy from others for your own benefit."

"But the children?" Adam asked as he looked toward the ceiling, shocked.

Angela knew his question to be rhetorical, but gladly answered. "Children offer eternal human life. They are tortured, murdered, and the adrenochrome drained from their bodies. That is then taken by our leaders to prevent aging. Have you ever wondered why some Hollywood actors never seem to age? They help spread our philosophy through seemingly innocuous movies. Awards organizations offer validation of their worth to society, and the masses fall into line, once again offering the troglodytes watching in their living rooms a sense of belonging and value."

Adam shook his head vigorously. "I don't believe you. There's no way."

Angela flashed her evil smile again. "And that's why the plan has worked so well. Seven and a half billion people will find out June twenty-fourth." She paused. "Okay, so it won't be immediate, but many will die over the next two years. That's just the day the event will be triggered."

"All of this began after World War I?" Sofia asked.

"A lot of this came together after World War II, only because that was the plan all along. Take the Black Dahlia. No one has ever been prosecuted for that heinous crime. It was surgical. It was evil." She confirmed the assertion in the Russian briefing. "Control the media magnate, control the world. The film industry. The police. The prosecutors. The judges. Everyone."

Angela looked at Sofia and thought for a moment. "In fact, the answer to your question is no. Our way of life has always been on earth, and always will be. After World War I is when all the various covens came together and began operating as one." She paused. "Do you honestly believe that a king would be forced to abdicate his throne for marrying a divorcee? The truth is he was too close to the plan. Look at the date of abdication and then the date my father came to power. For that matter, do you honestly believe a king on this planet doesn't receive the absolute best healthcare? Kings don't die suddenly, only to have their distraught daughter fly home from abroad to assume the role of monarch. It's all a show to create sympathy for evil doers."

Sofia interjected, "the British royal family and the Tsar were related. I've often wondered if there was a connection with the murder of the Tsar and his family. It was about consolidation of power, wasn't it?"

The old woman shrugged indecisively. In a weak justification, Angela replied, "You see, we weed out our own too—those who aren't onboard with the plan." She became pensive. "Truth be told, I view someone who holds themselves out as royalty as possessing supreme psychosis, only eclipsed by the sycophants who worship these so-called sovereigns. But that shows you why they are such an integral part of our plan. If humans feel themselves as sheep, or victims, it is our responsibility to herd, victimize, and slaughter them. That speaks to your energy spectrum, Dr. Phillips."

"My research was done in hopes of explaining our existence. It was educational in nature. Meant to benefit all of humanity. I'm not so arrogant to believe I was the first to come up with the idea, but you and your kind definitely suppressed the research. You people recruited me out of college with promises of eliminating evil…and exactly the opposite happened."

Angela only smiled in response.

"Who is onboard with the plan?" Adam asked.

"Every leader across the globe, now." She paused. "Think of all of the assassinations since 1958. JFK. MLK. RFK. Malcom X. Tupac. And the list will go on. These are all people who had reached a pinnacle of influence in their careers, were approached by the cabal, and refused to sacrifice mankind. And the beauty of these assassinations is that, through our media, we can cloak ourselves in their energy and have these sycophants believing we care for their well-being just like JFK and MLK did. It's a thing of beauty. Our media has the masses believing we possess the same benevolence as these great men. We promise Camelot and deliver Auschwitz." She giggled fiendishly.

Adam shook his head. "People are too intelligent for that to be true. No one is simply going to give over their critical thinking skills."

The old woman nodded. "For half the population that might be true. The disadvantage we had in the sixties was that once these people were murdered, we had to cover it up. We've reached that moment in time where we can take out an unruly public figure and have them replaced with a submissive clone we completely control."

Sofia interjected, "that's not possible, at least not yet."

"What do you think the Nazi twinning experiments were all about? It was the part of the plan we protected most. It's not hard to conceive, even for those with minimal intellect." The intensity of Trinity's giggle increased. She shook her head. "You're displaying the disbelief we count on. Humans won't believe someone is trying to harm them because it isn't in their nature to harm. There are tens of millions of old women who were in love with JFK, and still are. We gave them a bad guy to hate in Lee Harvey Oswald. He's the one who took Kennedy away. Today, it's common knowledge the CIA was involved in that assassination, and they still embrace that hatred for everything Russian." She turned to Sofia. "No offense, dear."

Adam nodded his understanding. "It's the old magician's trick. Look at my right hand, but not at my left."

"Exactly."

Sofia nodded. "And like an Einstein-Rosen bridge you construct a wormhole connection the positive and negative ends of the spectrum. People who support your narrative are absorbed by evil without even knowing it."

The old woman nodded. "I like that analogy."

"Purely evil," Adam replied.

"There are bleeding heart artists and musicians who don't realize the money behind them is ours. We've had a few that've tried to expose our deeds only to meet their own demise. No one will ever know if Tom Petty really died of a natural heart attack. Our assassinations will not stop until everyone alive realizes we control the world. Actors, musicians, media—most are involved now, and they will be an important part of the structure after the fall, acting to pacify remaining masses."

Adam looked around the space once again. He tried to imagine the intensity of evil in this room when elites were present. Did they salivate over their plans? Did they become sexually aroused like in Kubrick's film? Every thought Trinity expressed was base level. Humanity had gone through an enlightenment once before. It was imperative they do so again for mere survival. Although he'd gained an understanding of the forces at work, it was paramount he not get lost in its minutia. There was a game afoot, and he needed to win.

Angela laughed. "Actors are the easiest to control. They are vain, insecure, and—think about it—they have to have someone write the words they speak, another person to dress them, and another to tell them how to speak and where to walk. Insipid characters, if you ask me." She grinned. "Who better to control a mindless population, than mechanical and false icons?" The evil glint in her eyes disappeared. "Musicians are the hardest to control. They seem to employ their intellect to its fullest, and deal in frequencies that positively stimulate souls. Once again speaking to your energy spectrum, Dr. Phillips."

"Thank you again for the kudos, but all you're doing is giving the world a cadre of false idols that appeal to individual tastes," Adam added.

"Where did we fail?" Sofia asked.

Angela nodded. "I'll tell you where you failed. Two things. First, everyone fell asleep and took the American dream for granted; something to be passed down through generations. Our politicians did a masterful job of making people believe their intentions were to provide everyone a standard of living without individuals having to create anything of value. Second, our plans were put forth in thirteen-year stages. From 1945 to 1958, when this complex was completed. Then from 1958 to 1971, when the World Economic Forum was created. America was taken off the final vestiges of the gold standard in 1971. That meant we could print money for whatever purpose we wanted. Of course, after that it became much easier to buy politicians and timelines became compressed."

Her evil grin expanded across her face once again. "A happy consequence of all that money sloshing around in the economy was that home prices continually increased. People felt themselves geniuses for making such wise investments. In reality the value of their dollars were crashing faster. People think economic booms and busts are as random as any hurricane, but the destructive nature of both phenomenon are as controlled as this keyboard in front of me."

Angela held up an open hand in apology for her digression. "Anyway, before these ideas became reality, father placed in motion every aspect of a plan to launch nuclear weapons from Colombia into the center of Manhattan. The New York based family put a halt to that. Its patriarch put us on this long-term time horizon. His genius was understanding if we controlled human thought, people would eagerly load onto proverbial railcars. Humanity needed to accept their demise willingly." A pensive look crossed her face. "I guess he knew something I didn't."

She shook away the distraction. "Anyway, to get to that level of control for a global population would take decades. Ten years ago, we had a Nazi neurosurgeon approach with a nano bot. He promised that if we could get into the bodies of all humans, signals sent from satellites would cause these tiny computers to attack each individual human at its weakest point. Some will die instantly from heart attacks and strokes. Others will get aggressive forms of cancer—lung, brain, cervical, ovarian, breast. Most will die within four months. The entire process will take nearly two years. We'll blame it on something else to pacify those who remain. Plausible deniability." The old woman grinned. "We have finally reached the culmination of our plan, and our timeline finally nears its end."

"And by inserting these bots through vaccines gave you the permission you needed?"

The woman simply grinned and nodded her head.

"Jesus!" said Adam. "How is all this possible?"

"We created stress in the human population, and they naturally looked for help…to their government to solve their problems. When you realize the best way to weaken a family is financially, that's what we did. Klaus Schwab, the founder of the WEF, persuaded Nixon to remove the United States from the gold standard. Families' access to gold backed wealth was replaced by worthless paper. Wives who weren't persuaded they needed to pursue a career were still forced into the workforce. Poor household economics dropped the average family size from six to three since that time. The money people earned and saved was slowly made worthless by the continual printing of currency. We printed as much money as we needed to pay for our programs, and it was all unwittingly paid for by the American citizen." Angela flashed her evil grin. "And don't think the fact Roe versus Wade began making its way through the court system in 1971 was coincidental. If we couldn't prevent pregnancy, we could abort as many as possible. Women are the most valuable beings in the universe. They hold the fate of all life in their wombs. We cannot allow them to understand how treasured they are by God. They must be made to feel inferior; a victim of their gender." Seemingly unrelated facts were seen as part of a grander plan. The old woman nodded. "Can you now see how complex this plan was? We have the brightest minds working it to fruition. We have come at humanity from all conceivable angles."

It irritated Adam to hear Angela adopt a tone of legitimacy when speaking of the cabal's agenda. The complexity of their plan was easily conceived when he realized every segment of society was centrally controlled. He'd only suspected people operated in the shadows. It had been confirmed by Hitler's daughter. His awakening would be short lived unless Project Trinity was stopped.

Angela's boasting continued unabated. "The funny thing is we had enough politicians bought and paid for in key roles before 1971 that we had already started printing more than the gold reserves backing the dollar. Then Charles De Gaulle called the United States out and demanded France's gold in settlement. That provided the perfect cover. Nixon announced that speculators were manipulating the market and the gold standard would be temporarily paused for the markets to correct themselves. Temporary? That was in 1971. It's not a coincidence that the Georgia Guidestones were erected in March 1980, and that the Mariel Boat Lift happened between April and October 1980. We published our intentions in granite and began executing the plan right away. In 2024 it isn't a coincidence that your Secretary of Homeland Security was born in Havana, Cuba, and that he keeps the border open for tens of millions of unsettled souls to stream across the south Texas border. America is the sole beacon of freedom for the world and we are going to destroy it." Angela laughed wickedly. "And here we have come full circle. The birthplace of Naziism was in the Ukraine. Now, inside parliaments and congresses throughout the world you'll find Ukrainian flags and lapel pins; and not the flag of the home country. We even had the Canadian Parliament, liberal and conservative, stand and applaud a ninety-eight-year-old Nazi who participated in the Holocaust in Poland." She smiled. "You see, the infiltration is complete."

Conceptualizing the decades long timeline brought forth a melancholy associated with the once Germanic people who occupy modern day France. "It was sad that we had to kill Uncle Charles, but he would have exposed us."

"But he died of a stroke," insisted Adam.

Angela shook her head. "Before the cabal began utilizing Vril driven Nazis as their foot-soldiers, we unearthed many ancient texts, and we had reverse engineered several alien space craft. We have many technological secrets, some of which are directed energy weapons."

The old woman stood and walked around the conference table. She shook her legs individually as they had become numb from sitting for so long. "We can murder anyone and make it look like a stroke, a heart attack, cancer, what have you. We keep that part of human history for our benefit. Truth be known, there will be an ongoing attempt to destroy historical records that have nothing to do with advanced technology. You see, if we can remove the past from humans, they'll have no future. If they have no idea who they are and how they fit into humanity, they'll look to us for answers. And we'll gladly supply them. That's why history classes in the school system are nothing more than rote memorization of events and dates. Nothing about humanity's true antiquity can be disclosed. It would cause chaos. Can you imagine if humanity found out that Atlantis wasn't a myth, and that a utopian society was possible? That was Jimmy Carter's contribution with the Department of Education. From Washington DC we controlled the messages sent out to all schools. Once again, it all goes back to centralized control."

"Isn't there something in your code of ethics about lying?" Adam asked.

The old woman shook her head. "As long as we disclose our plan, no matter how obscure the reference, we're good."

Angela made her way back to her chair and sat once again. She laughed. "Politicians have gone on television for decades talking about the need for government-run health care. Do you think they really believe humanity deserves healthy lives? Hell no. It's all about control, and we are at the end game. Vaccinations have weakened the herd immunity that had become so resilient over the last few millennia." She smiled. "We are being honest when we speak of the carbon that needs to be reduced on the planet. It's just that humans are the carbon to which we're referring. Semantics can be useful."

Adam wrapped his consciousness around the reality that sat before him. He spoke rhetorically. "Carbon is the most essential element on earth. Plants need it for mere survival, and yet you've convinced humanity it's a bad thing…and by extension, humans are bad."

"So, you've pumped drugs into the entire population for the purpose of making humans more susceptible to disease?" Sofia said.

"Some of that, yes, but the program is much farther reaching. We've had nanobots placed in many injections, and the gelcaps of your favorite headache medicine. These computers will be activated by our network of a thousand top secret satellites circling the globe, and all has been paid for by the US taxpayer." She laughed. "Haven't you noticed that Big Pharma's ads on television don't tout cures but only monthly maintenance? There are cures for every known malady. Think about it. Our bodies are made from the elements here on earth. If someone's body is deficient in some element, the remedy is readily available. If someone develops a cure for a disease and they don't fall in line with us, then they are done away with. If they do work with us, we make them very wealthy with printed money paid for by the US taxpayer." She smiled. "It's good to control the printing presses."

"You're keeping cures from people?" asked Adam. He didn't think it was possible, but the height of his unwitting hypocrisy increased at that moment. What began as a quest to stop a singular and massive genocide revealed murders for nearly a century. People needlessly dying of all forms of cancer, and other maladies that could have easily been prevented. Another stress point on the family had been revealed, but to what end if he couldn't prevent the desired outcome of Project Trinity? Adam spent the last decade gauging the pervasiveness of iniquity in the world. Not until he met Angela, was he able to fathom its intensity.

"Mass formation psychosis," said Sofia, staring across the room. "People are happy to take their monthly pill, pay the bill, and complain without resolution; ever." She turned to Angela. "And I suppose these pills, vaccines, flu shots are laced with something that hinders cognitive ability?"

The Nazi smiled. "Of course." Her grin grew more devious. "We've finally perfected our technology. These latest rounds of Covid vaccines were developed such that the third shot is the kill shot. You see, God does not control the trinity. We do."

Adam seethed but didn't show it. He believed even the woman that sat before him possessed the goodness to overcome her evil upbringing. It was his philosophy all humans were valuable, but he found it more difficult to seek out Angela's value. If she indeed had more information to offer, it was his job to extract it. At the very least, he needed to make amends for a career working for the likes of her and her bosses. "I must offer kudos. You've accomplished exactly what you were born to do." His compliment was meant to soften Angela's defense of information leading to the trigger for Project Trinity. He decided on coming from a different angle. "For the sake of academic exercise, if you were us, how would you counteract everything you've done in order for humanity to thrive?"

She sat back in her chair, smirked, and shook her head at Adam. But then her confidence burst forth. "There is no way for you to stop what is coming, so I might as well tell you. Simply reverse everything we've done. First, go back to the gold standard so that politicians are limited in their spending. Decentralize all markets and even governments so that no one controls them. Localize all decision-making apparatus. This can all be easily accomplished with the blockchain." She seemed lost in thought for a moment, and then she shrugged. "That Satoshi was the only one that ever truly got away from us. A currency built on a blockchain that is fixed in number and controlled by the decentralized home computers of citizens across the globe would eliminate the majority of our control mechanism. Life on earth could become stress-free." She tilted her head and asked, rhetorically, "I wonder if Atlantis had blockchain technology?"

She continued as if she were a professor scratching out notes on a white board. "Place value on the family. For humanity to succeed, you need families with a lot of children who know God. Finally, humans need to look upon one another based on their souls. Perspective needs to shift from the physical to the eternal. What was it MLK said? 'Judge a man by the content of his character?' I think that was the easiest task for our news media, pitting races against one another. Humans will embrace their physical selves and shun God all too easily. That was our greatest accomplishment—persuading humanity to focus on the fleeting orgasm and not that which is eternal. Focusing on all that is carnal can only bring eventual destruction and plays right into our plan."

"So, what does your post-apocalyptic world look like?" asked Adam.

Angela sat up straight and proud. "It will be glorious. Barely five hundred million people, just enough to maintain all of the fantastic resorts that have been built in the best locales. We'll be able to jet from grand airports without having to deal with the herd of animals around us."

"What about the children?" said Sofia. "Servants will need to reproduce in order to maintain your workforce. Won't population get out of control yet again?"

"We are the gods of earth. We have planned for that contingency." Immorality returned to her eyes. "Seventy-five percent of all children born will be consumed by us to maintain our immortality and sexual desires. Half of those will be aborted like veal. The stem cells we harvest from those fetuses will keep us perpetually young. We'll cheat death as long as possible. The other twenty-five percent will sustain the slave race population. Half of those will be tortured."

"Why?" Adam's inquiry rose to the level of a shout.

"Because children are the closest manifestation of God on earth." She glanced between the two agents. "You two are older and will admit you've been corrupted by the society we created. By torturing children, it is a direct assault on God. That pure, uncorrupted energy echoes in pain throughout the universe. It pains God, and we delight in that." She paused. "That is, at least until we perfect the singularity—when we can extract the soul and place it into a machine. At that time, we will trap all souls inside technology and control them for our many sadistic pleasures. We will have eternally separated those souls from knowing God." She put her hands together, as if in prayer and cocked her head to the side, imitating images of Mary from Christian iconography. "But just think of all the souls that will be freed into the universe before our plan reaches perfection." Stated benevolence was completely muted by sarcasm aimed at the very nature of God.

Adam heard enough. His face was hot with rage. He rolled his chair around the corner of the conference table, grabbed Angela's chair by its arms and turned her toward him. There was no way the old woman would disclose anything that would aid their mission of stopping the project that was decades in the making. He drew back a fist and swung it with every ounce of energy he could muster. He punched the evilest person he'd ever encountered in the throat. Her larynx disintegrated beneath his knuckles.

Her eyes grew large as she gasped for life-giving oxygen.

Adam was all too familiar experiencing life as it departed a person's eyes. He leaned in and whispered in Angela's ear. Her frightened eyes followed the movement of his head. "There is no way I'll allow you to live long enough to escape God's wrath through some technological singularity. You have a couple minutes before you die. My God is a forgiving one. If you repent now, maybe, just maybe, your soul can be saved and experience a productive and creative everlasting life. If not, I like to believe your soul will be ripped apart one long strand at a time, kind of like string cheese. Or, better yet, as if your soul is entering the event horizon of a black hole. That's the nature of the black sun you Nazis worship, isn't it? You'll experience massive pain for a thousand years, equal to the destruction you've caused here on earth. After that, nano particles of your soul will be shat into the universe like sewage by a gloriously cleansing quasar; never again to coalesce."

Angela thrashed in her chair. But as her time drew near, she settled into her fate. Moments later her eyes stared blankly and without life toward an unknown inevitability.

Adam and Sofia stood and moved toward the door. The Russian turned to her partner. "Didn't your mother ever tell you you're not supposed to strike a woman?"

"Yes, she did, but she never mentioned the pure evil that exists in the world." He looked at Sofia. "I'll call that a push."

Adam had just murdered the object of their mission without gaining any insight into what or who would trigger the mass genocide of June twenty-fourth; or how to prevent it. Dread soaked his soul at the realization seven billion humans were unknowingly dependent upon him and Sofia. He resolved to move forward in life and carry out his duty until the ultimate conclusion of either.

15

Three decades without a failed assignment. Within ten days, Adam committed two unsanctioned murders. Assassinating their captive was not his job, but he knew the risk of a compromised judicial system. Even military courts couldn't be trusted. Rudolf Hess had been allowed to live solely in Spandau prison from 1966 until his death by suicide in 1987. He lived to be 93 years old roaming palatial grounds. Evidence of how those who executed the elite's plans benefitted was available for the discerning mind. He couldn't risk the daughter of Hess' boss receiving the same leniency. Anger had never gotten the better of Adam. It had been trained out of him as a young, impetuous agent; at a time when he was filled with vim and vigor. Conscience rationalized it was the right thing to do.

Empathy never led to a successful outcome, but throughout his career he'd allowed himself to embrace a compassion for family members who lost loved ones by his hand. He questioned how much he should allow himself to feel for the innocent. Emotional struggles to understand who was truly blameless in all matters concerning terrorism across a global chessboard were ever-present. He bullshitted himself briefly. Mental debates raged. Eason would understand they weren't concerned with a family of terrorists, but the entire human family. Wouldn't he?

He'd killed Trinity. There was no reason for Eason not to put a bullet in his head for the mere satisfaction of eliminating a liability. Would the general's superiors sanction that course of action? Of course they would.

Adam's superiors had left him in the field as he aged out of the position. They just wanted someone to do their wet work for them. His only consolation was there appeared to be a different power structure. People he did not know were in charge of not only his movements but those of allied nations.

The CIA cocaine plane once again ferried Adam, Sofia, and Maritza to their destination. It was the reverse of their previous journey: Bariloche to Buenos Aires to Havana, where everyone gathered at their makeshift headquarters.

Kennedy and Reinier stayed behind to staff the Argentinian data center. Redundancies between that location and the one at Finca Vigia were required in order to build a robust network. The goal was a system that would span the globe, but only if they could prevent the greatest genocide in Earth's history.

Adam rehearsed bullshit story after bullshit story; excuse upon excuse. None of them really made sense. It was fear that caused him to think irrationally. You can't lie to an intelligence agency that has eyes and ears everywhere. As he conceived what he'd done, he understood his mind had regressed to a time when there was no responsibility, and he could get away with anything if he just gave his parents a shrug of the shoulders. Juvenile notions filled Adam with hope he could avoid reality.

The same car and the same driver picked the three up at Mariel Airport and transported them back toward Lookout Farm. Cuba was enchanting to some people, with its lush jungles, its massive green mountains, and the occasional colorfully painted shanty town. The only feeling these familiar sights elicited for Adam was stagnation. Sights he'd taken in days earlier spoke to the fact he'd accomplished nothing. It was a rare sensation for him.

He glanced toward his granddaughter on the other end of the back seat and snickered at the sight. Her obligatory AirPods were firmly planted in her ears, and her body undulated to the familiar beat of her existence. Nothing seemed to bother her. It was a strength Adam displayed throughout his career. His psychological quiver was devoid of the piercing arrows once drawn upon to ensure continued existence. Impending demise of humanity rendered tactical measures inert. It was all he'd known. Contained within the countenance of his granddaughter was a vision of the future. She represented humanity to the man, and he needed to do all in his capabilities to prevent Project Trinity from strategically altering the composition of civilization.

Adam's mind raced as the car sped down the long driveway toward the estate where his ultimate fate awaited. The farmhouse had been built in 1886 and was obviously made to last. Everything in today's society was disposable; even humanity. How had it come to this point?

Experienced men's hearts don't race. Adam's testosterone level had simply diminished with age. The catalogue of experiences in his life and career helped him stay centered. His soul had been molded and shaped into an energy that allowed him to approach any situation gracefully.

Facing Eason for the murder of Angela Braun presented a situation he'd never before encountered. Adam's heart pounded through his chest as he emerged from the car.

He lost track of where Sofia and Maritza were as the three drifted up the front steps to the house. His focus was on the confrontation awaiting inside. As they climbed and moved toward the front door, the three came together once again.

Walking through the foyer and past the formal living room, the group made their way toward the rear of the home. Entering the sitting room, Adam spied Eason's familiar bald head. The general sat with his back to the group of travelers.

Adam stopped, clinched his fist, and looked down at the knuckles that destroyed Trinity's larynx.

He didn't care to recognize the woman sitting across from his boss. She wore a wide brimmed hat and held her head down as if a movie star who didn't wish to be recognized. Shaking out his clenched fist, he once again moved toward inevitability.

Slowly, he raised his gaze toward the man who controlled how the rest of Adam's life played out. There was no other way to handle the situation than face it. He was so focused on his fate that he continued to ignore the woman on the sofa opposite Eason. He made his way around the far end of the couch and turned to face the general.

Surprisingly, the man stood, smiled, and offered a welcoming handshake. Adam reached out hesitantly, trying to convince himself the warm greeting was genuine. Finally, he clasped the general's hand firmly.

Eason kept up his smile as he gestured toward the guest seated on the adjacent couch. "I believe you know Mary Miller?"

The mere mention of her name brought forth a myriad of emotions within Adam's psyche: love, respect, compassion, curiosity.

His old friend stood to greet him. Goosebumps raised the hair on his arms. Adam had never been demonstrative with his feelings, but he closed the distance between them in two huge strides and threw his arms around the only person he knew whose strength eclipsed his own.

"What are you doing here?" he asked as he broke the embrace.

"Saving your ass, once again," Eason remarked, from behind the couple.

Adam did not respond. He smiled as he took the time to drink in the beauty of his friend. The ISIS gang rape and beating had taken a toll on her physical beauty, but the person he saw standing before him was stronger and conveyed peace. Her eyes remained bright, clear, and strong. "How's Lester Goldman doing?" He asked, referring to her husband.

"You know, Adam, I'm lucky to have such a wonderful husband who stood beside me. He provided strength when I needed it most." She laughed. "He wasn't really sure why you ignored us that night in Key West."

"Did you tell him?"

She shook her head. "Your secrets are safe with me."

Adam nodded his appreciation. "Are you okay?" he asked softly.

She nodded.

Adam lowered himself slowly on top of the coffee table positioned in front of the sofa.

Mary reclaimed her seat.

Adam continued to sit without another word spoken.

The woman sitting on the sofa across from him rejuvenated his spirit. Her physical manifestation was pleasing. It was her energy that emanated purely, and positively affected his state of mind. Five days of cumulative fatigue slowly drained from his body as he drew inspiration from the only human capable of instilling vitality into his weary soul. Youthful beauty faded and had been replaced by the seasoned face of the woman that sat before him.

Adam held himself responsible for placing her in harm's way. He'd endangered the two women he loved most. He questioned the obvious flaw in his character. For all of his desire to snuff out characters possessing malcontented energy, he feared his destructive nature infected humans possessing impeccable integrity. Mary's station within his universe gave her carte blanche to do or say whatever she wanted. He would defer to her wishes without question.

As the two sat oblivious to the others in the room, Maritza and Sofia took their seats next to Eason on the sofa across from the one Mary occupied.

General Eason broke the silence. "Maritza, you need to go to your room."

Hearing this broke Adam's trance. He quickly pivoted on the coffee table and spoke to his granddaughter. "You stay right there." He then turned again and faced the general. "She's a valuable asset—person. And she needs to understand what we're facing."

Eason held up his hands in surrender.

Seeking Trinity

The trance between Adam and Mary had been broken, so he moved to the spot on the sofa next to her, strategically but unconsciously aligning himself across from Eason. He shifted his gaze from Mary toward the general, seeking direction for their meeting.

Eason dropped his hands so that his left rested on his leg and the right on the arm of the sofa. "Mary has some…interesting news."

Adam shifted his attention from the general back toward his friend and smiled. He was ready to accept whatever she offered.

Mary scooted forward to the edge of the sofa. She looked all four members of her audience in their eyes. "My road to recovery was helped by having Lester in my life, the most wonderful husband and father to our children. But the overriding strength I felt came from something I'll call supernatural." She paused to allow the group to digest the small bites she offered.

Sofia and Maritza sat on the sofa on the other side of the coffee table. Both looked intently at the narrator; resolute to listen to everything she had to say.

"As I was being raped by those ISIS soldiers, I closed my eyes and imagined a disconnect between my physical self and my soul. I prayed to God he preserve that which would live eternally." It was a story replayed daily in her memory, but she paused to gather the right words. "It was as though I affected an astral projection. I found my consciousness floating above me and watching the entire rape take place. No longer did I feel the pain of the beating or the humiliation of the rape. As I floated in place, I sensed a light next to me—a being of light—a consciousness. It was—reassuring. There were no words spoken between us; we seemed to communicate telepathically. My luminous friend seemed masculine, warm, caring, and strong. He said I could call him, Mintaka."

Adam whispered under his breath, "the third star in the constellation of Orion's belt."

Mary nodded. She glanced over at Maritza, who began tapping rapidly on the screen of her phone.

Adam smiled. People who didn't know the seventeen-year-old might have thought she was playing a game. Adam knew she was following everything being said and supplementing it with online research.

"I felt a tremendous reassurance that everything was going to be okay," continued Mary. "I knew I would come out of it with a greater purpose. What I couldn't do was allow these men, and those who controlled them, to take away my value; to break my spirit. Our conversation was carried out between two energies, two consciousnesses. It was pervasive and palpable, so much so it seemed physical to me. It tingled my perception like goose-skin, even though I had no physical manifestation in the state I was in." She shrugged. "Maybe there is a greater relationship between our bodies and souls than I previously thought. These are thoughts I'll continue to assess for the rest of my life. I've never seen Mintaka, or had a similar experience since that day."

For the briefest moment, Adam lost all conscious thought of Angela Braun and the mess he'd created in Bariloche. Communication lines had been established between Buenos Aires and Finca Vigia. The information had even been shared with the Russian Embassy down the street from their location in Argentina. Everyone in their rebel alliance knew of his impetuous mistake, but Adam didn't care.

Mary turned to Adam. "When you killed Angela this morning, Mintaka reemerged. He said you were being called before the Council of Three, in the Antarctic."

Doubt returned to Adam's psyche. As he moved closer to universal truth, he encountered situations he was ill-prepared to manage. He attempted to cover his insecurity with humor. "Was he still warm and kind?"

Mary sighed. "He was definitely stern. When I got his message, I called Eason, and he sent a plane for me immediately. You see, it was General Eason who rescued me from the ISIS soldiers with a platoon of men under his command. We've kept in touch ever since."

Adam looked from Mary to Eason and back again. "I don't understand what this trip is supposed to accomplish."

Mary shook her head. "All I know is that his energy spoke to a sense this would be the last opportunity to intervene before the execution of the Trinity Project." She smiled. "Poor Lester. He thought I was having a seizure. He said I was sitting on the sofa at home and stopped talking. Unusual for me." She laughed briefly. "My eyes rolled back in my head, and I began to tremble. I guess the amount of energy it takes to project thoughts from Orion's Belt to New York tends to overtake one's ability to multitask."

Adam processed all that was said and reduced her presentation to a singular plan of action. "So, we're heading to the Antarctic?"

She shook her head. "No. Just you and Sofia. You were the only two there at the murder. Aside from that, I have to get home to Lester. He doesn't like it when I'm away. He fears for my safety. If I'm gone too long he asks a lot of questions." She smiled. "I'm so lucky to have someone who cares so much for my well-being."

Adam's words were serious but delivered in jest. "Are they going to execute us after some sham trial?"

Mary smiled at her dearest friend. "I've never read Mintaka's energy as vengeful. I did however get the sense the outcome of your meeting would affect all of humanity."

Adam sunk a little lower in his seat. "Grrreeeaaat."

16

The situation Adam faced in the Antarctic reminded him of one of his childhood heroes. Operation High Jump had been relegated to the dustbin of history; so much so the expedition led by Admiral Richard Byrd was considered more myth than factual military expedition. It had been so successful Byrd was made the youngest admiral in naval history. Rumors of him flying a full-sized aircraft through holes in the ice and exposing a cityscape beneath persisted among those who had little trust for history taught in schools.

As Adam stared through the plane's window his thoughts were of how his early education failed him. Only when he took personal responsibility had he excelled beyond his upbringing. Success of their mission would only be measured by the prosperity of humanity.

Contributions to society of great men like Byrd and Nikola Tesla had been muted or covered up for the sake of the elite's continued global slave model. Discoveries that would have easily benefitted all of humanity were hidden. No one possessing similar benevolence would be offered access to their research. Hope would never be offered for the benefit of humanity.

Adam's childhood research into Tesla instilled the understanding there was no real energy shortage. The basis of the universe is energy. It's ubiquitous. Societal dogmas of scarcity made it nearly impossible to imagine how well off the earth's population would be if everyone had access to free electricity. Adam smiled at the thought, choosing to believe that possibility still existed.

Seeking Trinity

Awareness of the positive thoughts he embraced in the midst of darkness closing in around him extended his smile. He'd only come to realize a career spent causing death manifested unto itself. Like an avalanche gaining momentum he found himself being hurled toward a global genocide. Those who'd played on the negative energy within his soul recruited him into the life of an assassin. Adam realized shifting to positive thoughts manifested positive outcomes. He needed to move quickly from his past. That must be his pitch to the council. It must be acknowledged there is a great deal of positive energy on earth; therefore, the human race should not be exterminated.

Greed of robber barons dragged positive people toward their evil ways with promises of wages and continued sustainability. Societal constructs were meant to trap unwitting participants into an apparatus that enriched the elites. Adam was all for fixing the system so everyone had an equal opportunity to compete. At his time of greatest despair, Adam felt his faith in humanity overpowering thoughts of failure.

The long flight offered a great deal of time to think how the current system could be changed for the betterment of humanity. The lives of seven billion humans hinged on his ability to effectively communicate with the council. Trinity offered a frank assessment during their conversation. Kennedy introduced the possibility of a currency controlled by the people. Adam felt decentralization via the blockchain was the most logical first step. It was a system of infallible governance. Identity theft would be a thing of the past. Corruptible flesh-peddling politicians could be replaced by machines. Currencies could no longer be inflated toward obsolescence. Many had postulated the final world war would be financial in nature. He wasn't a businessperson, but he understood that economic control of humanity emanated from hegemony over its currency. Authority over its creation resulted in a global slave race offering little resistance. Financial stress created compliant souls.

Muammar Gaddafi had been assassinated because of his plans for a pan-African gold-backed currency for the benefit of all Africans. The US secretary of state lied about weapons of mass destruction to disguise the true nature of the need to eliminate Saddam Hussein. The former CIA asset turned on his handlers and began accepting currencies other than the dollar for his country's oil. The dollar had been the central control point for the global elite. It had been defended at all costs, and Adam was culpable in those actions. Service to an unelected cabal of elite became clear when viewing the global chessboard from a universal perspective.

Humanity placed itself at its greatest disadvantage by allowing a central authority control over the issuance of its currency. The elite built wealth by printing money for themselves and converting it to precious metals and real estate; hard assets. At the same time, they destroyed the value of fiat currencies the average person worked hard to save. One of the most well-defined pieces of Adam's mosaic came when he realized it wasn't the value of his home going up, but the value of the currency its value was stated in declining. Trinity confirmed his assessment. Would the Council of Three listen to reason? Would they even care about currency and market issues? What would make them care about humanity?

Adam doubted he'd have the opportunity to express these thoughts. If he were one of the final five hundred million survivors, he would fight to implement such changes. Humanity's purpose must be shifted toward improving life on earth. The planet needed to become a welcoming place for all souls who found their way into a human existence.

He laughed at his own naïveté. A career spent ignorant of the true nature of the global power structure overtook his thoughts once again. With it came the understanding a fraction of new souls would be just as evil as those he hoped to eliminate. The fight of good versus evil was eternal.

Trinity offered proof humanity must become more active in the fight for its own survival. People had to educate themselves in economic matters. That was the driver of human enslavement. All markets, and all power must be decentralized. The twenty-first century provided the technology to accomplish access to global wealth by all humans. No more fake buys or sells meant to create peaks and valleys in prices so those who controlled markets could systematically scrape away the world's wealth. It was chaos upon which the elite relied. As long as they convinced humans they were the enemy of one another, focus was removed from those profiting from human energy. In all aspects of life, they created a population begging for stability that would never be provided.

 Adam's thoughts were unorganized at best. He resolved to the same approach he'd taken in conversations with Maritza. He would allow the discussion between him and the council to grow organically.

 The Boeing 707 suddenly banked to the right, and the intercom burst to life. "There are several holes in the ice we could fly through," explained the pilot. "But in order to do that, we'd have to dive straight toward earth. For you uninitiated, that might be pretty scary, so I'm going to take us through the hole in the Transantarctic Mountain Range. You can see it in the distance off the starboard side. That will offer a more level approach."

 Adam unbuckled his seatbelt and moved from the left side of the plane to the right. He took the empty window seat in front of Sofia. In the distance he saw a giant black hole in the side of a mountain. There was no way to ascertain whether the passage was broad enough to accommodate such a large plane. The vessel only carried three passengers. Experience spoke to the fact the plane had probably been fitted with specialized equipment to accomplish its task.

 Adam's heart pounded as he and Sofia watched the giant black patch grow larger as the plane approached what he conceived as an event horizon. He surveyed the terrain around the hole and began to wonder if the pilot really possessed the skill needed to pull this off. Was he suicidal? Was there even a hole there?

To Adam, the shape he was looking at could just as easily have been a dark patch of rock possessing the potential to rip apart and consume the plane. Visions of being reduced to thousands of small pieces and drifting down the side of the mountain like a cluster of dandelion spores tortured his soul. Relinquishing control was not a task he suffered gladly.

The pilot banked the plane to the right, adjusting its path for a direct approach. When they lost sight of the target Adam sat up and looked over the back of his seat at Sofia. She raised her eyebrows. There was nothing they could do to influence the fate that awaited them.

Adam moved back to his seat on the left side of the plane and buckled himself in for whatever occurred next. He pressed his head against the window, trying to achieve a better angle of sight upon the so-called hole in front of the aircraft.

The intercom crackled. "Make sure you don't sleep through this," said the pilot. "It's a sight few humans have witnessed."

Adam looked beyond the pilot and through the plane's windscreen. His vision was filled with what appeared to be a giant black wall. There were no contours or surface anomalies one would expect to see on a mountain face.

He glanced at Sofia and saw his concern reflected in her face.

Adam shifted his gaze through the small window to his left. Relief came when he saw rounded edges on the left side of the hole. Maybe the pilot wasn't crazy. His heart pounded as the black, rocky face of the inner wall of the entrance came into view. The plane entered the opening, and for a few brief moments, he wondered whether the mountain would simply swallow them or offer up the advanced civilization Mary promised.

As the plane continued on its glide path, the mountain gave way to openness. The most massive self-contained environment was there for Adam and Sofia to behold. And in the distance, an amazing cityscape. Rows of lighted windows, stacked one atop another, gave definition to the façades of several skyscrapers.

Together all of the buildings rivaled the size of many great cities of the surface world.

Sunlight piercing the holes in the ice to which the pilot referred streamed to searchlight like devices on the city floor. Rays were amplified toward millions of mirrors positioned under the icy ceiling. Ambient light was bright, soft, and unobtrusive. The underground environment was so expansive, large planes regularly flew in and out of the enclosed habitat as they would in any metropolitan area.

Adam looked up in amazement at areas where the overhead ice canopy wasn't thick enough to completely block the sun's rays. The light that penetrated the dome gave off a blue hue, just like any cold, clear, crisp winter sky.

"Come look at this city, Adam," Sofia called.

He unbuckled his seatbelt once again and moved to the seat in front of Sofia. He was amazed to see a metropolis that appeared to be the exact same cityscape as the one viewed from his window.

Adam returned to his seat and began to ponder the genesis of this subterranean civilization. Was this Atlantis? Had the city's location shifted to the South Pole via a tectonic anomaly thousands of years ago? Were its inhabitants aliens? If so, did that mean aliens were the original residents of Atlantis? How did they generate power? Did they have a nuclear technology that rivaled the sun's power only on a smaller scale? Were the sun's rays collected by the searchlights the source of their energy? An assistant professor at Virginia Tech discovered an anomaly whereby cosmic rays and neutrinos intermittently emanated from Antarctica. What did this concentration of high energy have to do with that phenomenon? All the right questions presented themselves, but he was incapable of conceiving answers.

Adam noted the lack of turbulence in the controlled environment. Absence of winds along with the relatively stable atmosphere offered a smooth approach and landing.

Just before touching down, Adam saw what appeared to be a port in the distance. There were no ships, but the conning tower of a submarine was visible.

Adam called to the pilot through the open cockpit door, "Could we have taken a submarine instead?"

The pilot nodded. "Yeah, but you've never really lived until you've flown through a mountain."

Adam smirked. "Asshole," he muttered.

The plane touched down and taxied to a stop. Adam didn't see any support personnel or machinery. He decided against asking any more questions. Heavy was his psyche as his thoughts shifted once again to the meeting with the Council of Three.

When the pilot opened the door, Adam noticed a stairwell seemed to have been magically placed next to the plane. "That's odd," he thought.

Sofia descended the stairs first.

Adam stopped at the top of the stairs. "Where do we go?"

The pilot shrugged and gestured to a spot beyond the nose of the plane. "Every person I've brought down here simply walks down that sidewalk."

Adam peered down the long footpath. It appeared to lead nowhere. It was flanked by large well-manicured green spaces. He descended the stairs and stopped next to Sofia. "Shall we?" he said, tossing his head toward the vanishing point of the sidewalk.

Without a word, the two began walking, moving toward the most important meeting in the history of humanity.

17

Adam and Sofia strolled casually, without knowledge of an ultimate destination. They were merely aimless pedestrians moving through the city as if it were any metropolitan area above sea level. Sofia conceived buildings whose architecture included familiar onion domes. Adam focused on those that resembled skyscrapers. Neither was in a particular hurry. There was a peaceful energy unlike anything Adam experienced walking through a strange American city. He judged the temperature to be in the high sixties. That must have been by design. A perfect temperature for one's choice of aerobic activity.

As they moved, Adam felt the kind of high he'd only experienced when running long distances. He wondered if the effect was created by an oxygen enriched atmosphere. He strode effortlessly down the sidewalk. Gravity in the subterranean metropolis affected the natural pressure of weight differently. Strides landed without shock. The couple glided across the surface.

Everything about the environment offered perfectly balanced comfort. Harmony between physical and ethereal blurred senses of reality. Balance within the surrounding environment offered the feeling they could fly from place to place if they put their minds to it. Save the feeling of moving effortlessly, the skyline and façades contained therein never appeared to grow closer as the couple moved.

Adam sensed Sofia felt the same dread he did about the council meeting. Before he could ask her about it, a third sentient being entered their collective thoughts. Their consciousnesses were offered assurance they would be made available when the time was right. Both embraced faith that what they were doing was right.

Adam looked at his Russian counterpart. "Everything here seems geared toward the ethereal. The buildings seem more like holograms than brick and mortar."

She nodded. "Yeah, it's like there's a perfect balance between mass and energy."

Feeling unusually peaceful, the couple continued walking. Adam felt no need to express himself verbally. Silence was not uncomfortable, and there were no proverbial elephants requiring discussion. Adam surmised his experience was rooted in the kind of peace offered by a truly settled soul.

As the couple continued down the sidewalk, Adam noticed Sofia gazing at something off to her right. Without a word, she left the sidewalk and moved across the expanse of green grass. He was at peace with their separation.

Curiosity abounded as his attention was suddenly drawn to the left. He moved across the large green space. He didn't know where he was going but was drawn by a powerful energy toward an eerily familiar objective. Its spirit spoke of a lost association.

In the distance Adam noticed a singular doorway. As he got closer, he recognized the entrance as being from his house on Southard Street in Key West. There were no stairs leading to a front porch and ultimately the door. It simply stood century atop a slightly elevated hill on the green grassy field. The top half of the door contained etched glass with the initial 'P.' Nothing of the remaining façade of his home was visible.

In his professional life, each time he'd made his way through a strange entrance, healthy apprehension coursed through his soul. But this time, he was consciously aware of trepidation's absence. The entry ahead projected peaceful energy.

Adam sorted through the logical progression of possibilities awaiting him. Then he embraced the bold and moved toward its threshold. He reached for the knob and walked through the entrance as if he were coming home from a day's work.

Materializing before him was a complete manifestation of his home. Intellectually, he knew it to be nothing more than an ethereal representation of his most comfortable environment.

Physical sensations exploded once he saw his most familiar companion. It had been nineteen months since her death, but he felt no sense of longing. It was as though their souls were linked across the universe. The time that passed since he'd last seen her was nonexistent.

She stood in the kitchen, next to the sink, as if dicing vegetables for dinner.

The ethereal quickly transformed into the physical. Goosebumps rose on his arms as he heard a familiar song coming from the kitchen. It was "Caribbean Blue," by Enya; a song they played while making love when their relationship was young. Music resonated ethereally and connected their souls once again. His feelings for his wife were just as fresh. His fingertips tingled, longing to hold her one last time.

His heart raced so fast he thought he'd pass out. Just as his consciousness was fading, he felt his body change from that of a physical mass to an otherworldly apparition. Adam experienced the astral projection Mary Miller spoke about. He reasoned in order to interact with Carolyn, he needed to leave his world and join hers. He was grateful for the opportunity.

After his transformation, Carolyn sensed his presence. She turned and greeted him with a smile. Both manifestations were ghost-like and undulated with pulses of energy that were their conscious beings. Without taking a single step, he moved closer, drawn to her as she glided toward him.

He reached for his wife, but was incapable of putting his arms around her. Frustration intensified as he was unable to enjoy her tactilely.

She smiled and motioned with her arm, leading him to the rear of the house. Through the sliding door he saw five childlike spirits playing around a pool in the back yard. They all appeared to be the same age, which struck Adam as odd. Nothing spoke to varying birth order, or differing rates of maturation. Souls appeared imprisoned in childhood; incapable of growth experienced during a human lifetime.

"Grandchildren?" he asked telepathically.

She shook her head and motioned with her luminous hand between their ethereal manifestations.

Adam became frustrated. He couldn't figure out what she was trying to communicate. Then he thought about the calendar he'd found after her death. Emotion burst forth and he experienced what it was like for his soul to weep. Personal energy weakened to the point he felt there was nothing left to accomplish in life. The pain of regret mixed with a new kind of pain—one he'd never felt before. It was the pain of not being able to show her that his love for her was stronger than ever. There was no embrace, only words. "The souls of our children?" he asked silently.

She bowed her head. "Yes."

Adam finally realized the manner in which the universe punished him for his for evil deeds. The anger he'd felt toward his wife's calendar dissipated. For the first time, Adam was certain their energies would continue to grow together eternally. Other opportunities to affect positive growth in the universe would present themselves in an assured future together. What he felt was confirmation their love for one another was pure.

Adam became extremely fatigued and was no longer able to muster the strength to exist in his energy-based manifestation. His wife's visage began to fade as he struggled one last time to embrace her. Physical affection was impossible. His longing dissipated just before he collapsed; exhausted.

He found himself laying on green grass; once again in human form. It was his flesh that once again caged his soul and separated him from the one he loved.

He lay there for several moments trying to understand all that happened. When there were no more epiphanies he struggled to stand. He realized the Southard Street home was gone, as was his wife. He found himself standing alone on the vast green scape.

Adam stared at the distant skyline before dropping his gaze to an isolated figure that moved toward him. Sofia.

They moved toward each other and came together once again on the sidewalk.

Adam was hesitant to express his vision. Doubts echoed in his mind whether his experience was real or based in an ethereal dream sparked by the unusual environment in which he found himself.

Adam had been changed by the experience. The coupling of his energy with that of his dead wife left him with a deep carnal desire for flesh. Only the Russian stood before him.

Without hesitation, he leaned forward, embraced Sofia, and gave her the softest, gentlest kiss he could muster. His desire was not about consumption of her flesh, but to combine their souls in an effort to embrace un-satiated and intense love for his wife. Internal feelings that accumulated without gratification since the time of her death pulsed and burst forth beyond self-control. It was all so misdirected, and he felt it in the awkward kiss.

When he loosened the embrace, Sofia asked, "Why did you do that?"

Sheepishly he shook his head. "I've always wanted to know what it was like to kiss Ingrid Bergman." He desperately wanted to change the subject. "Where did you go?"

For the woman who was the object of every man's lust, Adam's explanation appeared feeble, and was brushed aside. She preferred to discuss her experience and Sofia blurted out, "I saw my dead grandfather."

"Did you talk to him?"

"We communicated, but not with words."

"Did he mean a lot to you?"

"He is the man I most love. He was KGB long before it became a puppet agency of the elite."

It was an admission Adam's new partner never shared before. There had to be many more agents like the two of them in intelligence apparatuses all over the world. Men and women willing to die for their country coming to the realization all was not as it seemed. Neither counted on the supposed cadre of highly trained individuals coming to their aid.

    Without further discourse, the two continued their walk toward an unknown destination. Adam once again began to think about the task ahead. He continued to feel wholly unprepared; like a stooge moving toward universal diplomacy.

18

Like a hazy desert mirage, two chairs simply appeared on the sidewalk before them as they continued toward their unknown destination.

"Do you think we should sit down?" Adam asked.

Sofia looked between him and the apparitions in front of them. "I don't know. In Russia, kids play a game where they pull the chair from beneath you as you commit your weight to sitting down."

Adam nodded. "Yeah, American kids do the same thing." He thought momentarily. "Maybe this is the invitation to the meeting?"

They both sat, employing extreme caution to not commit weight into a free-fall. They looked at one another as they settled into place.

As their collective weight rested in the chairs, Adam and Sofia found themselves inside a white room. The walls, the floor, and the ceiling were all the same hue. Their eyes became irritated and watered. Both shifted their sights, darting back-and-forth seeking relief from glowing intensity. All boundaries that created their cell appeared to be nothing more than light. Adam felt as though the room was nothing more than an hallucination. He grasped for logic, but nothing seemed rational, and that further tested his sanity.

He and Sofia stood and wandered curiously about the room. The chairs disappeared behind them. As Adam moved toward what he perceived as a wall, increasing intensity of the barrier of light aggravated advancement, repelling his progress. No matter how powerful the obstacle, there seemed to be nothing material about it.

Concentrated energy prevented him from moving beyond the room's confines. When he returned to what he knew as the center of the room, the emotional discomfort of confinement subsided. He witnessed the same effect in Sofia. They resigned themselves to remain in the perceived middle of the room to simply mitigate discomfort.

"It seems something, or someone, wants us to stay in the center of the room," Sofia mentioned.

Adam shrugged. "They took our chairs away."

Unsure how to proceed, Adam and Sofia stood silently, occasionally glancing at each other.

Adam sensed a calming of the energy governing the room. When neither human seemingly possessed the desire to move away from center, two chairs reappeared next to them. The second manifestation of seats had no legs for support and seemed to hover above the floor. It was as though an unknown entity desired they show a higher level of trust. The absence of physical support didn't bother either attendee. They became comfortable in their ethereal environment.

Adam looked at Sofia and motioned with his hand for her to have a seat. Ever the skeptic, she lifted her leg, placed her foot on the chair's seat and pressed down to see if this apparition indeed offered support. It did.

Adam watched as Sofia turned her back toward the chair and slowly eased herself into it. Adam followed suit.

Having been conditioned as a kid, he couldn't shake the fear someone or something might pull the chair from under him as he sat. Instead, the chair not only accepted his weight but molded perfectly to his shape. It provided the most comfortable support of any chair he'd ever occupied. He looked at Sofia and saw by her reaction, she experienced the same relaxation of tension.

Adam sensed every thought in his mind was heard and recorded by the entities that controlled this underground city. There was really no reason for he and Sofia to not speak freely. "Do you think we can actually make a difference with the council?" he asked.

"Not if we can take Trinity at her word. She seemed to think mass genocide was a forgone conclusion."

"Well, I'm not gonna give up. I'm going down swinging. The elite's greatest weapon is fear. The universe is mathematical perfection. There is a constant state of balance. If they try to overwhelm us with negative energy, we must draw upon the positive in our world. I have to believe logic will win out."

"What will you say?"

Adam chuckled. "I know I just said that logic is the best weapon, but I guess I'm gonna have to read the room and see what emotion there is in order to put forth the best argument." He waited for her to respond. When she didn't, he asked, "Is there anything you think needs to be said?"

Before she could respond, the room they occupied morphed into what appeared to be the council's chambers. Its color changed from pure white to red, and conveyed malevolence.

Adam and Sofia remained in their respective chairs. A horseshoe shaped conference table surrounded them. Five individuals were spaced evenly around it, yet far apart from one another. They wore tuxedos and appeared human. Each of the five wore animal-head masks that hid their identity. Adam carefully examined each, noticing the heads were of goats and sheep and antelope; animals considered prey on earth. Elites appeared to cede control to a higher authority in this environment.

At the open end of the table, three figures sat upon three very large thrones. Their raised level conveyed dominance. The trio appeared human as well, yet the animals they chose to wear upon their heads represented the fiercest predators on earth—a gray wolf, a hawk, and a cheetah.

Adam's aggressive nature dictated he take the fight to the council. He stood, but when he tried to speak, he found he was unable to do so. Frustrated and concerned, he looked at Sofia, who seemed to be experiencing the same phenomenon.

A voice echoed in Adam's mind. He understood it clearly. He wasn't hearing sound with his ears. Someone on the council was communicating telepathically. He rubbed his head vigorously to sooth the tickling sensation in his brain. It was not painful but unusual and uncomfortable.

Sofia rubbed her head too. She seemed to be experiencing the same sensation.

"You will be allowed to speak only in response to our questions."

Sneers of derision echoed faintly in the back of Adam's mind; obviously from the five prey. He was undeterred and determined to assert himself. He concentrated intently, focusing energy on his pineal gland, which he believed was humanity's bridge between the physical and the ethereal—a connection to the universe. Ancient cultures spoke of the third eye possessed by all humans. At a time when the human race communed constantly with nature, an astute understanding of their place within the greater universe took shape. Adam deferred to their wisdom.

After several moments of intense concentration, he managed to muster his first telepathic utterance. *"Can you at least tell me how it is the three of you head the council?"*

Slowly, vibrations built inside his brain, and the answer arose. *"Each of us are from a different solar system. We all contributed members of our populations to create humanity on earth."*

"May I ask which stars?" His second query came more easily.

Their response was devoid of emotion. *"Alnitak. Alnilam. Mintaka."*

Satisfaction swelled within Adam's spirit. However tenuous the association, there seemed to be a connection between ancient structures across the globe and their relationship to Orion's belt; among them, the pyramids at Giza and Teotihuacan. His satisfaction dissipated when he realized humanity was most likely going to be done away with and reestablished by similar beings.

Adam focused his telepathy directly at Sofia. *"Can you hear what I'm hearing?"*

She nodded.

Adam desired to keep the connection between himself, Sofia and the three aliens. The five around the conference table seemed nothing more than spectators; almost disinterested in the purpose of the meeting. *"I would like to request that everyone in the council, including the spectators, remove their masks?"*

"We will not," the wolf's voice rang in Adam's mind near the level of a shout. He sat tall upon his throne and didn't bother acknowledging his two counterparts on the council.

Adam didn't wish to upset their hosts, but decided to press the issue further. *"But you have us at a disadvantage. I was always taught when you're negotiating with someone you should always look them in the eye. I want to be able to assess the quality of your soul. Besides, you can perceive all there is to our beings, physical and emotional."*

"There will be no negotiation."

Adam turned slowly and looked intently at five animal heads that sat around the conference table. Once he had gone full circle, he turned toward the thrones and rested his gaze upon the Council of Three. *"There are seven and a half billion human lives on earth. I would like to ask that, if your race has a conscience, and I believe it does if you are truly our progenitors, you give us the opportunity to prove humanity is united against the coming genocide."* Adam gestured toward the other five. *"And that these five people, whoever they may be, do not represent the human race."*

Simultaneously Sofia and Adam grabbed their heads and rubbed, trying desperately to alleviate the discomfort of the intense vibrations they felt.

Sofia was able to gather herself and looked toward the council. She saw something that intrigued her. The female agent reached over and grabbed her partner's arm.

The three aliens were removing their masks.

Adam watched in amazement as the faces of their captors came into view. Although the three beings came from separate solar systems, their countenances were quite similar. Their mouths and eyes were larger than those of humans, yet their noses were smaller. Creases in the upper and lower lips gave them a somewhat reptilian appearance. Their skin was iridescent.

Subconscious curiosity pushed Adam closer to the thrones. He moved slowly. It was obvious he possessed no ill intentions, and they allowed him to proceed. Adam ascended the first two of three steps to the middle throne. Slowly he reached out to touch the face of the being that occupied the seat. As the tips of his fingers moved closer to its skin, scales appeared and became much more prominent and protective. The skin lost its iridescent quality and became hardened, defensive.

Sensing the more confrontational stance from the alien, and having satisfied his curiosity, Adam stepped down and re-took his position next to Sofia. He turned toward the beings again. *"For millennia the families represented by these five individuals have destroyed and rewritten history so that humans would not know themselves, and to cover their ill deeds. They acted individually, destroying civilizations for their own benefit. At some point in history, they encountered one another. Since they all possessed the same level of malevolence, they decided to work together and divide the earth's resources among themselves. The coverup began with the destruction of the library at Alexandria, the destruction of many artifacts throughout the Middle East, and through false teachings in classrooms all across the world. They knew humanity's natural curiosity would drive them to seek answers. These families provided a bastardized connection to earth by putting forth false narratives and idols. I know for a fact your races are governed by the same Godly energy as we humans. You must provide humanity the opportunity to prove we can coexist and thrive. If allowed to do so, I am certain you will witness beauty beyond comprehension."*

"What is this Godly energy you speak of?" the cheetah asked.

For the first time, the tuxedoed, goat-headed human spoke harshly and with authority to the council heads. *"You three. You three are the only extraterrestrial Gods that are to be worshiped."*

Calmly, Adam turned and faced the goat. *"God is the consciousness of love that is ubiquitous in the universe. That coalescent energy doesn't need to be worshiped because it is inside all of us. It simply needs to be recognized in order to thrive."*

Adam heard the five chuckling their derision in the back of his mind.

The antelope-headed human spoke, hoping to suffocate any further discussion of God. *"We have shown our intent in the news, movies, television shows; any way we can communicate. In 1980, at the Georgia Guidestones, we even carved, in granite, the need to reduce the earth's population to five hundred million in order to sustain it. We can't continue with this experiment much longer. We need to start over now."*

Adam smiled at Sofia then turned and faced the Council of Three. *"I would like to put forth to the council the entity that we,"* he motioned between Sofia and himself, *"and the five prey disagree are indeed based in energy that is ubiquitous in our universe. Our God is a benevolent consciousness that offers everlasting life to those who embrace love and light. The global elite place their faith in all that is physical, because it is only matter that can be destroyed. Devastation is what drives them. The Godly end of the spectrum is filled with infinite love, universal truth, and creation. It's up to each individual human to live a Godly life. Embracing those characteristics and allowing our brothers and sisters to create their own value produces a sharing environment. Earth is not meant to be destroyed by those who are consumed by malevolent energy."* Adam motioned toward the five prey with a sweeping gesture. *"From their own mouths, they admit they reside on the evil end of the energy spectrum. They covet destruction, deception, and the persecution of their enemies."*

The rabbit-headed human stood and addressed the council. *"With all due respect to whomever this person is, we have broadcast our intent to the population of earth. Everyone knows the earth is overpopulated. Humans are murdering the earth through global warming. No one has offered contradictory evidence, so we have their consent. Every medium has been exploited. We've made movies about it. We put messages out in the news about it. A large percentage of the population is voluntarily being vaccinated. Hell, we even carved our intentions in granite. What else is it we need to do?"*

"*All contradictory evidence is suppressed. You own and control all media outlets. Every talking head you employ are false idols. Sports stars, news media, musicians, actors—they all act contrary to the good of the human race,*" Adam said. "*These elites have computer bots that deny and suppress humans who do dissent. Others are never given the opportunity to listen to alternative points of view. They've stacked the cards in their favor.*" Then he turned toward the council. The figure in the center, whose hawk head rested on the floor next to his throne, raised his hand. Suddenly, Adam experienced the same warmth he'd felt when Mary was relating her story of Mintaka. It calmed him.

"*My duty on the council is that of historian,*" he said. "*Throughout earth's history, there have been six prior human civilizations, all of which were destroyed upon request of the council of humans in one manner or another. I have researched the history you teach your children on Earth, and it is not a true accounting of the events on your planet.*"

Adam began to feel better about his chances of stopping the genocide. Maybe Mintaka realized the error of prior human eliminations. He'd helped Mary in her time of need. Maybe the alien was aware the confluence of events would lead to this confrontation; through Adam's association with Mary.

Mintaka continued. "*However, Dr. Phillips has spoken about honoring the wishes of his fellow citizens, and I cannot go against what I see as the consent of the human race.*"

Adam's heart sank.

Sofia sensed the emotion surging within him and took over the conversation. She tempered her argument with logic and reasoning. She knew that would be the only way to sway the council. "*If I may? To your point that human history has been falsified in order to manipulate our race, I would respectfully submit humans have not had a fair opportunity to make an informed decision. These five deal in falsehoods and manipulations. All we ask is the opportunity to bring universal truth to our planet.*"

Sofia looked at Adam. They both grinned with satisfaction, and then Adam gave her a fist bump. They may not win, but each was shooting their shot.

The Counsel of Three noticed this. The historian asked, "*You really do care for each other don't you?*"

"*Yes,*" they answered in unison and without hesitation.

Mintaka paused, looked toward his colleagues, and blinked. His eyelids closed vertically. He spoke directly to the other council members. "*I am inclined to believe they have the same strong desire for the others that populate their planet. I am willing to forgo the genocide.*"

Faces of the other two alien council members were studied, seeking any sign of contrition. Adam could find none. Once again, the skin of the council members shifted from the soft iridescent glow to their scaly, armor-like complexion. He didn't consider that a good sign. They appeared to be hardening their defenses. Adam turned toward the historian and noticed that his skin still exuded its faint luminosity. He hoped at least one member would stay compassionate to their cause.

The cheetah head council member spoke sternly. "*I am not willing to set aside relationships that have been developed over millennia for someone who only appears before us today.*"

Adam stood tall, lifted his chin, and looked the council-member directly in the eye. "*Have you been alive the entire time in which this relationship existed?*"

Proudly, he answered, "*Yes.*"

"*In your culture, is it the responsibility of individuals to educate themselves to the facts in every situation?*"

"*It is.*"

"*Can you show me the reference material you've used to come to the conclusion that humanity has consented to its fate?*"

"*Why it is this complete council.*" He made a sweeping gesture to include the other five. "*The eight of us have final authority in all matters on your planet. That authority is born of the fact we are the progenitors of life on your planet. All seven human civilizations.*"

Adam dropped his gaze to the red floor, shook his head, and chuckled. He witnessed the arrogance he feared going into the meeting. No scientific justification could be evidenced for the need of mass genocide. The aliens were proving themselves as intellectually inferior as the humans they seemed to despise. He couldn't shake away the thought this race to whom he pleaded were tantamount to schoolboys burning ants with a magnifying glass. It was all about control. Clarity ascended to a universal level. Few living beings aspired to spirituality.

He must continue with a logic they could understand. "*So, then you would agree that humanity, in all of its iterations, is a reflection of your own culture?*"

"*Of course.*"

"*Am I mistaken in my assessment that your culture is guided by a very hardened logic?*"

"*We live in a universe that is very harsh. There are entities spread throughout our galaxy and beyond that will do us harm if we allow it. It is incumbent upon us to assess their intentions and act swiftly.*"

"*So from where in your culture do you derive beauty?*"

"*Beauty? Explain.*"

Adam spread his hands. "*Do you have people who are considered artists and are allowed to feel and create? Do you ever take the time to stop and watch a sunset, whether it be on your* home planet or here on earth? Do you ever look beyond the physical manifestation of another individual to identify their souls as pure and establish an unbreakable connection between the two of you? The examples are infinite. Everyone embraces their own concept of beauty."

Without any sense of smugness, the council member responded. "We do have a connection. All entities in the universe are connected by what you refer to as a soul. That is why good attracts good, and bad attracts bad. It was your Einstein that defined it as quantum entanglement. That is why humanity must be eliminated once again. Their energy has descended into a base state. They've dragged each other into that abyss. High level thought is not present on earth."

"There is a saying we have on earth that, 'beauty is in the eye of the beholder.' There are two types of beauty, physical and emotional, or that which resides in our souls. Artists have the ability to capture that beauty in whatever medium they choose to express themselves. Exceptional artists can make their works soulful by capturing the universal energy that pulses within their subjects. Any patron who appreciates their work raises their level of consciousness beyond merely physical appreciation." Adam pointed to the five members of the council from earth. "These people for millennia have represented to you that humans are merely fleshy beings roaming the earth without purpose. I'm going to posit that Sofia and I can prove to you humanity is much more than that. Yes, we have physical flaws that send each of us along personally destructive paths that possess the potential to harm others. However, it's our human existence that's been given to us by the universal consciousness that allows each of us to learn and grow our souls. All we ask is to be given the opportunity to prove humanity possesses seven and a half billion souls, but we all have a common bond that is the Godly soul. Humanity exists on a level far above mere livestock as these five have represented to you."

The wolf spoke authoritatively. "*But we have seen no growth in your species. That's why we need to scrap it and begin anew.*"

Adam paused as his epiphany grew inside his conscious mind. "*It just dawned on me. Every human empire at its collapse placed an emphasis on gender. As Rome fell the most pressing argument was whether angels were male or female. Tell me, is your DNA made up of complimentary chromosomes that determine gender?*"

"*Of course not. We are not burdened by your need to mate in order to procreate.*" The cheetah-headed reptilian scoffed. "*That's why you are mere animals, rutting for pleasure.*"

Adam smiled. "*It makes sense that you don't have the twenty-third pairing that determines sex; that which binds humans ethereally. I'll posit to you that fact actually makes us a higher level being. Humans have the ability to seek beauty in others and that strengthens our bonds with one another. You are all simply adrift in the universe. You'll never be capable of creating or strengthening an emotional bond.*" He turned and swept his hand toward the five silent council members. "*It makes sense why these families have chosen to worship a single god with both male and female genitalia. They are attempting to create a bridge between your race and humanity. They are trying to put forth to you they are gods on earth like you. The truth is they are simply placating you. All they want is control. Your technology that allows for global genocide and gene editing and God only knows what else, offers just that. These same families have destroyed six previous iterations of humanity. Don't allow for a seventh.*"

The three reptilian lords shifted positions on their thrones. Each one scanned the faces of the five sub-members of the council. There wasn't a single word of protest. Silence acted as confirmation of Adam's theory.

"*Thank you for helping me,*" Adam doubled down. "*I understand now. Your civilization exists as logic dictates. There is no joy. There is no pain. You just exist. But what you need to* understand is that on Earth there's a great deal of joy, and there's a great deal of pain. You've never been allowed to witness it." Adam motioned with his right hand between he and Sofia. "*If you'll allow us, we can show you just how wonderful humanity is.*" He pointed to the others around the conference table. "*These five council-members, in whom you place all your trust, exist to maximize anguish felt by humans. They are about destruction for personal gain. They are about consumption and not creation. They are about manipulation versus free thought. If you allow the genocide to occur, I only hope you can hear and feel the agony of billions of innocent humans being released from their earthly bodies. When you understand that kind of pain, maybe you can then understand that unbridled joy is the opposite feeling. That's the only way the universe will remain in balance. These five people, whoever they may be, are telling you the only way to make Earth a better place is to eliminate seven billion people, referred to as weeds. I put forth to this council we can eliminate only ten thousand elites, and the remaining seven and a half billion will exist in perfect harmony.*"

Adam and Sofia again grabbed their heads and rubbed vigorously to alleviate the discomfort of the council-members speaking amongst themselves in their own language. The intensity of the conversation exacerbated the irritation.

Through the discomfort Adam was able to put forth one last thought for the council's consideration. "*Do not forget God's will.*"

Without any acknowledgment of Adam's plea, the leading members of the council concluded their conversation and shifted their attention back to Adam and Sofia.

The wolf spoke authoritatively. "*We have decided to give you the opportunity to prove to us humanity indeed does not consent to the actions of the five earthly members of this council. On July twenty-first, at seven twenty-one p.m., you will know our answer. You'll receive our message at the Georgia Guidestones then.*"

Without another word, the council room and all of its fixtures dissolved. Adam and Sofia once again found themselves alone in their white cell.

After a few seconds more, the room disappeared, and they found themselves standing on the long sidewalk facing the plane that brought them to the subterranean world. It stood in the distance, ready to ferry them away from the ancient metropolis.

19

Sofia and Adam were silent as they made their way onto the tarmac and toward the plane. Before climbing aboard, Adam stopped to take one last embracing look at the underground city.

Once the couple was inside and strapped in, the plane sped down the runway and rose into the subterranean sky. The pilot banked left and then right as he aimed for the hole in the mountain that delivered them above the earth's surface.

The first stop was Jorge Newberry Airport in Buenos Aires. Adam waited on the plane while Sofia went to check in with her station chief. There'd been little conversation on the plane. Each knew what Trinity said had been validated by the council.

Global media had been so profligate with spreading elite propaganda that humanity stopped seeking news from establishment networks. Humans understood the rosy picture delivered on the nightly news didn't jibe with a society in decline they witnessed every day.

There was no centralized mechanism for communicating earth's dire circumstances. All contact with humans was controlled by the elite. They were constantly monitored and tracked like so many cattle. How many needed to be split from the herd to satisfy the Council of Three? Adam failed to envision a manner in which to wake the global population to its ultimate fate. Hopefully, the communications experts at Finca Vigia and in Buenos Aires could come up with something effective. He wasn't sure it could be done.

The meeting had been intense. Adam's scientific mind knew it would take as much energy to dismantle the deep state apparatus as had gone into building it. Even if all of humanity listened, what would be the message? Prepare to die? There simply was not enough time for dire consequences to be communicated. Regardless, somehow the population's consciousness must be raised to a singular interest ensuring global preservation.

None of the possibilities he envisioned ended well. He'd always worked as a lone wolf. It was an easy job to excise people from the planet one at a time. He had to find a way to emancipate seven billion in one felled swoop.

The message was clear when Sofia returned to the plane. The SVR recalled her to Moscow. She feared her country had once again withdrawn from the global community and were developing a plan of their own. At a time when humanity must coalesce, she knew her war had a second front upon which to do battle.

Once they reached Havana, a Mig awaited Sofia to take her to Moscow. Adam bid adieu to his temporary partner and focused on those tasked with saving humanity; Eason, the team at Finca Vigia, the one in Buenos Aires; and his granddaughter. For the first time in decades, he felt as though he had people upon whom he could rely. It was a good team, but it paled in comparison with the deep state apparatus that spiderwebbed the globe.

The Nazis used the term *die spinne*, to describe their web of multiple rat lines that engulfed the globe and helped high-level World War II criminals escape. They lived out their days indoctrinating progeny and developing the soon-to-be executed plan. Their network was decades in the making. Adam and his group had weeks. He envisioned himself a global Paul Revere.

What manner of ringing bell could he possibly employ?

Having globe-trotted half the length of the western hemisphere in prior weeks, Adam and Maritza once again found themselves at home in Key West. The last leg of the trip was a short hop from Havana to the Conch Republic on a Learjet. Adam and Maritza took a Seven 7s cab from the airport to their home on Southard Street. It was a home Adam hoped his granddaughter would never have to leave.

Instability of circumstances contributed to his unsettled soul. As an older man, he recalled and took stock of the important moments in his childhood. He'd made plenty of poor decisions early in life, and taken one at a time, they seemed innocuous. When he reminisced, he saw how completely they laid out on his personal timeline. The result was an entire mosaic, cracked and imperfect. It was the way he'd led his life that brought him to this moment. He did not wish the same fate for his granddaughter. She needed stability. Humanity needed stability.

Adam and Maritza removed luggage from the trunk of the cab and schlepped it inside. The grandfather left his bags at the foot of the stairs and walked back to the kitchen to peruse the mail that had been left on the counter by a neighbor.

He laughed as he heard Maritza ascend the stairs banging her heavy bag against each step and occasionally a baluster. He chuckled again when he heard his granddaughter's bedroom door slam shut. For all she'd been through, she was still a teenager possessing a future filled with positive growth opportunities.

Adam made himself a vodka, club soda and lime juice cocktail, then carried it through the back door. He kicked off his shoes, settled onto the pool deck, and dangled his feet in the water. He thought of death-row inmates; those facing ultimate demise. Was it time for him to come up with his last wishes? What could he do? What should he do with the brief time remaining? He considered the possibility he was nano bot free.

Adam hadn't taken any injections his entire adult life. Fresh were memories of being jabbed in the ass by pediatricians. So traumatic the experience, he vividly recalled being told he was such a grown-up boy when the doctor was able to inject him in the arm instead.

He'd purposefully halted the advancement of invasive procedures touted as good for him. Trust had never been afforded anyone in his life beyond Carolyn. He could actually survive the coming genocide. Would Maritza? Without her he had no reason to live. Without him, she needed someone to watch over her. There were two people within his island realm he trusted would make sure his granddaughter would be looked after if he was no longer around. A contingency plan formed within his mind. Checking off the last item of personal business from his mental to-do list offered comfort Maritza would have the opportunity to prosper if left alone.

He just wanted everything to be normal for her. Thoughts of the mass genocide of seven billion people darted in and out of Adam's mind. He knew he couldn't get beyond it, but he wanted one more slice of time in which to experience something that might be considered ordinary. Whatever that might be, it had to be bold. He had to find a way to drown out the constantly echoing death screams in his psyche.

Adam drank the last of his skinny bitch and rattled the ice.

He stood and walked through the house, placing the tumbler on the kitchen counter as he passed by it.

Standing on the front porch, he texted Maritza his plans. He got an almost immediate response.

It was Saturday night, and Duval Jazz was packed with folks wearing cargo shorts and Hawaiian shirts. Live music offerings in Key West stood in stark contrast to the jazz clubs Adam frequented in New York. That night, Chrissy Fitzgerald was performing.

Adam spotted Chrissy's husband, Jack, seated at the end of the bar, and there seemed to be an empty barstool next to him.

As Adam walked the length of the bar, he and Jack made eye contact. Jack tilted his head toward the empty stool. After rounding the corner of the bar, Adam mounted the stool, and the two men shook hands.

Jack was a man of few words. He was a veterinarian and proud Ohio State Buckeye. He also ran the Dolphin Research Center in Marathon and had been gracious enough to allow Adam and Maritza the opportunity to swim with dolphins.

Encounters with sea-going mammals provided great joy and a much-needed respite from encounters with humans. Adam imagined dolphins experienced as much joy as he during their encounters. He theorized it was because two physical beings with great intellect were interacting without physical expectations. Is that what one feels when two souls with advanced intellect come together without flawed desires?

Encounters consisted of souls seeking pure and authentic interaction. Adam's encounter with Carolyn in the Antarctic spoke to eternity beyond flesh. Such associations became possible in his mind, but only if humanity could behold one other beyond physical encounters motivated by primitive desires.

The noise in the club all but eliminated casual conversation. Regardless, Adam asked the obligatory question of a football fan during the summer. "Are the Buckeyes going to win the National Championship this year?"

Jack folded his arms across his chest, drew down the corners of his mouth, gave Adam a side-eye, and nodded.

Adam smiled.

Both men turned to the stage when Chrissy was introduced. The crowd erupted in applause. She commanded an audience from all over the world. Tourists on repeat trips to the island made a point of attending her shows. Her talent was obvious to even the most amateur observer of music. What Adam appreciated most was her ability to rewrite the lyrics of popular songs into hysterical and topical compositions. From his layman's perspective, she was the Robin Williams of jazz singers.

Adam watched the show intently. Every move Chrissy made, every lyric she sang, he knew was repeatedly rehearsed by every member of the band so that each note would be performed without flaw. Her performance satiated his desire for exacting standards.

Sometimes images were projected onto the screen behind the band. It was all so well thought out. She was a settled soul working hard and giving of herself for the betterment of others. The interaction between humans was genuine.

Chrissy's set ended with her most popular rendition of "You're Nobody 'Til Somebody Loves You." After thanking her band and the audience, she hopped off the stage and snaked her way through the tables to the rear of the club where Jack waited. Her husband wore an expansive and proud grin on his face.

He hopped off his stool and gave her a kiss. "Great set, babe."

"Thanks," she said. Then she turned to Adam. "Hey, stranger. Haven't seen you in a while."

"Yeah, I've been jetting all over the place. Shot down to Antarctica for a quick trip." He knew Chrissy and Jack would take his comment as a joke.

They laughed. For the couple, the world wasn't ending; it was just Adam goofing around.

"Well, I'm glad you could make time to come see my show."

"I just love your talent, Chrissy. I've always appreciated music, but I've never known a musician until you."

"You're very kind, Adam. I can tell you it takes a lot of hard work."

He nodded and remarked pensively. "Any worthwhile task is worth the effort."

Chrissy gave him a dubious look. She knew something weighed on his mind but possessed no appetite for a philosophical discussion. "Welp, I'm glad you came to the show."

Of all the people he'd known who composed his life's mosaic, she possessed one of the few truly pure souls. He thought of her as the spiritual sister he never had. Should he inform her of the potential impending doom?

He sat up straight on his barstool and strengthened his resolve to shoulder the burden of imminent genocide alone. Experiences between humans, as with dolphins, are often better appreciated in silence. There was no need for him to scare friends.

But he had one more thought he needed to share. "I need to ask you two a favor."

Jack offered, "of course."

Adam looked from one to the other for a long moment. And then he spilled it. "If anything happens to me, can you check in on Maritza? She'll have the house on Southard and enough money to survive. She won't be a burden to you. She'll be eighteen in less than a year. It's just that Key West is filled with unsettled souls. She's strong, but I want to make sure she has parental figures in her life."

"Your words have an air of finality. I don't like that," Chrissy assessed. "You're not going to do anything stupid are you?"

"No. I'm actually motivated by doing what is right. It's just that no one never knows what the future holds."

"Of course we'll take care of Maritza," Jack insisted.

Adam completed the final task necessary in case of his demise coupled with his granddaughter's survival. He moved toward whatever eventuality awaited, without reservation.

20

An emergency meeting awaited the Russian agent who'd been called back to Moscow. Sofia's flight was aboard a MiG-35 leaving Havana. She donned a flight suit and occupied the rear seat. The single seat version allowed for additional fuel tanks. The need for her second seat dictated mid-air refueling. Splinter intelligence agencies worked well together. However, threatened by global genocide required retreat and assessment of that which was best for Russian citizens.

Dedication to her job was paramount. Sofia's record had been exemplary throughout her career. Never had she acted contrarily to rules set forth. Nothing could be found on her body in case of death that pointed to her being Russian.

After her and Adam's meeting with Angela Braun, Sofia retrieved a trinket from her room at the Buenos Aires embassy. It had been given to her by her KGB grandfather. He told her to, "remember, this represents the highest authority." She risked her career if ever her bosses found the piece in her luggage, or worse, on her person.

She rubbed her chest, above her heart. The pendant's absence was troubling. Being only a passenger on the fighter offered a level of comfort, but she was not without guardian.

Sofia leaned left into the canopy and looked forward into the cockpit. The pilot seemed adequately engaged and otherwise occupied. She shifted to the right and leaned against the curved glass. Struggling against the seat in front of her, she was eventually able to cross her right ankle over her left thigh. Reaching into her sock she removed her Russian Orthodox Cross.

Reverently, she held the cross between her right thumb and forefinger and gently stroked it. Feeling her leg numbing, she pushed her foot off her thigh and back onto the cramped cockpit floor. She rubbed the circulation vigorously into her leg.

Sofia smiled as she looked at the trinket once gain. It was the only thing that offered comfort during the most trying assignment of her career. She held it tightly in her grip for the remainder of the flight; consequences be damned.

A private airstrip served SVR headquarters in Yasenevo, Russia. Regardless of being trained to do that which was right for all of Russia, Sofia's thoughts centered on the potential global genocide. Never had there been such a challenge to the agency.

When the plane touched down, she peered through the canopy at SVR Headquarters in the distance. She hadn't been in the building for over five years; moving independently from assignment to assignment across the globe. The edifice offered comfort in trying times.

Energy of a prodigal daughter returning home permeated her flesh. Nothing about her career spoke to production. Elimination of those acting contrarily to the interests of her homeland was a skill in which she was proficient. No expense was spared in the furtherance of stated goals. All she'd been given had been spent on such pursuits.

The architect, the contractor, and all laborers who built the building she gazed upon could point to something physical. Pride of workmanship filled fellow Russians with a sense of accomplishment. Nothing she could speak of alerted fellow humans to her existence. She would die and memory of her would fade into generational abyss. Recollections of her stunning beauty may prolong her existence in the thoughts of remaining relatives. Nothing she sacrificed for the world would be remembered.

Sofia studied engineering at university. Her life's goal was to build. Someone who contributed to a thriving Russia. Her looks attracted those who recruited for intelligence services. Men who used women as mere prostitutes to glean information from unsuspecting and libido driven politicians wrested control of her future. Pride was present in her sense of self-awareness. She'd done her job well and acted above reproach: as much as a spy was capable.

A divide had been constructed between her and the family she'd known as an adolescent. Unsure of their circumstances, it was easier to act as though their existence had been eliminated from her life. Memories faded with each passing year.

As the plane taxied off the runway and toward the open hanger, Sofia replaced her cross in the sock from where she removed it. Final thoughts of family were pushed aside in favor of the meeting into which she walked. She understood the collective work with Adam, General Eason, and Reinier would be subjugated to the Russian intelligence service's wishes.

As the plane jerked to a stop, and before any outside agents exerted influence, Sofia called forth between the seat in front of her and the canopy. "Dimitry, how long have we known each other?"

The pilot turned to speak into the gap between the two. "Maybe ten years."

Russian bluntness cast aside decorum. "If I told you my life was in danger, would you fly me away from here?"

"Oof. I don't know Sofia. I like my job. I like my life better."

"Okay, if I told you both our lives were in danger would you do it?"

The pilot's head bobbed between a nod and a shake. "I suppose." He opened the canopy.

Ground crew pushed a metal set of stairs against the fuselage.

Dimitry stood and looked at Sofia. "Is my life in danger?"
She smiled. "I'll let you know in an hour."

As maintenance personnel climbed the stairs, she rushed her final sentence. "If you see me again today, we need to leave…

quickly. Make sure the plane is fueled and ready to go." She climbed onto the stair apparatus.

Dimitry called to her. "Where will we go?"

She turned back. "Florida…USA."

The pilot exclaimed to himself. "Oof. USA. I will be dead."

Sofia was driven in luxury from the airstrip to the SVR building. She sat in the back of the Mercedes sedan stroking its leather seat. The smell conveyed quality. Again, workmanship and pride in a product confronted the fragile psyche of a person who had no tangible career of which to speak. If she could only talk about the many times she'd saved military personnel from certain death, or politicians from assassination. She resigned herself to the understanding the world needs spies, and she was good at what she did.

Entering the building she traversed the biometric and retinal scans before making her way to the bank of elevators and its lone express carriage that propelled her to the top floor.

Walking through the outer offices and into the conference room, she was met by the same cadre of officials who'd been at the embassy in Buenos Aires.

"Come in. Sit down," Major Medvedev commanded.

Sofia moved to an open chair at the end of the long table where the handful of men sat. Once seated, she sat silently awaiting instructions.

"We've all read your report from the Antarctic. That's a very interesting experience you had."

"Yes, sir."

"Have you ever delved into our World War II archives brought over from the defunct KGB?"

"No, sir."

"Hitler visited the Antarctic many times. The US sent Admirable Byrd on an expedition after the war to ascertain why." The old man smiled. "And now you know."

"You've known about the aliens and the Council of Three all along?"

The old man shook his head. "We've had our suspicions, but not until your exemplary work, did we have confirmation."

"And that of Adam Phillips."

"Yes. Whatever." The major dismissed the American.

Sofia leaned forward in her chair. "What are we going to do to stop the genocide?"

Medvedev scratched his right eyebrow. "What can we do? It was an immense failure on the part of American intelligence to allow this plan to be executed to near perfection."

"And we have no culpability?"

The major drew the corners of his mouth downward. "There may have been a few lapses on our part."

"Like trusting the Americans," Ambassador Chemyenko quipped.

Sofia failed to appreciate the humor. "So, what is Russia's stance?"

"It's the same as when Hitler killed twenty-seven million of our country's citizens. We will use every weapon in our arsenal to destroy the progenitors of global genocide."

"You're going to nuke the world?" She looked individually at all of the faces staring blankly at her. "Wouldn't we all be guilty of the same thing they're attempting? Hell, we don't even know if they'll be successful, and then *we* become the perpetrators of global genocide."

"Our aim will not be global. We will take out the massive castles these five families own and control…including the White House. We will track their movements, and make sure we get them no matter what hole they crawl into. Tactical nukes will be employed to minimize collateral damage."

Sofia sensed promises of excising only elites was meant to placate her. "Do you not have faith in humanity?"

"I have faith in most Russians. The west is lost in their profligate and pornographic lifestyles. Only that which provides orgasms advances their awareness."

She shook her head. "No. There are good people who struggle in order to instill in their children and grandchildren a sense of family. We all must embrace an eternity in which we'll be forever intertwined." She looked at all the old men around the table. "There are good souls that will be traumatized with your nuclear devices. Their souls will become disoriented in the greater universe. Once they re-form into physical beings, whether on earth or elsewhere, you will have created more unsettled souls who will lead destructive lives. Evil will have to be dealt with at an ever-increasing rate. Where does it end?"

Silence choked the atmosphere. Sofia expressed herself as passionately as stoic Russians allowed. She could tell by the looks on the countenances staring back at her, the decision had been made and was final. Why did they call her back? It would have been easier to allow her to perish with humanity.

Sofia's skin tingled and became goose-like. She realized there was at least one person at the conference table who wanted her to stop their plan of mutually assured destruction. But who?

She looked each man in the face once more. Jowly stares without discernable expression stared back. Then her epiphany grew. These men were ultimately controlled by the five families represented in meeting with the Council of Three. They all wanted her to know the gravity of circumstances. It wasn't the five families that were being targeted. It was most of humanity. They were the fail-safe. The men she worked for had been compromised by promises of life for them and their families.

Sofia stood, and scanned each face as she declared, "I'm going home to prepare for your eventuality."

The men all looked at one another. Grins were muted but discernable. They knew she'd been called to action. Their greatest weapon had been deployed without overt instruction.

"Sofia," General Ivanof called. The agent turned and faced the men again. "Our nuclear arsenal hasn't been tested recently. I'd hate for our missiles to fail."

Slow was the insight contained in his message. Her superiors intent was opposite that which she feared. Sofia realized it was her superiors' way of telling her they trusted she could stop the global genocide, and they would take care of the potential nuclear annihilation ordered by the cabal on their end.

The agent quietly yet quickly made her way down the express elevator, across the lobby of the SVR building, and into the warm Russian afternoon. Sofia knew she was on her own, and needed to drag Dimitry with her.

She jogged beyond the courtyard and across service roads behind the building before stepping foot onto the tarmac.

A clear path to the hanger was negotiated swiftly. Once inside, she ran directly to the plane that brought her home. Nowhere was the pilot to be found. She stopped at the fuselage and scanned three hundred and sixty degrees of the hanger. In the far corner was a door to a small logistics office. She ran toward it. Stopping sharply, she looked through the glass window and saw Dimitry asleep on a cot in the office's corner.

She tried to open the door, but it was locked. Rapping on the glass grew increasingly desperate as she saw he was not awakening.

Nearly a minute of constant knocking finally resulted in the MiG-35 pilot stirring.

"What?" he asked, sleepily agitated.

"We have to go. Get up," she yelled through the door.

Dimitry sat at the edge of the cot, rubbing his eyes. "Okay. Give me a second."

"Has the plane been refueled?"

"Yeeessss," he answered, groggily.

"Well come on then."

The pilot stood and stretched. His nap was only an hour, but exhaustion took him quickly into REM sleep. He was alert enough to make their situation humorous. "I feel like I've been drugged by the KGB."

Sofia smiled. She knew then her pilot was embracing the task ahead.

"Where are we going?"

"To Florida. USA"

Dimitry stopped and looked sharply at his counterpart through the glass window. "I just flew from Havana." He thought momentarily. "This is not sanctioned by the Kremlin, is it?"

Sofia's smile was beguiling. It had been used like a weapon throughout her career. Men found her irresistible, and her smile proved the tip of the spear that unlocked pleasures of the flesh. Some encounters were physical, and some only promissory.

Dimitry looked at his coconspirator. He waged his right index finger at her. "That won't work on me. Did you forget, I'm gay?"

A stern countenance replaced her pleasing expression. "In that case, let's go."

Both passengers still donned flight suits worn on the trip home. Necessary measures were taken to evacuate bowels and bladders. Energy bars were stowed in zippered pockets and bottles of water in a small duffle. Sofia had no doubt the bureaucrats she just left would provide a refueling tanker half-way through their trip. It was imperative they leave quickly to avoid grounding of all aircraft by the cabal.

As the two climbed the metal stairway to the plane, Dimitry used humor to deal with exhaustion. He sang loudly, Neil Diamond's song, America. "Far, we've been traveling far. Without a home, but not without a star."

Sofia laughed. "I know you're tired, but don't forget, I've been trained on this plane too. We can take shifts."

"Okay, Sofia," he replied, sarcastically.

21

    The prospect of making the transition from his physical manifestation to its ethereal grounded Adam. All influences that affected him throughout life became present in his consciousness. That which impacted his development at an early age became contemporary and vivid. Memories long forgotten stimulated the man to action.

    Economic despair seemed purposeful in Panama City. The tiny hamlet offered a stark contrast between the haves and have nots. The area was littered with smaller municipalities. Leaders guarded fiefdoms against talk of consolidation. No politician was willing to give away supplemental income in areas offering few possibilities for success.

    Adam's family struggled daily to make ends meet. Siblings were out of step with the man who embraced the concept of a greater universe. Brothers and sisters wallowed in physical stimuli and drug usage. Instead of joining them, Adam's resolve strengthened to prove that which was imperceptible. Desire for truth beyond forced circumstances set his life's path toward that of a loner.

    Intensity of corporal punishment meted out regularly stoked the desire to eliminate all that was evil. Adam's only conception was to eliminate physical manifestations of those using corruption for personal gain. Basic inequality witnessed as a child drove the adult. Escaping the small panhandle community only offered the illusion of advancement. For all questions regarding life, he never applied critical logic to the circumstances around global power networks. He went about his job as would a tradesman, completing task upon task without question. For all of his theoretical proofs of the eternal, the man settled into a global perspective.

Panama City's blue-collar environment instilled a work ethic in the young boy that proved invaluable. A man in his mid-fifties looked back on his brief time there during boyhood with an awareness of how it still impacted his life. In order for his granddaughter to have a complete picture of the man he'd become, she must behold the town for herself.

The weeks offered by the aliens passed without complete disbursement of an adequate message to save humanity. There were communication specialists at Finca Vigia and Buenos Aires better suited to global communications. Sofia and Dimitry took up residence at NAS Key West to aid in the global effort directed by General Eason. Only days remained before the July 21st deadline.

Like an item ticked from a to-do list, Adam wanted Maritza's soul to experience that which made him the man he was. A trip to the town which set his life's path seemed the only adequate way to communicate such a contrast in luxury she'd grown accustomed.

Inexplicably, Adam's time in the Antarctic manifested in a long gray beard he chose to keep. His mind marked the time spent there in hours. Its environment seemed to manifest wisdom. Adam cherished the beard as the sign of a sage. Maybe it was the changed visage that motivated Eason to bless the sojourn to the panhandle.

The members of the Finca Vigia team sent communications along every underground network to which they had access. Adam knew his skillset was useless in this situation. He must trust others to plant and nurture seeds that would give rise to a significant percentage of the population connecting Godlike energies. It would act as a shield against that which was emanant. It was hoped its intensity registered within the consciousnesses of the Council of Three.

Adam and Maritza reserved a condominium at Edgewater Beach Resort. It was the nicest resort of which he was aware. It had been built only a few years before his departure from town thirty years earlier.

He couldn't help finding humor in the realization that, in his return to the circumstances from which he'd escaped, he was arriving in a private jet that transported drugs all over the Southeast. His reasons for leaving were numerous, including his failed relationship with Kathy. Another was the palpable sense of despair among citizens who were purposefully kept at an economic disadvantage. The irony was that in his attempt to escape one desperate lifestyle, he'd stumbled headlong into another.

As he drove the rental car through the streets of Panama City Beach, he witnessed visual reminders of emotional despair he'd left behind. Misery manifested itself in the landscape, which seemed haphazard and barely functional. Buildings of varying style and age were cluttered together and offered no settled vision for eyes observing incongruity. Clapboard walls shifted and exposed decaying interiors next to newly built retail shopping centers. Any semblance of zoning or planning on the part of city fathers had been abandoned decades earlier. It was apparent to discerning eyes, standards had little to do with the issuance of building permits. In one block, a four-unit townhome building was built next to a thirty-minute oil change business.

Maritza slept in the passenger's seat. Adam shook his head at the realization of how easily she relaxed in an upright position. He'd brought her here to see his hometown and fought the urge to wake her. They'd been through a lot, and he knew she was exhausted. He let her rest.

He thought sarcastically about the glorious vision it must be to walk out of your front door every morning and see an oil change building right next door. He pondered the psychological effects of constantly beholding an unnaturally scattered environment.

Desperate landscapes flowed freely past the window of the rental car. Economic disparity changed little in the prior thirty years. He thought about the city council's desperate need for tax revenue and the blatant corruption and kickbacks that must have occurred. It was apparent any source of revenue was deemed acceptable in order to maintain individual territories. Neither seemed absolute, but there had to be at least a combination thereof. In a town offering little opportunity, political graft offered those achieving office opportunities few others possessed. Those in control used power for personal benefit. The result wasn't pretty.

Adam recalled unsettling rumors about the city's leaders from his young adult life. It didn't take much of a leap to understand how the love of money corrupts. UnGodly energy soaked into his soul. It saturated him during adolescence and caused the experienced man anguish. Panama City was a microcosm of all that was wrong in the world.

"Oh my God, Papa. Are you sure we didn't enter some wormhole and end up in Guatemala City or some other Third World country?" Maritza asked. She rubbed the sleep from her eyes as if the visions she beheld would vanish upon second sighting.

Adam laughed. His granddaughter's criticism, though well-founded, stung his fragile psyche. No matter how far he'd run or how hard he tried to break his emotional shackles, this town was still in his blood. There was something basic about its existence. There was goodness in most of the town's residents. He longed for pure connections experienced only during childhood. When people possess little of material significance, they value that which comes from within.

"I can't believe I came back to this town after leaving Stanford and Palo Alto." He shook his head. "Just look at the landscape. Buildings sit unoccupied and falling apart. If there is a business operating at a location, they don't even take the care to mow the small slivers of grass in their parking lot." He shook his head more emphatically. "It's a mindset of failure. I find myself wondering how deeply into my soul it soaked, and how it negatively affected me, sending me on a trajectory of destruction."

Maritza thought about her grandfather's assertion. "Why did you come back?"

"Well, it was only for nine months. For whatever reason I was drawn back to that which had instilled the energy of destruction onto which I so tightly clung." He thought about the intensity of the positive energy Kathy taught him to embrace, and how she helped close the early chapters of his life. Not wishing to discuss her further, he only offered, "I guess I just had loose ends to tie up."

The tour of the town continued for hours through various business districts and residential areas. There were three homes Adam lived in as a kid. His family environment was never rooted in stability. Moves were made quickly and without explanation.

The first house they visited had been built by his grandparents after World War II and was fittingly located on MacArthur Drive. Sue and Gran, as they were known, were married for seventy-one years. They were the only couple in his family that set an example of love possessing eternally binding energy.

As the rental car sat idling in front of the house, Adam observed the structure that hadn't changed since he'd last seen it. The physicist in him knew there was energy in those walls that had been positively affected by the lives and love of his grandparents. That kind of dedication had been passed down to his mother, two aunts, and an uncle. It was the love instilled in him by his mother that gave him a glimpse of the purity that could be inherent in all human relationships. Kathy reawakened that emotion, and Carolyn set it on its eternal path.

The second stop brought them to the small community of Saint Andrews. It had been a small fishing village in the early twentieth century, but the eventual sprawl by the larger Panama City engulfed the tiny hamlet. It was only recognizable as its own distinct community by those old enough to remember when it flourished on its own.

Adam's paternal grandparents' house was on Drake Avenue. He sat in amazement looking at the house that had been consumed by passion vine. The energy in the home was darker. Padlocks on bedroom doors secured rooms from the outside. As a boy, Adam stared at them contemplating the implications of the environment his father was forced to endure.

Memories of his father dissipated like fog in a hurricane as he shifted his thoughts to his paternal grandmother, Lilly Pearl Currenton Phillips. A smile engulfed his face as he thought of the woman. She'd loved the child in a demonstrative manner more than anyone ever had. He recalled as a youngster walking through the front door at which he stared. She'd spent most of her time in the kitchen at the back of the house. But if loved ones came to the door, she hurried through the house, wiping her hands on a dish towel, and gathered them into an embrace. She did this for Adam and all of his cousins. She gave the kind of love that lasted eternally. The calculating, cynical old man took great pleasure in the memory of his grandmother.

Adam lived in two other homes in town during adolescence. One in the Forest Park neighborhood; the other in Lynn Haven. Each of these locations only offered the opportunity to stare in stunned silence. Neither home existed beyond remaining slabs. Both had been taken down to the foundation by hurricane Michael in 2018. Apropos for the man who knew neither structure supported a loving environment.

Memories remained intact. Children of all races lived and played together in these neighborhoods. There were occasional scuffles between teens simply trying to assert individuality. Adam sat in an idling rental car thinking of those humans who'd been so close to one another. Had friends discarded relationships with one another as easily as he had? Did each go separate ways, seeking that which was right for them. The nature of isolation contributed to the lack of lifelong friends. Adam understood early in his life he simply didn't know how to be a friend.

Grandfather and granddaughter sat in an idling rental car, staring at his third childhood home. It was the second that'd been taken down to its foundation. The void in space creating by the home's disappearance filled his consciousness with an equally voluminous epiphany; homes built without love never last.

"Maritza, I have just one more thing to say, and then we'll head toward the condo. I've spoken to you about the energy in our bodies that is our soul, and that there is love in all of us. Some choose to ignore it for fleeting pleasures. Humans who foster loving feelings toward one another truly exist as God wants us. God is in all of us. Many people choose to deny God's existence, and those who do are denying themselves. That plays right into the hands of evildoers."

His granddaughter didn't quite understand. "How can they deny themselves when they are alive?"

Adam nodded. "Yes, they are alive but they're doing unGodly things, as I did during my entire career. This town propelled me toward that existence that was so divergent from the Godly. But by denying my eternal soul I almost lost the opportunity to exist forever with your grandmother."

"And me."

He smiled. "And you."

Adam shifted the car into DRIVE and began the trip to what would be their home for the next few days. The trip along memory lane had taken the pair from the airport, down Highway 98 along the beaches. Crossing Hathaway Bridge set their path along a route resembling an imperfect lariat. Through Saint Andrews and into the Cove. Shifting north into Lynn Haven and then looping back toward the bridge that set their path toward the beach once again.

Adam lived his life at blinding speed, never taking time to stop and reminisce. The time was right for him to examine his entire life. It was clear to him his mother tried to bring love into a home otherwise consumed by anger and hatred. Like a bed of embers that's been smoldering for decades, the self-hate he was schooled to accept consumed and limited him. It was not difficult to see from where he summoned the anger to execute rivals.

Nurturing acrimony paved the way for a lifetime of allowing others to manipulate his actions. His life had been a psyop, and he the victim. His mental mosaic was there in the present to examine every cracked and imperfect piece.

Adam maneuvered the car toward their beach destination and the condo at Edgewater Beach Resort. He glanced over at his granddaughter and smiled, realizing her soul was more mature than his had been at the same age. She'd given him many reasons to not worry. No matter her strength, he would still protect her until his dying breath.

He drove the rental car through the 15th Street business district. He surveyed the effects of decades of boom-and-bust economic cycles. A large number of businesses had been shuttered and buildings collapsed into foundations. As with the global community, the desperate nature of his hometown became more difficult to process knowing economic hardships seemed to be intentionally inflicted upon citizens. The result was hopelessness among residents. Being made to live in squalor prevented individuals from conceiving universal possibilities.

Adam believed strongly it was up to each local community to protect its citizens from such a broad reach of external governmental bodies. He'd been complicit in the elimination of opposition to such overreach. It was all done in the name of nation building. Propaganda to which he subscribed. Establishing global control networks was what his life's work accomplished.

In one block, Maritza gasped at the dilapidated buildings she saw. "Papa, how did this place become so desperate?"

"I'm not sure. My guess is it's a combination of an apathetic citizenry and a handful of wealthy families who know very well how to make things better for everybody but refused to do so in order to protect their own wealth."

"Can it possibly be made better?"

"Of course it can, sweetie."

"But how?"

"First and foremost, this town, and every town, needs to go back to Common Law and get away from the BAR system. The legal system we operate under is the British Acceptance Registry. It's designed to protect the interests of the elite by stifling individual expression in favor of the corporation...the landed gentry, so to speak. That's why Shakespeare wrote, 'The first thing we do, let's kill all the lawyers.' Regulations are dogmatically imposed to keep individuals from taking market share through innovation. At its very worst it's designed to take young black men from society and keep them in prison for minor offenses. Any community...humanity will only be strongest when everyone is participating in its success. The British crown has always been the greatest enslaver of humanity; it's just more subversive now. The five elite families are the most racist people on the planet. They loathe humanity and broadcast their hate-filled energy through global media outlets. It soaks into all of our souls, but only those strong in Godly energy can resist." Adam paused. "And that's why we need to take back control of everything. This town's economy doesn't need to be dependent on state or national politicians funding and controlling major dollar flows into the community. It's like controlling the flow of crack cocaine into a community. That kind of control only breeds corruption and its resultant destruction. We can be a part of Florida and the United States while at the same time being completely independent. There will be some pain to endure, but in the long run this town will be so much better off, and its residents will become resilient." He paused. "And if these residents are truly committed to making their community as strong as possible, they should issue their own gold backed currency. The blockchain would make that an easily accomplished goal, and one that residents could easily verify wasn't being manipulated to the benefit of any elite."

"It's sounds like you've thought a lot about this."

Her grandfather nodded. "I've had over thirty years of a career to gather evidence and consider the changes I would make."

He paused. "I've done a lot of bad in my life, Maritza. I need to do something Uber-good in order to make my time on earth worthy of continued existence."

As the car reached the apex of Hathaway Bridge, Adam pulled onto the shoulder of the road. He maneuvered so closely to the wall that Maritza couldn't have opened her door if she'd needed. "As much shit is I give the residents of this hamlet, I'm going to prove what good people they are." He gestured toward her phone. "Do you have a stopwatch on that?"

Maritza scoffed. "Of course I do." She pulled up the app and showed it to him.

Adam nodded and turned on the car's hazard lights. "Start the timer."

She pressed START and held the phone on her left knee and watched the timer advance. Adam was content to sit in silence and allow his thesis to play out.

His gaze drifted across the bay to a familiar point. On the landmass that jutted into the bay sat a beautiful, grand, and ostentatious white home.

Adam spoke as if to himself. "When I was a teenager, my father came to me and asked if I would pay for my cousin's abortion."

"Why?"

"I was the only one in our extended family who saved the money I worked hard to earn, and my uncle and aunt lived paycheck to paycheck, as did my parents."

"So, you were being made responsible for a pregnancy you had no part of?" Maritza shifted in her seat to face her grandfather. "Is that why you felt it was okay to be party to an abortion?" She paused. "That's messed up, Papa."

Adam nodded. "That's the kind of energy I was forced to exist in as a kid."

Maritza looked at her grandfather, uncertain whether she needed to say anything further. She did. "That certainly explains the last six weeks we've spent together."

He nodded once again. "When you're brought up to not value your own existence, you bullshit yourself into thinking a fetus is nothing more than a clump of cells—a mole that can be excised in order to enhance the beauty of a face…metaphorically speaking. There's a reason the souls given to children are brought to earth. The universe provides the opportunity to strengthen our souls throughout life. Children are the purest manifestation of life —a blank slate, so to speak. Part of that life is offering adults the opportunity to set young lives on successful paths. When we abort a child, it causes an imbalance in the universe. Adults in need of personal growth are rendered childless. There is a soul returned to the universe without the benefit of a life well spent…without the opportunity for growth. Adults are left to languish. We end up with the mess we're in today. Everyone is discombobulated except those who hate and wish to destroy the earth in order to gain control." He paused. "That's the only, truly, unforgivable murder I've committed, Maritza."

"So what does that mean? Do you think you're going to hell?"

Adam chuckled. "All I can do now is what I feel is right, embrace Godly energy, and hope God's mercy is part of that hue of positive energy." He turned toward his granddaughter. "You have to teach your children the kind of evil that's on the planet and always will be. We need to teach our children embracing positive energy and having love for all humanity doesn't make them weak. On the contrary, it will prepare them to fight their own battles. We need rugged individuals who know how to work together to eradicate those constantly spreading the seeds of evil in our otherwise blissful Garden of Eden."

"Do you really believe humanity can get to that point?"

"Yes," he said, emphatically. "If we continue to teach each subsequent generation how to be good and strong and love each other, but also to know how to recognize evil when it attempts to usurp personal value, we'll get there." Adam settled into the moment. "If we as a human race can get past July 21st, then I think we'll have proven ourselves worthy. That will give me a lot of hope."

Nothing was said between the two for several seconds. Automobiles passed speedily on the bridge as they sat parked on its shoulder.

"Can you see the white house on that point?" Asked Adam.

Maritza nodded. "Yeah."

"That's where Kathy lives."

"Should we go say hello?"

Adam laughed uncomfortably. "No. Her husband wouldn't appreciate that."

"She really meant a lot to you, didn't she?"

He nodded, and then looked to his granddaughter. "You'll have lovers, some will be in your life for the briefest of times. It's okay to carry them with you in your heart and soul. Only when you lust for their memory does it rise to the level of emotional infidelity."

"Have you ever lusted after Kathy's memory?"

Adam shook his head. "No. She's always been more like a guardian angel." He stroked his beard again.

"Where did you go when you left Buenos Aires?"

"Why?"

"Because you were gone for maybe twenty-four hours, and you come back with a long gray beard, like Rasputin."

He looked at the date on his watch and realized he had five days to complete the task assigned by the Council of Three. "You know about the subterranean metropolis in the Antarctic where Mary Miller set up our meeting with Mintaka. The energy down there seemed to transcend what we know as time. For some reason it manifested a long gray beard for me."

"You look like a Rabbi. All you need is a Yarmulke."

Adam smiled and nodded slowly. "It takes a lot more than a single religion to show your devotion to God."

Maritza's full intellect was on display as she drew their conversation to its only point of emphasis. "So, what was the task given to you by the aliens?"

"We have to prove to them the human race does not consent to the cabal's desire for a mass genocide in the name of saving earth. We have to raise our level of connection to reflect pure and unadulterated love. All the hidden messages the elite put in front of us daily are seen by them and the aliens as conscious consent." Adam looked sympathetically at his granddaughter. "We have until July 21st to show them a sign at the Georgia Guidestones, or they'll allow humanity's annihilation to proceed."

"How are you going to do that?"

Adam shook his head slowly. "I have no idea, sweetie."

There were many times over the years Adam joked about his granddaughter being so mature due to the fact she lived with her grandfather. She directed the conversation to not only a happier thought but a logical conclusion. "What did you and Kathy talk about that was so life changing?"

"Sweetie, those were all conversations we had when we were laying naked next to one another in bed, and I just don't know how to present it to you without feeling weird."

"Awe, come on! We've had some pretty brutal conversations in the last month. You can tell me what she said."

"I don't need to tell you. I've already shown you by being the man that I am. She helped set me on that course." He thought a little longer, knowing his granddaughter deserved a better explanation. "In a nutshell, she helped me understand that, although we view that which drives us as being protected by our bodies, in reality, we allow people to snip off pieces of our soul for their own use. Just like the guy who jacked-off while admiring her beauty. He was taking something from her without her knowledge."

"Yeah, I get it."

"Life is filled with remora that just want to glom onto something bigger than themselves in order to survive. Don't let that be you. Don't give your value away to anyone. We need to become more like the lion. We need to embrace the concept of pride. And that's exactly what I did, only I did it for the wrong reasons and the wrong people."

Maritza had grown to understand the man her grandfather was, more than any time in her life. "We're going to make that right, Papa."

Adam smiled. "My mistake was that I took orders from people who operate in the shadows. People I never looked in the eye. I never had the opportunity to assess the quality of their souls. I guess that's the reason I felt compelled to come here. All power should rest within each individual human. We all need to work hard and come together to solve the problems of our local communities. If I could only give you a single piece of advice, I would have to break it into two parts. It's all based on being the best human possible. First, embrace positive energy and develop relationships with other humans who do the same. Second, understand your place in the universe. View the earth from a universal perspective and understand how pieces are moved on the chessboard of life. I truly believe that if all of humanity did that, we could shun the evildoers by not participating in their games of control. Let them eat one another instead of feeding off of us."

Adam fell silent for nearly a minute. "That is if humanity survives July 21st."

Maritza didn't seem interested in her grandfather's trepidation. She continued with the issue at hand. "Do you honestly believe the aliens will allow the plan to proceed?" The juvenile notion bereft of the conception of death tinged her interrogatory. She embraced her own vitality and was incapable of comprehending its end.

Adam nodded. He couldn't bring himself to verbalize what he saw as inevitable.

"There must be something we can do to stop it."

Her grandfather smiled. "You know, through this entire adventure, we've been chasing the concept of a trinity. One thing

I've learned is that anybody can bastardize any concept for their own purposes."

Adam looked at his granddaughter. "I choose to focus on the trinity that exists between us. It's undeniable that our DNAs are completely different from one another. But ever since you became a part of our family, I've sensed an otherworldly connection to you. Even though you and I don't have the physical father-daughter connection, it's our souls that will bind us together for all eternity, and I'm convinced our souls have intersected at other times in history. Maybe God brought us together now so that our lives could be most positively impactful?"

Maritza smiled. "Be careful. You're speaking positively about your existence." She continued jesting. "The universe might not recognize you."

Adam offered a muted smile in response. His granddaughter was right. Without a word, he returned his gaze to a spot across the brackish waters of the bay; focusing on Kathy's house. The structure sat majestically upon the point.

Trance-like, Adam did not see an eighteen-wheel tractor-trailer combination approaching the car. Displaced air pushed from the truck's side as it sped past rocked the rental car violently, but Adam maintained his focus. "I believe the trinity is composed of two earthly beings connected by Godly energy. That's my conception of the trinity." He chuckled. "It may reflect my naïveté, but believing in the trinity this way does not contradict the Jewish shituf or the shirk in Islam. I'm not ascribing partners to God in my trinity. The trinity is all about humanity's interaction with Godly energy in a manner that ensures the success of the human race. I also believe those connections continue after death."

Maritza glanced at her phone. "Would you sacrifice everything you had to ensure humanity's survival?"

Her grandfather smiled. "Everything except my relationship with you…our personal trinity…gladly."

Maritza leaned across the seat and embraced her grandfather.

Seeking Trinity

As their grip on one another was released, Adam drew in a deep breath. "What we humans need to grasp is that all of our souls are connected. Visualize the universe as an ocean of water, and we live in that ocean."

"Like SpongeBob?"

"Sure," he replied not understanding the reference. "Physicists believe the universe is swimming in dark matter. We can't see it, but it provides an ocean through which all things are connected. Although, I prefer to think of it as light matter because that is how we are connected to all that is Godly and good." He paused. "There's a molecule in nature called Carbon 60. Its framework resembles a soccer ball. It is known as the best lubricant because its formation has proven indestructible. Two masses, no matter their size, can't destroy this molecule. They'll only glide past one another. That's how I envision humanity's billions of trinities connecting. If humans can stitch together their souls in the same manner as the pentagons and hexagons that make up a soccer ball, we can create an infallible structure of bliss that surrounds the globe." Adam glanced at his granddaughter. He nodded his head. "You know what? I'm going to stop being so damned technical and show a little faith. If humanity successfully creates the Flower of Life, it will be a mesh of humanity that is strong and enduring. Any time evil tried to destroy us, our infallible strength will hold tightly, and humanity will remain in a perpetual state of bliss."

He smiled at his granddaughter, knowing he'd communicated the best way he knew how, the visualization of a successful human race. Adam chuckled. "Back to the technical. If I were to express my trinity as a formula, it would be C_2E_g, two carbon life forms bound by Godly energy. At least that's how I envision humanity stitching together the ubiquitous fabric of light matter that permeates the universe. The human family existing in peace will proliferate through the ether without obstacle. I have never felt as much a part of the human race as I have since becoming your grandfather. Our bond is that strong. We're proof two humans who don't share a DNA can care for one another."

"Dad was adopted too."

"Yes, and he taught me to embrace the same human relationship."

Maritza challenged her grandfather yet again, extending the metaphor to the global community. "Yes, but what can we do?"

Adam tried to mask his frustration when he spoke. "I don't know." He looked in his rearview mirror and saw a pickup truck slowing to a stop behind him. Its hazard lights were on. "But we're about to see if my thesis proves correct."

A man in blue jeans and a green flannel shirt emerged from the vehicle. He walked briskly, toward Adam, cautious of the traffic approaching behind him.

Adam rolled down his window.

If the man's choice of vehicle and clothing weren't enough of a clue, when he spoke, Adam knew he was a local. "Y'all okay?"

"We're fine," Adam answered.

"She just quit on you?"

Adam smiled and shook his head. "No."

The man took stock of Adam and Maritza.

Adam witnessed the man's awareness grow. The differences between the two of them in terms of age and skin color were stark.

Finally, the stranger's gaze settled on Maritza. "Missy, are you okay?"

Adam tried for a moment to suppress his smile, but then gave up. A total stranger was willing to put himself in harm's way to protect an adolescent Latina; a complete stranger. His faith in humanity simply needed to be refreshed.

"I'm fine," said Maritza with a bright smile.

The man glanced at Adam, still not sure he understood the situation. "Well, if you're not broke down…" He seemed to be asking for Adam to make it make sense. "I mean, it's awful dangerous sittin' on top of this bridge like you're doing."

Adam looked around as if only then noticing where he was. "Gosh, I guess you're right." He turned the key in the ignition and the car's engine roared to life. "Okay. Thanks for checking on us. Very kind."

The stranger swatted the compliment away with both hands. "Naw, no problem, man. Just glad you're okay."

Adam let a bit of his hometown creep into his diction. "'Preciate it," he said. He shifted the car into DRIVE and waved through the window at the man. "Take 'er easy."

Adam stepped on the gas and merged into traffic. "You can stop that timer now."

Maritza looked at her phone and tapped the screen. "Eight minutes and eighteen seconds. Did your thesis prove out?"

Adam smiled and nodded. "There is good in humanity. Ninety-nine percent of the people in this town, and in the world, possess the same good heart as the man who stopped to help you. The secret to a successful life is knowing it's there and allowing it to express itself."

22

Adam and Maritza settled into their Edgewater Beach condominium. It was a two-bedroom unit. The long hallway bifurcated the sleeping quarters until it opened onto a large living room and kitchen that overlooked the Gulf of Mexico. Life had become a blur, and finally they remained in place that offered serenity for a few days. He took the Council of Three at their word nothing would occur until the 21st. Although two of the three seemed to possess the same malevolent energy as the earthly families who controlled humanity; all seemed to value a promise made.

The weight of the world rested on Adam's shoulders, and he had no idea how to make the Council of Three understand humanity was united. He didn't want to be a savior. That was no role for anyone other than Jesus. He'd reached a point in his life all he desired was to be one human linked to all others working toward a growing and prosperous universe.

Adam participated in daily conference calls between Eason and the other heads of the surreptitious intelligence apparatus. Pleas to major media outlets were rejected. Not a single talking head bucked a system paying them millions. Vapid creatures only skilled in reading eloquently from teleprompters chose to side with overlords. None seemed to possess critical thinking skills to question whether they'd be spiritually culpable in the global genocide.

Some smaller, independent outlets broadcast the rebel's message, but would it be believed by the small audiences they reached?

Thoughts of his wife were ever-present. The intensity with which she existed in his soul grew and pulsed since their ethereal reunion. Regardless of their interaction in the Antarctic, questions remained. Was she in a heavenly place; a place of infinite truth? Did she know he was nothing more than an assassin; a mere implement of a conspiracy? She'd been the only woman who'd supported him blindly, and her support grew stronger as their bodies grew weaker with age. If she knew the atrocities he'd caused throughout their time together, would her soul be receptive to another union during an ensuing reality? Of all that lay ahead of him, condemnation was his greatest fear. It possessed the potential to affect his ageless spirit.

Adam smelled the salt air as he sat on the condo's patio. A storm the prior week brought ashore tons of seaweed that had been bulldozed into piles near sea oat laden dunes. Rank odor of rotting vegetation drifted in and out of his consciousness. The less than comfortable environment did not chase him inside. This may be the last time he could enjoy such a view.

Names and faces of those he'd murdered during his life scrolled through his consciousness. Surely some were bad and deserved their ultimate fate. Doubts about Eason's true intent drifted through his mind. At his own peril, he'd trusted fully those he shouldn't. That would never happen again. Throughout his career, all Adam asked of God was that his life be protected; yet he found himself cast in the role of savior.

And then came the epiphany. God waited to give him this mission. Adam had been born at the exact moment in time to complete this undertaking many decades later. As if by divine intervention, the burden that weighed on his psyche lifted. He was ready.

He pushed away the vodka and club soda that rested on the balcony table. Looking at the exquisite sunset his eyes drifted downward to see his more beautiful granddaughter sitting at the water's edge. Her normally tightly bound long dark hair had been set free and blew in the wind; like tentacles engaging a thousand points of energy.

Adam concentrated his thoughts on her beautiful energy and uttered a prayer. "Please give me the wisdom and the words to bring people together. Please God give me the strength to do enough to persuade the council. Please, God, don't allow my efforts to be in vain. And please don't allow my prior sins to detract from the task at hand. My desire for humanity's well-being is sincere."

Unbeknownst to her grandfather, Maritza received a text from Mintaka. It contained a brief message: "True history must be maintained." Attached was a video of Adam and Sofia's presentation to the council. The teenager had no idea why he would be contacting her. She listened to the debriefing after her grandfather and Sofia returned from the subterranean metropolis. Taking all of their conversations together, she gleaned one of the three aliens that comprised the council possessed benevolence toward humanity. Her grandfather's imploring her to find the good in humanity grew and extended to all energy across the universe. Mintaka knew Maritza to be one who possessed the skills to build a coalition of consensus.

During their days at the condo, if Maritza wasn't on the beach, she was hold up in her bedroom. She knew her grandfather had grown accustomed to this pattern of behavior. But when she was in her bedroom, Maritza combined the video sent by Mintaka with several she'd surreptitiously taken of Adam during their many conversations. She felt there was no better way to communicate a single man's sincere love for humanity than through the use of his own words. Spreading them across social media was the only way the teenager knew to utilize global friendships. Shared amplification of the message she'd constructed was hoped for by the teenager who'd grown up befriending people around the world.

One of Maritza's favorite challenges was editing videos. She cut the various raw videos into singular thoughts and then brought them together a thousand different ways until she was satisfied. The finished product was uploaded on every platform to which she had access. The internet had been her connection to the world, and it became electric with the message.

The result was a work that showed a very human and concerned grandfather—a man whose actions were for the benefit of all.

She spent hours each night meditating at the water's edge. It was the positive energy her grandfather spoke of she wished to project into the universe without interference from steel skeletons, concrete walls, and glass sliders. She'd uploaded her finished video to every manner of social media on the third night of their week's stay. The message attached to the end of the broadcast was simple: It was time to engage in person and not via electronic media. If the world's youth desired to change the world; it was time. Young people couldn't rely on grandparents or even parents. The success of humanity always rested upon successive generations.

23

It was the morning Adam dreaded most; July 21st. He sat on the balcony of his condo watching the sky turn from black to dark blue to blue as the sun rose above the horizon. The star's path from behind the building would make its way to an anticipated beautiful setting beyond gulf waters. Adam witnessed his last such ending the evening before.

He opened Google Maps on his phone and had it plot the route to the Georgia Guidestones. It would take them seven hours by car. He continued to debate whether or not to take Maritza with him. He settled on being next to her when the evil elite sent the signal from their satellites triggering mass extinction. Maybe proximity upon death would ensure their being together eternally. A rare smile crossed his face as he thought of being reunited with his wife and son. Joy faded upon recognition that selfish desires meant devastation for humanity.

There were good souls on earth. Even those who'd made the most horrendous of choices weren't beyond redemption. Adam focused on the energy trapped inside his flawed human existence. Desperately he attempted to ensure its hue was that of a soul acceptable by God. He feared all of his deeds prevented a reunion with Carolyn. Had the aliens in the Antarctic teased him with the couple's brief reunion? He continued to question his future.

Adam visualized an eternal existence as brilliant white. Pure. Without darkness to soak away universal truth, infinite love, and eternal happiness. Those were the attributes he wished to embody and carry beyond life into eternity. He wondered if end-of-life thoughts were daunting for all possessing questionable character; or was it just him? Was the dark star; the galaxy's black hole awaiting his arrival?

Suddenly, Adam saw two F-22 Raptors from Tyndall Air Force Base before he heard them as they streaked loudly across the sky heading from south to north. Their speed had to be close to Mach one. Odd. Training flights were normally conducted at much lower speeds. Regardless, Adam loved the visceral experience of the engines' power and appreciated the men and women who flew those aircraft. He smiled at the consideration two pilots were merely showing off. He'd witnessed all manner of aggressive chest-thumping from military personnel during his career. It offered a visual representation of strength when he felt weakest.

He went back to checking the map on his phone but was distracted again. Two more F-22s streaked past the condo. There must have been some intense exercise going on. Those kinds of drills were normally performed over the Gulf and not around populated areas.

Eight more jets streaked past, two by two. Then it dawned on Adam. The elites' plan had been initiated. Dread came over him. He stood and leaned over the balcony railing, looking for other approaching jets. His shoulders initially slumped, but he stood tall and erect as he fully appreciated it was time to face tyranny.

He ran through the living room and down the hall toward Maritza's bedroom at the front of the condo. Before he got there, he heard the incoming text chime on his phone. The message from Sofia read, "Come out front."

As he approached Maritza's room, he heard and felt nonstop thumping repeatedly against the front door.

Adam knocked on Maritza's door. "Come on. It's going to take us seven hours to drive there, and we'll need to stop to eat and pee."

"Just a sec," she called out.

For seventeen-year-old Maritza, "a sec" could be thirty-seconds or a half hour. "Okay, I'm going to check something out front. Be right back."

He opened the front door tentatively, then stepped outside onto the front walkway. He stood at the railing watching an Army UH-1Y Venom helicopter as it landed across the street on the resort's par three golf course.

"Holy crap," said Maritza, who'd stepped outside and sidled up to her grandfather. "Ariana Grande, eat your heart out."

Adam looked exhaustedly at his granddaughter. "Come on."

The two ran to the stairs at the end of the walkway then hurried down the six flights and out into the parking lot. They crossed State Road 30A using the pedestrian overpass. As they reached the highpoint of the bridge, Adam saw Sofia waiting at the other end, using her entire body to wave them over.

When he reached the Russian agent, Adam asked, "How is it that you Russians have access to everything that's sacred to our security?"

"Believe me, the SVR is sharing all of our information, too."

Adam shook his head incredulously as the three jogged to the helicopter. He chuckled when he saw the looks of the three golfers stranded on the eleventh tee; waiting for the chopper to take off. Vacationers occupying patios lining the fairway for a quiet breakfast lay across tables holding down plates, cups, and morning papers.

Once everyone was buckled into their seats, the pilot revved the engines for liftoff.

The helicopter became airborne and the pilot thrust the ship forward, reaching a high rate of speed in no time. Adam watched through the window as the cars and buildings of the community gave way to purposefully planted forests of pine trees. A little farther on, he saw the assets and land owned by the St. Stephens

Company, another visual reminder of the concentration of wealth in this part of the world.

Sofia handed Adam a set of headphones and motioned for him to wear them.

As soon as he had them in place, she started talking. "You won't believe what is happening at the Guidestones. SVR headquarters is tracking satellite imagery of a mass migration of humanity to North Georgia."

"Your Georgia?"

She shook her head and pointed to the northeast. "The other Georgia. Millions of people have come together. All over the world, they chartered aircraft to make the trip. Commercial airlines couldn't handle the traffic. Pilots gladly worked overtime flying from the four corners of the globe and back several times, using their skills to save humanity. This migration cuts across all religions—Christians, Jews, Muslims, Russian Orthodox…It's beautiful."

She fell silent, then she reached out and gave Adam's long gray beard a tug. "You decided to keep that, huh?"

"Yeah. I think it makes me look like Ras-Pew-Ton." He purposefully mispronounced the name of the Tsarina's consort, just to tease Sofia a bit.

Sofia's face hardened. "Ras-Poo-Tin," she said, enunciating each syllable carefully.

Adam couldn't subdue his smirk.

"Ha, ha," she said. "Very funny. Besides, I don't see what's so special about him. Why do you Americans worship him? He simply had the ear of the Tsarina."

"It's not that he was some mystic or had magical powers. It was the fact Russian assassins poisoned him, shot him in the back of the head, threw him into a frozen river, and still couldn't kill him. That speaks to American strength and individualism."

"Well, my friend, you're about to witness the collective strength of global individualism," Sofia said.

The pilot maneuvered the craft to an altitude deemed safe for top speed and spoke into the microphone that extended from his helmet to a point in front of his mouth. The noise of the rotors were cancelled by everyone's headphones. "Hang on." He thrust the ship forward.

Adam knew the Venom's top speed was three hundred kilometers per hour, and assumed the pilot was pushing as hard as he could to get them to their destination as quickly as possible. He stared out the window at the many small towns he'd traveled through as a kid. Landmarks looked different from up here, but were unmistakable.

Adam spied the circle created by Alabama Highway 210 in Dothan in its entirety. Just west was Andalusia, Alabama, and the Veterans' Memorial. It was easy to pick out because it was another obelisk modeled after the Washington Monument. Adam pondered the ramifications of seeing another such replica in Buenos Aires. Knowing there was energy in all mass, he hoped it would bode well for their journey.

Adam knew the pilot must have been prohibited from flying above populated areas, but he continued his game. For a southern boy who'd traveled the world for nefarious purposes over the course of decades, it amazed him how fresh were his memories of childhood locales.

He pondered the course of his personal energy throughout life. Were the endpoints of his lifeline joined, making a circle? Had he completed the round trip of his life? It made sense to the physicist who understood there was no end to energy. He could only hope it remained coalesced eternally.

Adam repeatedly posited that human energy must follow a similar elliptical path as the earth around the sun. It explained his drive to move forward constantly throughout life as a youngster. Having eclipsed the apex of his time on earth, he reflected along the timeline of his youth. A time of tears and sadness easily and vividly recalled. Moments already spent and consumed by both good and bad deeds. It made sense those memories were a large part of his makeup. This epiphany gave Adam a great deal of strength. It was the strength of forgiveness for all those who'd wronged him, and for the first time, he forgave himself for those he'd wronged. Absolution came from within.

The helicopter's main rotors chopped the air around the vessel and thrust its draft downward; convulsing the cabin in which they travelled. Regardless, the craft continued at its breakneck pace which made for an uncomfortable experience. Adam continued to stare through the window, picking out towns and landmarks.

They passed over Albany, Americus, and Cordele. Warner Robbins was the hometown of his college roommate. When they reached Athens, it was easy to pick out Sanford Stadium. It was where the Georgia Bulldogs competed at the highest level of college football.

At that point, the landscape changed drastically. No longer was Adam's attention focused on buildings and roads. Man-made structures gave way to rolling hills. He looked back over his shoulder at the parking facilities for the football stadium before he lost sight of it. The lot was as full as on any game day. Farther ahead, cars were abandoned on the side of the road; six and seven deep in some places. It was a recklessness like he'd never witnessed.

He watched as people walked toward the largest mass of humanity he'd ever seen. Empty spaces were filled in an orderly fashion. Individuals became a part of the greater mass. The only time he'd seen humans so happy to be tightly packed together was on a beach in Rio de Janeiro. Adam estimated the crowd was thousands of times larger than any he'd ever observed. The number of people was simply incalculable and unfathomable. The rolling landscape had become a life-scape.

Astonishment grew with the continued realization that streets and fields of green were packed with people, seemingly content to move no further toward their destination. The sea of humanity undulated like a single living, breathing animal. Adam imagined the souls of each human below, linking and stitching together the strongest human fabric possible. Was each person's elliptical energy linking with those around them? Were they all forming an indestructible chain together? Adam continued questioning because he needed to know.

The grandfather felt a nudge against his right arm. He turned and saw Maritza holding a small blue box. Tiffany blue. Many times, he'd bought his wife jewelry. He continued the tradition with his granddaughter.

"Open it," she said, excitedly. "It's from Tiffany." The teenager saved her own money to purchase the gift for her grandfather.

Adam smiled. Cautiously, he removed the white ribbon and opened the box. Inside was a silver cross, simple and understated, but beautifully impactful.

"I know how much you've examined the cross and how it fits into your philosophy, and that you've given it meaning for yourself. You told me that, for you, it applies to all humanity, regardless of religion." She smiled. Pointing to the cross she continued, "The horizontal beam represents humanity, of all races and religions. The vertical represents the energy spectrum in the universe. Our job as humans is to keep our beam as close to the Godly end of the spectrum as we can. That's why those embracing evil wear the cross upside down." She smiled. "You see, Papa. I listen to you."

Adam had never been prouder. He put his arm around his granddaughter's shoulder and pulled her close. He gently kissed her forehead. At that moment, his only thought was of the inextricable and chainlike linking of their elliptical souls for eternity.

Shaken back into reality, Adam watched as F-22s buzzed the sky at a safe altitude above the helicopter and the mass of humanity. They had an established pattern, offering protection from potential evil threatening from the skies. The elite wanted them all dead and would stop at nothing to accomplish global domination.

The pilot slowed the helicopter to a mere crawl above the crowd. He kept the craft high enough that the crowd wouldn't be impacted by its downdraft. They circled the Guidestones several times.

Adam's headphones came to life. "There's no place to land down there," said the pilot. "I'm going to have to go back to the football stadium to find a place to set down."

A couple of minutes later, the pilot set them down inside the stadium at midfield. Adam stepped out of the chopper, Maritza's hand in his. The grass had grown thick throughout the spring and summer, and the midfield logo disappeared months prior.

Childlike jubilation overtook Adam. His life had been about embracing darkness in order to bring himself to the point of murdering another human. A positive spirit possessed the man who knew it was required to save humanity.

Adam dropped Maritza's hand and ran down the field toward the end-zone. He looked back at the pilot and held up his hand to signal he was open. The pilot dropped back and threw an imaginary pass, which Adam caught and carried across the goal line for the score. He then spiked the imaginary ball and struck the Heisman pose. The pilot smiled, shook his head, and went back to his craft to monitor radio communications.

Adam had never felt more comfortable with fate. He knew even if the elites activated their satellites, or if they employed nuclear weapons instead, humanity was good and pure and would embrace eternity. He understood those he'd known throughout his life who possessed a sense of calm. They understood the eternal nature of humanity. His soul had been unsettled for so long, yet he understood the power of redemption.

The pilot suggested they lift off from the stadium at 6:21 p.m., an hour before the council's deadline. Humanity covered the peaks and valleys that formed many undulating hills between the football stadium and the monument to evil. There was no other place for them to occupy other than atop the Guidestones. That required all three to repel from a hovering helicopter. Adam and Sofia had done this several times during their careers. Maritza needed training.

It might have been risky, but Adam's desire to have her next to him outweighed all other concerns. He spent an hour going over exactly what to do, showing her all of the equipment, and having her repeat steps back to him.

The murmuring of the crowd could be heard beyond the confines of the stadium. It had a pleasant tone. Feeling the energy of millions of people wafting over the stadium walls and cascading downward onto the field caused Adam to wonder if he'd been the last person on earth to realize the power of positive thinking? Had the rest of humanity come to that realization at the same time?

The pilot spilled out of the chopper and made a beeline for Adam. "Atlanta's airport is basically shut down," he said. "They have aircraft by the dozens in holding patterns waiting to land. They've come from all over the world and some planes are dangerously low on fuel. I hope they can get them all on the ground safely."

"I'm sure they'll divert the ones in need to other airports."

"Yeah. Let's hope they can identify them in time."

Sofia and Maritza approached Adam. "Have you got some sort of speech written?" Asked Sofia.

"I'm not sure what I could say that would be heard. The crowd is too large."

"They've heard all they need to hear," insisted Maritza. "I think your presence is what's needed to bring our experience to its natural conclusion. They want to see the man they've seen on the video who represents a passion for humanity not witnessed during their lifetimes."

Adam heard the helicopters engine fire up. He looked at his watch. It was almost 6:21. Sofia, Maritza, and Adam took up the same seats they'd occupied on their trip to the monument.

Maritza was about to buckle in, but she froze. "Can I sit in the front seat?"

The pilot motioned for her to come forward and take the copilot's seat.

It was a short trip to the monument, and the rappelling was completed without incident.

The crowd cheered as the three stood atop the monument. It consisted of four rectangular slabs standing on end and aligned from the center at each ninety-degree point of the monument's circumference. Atop the pillars was a rectangular stone slab that gave the structure stability. No one knew the significance of the structure's design to the evil humans who placed it there. In all, the monument stood nearly twenty feet high. Each occupied a vertical slab leaving the fourth empty.

A concentric circular wave began at the base of the monument and moved outward, as if a pebble had been dropped into a pond. Those up-close confirmed Adam's identity and communicated confirmation backwards to those unable to make the distinction. The wave continued over the surrounding hills and out of sight until everyone was aware the man they came to see had arrived. His existence moved from clandestine to the most well known figure at that time.

Occasionally, Adam moved atop the capstone and waved. He didn't know what else to do. He checked his watch repeatedly.

Adam saw several people holding processional crucifixes aloft. Others held the Star of David high. Religious symbols from all over the world were proudly displayed. Adam directed Sofia's attention to the nearest Russian Orthodox cross. Elements representing individual and collective relationships with God could be seen from their vantage-point throughout the undulating sea of humanity as it disappeared over the horizon in all directions.

Adam noted all manner of dress in the crowd, from black khimars and hijabs to—well, nothing at all for those who felt compelled to experience the gathering in the same manner in which they'd entered their human existences.

Nearing the top of the hour the Christians began to sing "Amazing Grace" in unison. It was obvious not all attendees knew the words, but as additional stanzas were sung the collective voice grew stronger. Those who knew the lyrics taught those who didn't. The same thing happened when the crowd sang joy-filled songs representing every religion on earth. Cultures and faiths were so evenly dispersed throughout the crowd that people of the faith whose song was being sung taught those around them. It was an amazingly unifying gathering.

The crowd became aware time was drawing near. They finished their hymns, and the entire crowd began to chant, "We do not consent. We do not consent. We do not consent."

Adam became mesmerized by the spectacle until it neared time for the council to issue their final ruling. He knew not how the message would be sent, or if those who controlled their fate would offer a warning.

He looked at his watch and was surprised to see that it was 7:21. Fear dictated he question the Swiss precision that went into its making. He faced potentially the most devastating act in history and felt ill-prepared. His heart raced, and he did the only thing he knew. Adam looked up, toward Orion's Belt.

Each star began to glow red. It was soft at first, but it grew more intense; more ominous. The crowd witnessed the same phenomenon and continued their chant. It became louder with every sentence spoken in unison. Purposeful was their disdain for being made targets of evil.

Adam moved from atop a column to the monument's capstone. He motioned for Maritza and Sofia to join him. They held hands with Adam in the center. They gazed up at the red stars and faced their mortality bravely.

The energy that emitted from each of the three stars came together at a center focal point and grew in intensity. A previously unseen satellite absorbed that energy until it burst forth in a single, intense beam toward earth.

Suddenly, the red laser-like stream shot down and engulfed the monument and its three occupants. No one in the crowd was affected; not even those immediately adjacent. It was focused and intense. The crowd grew silent.

Adam looked down and witnessed the granite beneath his feet slowly melting. It would take temperatures over twelve hundred degrees Fahrenheit to accomplish such a feat. He felt no ill-effects and looked at his granddaughter and Sofia. Both appeared jovial at the realization their health wasn't threatened.

The crowd watched as the granite monuments that had been a part of the landscape since 1980 slowly melted into a single flat slab. Once the structure was leveled, the red beam dissipated leaving Adam, Sofia, and Maritza standing, unharmed, atop the newly formed marker.

Stunned, the three shook away their disbelief and walked slowly along the surface of the marker. It was rectangular, fifteen feet by ten feet, and stood eighteen inches off the ground. Beneath their feet, they read the new inscription: HUMANITY.

24

The intensity Adam experienced over the last month was diametrically opposed to relaxing in a rocking chair on his porch on Southard Street. General Eason sat across from him. The table between the two held a chess board. Pieces were arranged for a new game.

Adam had been debriefed at the Naval Air Station Key West. He had no confidence his experiences would lead to change. The struggle against those who possessed the psychosis to cause harm would never cease. He expected those who experienced what was being called the Georgia Guidestones Event would understand this as well. A change in the way parents expressed life lessons to younger generations must include ever-present malevolence. The battle between good and evil was eternal and universal. Having experienced it firsthand, he felt as though his soul had been strengthened. He hoped wherever his energy traveled after death, experiences would stay with him. He believed positive encounters would lay the foundation for a strengthened soul.

Adam never played chess competitively. There was a pad and pen next to the board. While in a Sensitive Compartmented Information Facility, he and Eason developed a method of communicating via a seemingly innocuous game of chess between aging men. No one strolling down Southard Street offered a second glance. Squares and pieces were coded, and moves were combined to develop messages that would not be recorded anywhere but within the minds of those who played the game.

Glasses of lemonade sat on coasters to the right of each man's position at the chessboard. Adam watched as condensation repeatedly beaded on his glass. Occasionally, a droplet slid down its side and soaked into the coaster. Life slowed considerably.

Peripheral players to the planned genocide still roamed the earth. The splinter team identified two and traced them to Key West. Eason had not made Adam aware of their presence. They'd developed a method of communicating in person, immune to listening devices. He used Adam as the control function of his test. Would this method indeed work?

"Shall we begin," Eason said as he leaned toward the chessboard. The general made a series of moves. Thinking the game was merely a practice test, Adam scribbled dutifully on his notepad until the dispatch became clear.

He read the message and shifted his gaze to a spot across the street. There were two men walking south toward Duval Street. One man was tall and slim. The other was just over five feet and muscular. Each wore leather fetish caps with chains around the brim, leather vests, and ass-less chaps. The taller man walked behind the shorter one. He held a leash, attached to the studded leather collar around the neck of the short man in front.

Eason began another series of moves. Adam dutifully scribbled the message to its completion and then read it silently. "The tall man is a neurosurgeon in Berlin. He is the descendent of a Nazi doctor who researched pharmaceuticals on our Jewish brothers and sisters during World War II. He has continued that research on homeless and indigent people. He's also the one who developed the nanobots that are coursing through the veins of billions of humans."

Eason continued to lay out intelligence about the men who were the focus of Adam's next assignment. They'd been under surveillance by military intelligence for nearly five years. The government's various three letter agencies possessed the same evidence, but continued to bathe in the corruption that made them wealthy. Intelligence had been suppressed in favor of future attempts to cull humanity. Various technologies were continually developed to tailor homicide such that circumstances could be easily explained by media talking heads. Heart attacks, cancers, and other maladies were touted as naturally occurring phenomenon.

"So do you think this method of communicating assignments will work?" Eason asked. "If not, I'm sure we can come up with something you're more comfortable with."

Adam chuckled. "Yeah, but try and be brief, or slow your role on that chessboard. It's tough keeping up with these long messages. I need to get the point of not relying on written notes."

Eason smiled and nodded.

"Is it true what you said about those two Germans?"

"Sadly, yes. As you've experienced, our greatest societal failure is that we were taught evil was exterminated when Hitler committed suicide in that bunker."

"Which we know didn't happen."

"Exactly." Eason smiled. "The five families you encountered at the council meeting utilized Hitler, and they will continue seeking out those consumed by evil to do their bidding."

Adam glanced across Southard once again. The two men made the turn onto Duval Street. Nodding his head in their direction he asked. "Those two. What's the mission?"

"First, you have to be aware of the small one. He's volatile. It could be the DNA changing steroids they've used on him, or it could be the fact that he's a mix—German and Colombian. Man, can you imagine the conflict that rages inside that guy with such disparate DNA? Regardless, he's like a little chihuahua. Once he gets set off, you'll never be able to rein him in. You might as well put him down."

"Is that the mission?"

Eason shook his head. "No, the doctor is definitely more valuable, but we need to keep the tiny man alive. There will be a lot of information gleaned from him once we infiltrate their organization." He debated whether to divulge details and decided to do so for the sake of full disclosure. "We've got all kinds of surveillance video on these two. The little guy is always the receiver in their sexual relationship. Maybe that's what triggers his anger."

"Wait, so you guys have been videoing their encounters?"

"God no. They make videos with their phones. We've just been surveilling their devices." Eason shook his head. "What kind of creep do you think I am? Besides that, the little guy uses it as leverage against the doctor. He could ruin that man's reputation in Germany. The doc pays him ten thousand dollars a month for his silence." His smile grew impish. "Now, we have the same leverage."

Adam displayed his ever-present love of humanity. "I'm really not comfortable targeting people because they're gay." Once the words left his mouth, he realized he had once again contradicted a superior. He'd also shown compassion, a trait contrary to an assassin's existence.

Eason shook his head. "It's not that they're gay. We can use leverage based on them not being honest about who they are. It's the same as the doctor putting himself forth as a neurosurgeon when ninety percent of his income is earned by producing tainted gelcaps. It's the lying. The leverage created is by their own deeds. Those are their lies, not ours."

Adam nodded. "Well said. But how does the little guy's anger manifest?"

Eason gazed beyond Adam. "There was an incident at the Adam and Adam Club at the east end of Duval a couple months ago. The doctor was in Germany and was not there to rein in the little guy. It's common knowledge in the gay community the doctor owns a small manufacturing company in Fort Myers. That's where they make the gelcaps laced with nano bots. He placed the little guy in a position of authority at the factory until his chihuahua attitude alienated everyone there. The doctor removed him but kept paying his ten thousand dollar a month stipend. All the guys at the A & A club were giving him a raft of shit one night about being nothing more than a bitch and a whore." Eason paused. Thoughts of the many affairs he carried on throughout the world when he was dependent upon alcohol occupied his mind. He knew he was just as hypocritical. Many weaknesses could be leveraged against him. "I guess being a whore in the gay community is just as bad as in the straight community. Anyway, he was drunk, and I'm sure the steroids helped. A friend pulled him out of the club to drive him home. The little guy insisted on passing the club on Duval Street on the way home. As they passed the building, the little guy stood up through his sunroof and emptied his .38 revolver into the building."

"Oh, my God," said Adam. "And he's still walking free?" He thought more. "I remember reading about that in the newspaper, but there was never an arrest made."

Eason shrugged. "Normally when a newspaper buries a story, it's because the bad guys squashed it. This time it was us who played the national security card. The doctor is way too valuable, and the little guy is his weakest link. A very weak link. There's a lot of leverage there."

No one said anything for several moments. Silence became uncomfortable. The proverbial elephant on the porch grew larger. It was an energy Adam felt before from his superior. "Do you have something to say?"

Eason glanced at his newfound friend and once again down the street. In the distance he saw two figures making their way toward Adam's house. "I'm not sure how you're going to take this, so I'm going to blurt it out. It's your age. You're too old for the field."

Adam stared at the intersection of Duval and Southard. It bustled with people crossing the street and dodging cars. An occasional horn overtook the sound of music blasting from open car windows. "So, what was the purpose of all of this?" he said, as he swept his hand over the chess board.

"Oh, you're going to lead a team. But not in the field."

It was an eventuality Adam knew one day would become reality, and he welcomed it. "What's my role?"

"You'll operate from your home." He hitched a thumb over his shoulder at the house behind him. "We are going to do a remodeling job, but not inside. Beneath your home we'll carve out the limestone into an operations center and SCIF." Eason smiled, smugly.

"You want me dealing with sensitive compartmented information?" An issue arose in Adam's mind. "But I just spent a quarter million dollars remodeling this home less than two years ago. Pulling permits might be difficult. Won't it look suspicious?"

"If we have to blow a hurricane through here to destroy the home so that we can rebuild it, we will." Adam knew it wasn't a joke. Their rebel alliance had picked up a secret or two from the five families and their research institutions.

Adam shook his head. "That would destroy the local economy." Love for his fellow man had been intensified by the experiences of the last month.

For the first time in their relationship, Eason said something that caused Adam to doubt the man. His trust in his leader was damaged. The general had access to weather modification technology developed at DARPA. Had he become mad with power? Adam vowed never to trust anyone completely, but inability to trust those with whom he worked spoke to a potentially greater set of negative consequences. Would Eason judge Adam harshly for caring too much for his fellow conchs?

"The cleanup will keep people busy so they won't have time to question our actions."

To Adam, that sounded more like a justification conceived by a member of the elite speaking about peasants.

Adam's concentration was broken when the two people walking down Southard began to ascend the stairs that led to his porch.

Once he heard their steps behind him, he turned to see who it was. He smiled at the sight of Sofia and Reinier. The two younger operatives made their way between the older men and leaned their butts against the railing.

"It makes sense now," Adam said, jesting arrogantly. "Maybe—just maybe, these two together might become as prolific an agent as I have been during my career, but I'm not so sure."

Adam smiled as he looked from one to another of his three guests. He harbored some suspicion. His life had been hard—harder than the destiny meant for any human. During his childhood those who were supposed to love him doled out corporal punishment liberally. It left him possessing a skewed sense of loyalty.

Reinier jostled Adam from his contemplative haze. "Where's Maritza?"

Adam tossed his head toward the second floor of the house. "She's upstairs in her bedroom. Where else would she be?"

Sofia smiled and interjected. "Is she hacking into elite gaming platforms?"

Adam drew in a deep breath and exhaled. "I hope not. She just needs to be a teenager now."

There was one irrefutable truth Adam discovered entering his sixth decade. His life had been spent wandering aimlessly and without meaning until inspiration from God spoke to him as clearly as physical manifestations and stimuli shaped him throughout life. The young man sought out corporal and carnal experiences for the purpose of advancing life in a purely physical sense. He thought finding the perfect physical partner would bring him peace. What Adam didn't realize in his youth that the physical was meant to die and be returned to the earth. In reality it was an eternal connection he desired. A place in the universe. He wished the same for Maritza; to know her grandmother once again, as he had in the Antarctic.

Reaching into the depths of his soul was never taught to the young man. Was it supposed to be innate? Pulp experiences adhered to the flesh. Sensations dissipated, and his mind desperately sought continuity of stimulus. Sensual encounters saturate, and one's flesh becomes gin-soaked with wanton desires.

For some men, misguided affairs led to endless wandering and increasing skepticism concerning the existence of their souls.

Emotional lucidity eluded Adam for most of his life. Finally, he realized he could only attain clarity by embracing the purity inherent in human souls. At that point, he realized he could do more than just survive. He could live a life filled with meaning.

Each human life was given by God for the purpose of strengthening one's soul. Misdeeds could be forgiven, but only whenever positive change resulted from experiences. Unforgivable were those who never embraced the concept of growing eternally.

Adam felt a great sense of fulfillment. Eason, Sofia, and Reinier watched as a serene grin slowly grew on their friend's face. His consciousness was nowhere near the house on Southard Street.

Adam realized all humans were forced to participate in a system driven by dogma. Every institution was built to move forward on the destruction of the individual, and not what was right and good.

The rapacious nature of corporate America compelled individuals into acts never considered without the dogma of losing one's livelihood. Adam had never been given the tools to embrace the positive—not by his parents, college professors, or clergy. Instead, he was taught proverbially to tread water for survival. The source of Adam's outward satisfaction, evident to all, was borne in the recognition Godly energy always wins. A man and his seventeen-year-old granddaughter made a difference. His life had never been his own, but when he'd taken control, it opened his soul to flourish eternally.

Adam spent his entire life seeking truth to explain the reason for his existence. He thought of his encounter with Carolyn in the Antarctic and understood it only existed in the ethereal. He wasn't sure whether it was merely a dream or a creation only his mind could conceive. Regardless of how intensely he meditated, he was never able to recreate the synthesis of their eternal beings. What he was certain, was that pure energy was necessary for successful relationships.

As he reflected on the timeline of his life, he found more positive human interactions to embrace. Kathy. His wife. Maritza.

And then he looked at the three associates staring at him curiously. He knew that if their relationships were based in truth and pure love for one another, they would succeed in every endeavor undertaken.

Other Titles by Louis Berry:

The Surrency Affair

Task Force Vigilante

Seeking Trinity

Madeline

Printed in Dunstable, United Kingdom